Panting again, Lorin paused, then looked down through one of the air slits. His heart sank. Nothing. Nothing but more foul straw. *Idiot, idiot,* his brain began singing—

There was a movement . . . and the eye was gazing up at him. It was a dull eye, slitted . . . and about as big as Lorin's head.

His breath got caught somewhere south of his ribs.

There was the sound of a whuff of breath— then another, and another one, quicker than the second.

It's waking up! he thought, and snatched the piece of parchment out of his cloak, and held it up . . . and then realized that it was too dark to read the spell.

Oh Gods! he thought, shoving the parchment back into his cloak—no good dropping it where it might cause questions, or worse, get someone to look inside this box. Hurriedly he recited the rune. He dared not look down into that air slit again to see what was happening inside. But he could hear the sound of the liskash's breathing getting faster in there. . . .

**Ask your bookseller for the
Bantam Spectra Books you have missed:**

GUARDIANS OF THE THREE, VOLUME 2

KEEPER OF THE CITY

Peter Morwood
and Diane Duane

BANTAM BOOKS
NEW YORK · TORONTO · LONDON · SYDNEY · AUCKLAND

KEEPER OF THE CITY
A Bantam Spectra Book / August 1989

ISBN 0-553-28065-1

Published simultaneously in the United States and Canada

Bantam Books are published by Bantam Books, a division of Bantam Doubleday
Dell Publishing Group, Inc. Its trademark, consisting of the words "Bantam
Books" and the portrayal of a rooster, is Registered in U.S. Patent and
Trademark Office and in other countries. Marca Registrada, Bantam Books,
666 Fifth Avenue, New York, New York 10103

PRINTED IN THE UNITED STATES OF AMERICA

0 9 8 7 6 5 4 3 2 1

For the Chicago Mafia,
with love from the usual suspects

And for Smokey and Spock
and all the other mad cats who've graced our lives

PROLOGUE

He stood there among the lesser hills just after dawn, just before the edge of the desert, and in silence looked down through the shallow valley at the little city. *Perhaps this will be home at last*, he thought. *Gods, I'm tired.*

It was hardly the largest town he had ever seen. Basically it was nothing more but a group of little hillocks—one of the last before the land became perfectly flat and the green of the lowland country turned to the scrubby brown of the desert. Those three small hills were still green toward their tops, flowering into houses farther down the slopes. One hill was taller than the others, and had the remains of some old ring-fort at the top of it, all dark stone, ruinous. Around the hills was built a wall, and inside it, almost swallowed by building, were signs of several others, smaller ones, long outgrown. This town had done well for such a tiny outpost, so far from the lands where none but mrem dwell. It was dangerously far east, this town: too close entirely, by the reckoning of the old days, to the lands across the desert, the lands where ran the writ of the Lords of the East, the unfurred ones, the ones who used magic.

He shivered a bit, remembering. It had not been all that long, a matter of some years, since he had met and fought alongside Talwe the hunter, who became Talwe the lord of Cragsclaw city, a lord among the other Lords of Ar. Reswen had been several things himself at that time: a commander of mercenary mrem, but also a friend to the Kings of Ar, and to one king in particular.

"Will you do it?" Andelemarian had said all those many

months ago. It was late at night in the palace of Ar, in the
king's rooms. Nothing stood between them but a flask of
wine and a couple of glasses, often filled and often drained
that night, and a lamp with a wick that needed trimming.
"It is a long way from here, but if any city needs our paw
held over it secretly, it is that one. Niau is a bastion, one
of the most distant and most threatened ones, against the
encroachment of the East."

It was always hard to argue with a king, but the wine
had made Reswen feel a little scrappy that night. "Nothing
from the East has been near Niau for many years," he
said. "The desert is wide there . . . and there's nothing
there to attract their attention. The place is tiny. Herders,
a few merchants—"

"It will not always be tiny," the king said. "Those
merchants are becoming too successful. Time will come
that the Easterners will look that way . . . and they may
look at Niau as a likely place to attack, since as you say
they have not been seen or heard of in those parts for
many a year now. For who takes serious defense against
legends? Who believes in dragons, who hasn't been burnt?"

Reswen twitched. He had been burnt, more than once.
He had no trouble believing in the liskash, the lizard-
things of the East, in all their many kinds—lords and
servants, the wise-worms, and the dragons that breathed
fire. There were no deadlier enemies to mrem, except fire
itself, which mrem used with a care born of old fear.

The king leaned back, switching his tail slightly, and
then shrugged. "And then they may not come at all," he
said, glancing up; the light of the little lamp gilded his
white fur, and caught in his eyes. Their look was humorous for the moment. "But that's not a chance that we can
take. If they don't come, well. But if they do, I would
have someone there who can find out what they're up to
before they know they've been found. And I can think of
no one better fitted to defend a city, whether it knows it
needs defense or not. Will you do it, Reswen? I would be
glad to know that city was being watched over by one of
my own. And whoever follows me would be glad to know
it as well."

Reswen had sat and thought about that for a while. On

the one hand, he wanted to please the king. He would not
be holding office in Ar much longer. His age was troubling
him, had been for some time, and he had begun to remind
people more and more often that it was time the kingship
rested in younger paws. On the other hand, there was
nothing much to look forward to in this mission. Ahead of
him, in that little city, would lie nothing but secretive-
ness, a long hiding while he became used to the ways of
the city, became one of its people, and used that oneness
to protect the place from what might happen . . . or what
might not. It would be a surveillance of considerable length,
on the edge of an inhospitable desert, a long way away
from the more cosmopolitan cities of the world.

But there were other considerations for him than his
own comfort, these days. He had been rather shocked to
find that he had developed a taste for being the defender
of a little piece of the world, the one responsible for
keeping it intact, no matter what others, perhaps in higher
places, might think he was doing.

"I can offer you no overt help," the king said. "No one
can know that Ar is working inside the walls of Niau. The
independence of these small border cities is a great thing
. . . in some ways, their chief defense. I would not have
that interfered with. As far as they are concerned, you will
have left my service—understandable, for what use is a
mercenary in peace?—and gone seeking other employ. But
if you accept this charge, I daresay you will find other
compensations for your stay in Niau. Somehow I doubt that
you will stop at being a mere captain of mercenaries."

Reswen grinned at that. "No, King," he said. "I would
doubt that myself. I'll find some position, sooner or later,
that suits my talents."

Andelemarian had smiled. So simply, and without any
explicit declaration, the decision had been made. After a
few days' worth of good-byes, Reswen had begun his long
journey to the easternmost parts of Ar.

And now the journey was almost done, and he stood on
the scrubby little hillside and looked down past Niau's
grazing lands and townlands, to the city itself. It looked
very lonely, very isolated. Beyond it, the desert shimmered in the first heat of what promised to be an intoler-

able day, and the hard blue sky came down and met its distant edge with brutal sharpness. It would not do so for long, he knew. The heat-haze would rise, and the horizon would become a blurred silvery thing, out of which anything might emerge without warning. Of course, hardly anything ever did, the people of the city would not be too cautious about the edge of the world. But Reswen would have some time, some years perhaps, to change that, before the threat that the king foresaw came true.

From far down the valley, from one of those three walled hills, came a low deep sound: a horn, the signal for the opening of the city gates. He smiled a little to himself . . . they were still, at least, *that* cautious. Reswen bent down to pick up the pack he had been carrying, and shouldered it again. Then he went down the hill, toward Niau: Reswen Kingfriend, hero of the battle of Cragsclaw, soon to be merely Reswen, unemployed mercenary, looking for a place. The city guard, perhaps, if they had any vacant posts. It would not be a bad start for one who would slowly and carefully work himself up through the ranks, always keeping his oaths to protect the city. . . .

But never quite revealing the truth about for whom he was protecting it—and from what. . . .

▲

Chapter 1

▲─────────────────────────────────────▲

Dawn in Niau was probably no different in its more basic aspects from the same time of day in any other city-state all across the world. A bit cold, a bit damp if it had managed to rain in the night, the brightening sky clear or dull as the weather dictated. This morning was pleasantly cool and fresh under a blue sky, the coolness and the freshness both legacies of a small, noisy, desert-born thunderstorm that had rattled shutters and shingles about the third hour. The quick, fierce downpouring of rain had left the air smelling sweet, clean, and for the moment dust-free, though that would change as the sun and the heat rose and the wind that always whispered in across the Eastern Desert carried the lightest motes of that desert in its wake. Its citizens—except for the fortunate few who had no need of such early rising—would stir from their pallets with pleasure or reluctance, yawn, stretch, eat something, and then be about whatever business concerned them. Except for those mrem employed by the secret police, because their business was concerned exclusively with that of other people. . . .

"Quiet night, sir." If Reswen had heard that once since he entered Constables' House, he had heard it twenty times. Not that he would have preferred more action. Far from it. That sort of attitude came in with new recruits and left them rather precipitately after their first eightday on duty. By the time they reached his side of the chief's desk, those few that did, they had seen enough action in one form or another to keep them content with peace for the rest of their active lives.

Reswen acknowledged the salutes of his two personal

guards with a neat little flourish of his baton-of-office—a
gesture unashamedly stolen from one of the players in a
favorite dance-drama—and stalked up the curved flight of
stairs that led to his office and his private duty-chamber.
And to the file of observation reports which, regardless of
whether the night had been quiet or busy, invariably
spread themselves all across his desk.

Today was no different. Reswen mewed softly, an inar-
ticulate sound of pure disgust, as he closed the door behind
himself and took first note of the piled-up documentation.
Chief of Constables he might be, paid in gold where lesser
mrem might see no more than silver, honored, respected,
and invited to all the best parties. But the clandestine
duty that accompanied the post, command of the secret
police, always seemed to need not the brain that was
renowned for its cunning, its wit, and its mordant humor all
across Niau, but a plodding, methodical mind like that of
the most menial file clerk.

Reswen had been a file clerk once, long ago. He had
been most things, since that morning outside the walls.
He had indeed started *on* the walls, as a mere spear-
carrier. At the time he had wondered what people back in
Cragsclaw would think of it—the leader of small armies,
now himself doing sentry-go, watch on and watch off, turn
and about, and taking the same pay as any of the other
guards. But what people back in his old haunts would have
thought wasn't the issue, doing his job well *was*. He paid
no attention to the gibes of some of the younger guards,
that someone his age should be dozing by the fire, or
setting up in a shopkeeping job somewhere. It *was* a gibe,
of course; he had barely five years on any of them. But
those who chose to try to push the battered-looking mrem
around a little, just for fun, shortly found out that fun was
not part of what happened. Ears torn to rags were—for
Reswen, unwilling to start an incident with one of these
infants, batted them around like the half-wet kits they
were and left them stunned, scarred, and mortified, but
nothing worse.

And word got around, as he had intended it to; mention was made to one superior by another, mention of this
scarred guard-mrem with the patient temper and the quick

eye. Someone suggested that he might be better employed than on the walls. Reswen had no idea who it was.
On occasion it occurred to him to wonder whether the
king might have had another friend or two in the city—
friends who had no idea who he was.

But it didn't matter. The guards on the wall were part of
the city police force of Niau, not part of the standing army
(not that the army stood in any good order just then, a fact
which caused Reswen some concern). Reswen was promoted (if that was the word) to file clerk, and secretary
(having taken the time to learn a creditable shorthand),
and then to beat policeman in one part of the city and
another, and finally to posts within the constabulary itself,
investigator and under-chief. And finally, after ten years or
so, Chief Constable, when old Trrl died, and there was
ostensibly no one better equipped to hold the job than he.
Now, some twelve years into his tenure in Niau, Reswen's
was a name to conjure with in the town, not because of
any battle ever fought back in the mists of time—for mrem
on the borders of the world, Reswen sometimes observed
to himself, have short memories—but for his own success
at his job. He had won reasonable fortune, honor, and
recognition from the worthy, the high, and the holy. To
say nothing of a different mistress for every night of the
eightday if he felt so inclined, a fine town house of his
own—not a grace-and-favor house, either, but paid for out
of his own pocket in ready money—and a noble's title to
wrap it all up in. He did not particularly like being reminded of past parchment-pushing chores each and every
morning, and that he still derived a certain sour satisfaction from completing such a mediocre task as well as he
was able struck him as one of the great ironies in a world
filled with them.

He sat down on the low chair, switching his tail into
the recess left for it in the chair's bentwood back, then
smoothed the pleats of his military-cut kilt, laid jaw on
paws, and considered the more or less orderly documents
piled before him. Parchments, rag papers, wax-on-wood
tablets; most of it would be useless or at very best only
interesting gossip. From the rest he would collate the
information gathered by his minions during the course of

the preceding night: bits of usefully incriminating evidence against those whom either the Secret Police or the Council of Elders might at some stage need to exercise leverage; standard surveillance reports from the various consulates, embassies, and legations that Niau's position invariably attracted; and, every once in a while, as a bribe or more simply as a juicy morsel uncovered in the course of some other investigation, something useful that would let him close a long outstanding case or (Reswen's whiskers curved forward in a smile as he remembered the last time) even win some money by the placing of judicious wagers. But most often nothing especially dramatic. And that, most often, was the way he liked it.

Reswen worked for two hours in relative silence, organizing the paperwork into separate heaps: one heap to be thrown away, another to be further checked before a decision, yet another for immediate attention. Once that was done he allowed himself time off for a snack of dried meat washed down with water, an austere little meal that made him feel quite virtuous. Chewing on another strip of the smoky, salty, tasty flesh, he strolled to the office window and gazed east toward the desert and the great silent threat beyond it. His tufted ears twitched involuntarily and flattened just a bit at the thought of one day looking out from this same window to see the wavering heat-haze darken and solidify into the invading armies of the Eastern Lords. If they came, when they came, they would come this way, following the caravan·trail from oasis to oasis until they reached Niau and made the city the anvil to their hammer. But the oases, thank the gods, were few, and hard to find at the best of times, and also prone to failure. *Not even the liskash would be very sanguine about trying that approach. . . .*

Despite the glare from the sand that made everything dance as if reflected in a bowl of quicksilver, the narrow pupils of Reswen's green eyes dilated very slightly in response to the picture that his mind had painted. He had an imagination, had Reswen, and unlike most military mrem who aspired to high rank, he had never been afraid to let that imagination color his thinking. That was why he was so very good at his job. Reliance on the tried-and-true warriors' skill was all very well in skirmishes and the traditional sorts of battle—it had certainly helped Talwe, all that while ago. But then that kind of approach had seemed to work better in those days and places; violence and luck granted either rapid success or rapid extinction. Reswen knew all about the judicious—and judicial—application of violence, but he was no longer sure he believed in any such thing as luck. And he doubted that such an approach would work against the Easterners. Home-grown warriors were all very well in highland skirmishes. But to fight armies a city needed soldiers—drilled, disciplined soldiers, backed up by efficient intelligence and the knowledge that their homes and families were protected by a force that rooted spies and saboteurs out of their city. A force like that which Reswen covertly commanded—the H'satei, the Quiet Ones.

Reswen worried off another small piece of meat, and he continued to gaze out at the desert glare. His people were out there somewhere, two octs of the newest recruits, sent out two days ago for what they thought was just another of the exercises that their commander was so notoriously hot for. A survival exercise, they thought. Only Reswen and his senior staff knew—and had made certain that the exercising recruits didn't—of the approaching caravan supposely due into Niau today or tomorrow. If it got within sight of the city before a report of its presence got within sight of his desk, the recruits were going to find that their commander wasn't just hot for exercises per se, but for the "vigilance constant and unfailing" written in shiny brass letters around the crest carved on the frontage of Constables' House.

So far there had been neither caravan nor breathless, draggle-furred reporter of its sighting, but Reswen remained unconcerned. Besides, he had other things to do than stand at the window watching the world bake. Today was payout day for the spies and informants working Northside, and if he didn't get along and authorise their retainer chits, there was going to be a lot of anonymous but deeply felt dissatisfaction in the city.

He swallowed down the last bit of meat, all its flavor chewed away by now, and turned from the window. Then turned back again with a snap as he saw—or thought he saw—something that hadn't been there before. Nothing moved now, except for the horizon's unending slow shimmer, but Reswen narrowed his eyelids until they were mere creases in the ginger-russet fur of his face and stared at featureless brilliance until spots began to dance between his eyes and the world, and until the beginnings of a headache nagged between his brows. And until he saw again what he had seen before.

The distant speck was still too far away for him to discern who it might be, but Reswen felt betting-certain that it was one of his recruits. "Good," he said for no reason other than his own satisfaction. "Very good." He gazed a moment more, then went downstairs to wait for what the courier had to say. And to deal with the wretched informers' wretched chits.

▲

"How much lead time do you expect, sir?" asked Sithen. Then he consulted his list and said, "Ten silvers to Reth One-Eye."

"Ten to Reth," Reswen echoed, marking the chit and stamping it with his personal seal. "Too much for the little he provides. Either something useful next month or this is cut to five." He put the parchment slip aside and yawned leisurely, all rough pink tongue and sharp white teeth. "You said . . . ? Oh yes. Time. I don't know, but if it's enough time for the city to get onto a defensive footing, then I'll petition the Arpekh for a standing guard out there at all times."

Sithen's whiskers twitched. "They won't like it."

"Who? The Arpekh or the guard?"

"Neither, probably. I wouldn't like that posting myself, and as for our sage Council of Elders—"

"—'It's too expensive, it's not necessary, and we didn't need such a thing in my sire's time anyway.'" Reswen laughed softly, but the throaty purring trill that was mrem laughter sounded sour even to his own ears. "Yes. All their favorite arguments. But times change, and now it *is* necessary, and nothing so necessary is too expensive. Unlike these idlers." He gestured at the stacked payment chits with an irritation made plain by the way his claws slid briefly from their sheaths. "Apologies, Sithen." The claws retracted again. "My manners are slipping."

"Understandable, sir. Sometimes I feel like spitting myself."

Someone knocked outside the closed door. "Our messenger, I trust," said Reswen. "Come in."

The guard who came through the door was armored in the cream-colored uxanhide of a duty constable, functional and unimpressive in the ordinary course of things, but looking positively magnificent by comparison with what he was escorting. The mrem by his side was even more scruffy and breathless than Reswen had imagined he would be, and the fair quantity of desert he carried about his person added to the general air of dishevelment.

Reswen looked at him with mild surprise. "Mrem in the Constabulary are above average in their intelligence," he said. "Usually that suggests enough native wit to avoid running through the desert after the sun's well up." He glanced at the guard. "Heth, bring this gallant idiot some water. And you, sit down before you fall down."

The scout collapsed gratefully onto a seat and Reswen had to pretend sudden interest in the expense chits to hide his smile. There was something amusing about the way this so serious, so intense young mrem—little more than a kitten, in truth—left small clouds of dust hanging in the air with every move he made, and Reswen knew perfectly well that smiling at the kit's discomfiture wouldn't make the youngster feel any better. He looked more closely, and pulled a name out of the cluttered files that comprised his mind right now. "Creel, isn't it?" he said.

"Yessir, Second-Oct Recruit Creel, sir!" The scout bounced upright again—another cloud of desert sifting from his person across Reswen's desk—and saluted as briskly as his weariness allowed, from the set of his ears and whiskers very proud that this most senior of officers should remember his insignificant name. He wobbled as he stood.

If Reswen had misremembered he had been ready to cover it with a joke about the concealing qualities of too much dust worn as a garment, and was as pleased as the

youngster to have gotten the name right first time around.
Remembering the names of each and every one of his
constables was another matter—they were fully qualified,
enlisted, and worthy of that sort of small consideration—
whereas recruits . . . Well, luck had a lot to do with it, if
he really believed in luck, which he didn't. But it did no
harm. "Sit *down*, Creel, for pity's sake. Don't stand there
weaving about like that. We'll consider all respects and
honors taken care of. Now, in your own words: What have
you to report?"

Second-Oct Recruit Creel blinked a bit at being treated
so gently. Reswen's reputation as a fire-eater was all over
the recruit barracks, both verbally and as graffiti scratched
at unlikely angles on the latrine and bathhouse walls. He
was well known as a piss-and-sour-wine old bastard—the
"old" again more a part of the disrespect than an accurate
judgement of Reswen's age. As usual, those newly adult
considered those less newly so to be relics of an ancient
age and ready for retirement. Yet Reswen's reputation also
said that his nature was even more full of ginger than his
orange-tawny pelt suggested—but here he was, smiling
right to the tips of his whiskers and being just as nice as a
piece of fish. Probably, Reswen thought with mild satisfaction, Creel was quite confused.

"Err . . . ," said Creel, and swallowed. Then he coughed
and drank more of the wonderful cool water that Old
Ginger had summoned for them all to drink, because
there was more dust than spit in his mouth and throat.
"Sir, we, myself and the others, went on station and I
suggested, I took the liberty of suggesting, sir, that if we
were out in the desert we might as well look as if we
belonged, so I, that is we—"

"Creel, try this—because I think if we listen to your
own words we'll be here all day. Reply simply. What did
the squad do?"

"Sir, we disguised ourselves as herders, sir."

"Herders?" Sithen glanced at Reswen and then at the
recruit. "And what were you herding, pray tell? And
how?"

Reswen looked at his second-in-command and decided
not to reprimand him for the interruption. At least not

yet, not in front of young Creel. He made a mental note to hold the impoliteness in reserve for when it would be needed—as it would, sooner or later, when this mrem and his ambition overstepped the limits Reswen had already laid out for them—and instead nodded benevolently. "A very good point, Sithen. One I had considered myself." *And dismissed as not so very important right now,* ran the unspoken rest of the sentence, clear enough for Sithen to read it whether spoken or not.

"Sir, we were herding bunorshen, some of his father's herd that Deiarth borrowed. He knows how to herd them, sir."

"Well done, Creel," said Reswen and meant it, because the plan was a neat bit of protective coloration if anyone had to spend time out in the desert. The bunorshan's fleece was valuable, but the animal itself was a damned nuisance, eating only the harsh pasture plants that grew in and along the edges of the desert, and grew so sparsely that the herds and herders were constantly on the move to the east of the city. "An excellent plan. And what did you—your squad, that is—discover? Foreigners, maybe? Invading enemies, perhaps?"

"Sir!" Creel's eyes had opened very wide, their pupils expanding enough to swallow up all but a thin green rim of iris. Evidently with this single observation, Reswen's reputation for sagacity had increased by leaps and bounds. "Yessir! Not invaders, sir, but there's a caravan approaching the city—and sir, there are Easterners traveling with them!"

Reswen's features betrayed nothing. "Which kind of Easterners, son? There are several. . . ."

"Oh, you don't mean liskash, do you, sir? They're extinct!"

Reswen did not change expression, but under his fur his skin itched a bit, as if remembering some old burn. It was just as well that people here thought that there were no more liskash. Panic could work against a city as effectively as invasion. But Reswen had been keeping his ears and eyes open for the lizards for years, and had (he had to admit) never seen so much as a scale's worth of one, or heard even a breath of a rumor of their presence either here or among the cities of the desert's far side. "Just Eastern mrem, sir," said Creel. "Their clothes are easy to spot, and the harness on their burden beasts. Also the breeds of beast are different."

Reswen nodded. Though he asked only a few more questions there was no suggestion of haste in any of his words before he dismissed Creel with kindly voiced instructions to get cleaned up and rest. "Well now, Sithen," he said after the scout had left the room. "What do you think of this, then?"

"Interesting."

"Is that all?"

"Not quite. Fascinating." Reswen gave him a funny look and Sithen's pointed ears twitched back. He made a steeple of his forepaw fingers and stared at them as if expecting they would contain all the answers he might need. "I mean, that the Easterners should show up in a manner so easy to track as a caravan . . ."

"Perhaps they aren't worried," said Reswen helpfully. "Perhaps they don't intend us harm. Perhaps—" the points of upper and lower fangs showed for just the merest instant, "—their mission is peaceful."

"Perhaps it is." Sithen jumped on that bait far too readily, betraying—to Reswen's mind at least—an absence of any personal opinion whatsoever.

"And if so, what should we do about it?" Reswen was needling quite deliberately now; both of them knew it, and both knew equally that he was well within the rights of his rank to do so. He stared at the junior officer and waited patiently for some sort of comment.

"We should, we should, we, er . . . ," Sithen said, "we should make them welcome." He paused, but in that pause read nothing either of agreement or disapproval in his commander's face. Evidently Reswen wanted more. "And make sure that they know we knew of their approach."

"Excellent. Well thought out." *Eventually.* "Then you'll be in full agreement with what I think we should do now." Even though Reswen hadn't said what was in his mind, Sithen nodded almost as a reflex response. "Runner." Reswen looked at him, then at the door, and this time yelled. *"Runner!"*

The mrem whose head came hurriedly round the door was wearing the yellow cross-belts of an offical courier. He was also wearing a rather startled expression, because Chief of Constables Reswen wasn't one to raise his voice for anything other than the gravest of emergencies. Reswen knew quite well that Sithen was staring at him for that very same reason, and he didn't particularly care. "You," he told the messenger, "get your tail in here right now."

He reached for a wax-faced writing tablet, looked at it, and glanced about for a stylus. There were none in sight; he and Sithen had been using brush quills for their work on the expense chits, and Reswen, whether for the sake of immediacy or drama he couldn't have guessed himself, wasn't inclined to waste the time to fine one. Instead he unsheathed the claws of his right paw and scrawled words swiftly on the wax, quite aware of the stares that his gesture was drawing from both Sithen and the courier. "Speed first, manners second," he said briskly to no one in particular, then struck his official seal into the wax, snapped the tablet's protective covers shut, slapped his seal again against the wax-impregnated leather strip that held it shut, then shoved the whole thing at the courier-mrem with an incongruous smile to back it up. "That to the Arpekh Session-Chamber, fast as your legs will take you. Send in another messenger as you leave."

"Sir?" Sithen ventured, very quietly, very cautiously, not quite sure what flea was in his commander's fur and reluctant to get in the way of whatever was needed to scratch it.

"Sithen," replied Reswen. He didn't look at the junior, already using his extended claws on the surface of another tablet. Stamp of seal, snap of covers, stamp of seal again and another brusque shove towards another waiting messenger. "That to the Garrison Captains. All of them. Action, immediate. It's all there anyway. Move!"

When the door had slammed behind the second messenger, Reswen's relaxation was undisguised. "There," he said. "That ought to cause the right sort of stir."

"What, sir?"

Reswen yawned before he bothered to answer, yawned, and stretched, and flexed so that sinews clicked in his back and neck and his claws slid involuntarily from their sheaths in his pads to leave small, pale parallel gouges in the surface of the desk. None of it was to insult Sithen, or to show superiority of rank of birth or anything else, and both mrem knew it from the set of ears and tail and whiskers; it was just so that Reswen could work the slow tide of tension out of his muscles and ready himself for whatever came next. Whatever that might be. "Oh, nothing much," he said, far too calmly. "I've just given the Easterners something to see that I greatly hope they're not expecting. And won't like." He paused a moment as a new sound filtered in from the city outside, then observed calmly, "That was quickly done."

As the sound, a muttering of rapid drumbeats, became plainer and louder as it spread across Niau from one garrison signal tower to the next, Sithen recognised the pattern of its rhythm and stared at his commander in disbelief.

Reswen met the stare, held it, and then nodded. "Yes, Sithen. I am calling battle stations. Throughout the city. Let them think that Niau is like this all the time—and then let them start to wonder what our combat readiness is really like!"

"The Arpekh won't like it, sir."

"Yes. I know." Reswen eyed the uncompleted expense chits as if they were a stack of used latrine wipes, and smirked a sort of self-satisfied smirk that Sithen had never, ever seen before. "I don't expect them to like it. But I do expect them to wake up, just this once. Otherwise why do they need us at all? For this?" He gestured at the chits, then reached for his brush quill with a resigned air. "I hope not. We'll find out soon enough."

"Your message?"

"A hot dish of charcoal at the tail root of every elder presently dozing through whatever they've decided to discuss today. Well, they'll have more to discuss then transport duties once that gets to them, and they'll have to discuss it with me."

"Sir?"

"Yes. It's not quite martial law, Sithen my friend—but it's close enough not to make a deal of difference. In the

meanwhile, how much did you say we were paying Torth—
three silvers?"

"Yes, sir. Three, sir."

"Too much. I've always said so. Far too much . . ."

▲

Chapter 2

▲———————————————————————————————————————▲

She lay in the dark, unmoving, feeling the warmth. It was pleasant, but she knew it would not last much longer. Soon her surroundings would become cool, and thought and action together would be more difficult. This was, in a way, just as well; it would not at that time be to her advantage to move, or to think. There would be those on the lookout for either occurrence.

Not forever, of course. Vigilance would relax, and that would be her time, to command as she would. Her heart grew quick and hot within her at the thought of how it would be then: the scurrying before her, the terror, the delight in the hopelessness of her prey. But for this while, her life would move more slowly.

I shall indulge myself, therefore.

It was a moment's work for one of her training. She let her body go. It was her people's art, no more a matter for thought, as a rule, than to move or eat. But she had had that innate talent sharpened for the work she had to do. For her, the bonds between body and soul were more tenuous than usual, more easily stretched to the limit. And her limit was farther out than others'. Where many another might strain and die of what she was doing, *she* could leap at the end of her soul's tether and stretch it over years and miles in a matter of seconds—then do works that others would find heavy going were they still in their bodies, and more firmly attached to the sources of their power.

One movement of the mind, it took, to cast the skin: a shaking-off, a splitting. A moment of peculiar sensation accompanied the movement—a sort of fear at the prema-

ture shedding of a skin that one (theoretically) was not
through with yet, the body's terrified reaction to needs it
did not understand. But at the same time there was a sort
of bizarre pleasure about it, like the pleasure of shaking off
a true cast skin, getting the wretched, stiff, dulled, scratchy
business stripped off one's limbs and body, and coming
out sleek, cool, and shining at the end of it—made new
again, as the gods had intended, youth periodically renewed, forever and ever.

And when she came free of the sensations, the feelings
of fear and pleasure, it was no longer dark. She reached up
and out and looked around her, peering through the warm
light of the overworld. Half regarded, below her, her body
lay in its darkness, unmoving.

She turned away from it and set her will on her desire,
commanded the light to carry her to the place she wished
to see. And instantly she hung far above it, gazing down as
if she were one of the winged ones.

It was a small place. It was cold. There was little fire
about it. It lay on the fringes of the world, the farthest
frontiers of the warm places. A bad place to want to have
dealings with. But she had her commands, and in the
manner of her people, the commands of her lords were as
her own will.

The town was a wretched little thing, barely more than
a collection of hovels, by the standards of her people.
Water ran in its streets—if one could dignify them by that
name. The buildings were crude. The walls were thin
things; surely an army could breach them without much
trouble. Just once, just for a moment, she teetered on the
edge of rebellion and wondered why one of her talents had
been required to deal with this pitiful place, overrun with
vermin, these vermin with fur. . . .

But the rebellion lasted only a moment; then her obe-
dience found her again, and she settled into it gladly. She
did not mind doing this work, though it seemed a small
one. Vermin these creatures were indeed, and not to be
considered in the same breath with her people; but at the
same time, vermin had to be watched, lest they breed
more swiftly than they had in past years, and become a
threat. And these were in some danger of doing so, she

had been told. That was why she had been commanded to look into them—to consider the matter, and see what attention and action might be needed.

For a while she simply watched the place, as one might idly watch a nest of insects, just before kicking it. From this height, certainly there was something of a resemblance. The half-built, crude look of the place, as compared to the elegant architectures of her own people; the scurrying of the little creatures in the street, wearing their ugly scraps of clothing, doing their toy businesses, as if they were real people—it was all rather pitiful, rather loathesome. *Upstarts,* she thought with scorn. Sometimes she found it hard to understand how they had ever come to be a matter of concern to the Lords in the first place. Who had taught them cities? Who had taught them language, or the use of tools? It had to have been some tribe of her own people; certainly there was no way that these beasts, these furred things, could ever have managed the discovery of civilization by themselves. She wondered whether the Lords in their wisdom did indeed know who was responsible, and whether they had been punished, and how many years the punishment had lasted, in its manifold subtleties. Some she had heard of had gone on for a long time indeed. When one was as long-lived as one of her people, there was no surprise about that. . . .

She bent her attention a little closer. The action in the rough little streets grew more apparent, as did the lifefire of the vermin. A muddy-colored sort of fire it was, by her people's standards: something to do with the fur, she supposed, or their frantically hasty minds. Their lives made fires that burned quick, but not clear; they left an odd taste when her mind brushed them. She shook her head at it, as if trying to shake it away. She could not allow herself to be distracted by inconsequential things.

She let her true body sink lower, until she seemed to perch atop one of the squalid rooftops and gaze down into a teeming street. How they jostled one another, how they rushed, these creatures! No stately grace about them, no slow ponderousness of movement, hard-gained with survival to a dignified old age. Just scurrying, hurrying, all to no apparent purpose. *Though,* she thought scornfully, *doubt-*

*less they think their own inconsequential businesses to be
important enough.*

No matter. That will change soon enough.

Indeed it would. Stretching her senses out in the pallid
light of this place's overworld, she could smell the minds
she wanted, the ones she had been told to look for. Not by
name—did they even have names?—but the emotions were
clear enough to her: clear as the track of a tail in the sand.
Though poor little rodent-scratchings their petty passions
and desires were besides the thoughts and feelings of one
of her own people—slow, subtle, careful, but fierce as the
snap of jaws at the end of it all. Her tongue flickered
reflectively at the taste of the little minds, the greed, the
hunger, the jealousy and impotent rage. They would serve
her purposes well enough. Her servants would seek out
the bodies in which those minds lived, and through them
she would work. It was a very choice irony. By their own
claws, would these vermin be brought down: by their own
acts, their own passions. And her kind would rule here
once again, as they had been meant to long ago.

What should have been, would now be. It was a good
thought. She sank back into her body, into the darkness,
and hissed with the pleasure of what would come . . . the
thought of the running blood. . . .

▲

The Arpekh's summons, in the form of a troop of their
larger and more imposing guards, was outside Constables'
House and hammering the door for admittance within the
half hour. Reswen was faintly surprised that they had
taken so short a time to send for him, for the Council of
Elders were very literally what their title suggested, wealthy
noblemrem of advanced years who ground slow and small
when reaching a decision over trading rights, but who
were equally renowned among the mrem of Reswen's
generation for turning that slow, careful consideration into
farce when rapid action was required. How much they
knew of how they were regarded, Reswen didn't know, or
care.

But he didn't keep the guard-troop waiting, even
so.

▲

"What the council is at pains to understand, Commander Reswen, is why you chose to order out the city cohorts without consulting us. And indeed, why you deemed the order necessary at all." Councillor Mraal looked from side to side, and his fifteen companions nodded as sagely as they could—all except Councillor Aratel, who had nodded off.

He'll have to go, thought Mraal irritably. Venerable old age was necessary in an Elder, but there were limits even to that most basic requirement. More to the point, Mraal could see that the Chief of Constables, far from looking suitably contrite, was gazing at the sleeping—and now both audibly and visibly dreaming—councillor with a barely concealed smile curling at his whiskers.

Aratel mewed shrilly in his sleep and paddled his forepaws a bit, upsetting the stack of terribly important-looking papers which he, like most of the other councillors, had apparently had placed before him before admitting their errant Chief of Constables for what had been intended to be mild verbal chastisement and which was now becoming an embarrassing comedy of errors. "Lord Arpak, the facts of the case speak for themselves," observed Reswen pleasantly, still looking in a very pointed sort of way at Aratel.

Mraal considered the various options which irritation had sent flickering through his mind, then reconsidered them and discarded the lot. Reswen, after all, had only said aloud what he himself had thought on several occasions in the past while. That Aratel was too old even to be an Elder any more, was long overdue for honorably retirement to his mansion, and even longer overdue for replacement by someone a good twenty years younger. Most to the point, Mraal knew just the mrem for the job. . . .

"Very well." Mraal conceded the first point with as good grace as he could manage while wishing that someone, anyone, would give Aratel a good hard nudge under the ribs before he did something to really spoil the Arpekh's dignity. "We allow that you felt time would be lost by endeavoring to consult—or dare I say awaken—" Mraal

smiled stiffly and was gratified more by Reswen's surprise
at the unexpected joke than by the appreciative soft laughter of his fellows, "—all the members of the council. But
what must yet be explained is your reason for sounding
battle stations in the first place. Niau is not under attack,
surely?"

"Not yet, Lord Arpak." Reswen's statement caused just
the sort of sensation that he plainly intended it should, for
Mraal saw relief and satisfaction quite unconcealed on the
policemrem's face.

What game are you playing now? Mraal wondered,
and said "Explain," with just the right impatient emphasis.
Reswen did, and with sufficient clarity for even the finally-
awake Arpak Aratel to understand his reasoning. Mraal
listened, sitting quite, quite still with not even the twitch
of a whisker or the expansion of a spindle-narrow pupil to
reveal what he was thinking. Inwardly he was applauding
Reswen as he had never suspected he would applaud any
of the Quiet Ones. If what Reswen said was true, and
there was no reason for him to fabricate something so easy
to disprove, then his high-and-heavy-pawed actions both
as Chief of Constables and Head of H'satei were no more
than an indication that he was doing the job for which the
Council and the city paid him.

As for the Easterners who accompanied the approaching caravan—assuming that Second-Oct Recruit Creel had
indeed seen them and not simply imagined their presence
after cooking his brain too long in the desert sun—what, oh
what were they doing coming here in the first place . . . ?
Mraal looked at Councillor Aratel as the name of the
old mrem's replacement drifted through his mind again.
Erelin. . . Always assuming that he could force the proposal through. Aratel had many supporters, or at least
many who would be reluctant to see so compliant a councillor removed from the Arpekh in favour of one so much
younger, and most likely much less amenable to bribes.
Almost of an age, indeed, with that impudent ginger-
furred whippersnapper Reswen. Mraal smiled a bit at that.
It would probably be no bad thing for the city, no matter
what anyone who stood to lose might say.

"This city lives by trade, Commander Reswen. If it is

seen as a perpetually armed camp, then the traders and
their caravans will take their business elsewhere; to Ar, or
to Cragsclaw, and judge the excess journey worthwhile for
the sake of their peace of mind. The Arpekh will withhold
judgement on this matter until it can be seen what advantage if any has resulted from your hasty actions."

Reswen appeared unfazed by the tacit threat, and Mraal
hazarded a guess that the Chief of Constables had already
balanced cause and effect before committing himself to so
irrevocable a course of action. Besides which, his police
spies could provide him with more than enough juicy
details to disarm even the most wrathful mrem on the
council. Mraal wondered about a few small indiscretions of
his own, realizing just how lucky he was to have nothing
serious to be left panting and bloody on the rug, then
caught the way that Reswen was looking at him and realized though the policemrem might not be able to read
minds, he could certainly make an uncomfortable amount
of sense from expression alone.

"I," said Reswen, rising from the small seat where he
had been placed at the beginning of the interview, "have
work to do. If there is nothing further then, my lords
Arpekh, I'd best go do it. Now. Good day to one and all."

Mraal watched him go, and made a mental note that
some day not too far from now, he would have to talk with
Reswen in private. About various matters pertaining to the
safer running of Niau city, and the mrem within its walls.
But that would come later. Right now Mraal was more
intrigued than he allowed himself to show over whether
there were indeed Easterners in the approaching caravan,
and most important of all, how they would react to their
first sight of a city where normal life seemed to include an
armed, defensive stance. Reswen had been right: "I don't
know what they told the caravan-master, but these Easterners aren't merchants. They're spies. I've given them
something to report, and though I know they'll suspect
some of it was for their benefit, they won't be sure how
much. I want them to believe that Niau's soldiery reacts
like this for every caravan; because I want them to really
worry about how we'd react to an invading army. Let
them tell their master *that!*"

▲

Reswen's excuse for going up on the walls was, naturally, to inspect the guard positions and make sure they were properly manned—"properly," in this case, meaning "too heavily for anything but a full-scale invasion." He was delighted to find that old Sachath the City Commandant had taken the challenge quite seriously. The walls could barely hold all the soldiery massed along them; spears and arrows bristled everywhere, and guardsmrem peered out through the crenellations as if they could hardly wait for the invaders to get within bowshot. This, Reswen suspected, was the truth. The snatches of conversation he caught here and there before being recognized gave him to understand that the guardsmen were wildly curious about the Easterners. That the curiosity would look, from a distance, like alertness, and maybe even hostility, bothered Reswen not at all.

He found Sachath right where he expected to, in the most dramatic possible spot, on the walk above the Great Gate, where a commander would deliver ultimata or ritually taunt the enemy before releasing a sally. *It's where I would stand myself, after all*, Reswen thought, and his whiskers curled forward again. There Sachath stood, a brawny brindled shape all plate mail and tanned leather, his helm tucked under one arm, gazing out at the approaching caravan, with the look of a mrem who wished they were an army, and wished they would start something, anything. Sachath's tail thumped hard and thoughtfully against one hind leg, under the lorica. It was a stump tail, half lopped off in some border skirmish back in the mists of time. Sachath had told Reswen the story a hundred times, at one offical function or another, and mercifully Reswen always managed to forget the details before the next policemen's feast or army dinner.

Sachath was growling in his throat, as usual; the joke around the barracks was that he had growled at his dam when she first licked him off. He turned to see Reswen, and the growl if anything got louder, but this was nothing more than recognition and pleasure. "Not enough of 'em," he said as Reswen came up.

"Pardon?"

"Not enough of 'em, my young friend. Where's the army we expected? Not enough fight here to keep us busy more than half an hour. Less than that, perhaps."

Reswen leaned between two crenellations and peered out. There was nothing more on the horizon yet than a yellow dust cloud, rising. "Probably not," he said.

"As you well know. *Certainly* not. Then again, maybe best they think that, eh?"

Reswen looked sidewise at Sachath. Old and torn-eared to the point of cliché he might be, but he was not stupid; the Niauhu Army had politics of its own that made some of the city's infighting look like littermates' squabbles, and Sachath had survived it all for three-quarters of a lifetime, losing nothing more than half a tail and his good temper. "Maybe so," Reswen said, and shifted his eyes to the horizon again. More was showing now than dust: a glint here and there, a pair of moving specks ahead.

"Scouts," Sachath said, squinting past him. "Spears there, too. No more than there should be, for the distance they've come. Maybe a few more carry-boxes, though." He pointed with his flail of office. Reswen could just make out the outlines of the first few slave-carried travel boxes. It was a large embassy, surely. "That's trouble for you," Sachath said, growling low.

Reswen shrugged his tail. "No worse than expected."

"Let us save you trouble and make short work of 'em now," Sachath said. "A mistake, you'll say later. Could have happened to anyone. Blame it on the army. Always spoiling for a fight, those types."

Reswen's whiskers went forward almost against his will. This was one of Sachath's specialties, this outrageous black humor that he would turn against himself and whoever happened to be standing nearest, both at once. Usually it had a purpose: to get you to talk Sachath into something he wanted to do anyway (or out of something he didn't). There was only one weapon against it. "Rrrh," Reswen said, purring. "Go ahead. Who first, then? Bowmrem? Feather 'em at a distance? Or wait and let the foot soldiery out? Swords' edges on all that silly giltwork?" For the gleam of gold and the shimmer of silk were beginning to be visible on the nearest of the boxes, and on the armor of the walking guards, and even the harness of the slaves.

"Fleas and mange on it, wait indeed," Sachath growled. "Who taught you tactics, kit-brain? Waiting is weakness, attacking is strength. Get the infantry out, let 'em run for it, do 'em good in this heat, they're too fat as it is, most of 'em. City life, it spoils a mrem. Get to be like *that* before too long." Sachath jerked the less scarred of his ears at the approaching caravan.

"Let's get to it, then," Reswen said, and made as if to call a trumpeter over.

"Hnnr," Sachath said, and this time the growl was half laugh; he slapped Reswen's raised paw down against the stone with his own, but his claws were in. "You'd drag string in front of a lame kitten. Not matter, let 'em be. *They're* dragging the string for the moment. Look at 'em."

Reswen did, and had to laugh himself. The intelligence report he had received earlier made it plain that most of the carry-boxes had been slung across the pack animals, and mrem had been handling the baggage, except for a few very large crates or boxes being dragged travois-style by teams of beasts. Now the beasts were carrying nothing but luggage, and all the carry-boxes were being handled, in some cases with great difficulty, by mrem; there was much staggering and breaking stride among several of the teams in the rear. *Slightly less important officials,* Reswen thought, *doing the best they can to make a big entrance. And having second thoughts about it in some cases,* as he watched one of the box teams stumble forward, ram into another, and both go down in a gilt-edged heap. The rest of the caravan continued its approach. Faintly, over the sweet chime of bells on harness, came the sound of swearing in Eastern dialects.

"Enough," said Sachath. "Let 'em play their play. Us to our own. *All right, you flea-ridden ratspawn!*" he shouted to the immediate wall as he strode off among his people. "What're you staring at, hast never seen a caravan before? Straighten up, the lot of you, wouldn't think you knew which end to hold a sword by, don't pout your ears down at *me,* my son— " Reswen heard the sound of Sachath's officer's flail being put to some use as he went roaring off into the distance, down the length of the wall. The soldiery stood straight and looked to a mrem as if they would much rather attack something than endure the assault being committed on them by their own side. The faces turned down to the caravan as it approached the gates were uniformly hostile indeed; the assembled guard considered all this upset to be *their* fault.

Time to play the play indeed, Reswen thought, and stalked along the wall to where the stairs to the Great Gate swept down. He brushed at himself as he padded down. He had dressed not so much for effect this morning as for lack of it. First impressions were important, and he wanted no one noticing him as anything but chief of police, a flunky rather than a functionary. He wore his plain leather everyday harness, somewhat worn, rather than the ceremonial set, along with the shortsword/knife of his (apparent) station—everything polished and tidy, but nothing rich. Even his family's old dewclaw signet he had left at home, not wanting the gold of it to distract from the unrelieved black leather and steel fittings. This, perhaps, bothered him most of all; his thumb-claw itched where the ring was not. It made him nervous. Of all the things he habitually kept about him—swords, purses, paperwork— the ring was the one thing he *never* took off except on undercover work. *Just as well I should be nervous*, he thought. *First impressions come through clearer*. But it was poor comfort to the itchy place. He kept feeling that his father, who had given him the ring, would cuff him on seeing it off. The feeling was not even slightly dispelled by the knowledge that his father was many years in the ground and gone Elsewhere.

No time for that now. Here they came, and to do them justice, they did it splendidly. The glitter of gold that had looked funny, off in the dust, now glanced almost too bright to look at; the dim sound of bells that had sounded ridiculous mixed with curses now came all in sweet chords; and the uplifted spears of the embassy's guards lanced light back at the sun, and gems caught the light and kept it and were little suns themselves. *Impressive*, Reswen thought dryly, because he really was impressed, and was slightly disturbed by the fact. What kind of people would carry such riches across the desert, careless of wind and sand and bandits? *This wants some looking into,* he thought, and stepped out from beside the gate into the hot sun.

The Lords Arpekh were gathering there. They at least had been able to dress for effect, and there was as much glitter of gold and ripple of velvet and satin as there was outside. Reswen felt the urge to snicker at the sight of them, but restrained himself. The guards at the gates hauled on the counterpoises, and the gates swung slowly open. The herald of the Easterners stalked in, a bizarre brown curly-coated tom all gems and moiré silk, and a cloak of black sendal spangled with diamonds like a desert night. His robes had the kind of excessive dagging, purfling, and superfluous tucks about them that cause sumptuary laws to be passed by cranky kings. His ears were each pierced three times and each ring had a different stone hung in it, and in one hand he held an ebony rod with a balas at the end—a round clear stone with a red agate embedded in it. Reswen found himself doing tallies in his head at the sight of the showy mrem, and he struggled briefly with exchange rates—and then had to break off suddenly on noticing that the creature's tail was hairless in a great patch near the end, as if he had been snatched bald, or had been swinging in trees like the little green primates of the wild forests. *If this is the herald,* Reswen thought, choking down his laughter, *heaven save us from the rest of the embassy!*

The curly-coated mrem bowed low, waving his rod of office with exaggerated grace. "In the name of the Lords of the East, great and terrible to their enemies, yet mild to their subjects and their friends," he said, "and in the names of the gods of the Lords of the East, who are secret but from whom no secrets are kept, well we greet the mrem of this city Niau and its mighty Elders, who are known from the sea to the sky in all of the world where mrem tell tales of their wisdom and power—"

Oh no, Reswen thought. *One of these.* He set himself in the balanced stance that would enable him to be a long time in one position without moving, and grew very resigned about what this morning promised. Why couldn't more cities be like the Northern ones, where people talked in sentences short enough to let a mrem breathe properly, and even diplomats tended to occasionally say "yes" or "no" outright? But he had half expected that this was going to happen. Damned flowery Eastern dialects—though he was slightly relieved to find that the herald's accent and way with Niauhu were more than passable. At least there would be no need for extra translators; his usual staff would be adequate to handle the business of spying on these people. A good thing. He hated to have to subcontract work out . . . it was expensive, and there were too many other people eager to talk to the subcontractors afterwards, about police procedures . . . or other, more private matters involving the H'satei. *Well, no matter. I wonder if the house in Dancer's Street is ready . . . it had better be. . . .*

The herald was going on, fulsomely and in mouth-crippling periods, about the wondrous stature and wisdom and wealth and whatever of the Elders of Niau. Reswen glanced sideways and found to his annoyance that the Elders were eating it up. *Something missing in their diet, perhaps,* he thought. *Maybe if we flattered them ourselves, on occasion, they'd be less susceptible to it from outsiders. Though why anyone would want to flatter these somnolent, crapulent, obsolescent—*

"—whose fame and glory shames the Moon and outblazes the Day—"

Reswen wondered if the herald would get around to mentioning why they had come before dinnertime, or perhaps sunset. *Maybe I'm being too paranoid,* he thought, *and the plot is something simple. To kill us by sunstroke . . .* But at that moment the city herald, Tehenn, stepped out in his own finery and outbowed the Easterners' herald, who came to an abrupt stop at the gesture, or perhaps at the appearance of his opposite number. Reswen had to admit that Tehenn deserved the astonishment; few outsiders were prepared for the sheer size of him. He was perhaps the biggest mrem Reswen had ever seen, with a build that seemed more appropriate for an uxan than anything else, and black, all black, not a white hair on him. From the shining blackness perfect golden eyes stared, molten and dangerous-looking. Tehenn was one of those heralds who looked fully inclined—and able—to take care of himself whether or not the people to whom he was sent treated him with the traditional courtesy. Too, for all the Eastern herald's finery, it looked slightly cheap and pale next to what Tehenn wore: a simple black leather strap-harness, and a supple loincloth. But it was hard to see that the leather was black, since every bit of it on the outside was encrusted with diamonds. Tehenn straightened, and the diamonds on the ancient Niahu heralds' livery flashed, blinding everybody nearby, most specifically the Eastern herald.

"In the name of the Elders of Niau, we give you greeting and bid you be very welcome," Tehenn said, and the other herald and the Easterners behind him reacted, as Reswen had suspected they would, to that astonishing voice, all honey and gold, slow and warm. "But the day is hot, and you have come a long way, and the Elders fear for your health and fear to fail in their hospitality to you. So say, I beg, what brings you unlooked-for but most welcomely to our gates, so that we may bring you in and give you refreshment—or do whatever else is necessary."

Reswen smiled as the Easterner looked momentarily out of his depth at the elegant hurry-up. He could see the other herald thinking: Could that have possibly been an undertone of threat to that last phrase?—but of course not— The Eastern herald bowed low again. "We come with gifts," he said, "for the Elders and the people of Niau, and with things of mart, things to trade and to sell; for we have made great wealth in trading north and south, and why not now west? We come with rare stuffs, and curious works, clothes and leathers and precious woods, rare beasts and jewels—"

"We sometimes have use for jewels," said Tehenn, offhanded and gracious, and bowed a little, blinding everyone again. "But such other things as you mention are pleasant to us, and the Elders and the people will be pleased to look upon them while you sojourn here. Enter, then, and be welcome, and the Elders and merchants will meet with you and speak with you personally, as they speak through me to you now. Be welcome once more, and may your stay be propitious!"

There was more bowing, and the Eastern herald finally turned and gestured his people in. In they came, piling into the courtyard, amid clouds of dust and the noise and lowing of beasts, the squeals of caged things, the chiming of bells, the smells of perfume and sweat and ordure. Tehenn had stepped over to the Elders and stood with bent head, conferring with them for a moment, then crossed over to Reswen.

"The house in Dancer's Street?" he said, in an undertone.

"That's right," Reswen said. Wryly he added, "Rare beasts, hmm?" For one of the gilded litters was being borne past them, and a curtain parted, and blue, blue eyes in a narrow, delicate gray face peered out, eyeing Tehenn with great interest. Then the curtains swung shut again.

"Courtesans, eh," said Tehenn. "A gift for the Elders, no doubt."

"She didn't look particularly interested in the Elders, Tehenn."

The herald looked ironic. "Nay then," he said, "you're climbing the wrong tree, master. My wife would have both my ears off, and kick out my guts. But doesn't anyone simply do straightforward trading any more, without bribery—" He fell silent.

"Gifts are traditional, in the East," said Reswen.

Tehenn looked more ironic than before. "So are knives in the back," he said. He gestured a quick farewell to Reswen, and went off the lead the caravan into the depths of the city. Reswen watched them curl away out of the square, a long line of swaying beasts and litters and dusty mrem, surrounded by curious, staring Niau people . . . and thought about knives.

He headed off to see about the house.

▲

Chapter 3

▲————————————————————————————————▲

The house in Dancer's Street looked not very different from the other houses there. It was obviously a well-to-do place, all white marble and intricate carving; those knowledgeable in Niau architecture would have dated it to the second wave of the city's building, when the prosperity of the place was beginning to gather speed, and people building houses were eager to show how well they were doing. It had in fact been built by one of the oldest merchantile families, the *rrh'Hhwaen*, who had made their fortunes in the import and treatment of hides. The stink of the tannery had never come near this place, though. Originally the one house had been alone in a small parkland, but the family's fortunes declined over several generations, and finally they began to sell off the land around them to priests and other wealthy people.

The area had become the high rent district: absolutely respectable, the other houses there owned by nobility, or other, even richer merchants. Finally even a few temples had been built there—the temple of the White Dancers was down at the end of the street in a quiet cul-de-sac. The street was perfectly clean; there was no filth in the gutters, and had not been for a long time, since the more innovative of the rich merchants had been the first in the city to install plumbing, and had had the novel idea of having their garbage hauled away and dumped somewhere else, rather than burning or burying it on their own grounds. Reswen knew parts of the city where he strongly suspected the garbage had wound up for many years, before even the poorest mrem rebelled and insisted that it be

dumped outside the walls. But the merchants had not
been too concerned about that; their own nest was clean.
Wherever you looked, there was marble white or gray or
polished black, everything gleaming; you could catch
glimpses of rich tapestries or figured hangings through
those windows thrown open to the morning. The sun fell
more gently here, through tall old trees that remained
from the ancient parkland and had been spared in the
making of the street. Even the cobbles, marble as well,
shone softly where they had been worn smooth.

Reswen, pacing down the street, considered that he
would not have lived here on a bet. The place was a little
too clean, a little too affluent, for his tastes. *Now is that
completely normal?* he found himself wondering. *Maybe
my police work has corrupted my sensibilities. What's
wrong with cleanliness? Little enough of it in most parts of
this town. . . .* But on the other hand, anymrem needed a
little dirt to survive, even if only to scratch in once or
twice a day while doing the necessary. And all the cleanliness here only served to accentuate the dirt when it did
show up, in people's lives. And it always showed up,
sooner or later. The people who could afford to live for
long in houses like these did not always come by the
money honestly . . . or did not always comport themselves
in honorable ways, thinking their riches excused them.
These people, some of them, were the reason Reswen was
obliged to overpay his spies.

But he put the thought away for the moment, as he
came up outside the house. The place had a wide, walled
courtyard in front, gated in gilded iron. Inside, the caravan people's beasts were milling around while the house
servants led them away, one by one, to the stabling behind the garden in the rear. Reswen waved a claw at the
gate guard, who opened it for him.

He went quietly up the marble flagging toward the
house, smelling the air appreciatively, for there were garden plots on either side, thick with herbs and sweet-
smelling flowers. They curved toward the wide portico of
the house itself. Its old name, "Haven," was carved in
simple, antique style over the portico. This porch had
pillars, in the manner of classic architecture, but between

them, shielding the house's unshuttered windows, there were marble screens pierced and carved with endless cunning: openwork trellises of marble, with marble vines and tendrils curling up and around them, flowering in white and blue and red and gold. The gold was real, and the blue and red were lapis and carnelian. Floating through the bright tracery, Reswen could hear the sounds of talk, laughter, astonishment. Haven was a place designed to astonish, which suited Reswen well. He went up the steps and stopped in the doorway.

In the great white-and-gilded expanse of the forehall, a cold collation had been laid out for the Easterners, since Niauhu hospitality stated that food should be offered even before rest to the welcomed traveler. The house servants, of course, stood ready for escort upstairs anyone who should wish to retire; the rooms should be in good order, and even an Easterner should find the luxury impressive. Soft couches, floors strewn with rare soft furs, rich hangings, and no common dirt closets, but luxurious rooms with water running through them, and every kind of toiletry that the fastidious Niauhu had been able to invent over many years. Reswen had made it his business to sleep, at least once, in every one of the rooms. His staff chuckled over what they considered a canny move by Old Ginger to have himself a few soft nights. Reswen let them chuckle. He had other reasons . . . though he was hardly fool enough not to enjoy himself at the same time.

Reswen strolled about in the forehall a bit, keeping to the edges of the room to have a look at the visitors. Many of them had gotten rid of their desert clothes, and were busy drinking up the wine in snow that had been brought for them. *Fine*, Reswen thought. *Loose tongues will make this job a little easier, no matter how cautious they are on the first day.* . . . He counted about thirty people who interested him; the other twenty Easterners in the forehall were servants, some liveried, some not. About twenty of the notables were noble, several of them priests of one god or cult or another; some of them were family, spouses or sons or daughters. Several of them seemed to be merchants —they had that sharp, noticing look about them—and there were a couple of others, advisers or hangers-on, that Reswen couldn't immediately classify.

And then of course there were the courtesans. Reswen stopped by one of the tables, indulging himself in a cup of cold wine and a tiny fried roll-cake with fresh fish in it—pool whitefish, by the taste of it, and quite well seasoned with something sharp and spicy. He resolved to have a word with the cook later; Reswen believed in complimenting his staff when they deserved it. He glanced over and saw Tehenn moving with his usual graceful assurance from one guest to another, smiling here, laughing and gesturing for a servant to pour wine there, and proceeding by his own careful methods to work out who here was in authority, and with whom he needed to make arrangements for the more formal meetings to take place later in the day and the evening. Reswen had to admire Tehenn's smooth operation. *I wonder, could I get him working for me?* . . . There were attractive aspects to it. To have the Elders' herald in the H'satei, a mrem privy to all kinds of sensitive information . . . Then again, if the Elders found out about it, they would certainly sack everyone involved, Reswen included. And it would be a shame to deprive the city of such a good herald. . . .

The thought faded out as Reswen found those blue, blue eyes trained on him again from across the room. The courtesan was extremely beautiful, but that was to be expected, or she would hardly have been brought along. She was wearing hardly anything—which was also to be expected—nothing but a wonderfully made harness of linked silver ornamented with aquarmarines and sapphires, over sea gray fur darkening to charcoal gray on face and ears and paws and tail. A dusky loveliness, hers, in which those eye burned blue as sky; and a lanky loveliness, long-limbed, graceful, and cool. Reswen let his eyes widen as if he were what he looked to be, a minor functionary of some sort, unused to being gazed at by fine ladies. Very hurriedly he gobbled the last of the fish cake, put the wine cup down, and headed toward the front door like a mrem caught doing something he shouldn't.

A few heads turned as he made his hasty exit, and Reswen was careful to notice which ones. One of the priests, a great gross creature splotched in muddy orange and white, wearing ornate robes and bizarre symbols in lead and gold strung on a silver chain around neck and girdle. One of the merchants, a round-eyed gray tabby in divided robes of white silk and cotton, his markings blurred, his eyes green and oblique. And another of the females, a dark and subty patterned tortoise-shell with golden eyes, modestly dressed, some servingmrem perhaps. Just now, when they had no idea who or what he was, such reactions were of interest. After Reswen had been formally introduced, natural reactions—or unconcealed ones—would be harder to come by; after all, who is utterly without some small trait or habit or misdeed that he would rather no one, especially not the Chief of Constables, knew anything about? Out he went, and down the steps, and out into the courtyard, where he paused for a moment and breathed like a mrem who had had a narrow escape. Then around the side of the house, past the stables, where the servants were putting up the visitors' beasts, and down one side of the stable block, being careful to breathe out all the way down.

This brought Reswen to a wall at the foot of the garden, and a little door in it that opened on the street behind Dancer's. He lifted the latch, stepped through, and pulled the door to behind him. Here was another white marble and polished granite neighborhood, but he gave it not a glance, heading across the cobbled street to a smallish town house between two larger, grander ones. Reswen went up the steps of the town house, knocked at the door, and waited.

The door opened, and a brown-striped tabby servant in civic livery looked out, saw who Reswen was, and stepped aside. "They're waitin' for you downstairs, sir," he said.

"That's good, Lelef," Reswen said, and headed down another white marble hall, much plainer than the last one. Down the staircase at the end, to a granite landing; down the granite stair at the end of it, to a wooden door set in stone; and through the wooden door into a tunnel, cool but dry, faced at first in rough blocks of black and gray stone, then in timbers. Occasionally roots stuck through into the tunnel between the timbers. It was a longish walk; at the end of it the tunnel terminated in another wooden door. Reswen opened the door and went in.

The room revealed was as long as the Haven house from back to front, which was no surprise . . . since it was directly under it. The walls of the timber-faced room had numerous metal tubes projecting from them, and at almost all of these tubes, mrem of Reswen's service were sitting, listening attentively, wax pads on their knees, making occasional scratched notations in the wax. The room was filled with a soft hollow mutter of voices drifting down from the floors above; still the innocent sounds of surprise and merriment that Reswen had heard, the little while he had been up there.

"Sir," came a voice, and one of his officers, Krruth, came up from the rear of the room to meet him. Krruth was an unlikely-looking mrem. He had lost an eye due to illness when young, and his upbringing, a wretchedly poor one, had left its stamp on him. Krruth was bent and blasted-looking, thinned right down to the bone, and his dull black coat did nothing to make him look any better. But Krruth had something a hundred times better than good looks, as far as Reswen was concerned—his memory was a room with one door in and no way out. He never forgot a face or a voice, and he was a repository of information more reliable than many a gilded parchment back in Reswen's office.

"Krruth," he said, and they sat down together at a table in the middle of the room. "Anything of interest?"

"Nothing as yet," said Krruth. "But from what we have been able to hear, I warrant there will be."

Reswen nodded. "The rooms are all in order?"

"All the listening tubes are working, yes, and last week we put a new set in to replace the old ones in the water closets, so the echo will not bounce back upstairs and make anyone curious."

"Very good. What are your impressions so far?"

"They're being cautious, sir," Krruth said. "But introductions can hardly be avoided, and some of them have let fall information they might have preferred to hold back a while. The delegation—for so they title themselves, not just a humble caravan—has eighteen body-servants, whom our own 'servants' will being working on as soon as convenient. Indeed, several of their servants have already tried to seduce ours, so this bodes well. We have here several priests, all of the same worship; they are involved with some kind of Eastern grain-god. . . . We will find out more about that later. They put about that they are required to travel with another of the party, a corn factor, to advise him on his business decisions. The one we judge to be the corn factor says nothing about that; he says he is here on behalf of several other guilds who are interested in trading with the Western cities, and he claims that this is not an unusual thing, this joint representation. But I heard his voice, and I have my doubts. He sounds too scornful and angry to be telling all the truth."

"Keep an ear on him, then," Reswen said. "And the others?"

"The corn factor has brought his wife and children with him, for a holiday, he says, but about this too I have my doubts," said Krruth. "The wife sounds to be the petted sort who has never seen the outside of her home city's walls, and has no desire to see it now. She came in complaining about the heat and how thirsty she was, and is now complaining about the chill, the crudity of the food, and the warmth and poor vintage of the wines. The children are barely adolescent, and brats both, from the sound. They are presently eating everything in sight, and spoiling to wreck the place. I think they have never seen such splendor in a house, and can hardly wait to destroy some of it to let us know that they are not particularly impressed."

Reswen rolled his eyes slightly. "Something their father put them up to, you think? To reinforce our opinion of the Easterners' wealth?"

"Hard to say. We shall see."

"Can the upstairs people handle it, or should we 'call the police'?"

"No need, I think. There are other matters of more interest, at any rate. Despite the fact that the one merchant—Rirhath—claims to speak for all, there are three other merchants—a clothier, a jeweler, and someone who deals in predictions of meat purchases in the East. Peculiar sort of trade."

"I have heard of it," Reswen said. "It does seem odd, betting on whether the uxen will calve properly next year, but the Easterners have apparently learned to make money that way . . . I suspect we may have to learn ourselves."

"I prefer dice. At any rate, they have been very impressed by the surroundings . . . a word or two was let fall that we appear to be better off then they thought, though they knew very well that we've given them this accommodation on purpose, to impress them."

"Among other reasons," Reswen said, and chuckled. It had been his predecessor's idea to get the city to buy Haven and turn it into a place where guests could be cosseted, pampered . . . and listened to very closely, not in the usual ways or at the usual times. Everyone in Haven was on Reswen's payroll, and these mrem he did not mind overpaying, not at all . . . considering the kind of work they had to do, and the dividends it produced.

"Then we have the higher-class servants—they are so, though they are dressed like nobles, and Rirhath calls them 'our associates.' Two scriveners and a mathematician."

"Spies," Reswen said. For some reason, they always came disguised as scribes.

"Possibly. We shall have a look at their shorthand over the next few days and see how long they have been writing it. At any rate, they have said very little for the time being . . . they've been too busy eating."

"Definitely spies," Reswen said. "Underpaid and underfed. Poor creatures . . . we should try to hire them."

Krruth grinned. "And then we come to the courtesans."

"Plural? I thought there was only one."

"No, two. Deshahl and Laas are their names. The first is the high-priced one. The second I judge to be a less highly, ah, seasoned sweetmeat, to be given to someone of less importance, or several someones. The second has said little, and done little but drink since she came in. The first is flattering Tehenn most outrageously, poor thing; she has no idea how few fish *that* pool has for the likes of her. But then she is flattering every other Niauhu male of rank she's seen. I wonder that she didn't make a pounce on you."

"She did, in a manner of speaking. . . ." Reswen thought of those blue eyes again, then turned away from the thought. "How has their unpacking been going?"

"Well. They had no objection to our people unloading their beasts and putting the bags and so forth in their rooms. We are still searching some of them, but nothing interesting has turned up so far. The usual mercantile goods. Vash tells me that some of the cloths and jewels are particularly fine, much better than Western make."

"All right. Continue as you have been. Anything of real interest, I want to hear about right away. Send a runner. Otherwise, so far I think we'll find out things in the usual order: Today and tomorrow and this eightday will be dry, and news of their covert intentions will begin popping out of the holes later in the month. All the same, see to it that all the peepholes are manned for the next few days, until we get these mrem's routines worked out. After that, check with me."

"Very well, sir. Now I will need descriptions for these voices."

Reswen spent a goodly while with Krruth at one or another of the tubes, identifying the voices his people had been listening to, and describing the owners. Krruth stood beside him, making no notes; he never needed them, and would pass the information on faultlessly to his people. Only once during the process did Reswen pause, as a silvery voice way above on the ground floor spoke up and laughed, asking for more wine. "Deshahl," said Krruth.

"Blue eyes," Reswen said. "Pale, darkening at the points."

"Rare, very rare," Krruth said. "Be a lot of lads fighting for her peephole, I should say."

Reswen looked askance at Krruth, who gazed back, perfectly grave and apparently without a trace of a salacious thought on his mind. *I should eat more breakfast in this weather,* Reswen thought. *I'm becoming lightheaded. Or lightminded.* "I dare say," he said aloud. "As long as they don't forget to watch everyone else as well."

He turned to go. "I've got the formal reception this evening," he said. "I'll leave an outline for you of anything interesting that our mrem should listen for."

"Very well, sir," Krruth said, and saluted informally. "Mind the wine, now."

"I will," Reswen said, but his mind was not on wine as he left, unless wine is blue.

▲

She had not bothered to go back to her body for a long
time. For one of a lesser talent, that would have been
dangerous. Indeed, to most of her kind who worked out of
the physical body, it was a constant danger. The less
physical body one wore in the overworld always seemed
somehow preferable to the body one wore in the world.
Perhaps it was because one's perfections stood out there,
where in the physical body they were hidden. Or at least,
the aspects of one that one *perceived* as one's perfections,
stood out. She had been shocked, at home, to meet some
of her superiors—great lords and wizards, terrible in their
power and beauty in the overworld, splendors and glories
of scale and flame—to find that they were actually crabbed
and ugly creatures. Or sometimes she found that they
were utterly ordinary-looking; that was somehow even
worse.

Though she had to admit that it was a novice's mistake,
to look at the physical body and assume that what it looked
like accurately indicated what was actually so. One who
did so much work outside of *essh'haaath*, the Hardest
Skin, the skin that took longest to cast, should certainly
know better.

Even more laughable, though, she had found those of
her kind who sought, in the overworld, to present themselves as unusually quick or clever or subtle. One might
fool oneself with such seemings, but others were not confused. The overworld revealed the truth. She had sometimes wondered how she looked to others, and had
shuddered at the thought that the way she perceived
herself might be other than the truth.

She hissed at herself now, softly, in mild irritation, and
turned her mind back to her business. This place was not
conducive to quiet work, this hive of mucky little passions
and strifes. She had spent the last few days and nights
slipping through its sordid streets, looking in the windows
of houses and souls, seeking her enemies, and her allies.
They were many, though none of them knew themselves
for such as yet.

She lay in the midst of one street now. The weak sun

of this place beat on her, pale shadow that it was of the sun of her home, or the true bright sun of the parts of the overworld that her kind called their own. She basked in that light, poor as it was, and watched with cool pleasure as the creatures walked through where her immaterial body lay. Actually, not many of them walked through; she got a certain wicked delight at watching how many of them shied away from the center of the street, as if something chill was there, something that watched them. And so there was, but poor pitiful things, they had no power to truly perceive what caused their fear. All around, the walks and the sides of the road were squeezed full of furry vermin, doing their businesses, but few of them were so bold as to go down the middle of the streets. Burden-beasts shied when they discovered her presence, and tried to flee. She watched with slow amusement as their pur-blind masters beat them toward her, and sometimes succeeded in driving them through where she "lay," and sometimes failed, causing the beasts to bolt and trample the passersby.

A good long while she lay there, under that firefly sun, looking into their faces to see if they had any. They did not. One and all, they wore the same hectic expressions: the idiot smile, the look of fear. Thought did not show in those faces. There was nothing on them but fur, and their eyes were not opaque and tantalizing like those of her own people, but pallid, shallow, and clear, like water. She hissed softly in loathing. At least water did not run down the center of this street, as it did down so many others. But it ran in the eyes of the passersby, and she detested the sight of it. Water was a curse on the world, and these creatures were too familiar with it. Fire, that was what mattered. Fire, and blood. At least some of them knew about *that*.

She rose up from where she lay, causing another small stampede down at the end of the street. There were parts of this city—one might as well call it that, having no better name, though it was a poor place—parts of this city which were of little use to her; the vermin there were too contented. But in the stews, in the poor streets where filth ran in the gutters, and among the high houses on the hill, where everything was stone and greenery, *there* her prey walked and plotted, and did her will without knowing it.

She reached out with her mind and laid her will upon the overworld, and in a swirl of pale fire, she was where she desired to be. The street was broad and shaded with great trees. Its cobbles and the marble walks were swept clean; the great buildings rose up on either side, many-windowed, terraced, still. Few vermin walked here, and those that did went hastily, and walked around her without even seeming to give the matter thought. *They are used to giving way to their betters*, she thought with a long slow smile, and her tongue flickered in amusement.

She glided forward to lie in the courtyard of the great building that lay at the end of the street. Great for these creatures, at least. She thought of the Halls of the Lords, back in her own land, the great glittering caves so huge that a dragon could fly in them and not cramp its wings, and the comparison between that grandeur and this hovel was laughable. Still, here her slaves lay. Here questions were being asked, and the answers would deliver this city into her claws. She reached out with her will, just for pleasure's sake, and threaded her thought down through the place, letting her slaves feel the fear of her, the presence of something that watched, though they did not know—most of them—that she existed at all. She felt their shivers, in what was for them a hot day; felt them, and rejoiced.

Other shivers answered the pressure of her will, and in those too she rejoiced, and her tongue flickered again in token of her hunger. Without even reaching out her mind she could feel them, the vermin buried under the house outside which she lay: the listening minds, thinking themselves so secure in their little lair. Well, they were not as secure as they thought; one of her slaves had already seen to that. The buried listeners would do her will as well, sooner or later. She would find that most amusing. She looked forward to the taste of their horror and despair on the air of the overworld . . . and the taste of their bodies afterwards, and as a final delicacy, their souls. She felt sure that some of them, at least, would be given her as her reward. She turned away, then, laid her will once more upon the stuff of the overworld, and the shady street gave way instantly to one of those small filthy alleys buried in the heart of the town. The buildings leaned together, and everything here was shadow instead of shade, decay instead of cool solidity. Muck lay against the houses, noisome water ran in the gutter down the middle of the street. Here no one had any choice where they walked, and every glance was furtive, every heart had the seeds of rage in it. The colors of the vermin burned far more sullen and muddy here than in the high houses. They would be easy to warp down into the soul-darkness that she needed. Greed and rage were rooted deep in almost every mind, and many of the vermin made no attempt to detour around her overbody; they walked right through her with the barest shudder. She smiled again, a wide expression, showing the dreadful teeth. None of them saw, and only a few shuddered. These were indeed apt meat for her use, and later, perhaps, for her tearing. It was not meat that one would bother eating, of course. But seeing the blood flow would be delightful, and hearing the screams as she indulged herself what she was not forbidden, and burned their hearts with fire.

Her tongue flickered the air of the overworld in pleasure. Then she paused, scenting something on that air, an annoying scent, sharp, alert. She looked about her. *Here?* she thought. *In this puddle, this dunghill?* Yet there was no mistaking it.

For a moment anger rose in her. *I was told there were none here,* she thought. *And how should I not have known there* was *one until now? How has that one been hiding from me?*

She slipped down the street slowly, tasting the air as she went. Yes, definitely, no mistaking it, that tang, that slight acridity. The slight whiff of flame. Not willingly used, not at all; that was one thing she knew about the vermin. Fire they held as an enemy, poor benighted things that they were. *Probably they are afraid it will catch in their fur,* she thought in amused scorn. And if it did, a cheerful sight that would be. And it would serve them right. They were barely more than the brute beasts, these things. They had somehow learned to think, to speak, to build houses, to write; how had they learned magic? And a magic different from the crude kind used by the beasts they hunted, in the wilder places? Magic! Magic was the right of the Old People, the Thinking People, her own kind. No upstart race, fur-wearing, verminous, should know anything about it, should be able to contaminate the overworld with its presence. It made her want to forget everything she had been bidden, made her want to let go right now and reduce this place to— But she calmed herself. Rage was not her way, not really. Far more entertainment was to be garnered by the slow steady pursuit, with one's eyes fixed unwearyingly on the quarry. Let her prey know she came, let it turn and twist and try to get away, let it know fully at last that there was no escape for it, no way out, all its paltry devices laid bare. Then, *then* the crunch of teeth, and the blood running.

Slowly she slipped down the narrow little street, through the shadows. By one door she stopped, seeing through its rickety wall the light she had tasted down the street. Through the wall she went, through the wattles and daub, and looked upon the small miserable creature that lay there, lost in its dreams at such a time of day, with the tiny flicker of muddy fire, burning so very low, too low to do much of anything with. The mockery of it enraged her anew, but she forced herself to find some amusement in it, that a creature so wretched should have magic, and know how little it could do with it. *A nightrunner,* she thought. *The worst kind of vermin, but the most laughable. Know me in your dreams, little beast, little mrem. Know me, and fear. All your struggling against me will not avail you. I am here, and nothing you can do will make me go away. I am your death, little mrem. I am you city's death. Sooner or later,* she thought, *I and my kind are your* world's *death.*

And she laughed, and the sound of her laughter filled everything as she willed herself away to let the death begin to unfold. . . .

▲

Chapter 4

▲──▲

He woke up in the middle of the afternoon, shaking, and stared around him. Something had been hissing. Hissing at *him*.

He looked around his room, breathing hard, and tried to force himself to be calm. Nothing was here, nothing bad seemed to be happening. But the sense of impending danger, of horror, hung thick in the room. Everything otherwise seemed quite ordinary. Dust danced in a stray sunbeam forcing its way in between two boards of the wall. Outside there was the sound of voices, and through the cracks in the shut door, the same old stink forced its way.

He breathed out and shook his head. The feeling had been growing on him for a couple of days, now, that something bad was going to happen. This sort of thing had happened to him before: The last time, it was a premonition of pain, an ache that had settled into his bones . . . and four days later one of his clients had taken exception to the way one of the Games that he bet on had turned out, and had taken out the frustration on his bookmaker, since there was no one else he could attack with impunity. Lorin had limped for days, had gone about his business with eyes swollen half shut, and his tail had never completely been right again, not after the way Jath had pulled it. Lorin had not done anything, of course. There was nothing he could have done that wouldn't have revealed him fairly quickly as what he was, and *that* would have meant a stake over the city gate with his head on it—or some part of him that would have hurt worse. He had gone to a lot of trouble making himself look small and

harmless, a bookmaker almost too small for the city to take
official note of, small enough to hide some of the takings
for his own uses. And if anyone found out what those uses
were, or suspected them, Lorin would have been as good
as dead.

But what he felt now made that aching of the last time
look like nothing by comparison. The past three days it
had been growing on him, the feeling of being watched.
No, not precisely that, he thought. *But of being just
barely overlooked . . . by something looking for me.* He
shook again, for a moment, as the thought brought the
sound of the hissing back into his ears. Whatever was
happening, the hiding, the being overlooked, was done
with. Something had found him—had found the whole
city. And it meant them no good at all.

Lorin sat up on the bed and rubbed mournfully at his
ears for a moment. They still hissed softly, and though it
was only the sound of his own blood running, it made him
think of that other hissing. He was very frightened—but
what frightened him more was the thought that had started
running in the background of his mind: *I ought to do
something.*

Like what? he demanded of himself.

No answer came, at least not right away. What could
he possibly do? Any work of *that* kind—any of his real
work—might reveal him and get him killed. On the other
hand, if he did *not* do something, he was betraying what
he was in a way that no mrem would understand. One was
not born with the talent he had, and as slowly and bitterly
trained in it as he had been, without responding to certain
threats. That hissing—

"Why me?" he muttered, and then hushed himself, as
if someone might hear.

No answer, of course. But usually there was none,
when a foreseeing of something like this came up—some
threat that was not of the body, something of the overworld,
something of wizardry. One was not given the answers.
One *made* them.

Lorin moaned softly to himself, an unhappy little yowl.
What am I supposed to do? he thought. *I don't have the
materials I need, I don't have the money . . . or the skill,*

or the time—that's it, I don't have the time— There were no less than three Games today; various of his clients had bets riding on every one of them, some of them fairly substantial for this part of town. He couldn't possibly do anything until much later. After the Games, possibly not until this evening—

He paused. *But the trail will be cold,* he thought, and breathed out in annoyance. There were some facts that could not be ignored. If something out of its body had just been in here looking at him, it would have left a trail of sorts in the overworld. Or it should have, at any rate. *Unless it was a wizard of considerable power . . .* But why would anyone like *that* be looking at *him?* Sometimes wizards did go on spirit-jaunts, traveling, just to see the great world without leaving the comfort of their homes. But that kind of immaterial journey typically burned four hours off one's life for every hour spent in it, and no one would waste such a large piece of life prowling around in—admit it—a slum. No, this had to be something else.

But why would some other wizard be looking at me?

And what *other wizard??*

That was the other problem. Niau was one of those places where mrem did not believe in wizardry . . . not really. That was one of the reasons Lorin had come here, long ago, after his parents had been killed. He had had enough of wizardry, wanted nothing but to hide away from the reactions of more informed mrem, who definitely believed in wizards, and mostly believed in killing them. *Fools,* Lorin thought, but the bitterness in the thought was old and dull. *As if an honest mrem wizard would stoop to the kinds of things that the worms and snakes did in the old days, when they ruled—* But that was exactly what too many mrem thought, and by and large, wizard-mrem survived by keeping quiet about their talents and their intentions. Lorin's parents had not; they had paid the price. And Lorin had learned the lesson.

But not well enough to leave well enough alone, he thought to himself, and frowned angrily at his own idiocy.

Then he sighed. The feeling of something bad about to happen was not going to go away; he knew that perfectly well. Neither was his bad conscience, which had not stopped chiding him, more or less in his mother's voice, since he woke up. *Will you make everything that every wizard-mrem has done since magic was tamed mean nothing? What use are you if not to protect your own kind?*

You died doing that, Lorin said silently to the voice.

It made no reply, but Lorin still had a distinct sense of a maternal paw, somewhere, ready to cuff him hard about the ears, if only it had a body to do it.

He sighed, and thought a moment, and then lay back again and closed his eyes.

I don't know if this is even going to work. . . .

But then he never did. It was always a strain, getting out of himself, no matter whether he used drugs and chants and smokes to help, or whether he did it the old-fashioned way, as his father had always insisted, and simply got *out. And anyway, drugs are expensive, and chants, in this neighborhood, would get you lynched. . . .* Therefore Lorin composed his limbs and relaxed them one by one, and then imagined his whole self to be a small glowing light at the top of his head . . . and concentrated on burning his way out through the top of his skull, into what lay beyond.

There were the initial few moments of embarrassment. Lorin was sure that no matter how hard you studied, and how often you did the technique, for the first few breaths you felt incredibly silly. He had tried other visualizations, on and off, but none of them had ever been any better: flowers, eggs cracking open, all the rest of them, they all just seemed silly. There was simply nothing to do but keep at it, and so he did, concentrating on melting the top of his skull off and letting that small fierce bright light out to run free about the world. The pressure built and built, and he got more and more nervous as he became certain (as always) that it wasn't going to work. He became even more nervous when he thought that he hadn't set up any wards—there was no protection for his body while his soul was out of it, and if someone should come in—say, another wizard—

Ridiculous, he thought—except that suddenly it seemed bizarrely likely. Why would a wizard have been looking at him in the first place?

—If it even was a wizard—

If you keep dithering like this, his conscience scolded him, *the trail will get cold.*

But I should at least set up wards—

And by the time they're set, the trail will be even colder. Stop making excuses!

And then of course Lorin's concentration was ruined, and he had to start all over again.

It took several minutes for Lorin to get all the chatter in his head to simply be quiet, so that he could sink back into the relaxation that started the process. Then he was back trying to burn a hole in the top of his head, and feeling embarrassed and foolish. . . .

The embarrassment fell away. The sense of having a body at all fell away. He concentrated on having his whole self be something small and white and fiercely hot, like a spark flown out of the forge onto a blacksmith's floor—

With a silent explosion of pain, his head fell to pieces and he blasted upwards out of it. And there was no more pain, and the usual odd calm of the overworld settled down over Lorin. He looked down at himself, lying there on the wretched straw pallet. *Mange,* was his first thought; the tone was more sorrowful than embarrassed, for once. His skin had always been delicate, and even when he was young and healthy, he had always been one of those mrem who seem to spend most of their time scratching themselves. And now the poor diet and damp accommodations of his present state had reduced his coat to a sorry condition. He had never been particularly handsome, though his markings were clearly enough defined; now the various bare patches made anything but pity out of the question. But perhaps it was a blessing in disguise. A handsome mrem might attract attention. Lorin wanted nothing of that.

He sighed and turned away from himself, looking around. No two wizards ever perceived the overworld the same way—that was what he had been told. His own perception always struck him as rather pedestrian, for what he saw was the normal world, but made pallid and ephemeral—ghostlike buildings, houses that were wraiths of themselves. There were peculiar departures from the

real world, though. Sometimes, it seemed, a house was
sufficiently lived-in to come alive, and then it would
appear subtly different in the overworld from whatever
actually occupied that spot in the city. He knew of one
hovel, several twisting streets away, which insisted on
manifesting itself as a fine mansion of a style that had been
popular at least a hundred years before. Whether that
mansion had stood there and was now demolished, or
whether the house had gone mad and was suffering from
delusions of grandeur, or whether someone *in* the house
was, Lorin had never been able to understand.

For the moment, though, he put the question aside,
since none of the houses in his own street was usually so
afflicted, and none of them was showing any changes just
now. He lifted his head and scented the air. The sky above
him was silvery; there was no sun. A slight breeze blew, as
it always did.

And on it, he caught the reek. It was not the smell of
the local streets—*that* he was so familiar with that he
probably wouldn't have noticed it at all. What he smelled
was something dry and faintly metallic. But mostly dry,
and the smell had a sound about it as well, in the way that
senses in the overworld often combined and confused
themselves in ways impossible under normal circumstances.
He smelled dryness, and a rustling: something soft in
places but also bizarrely chitinous, like some kind of insect. But big. Bigger than any insect.

*And what in the gods' good name makes a smell like
that?*

Lorin shook—even there, out of his body. But he
moved with the smell. One didn't have to physically move
with it, in the overworld. Walking was unnecessary—you
could drift, so drift he did, past houses and through them,
through the marketplace—*And why is it deserted this time
of day?*—out the far side; among more stately houses,
under trees that seemed half transparent and waved in
that slight breeze, trunks and all, like weed in water;
down stone streets that Lorin more than once sank ankle-
deep into, becoming mired in stone as if in mud, when he
forgot to watch where he was going. But the smell was
getting stronger and stronger. There was more of a sense

of *intention* about it—some whiff of the cast of the mind of whatever had left the trail. Lorin shook worse than ever, for it was malevolent, as wicked as he had initially sensed on awakening from sleep—and it *enjoyed* its wickedness. *Why am I following this person?* he asked himself, in increasing terror. *Why aren't I heading for home as fast as I can get there, and hiding under the floorboards?*

But there was no answer for that either. Lorin drifted on down the streets, among houses finer far than he ever usually saw. One of them in particular, a fine, wide-gated place, drew his attention; the smell was thick about it. Lorin paused outside those gates, unwilling to go any further. Something made him feel that, if he once entered that busy courtyard, the attention of whatever had left the scent would be unfailingly drawn to him.

He hung there, drifting just above the clean-swept cobbles, for what seemed like a long while, looking in. The mrem bustling about, seeing to beasts and carrying hampers to and fro, all ignored him, as was to be expected. Idly Lorin watched them. There were several large boxes, carrying crates of some kind, with beast harnesses still fastened to them. Servingmrem came and went about them, taking the contents—bolts of cloth, furniture, caged animals of strange kinds—into the great house at the far side of the courtyard. Several of the little beasts in the cages, as they were carried in, looking pitifully at Lorin, plainly seeing him, and called or mewed unhappily. He looked away. He had no idea what they were, but he felt sorry for them. It was not that long since he had been looking down at his own poor mangy body, and he knew what it was like to be in a cage.

And then he looked up, and saw the mrem staring toward him.

The mrem was standing by one of the boxes. He did not see Lorin, not clearly. But he clearly felt that something was where Lorin was, and his eyes searched the air, roved, uneasy. Lorin shook, more than ever. The mrem was no more physically distinctive, in Lorin's perception of the overworld, than any of the others. He was a ghost, a fat ghost in gaudy belled robes, a priest's robes, his fur patched in orange and white and mud-color. But the reek, the taste of insects, the smell of chitin, of hard scratching things, the metal smell, the burning smell, hung close about him, and wafted closer as he took a leisurely few steps in Lorin's direction, away from the big boxes, and then several more steps, more quickly. He was not the being that had been watching Lorin. But he was that being's servant, and he knew that that being had been trailed here by someone, and he was suspicious.

Lorin did not bother drifting anywhere this time. He seized the stuff of the overworld in his claws and laid his will upon it, swarming up and away through the fabric of it like a kit scrambling up a tree, then came out with terrified suddenness in his own miserable house again, and exploded back into his body three times as hard as he had tried to leave it. He had not cared much for the look of it before, but now he was as glad of his wrapping of poor mangy flesh as he had been of anything for a long time. One might look better out of the body, but in flesh, you could hide.

Gasping, he came back to himself. His head ached like pounding hammers where he had escaped it, and he shook all over like a kit just dragged out of icy water. The effort had come to nothing. He had not found what he was looking for. And in retrospect, perhaps it was just as well.

The smell of something scorching, of chitin, of ripping sounds, was still in his nose. He sat up on his pallet, sneezing, rubbed his watering eyes, and tried to think what to do. . . .

Stay far away from that priest, was the beginning of it. What the end of it would be, he had no idea.

He got up to tend to the bets.

▲

Reswen decided to take his time going back to the office. This morning, at least, with all the excitement, other people would be sufficiently distracted by the news to grant him a moment's peace away from his desk. The sun was still low enough that it did not strike directly down into the streets, so he strolled along at an easy pace, in the shade of trees (or at least on the shady sides of the streets). If anyone needed an excuse, he could easily say that he was about his business as master of police, seeing that there was order in the city. If anyone accused him of enjoying it, well . . . he could always deny it.

The city was becoming active. It was one of the six market days that took place every eightday, and the square at the heart of the city made a low murmur already; even here, blocks away, he would hear it. Reswen strolled along out of the high-rent districts, all marble and trees, into areas less shady but more interesting. Between the center of town and the market, there were shops catering to the wealthier clientele of this neighborhood . . . mercers and butchers, lamp makers, merchants dealing in leather and metal wear, knife makers. . . .

Reswen paused outside the cutler's shop, leaning against the carved wood of the folded-back shutters to admire the sharp little metal fangs lying on velvet and brushed leather in the window. He was something of a connoisseur of fine weapons. The interest had sprung up in him over years of taking crude ones away from various mrem, so that when a fine one crossed his path, he had come to appreciate it. One of them was something the likes of which he had never seen before, a curved edge-and-a-half knife made in a metal that seemed somehow to have been stained matte gold and deep rose. Reswen gazed at it in pleasant perplexity, wondering how it had been made; the color was not a plating, but seemed part of the metal itself. The blade was gold, inlaid in swirls and flower patterns with the rose-colored metal, and the hilt seemed carved of two pieces of the same metals welded together, the division between them flowing down the hilt in a long graceful double curve recalling the swirls in the blade. The thing drew Reswen's eye more than all the plainer knives there, for all their gleam of silver and steel. The problem was that there was no price on it, and he knew what *that* meant.

"A lovely knife," said the merchant, who had not wasted a moment and was out beside him in the doorway, leaning over to peer in the window and enjoy the sight of the knife herself. She was a stocky, dark orange, golden-eyed tabby with one ear missing about a third of its shell, and she had scars in other interesting places. "Do pick it up, master. Feel it in the paw, that lovely carved hilt."

"Not I," Reswen said. "Not on my salary, though I thank you, madam. But having said so, I will ask how much."

"For you, Reswen-*vassheh*, eight claws'-weight in gold, and we'll forget the change."

He laughed at her outright. "That's more than I make in half a year, but thank you anyway. And how do you know me by sight, anyway?"

The knife seller smiled at him indulgently. "Hard not to, when you come down here so often in your different outfits to check up on your foot patrols," she said. "The beat officers may not see you often enough to catch on, but all the shopmrem down here know you."

Reswen resisted a sudden urge to wash. He had thought he was fairly inconspicuous when he went out in townsmrem's dress, or servant's harness, to see whether his people were doing their jobs, and to make sure none of them were on the take in neighborhoods they were supposed to be protecting. *But maybe this is for the better. . . .* "Well," he said, "as long as you don't mention it to my people. . . ."

The cutler laughed outright. "After what you did to that lot over on the sunside when you caught them claws out? No chance, *vassheh.* Half the west of the city had been paying protection to those policemrem—you stopped it. You can sleep in our doorways any time."

Reswen's whiskers went forward, remembering the wretched food and cold nights he had endured that month, wrapped in stinking rags, pretending to be a beggar. But the pretense had paid off, and the ring of policemrem caught extorting money from the small shopkeepers on the west side had shortly thereafter been spiked up on the city walls. "Well," Reswen said, "I'll bear that in mind. A good morning to you, madam."

The shopkeeper bowed slightly to him and retreated into the dark and cool of the shop. Reswen walked on, thinking about the knife. And about blue eyes—

He stopped at the next corner and held his breath while a night-sand cart drawn by phlegmatic uxen lurched by, the drover whacking the creatures equably with a length of spring-stick and shouting unlikely obscenities at them. Holding his breath didn't entirely defend Reswen from the smell, and the smell didn't entirely distract him from thoughts of that female at Haven. He stalked across the road, beginning to feel vaguely annoyed with himself. He didn't usually lose his head over the shes, no matter how pretty they were. Oh, he enjoyed his nights out on the tiles: a dalliance every couple of days, if the urge took him—nothing wrong with that. But not an obsessive sort of thing like this—

He hissed softly to himself as he came to the stairs leading up to Constables' House, and his men came to the salute. *Maybe that's what I need,* he thought as he stalked up the stairs. *I've been working too hard, that's all. A little helling around—*

He was almost knocked over by the liveried runner who came dashing down the stairs at him. The mrem grabbed him, possibly as much to keep his own balance as to keep Reswen from falling down, and then brushed hastily at Reswen as he realized whom he'd run into. "Oh, sir, I've been looking everywhere for you—"

"You found me, more's the pity," Reswen growled.

"The Arpekh summon you, sir. Right now."

"Twice in one day," Reswen muttered. "All right, off with you and tell them I'm coming." And he pushed the oversolicitous runner away from him and kept on heading up the stairs; he needed a bit of sand, and not even the Arpekh were going to hurry him as regarded that. *Anything else, of course . . .* he thought sourly. . . .

Ten minutes later he was out of his plain harness into something more appropriate: a touch of gilding about his kit, a flow of day-blue silk down from the shoulders to remind them whom they were dealing with, as they sometimes needed reminding. Then off to the council rooms, and this time he banged on their doors with his staff of office as they had banged on his this morning.

He was admitted without delay, and this time was shocked and rather alarmed to find them in session, all talking at once—some of them rather loudly and angrily—and all awake for a change. He bowed and made his duty to them in a purposely leisurely fashion, giving them a moment to settle, and then said, "Lords, it is a busy morning for me. What is it this time?"

Councillor Mraal looked down the table at him and simply waited for the uproar to die down a little. It took a few moments, Aratel being the last to quiet down. "It's not *decent!*" his voice said, alone, into the sudden silence, and then he looked around guiltily and hushed up, embarrassed by this own loudness.

Mraal flicked one ear back in mild annoyance. "We have here," he said, "the preliminary note of intent from our just-arrived guests." He pushed the piece of parchment a little across the table, away from him, as if he disliked the feel of it. Even from where Reswen stood, he could see that the thing was a gaudy farrago of rubrication, seals, and gold; it looked the way the Easterners' herald had sounded. "It involves the initiation of trade agreements and so forth between ourselves and a consortium of the major Eastern cities. . . ."

"You hardly need have called me, Lord Arpakh," Reswen said. "I'm no merchant to advise you on such things."

"Not about the business of buying and selling, perhaps. But I want you to take a look at the schedule they're proposing."

Reswen reached down the table to take the parchment as it was passed down toward him. He scanned the crabbed brushstrokes, squinting slightly at the tininess of them. "Hm. Fourteen caravans a year—each to stay half a moon—and several of these overlap." He thought about that for a moment. "In both spring and autumn there would be three parties here at any one time— "

He looked up. Mraal was watching him. "I would wonder," Reswen said, "how many mrem they were planning to bring in these parties."

"So would I," said Mraal.

"It could be anything from a few innocent groups such as we have here—"

"Innocent!" Aratel said, and his creaky old voice cracked with anger. "They're nothing like innocent! Spies and deviles, these Easterners. It's folly holding out a paw to them that doesn't have a whip in it! We fought the Eastern cities when all you here were nothing but kits feeling for your mothers' milk, and I remember how we—"

"Aratel." Mraal sounded quite annoyed. "We have had

this discussion twice this morning already. The fathers of these mrem have gone to war with our fathers in the past, and some of us may even have fought in those wars. But there is no indication that *these* mrem are going to do anything of the sort now. They would be biting their own ears off."

"And just because their ways are different from ours, and we were taught to hate them," said Chezjin, next to Aratel, "is no reason for us to keep blinding ourselves with our sires' old hatreds—" He laid a friendly paw on Aratel's arm. Aratel subsided somewhat, but he still glared at Mraal, and from where Reswen stood, he could see the Arpakh's tail swishing.

Mraal hissed softly—he could see it too—then mastered his anger for the moment and let his breath out more quietly. "Aratel," he said, "the Eastern cities have changed their leadership many times since you went to war and we were all kits, and milk or no milk, times are not what they were when our fathers led us out to butchery against the East. These mrem want our trade. They need it: their own traditions have stopped them from making things that they need and we have in plenty. And we can use their trade. Sitting here at desert's edge, we could use another market for our stuffs, one that's not glutted for grain and cloths like the Western markets are. Our farmers grow more than they can sell West these days—not their fault; the West used to be grain-poor. But the climate's changed, and now our farming-mrem have to sit on what can't be sold, hoping it'll keep till the scarcities hit in the winter—or else they have to burn it all when the granaries get too full. You know all this—at least, you would know it if you hadn't been sleeping the past two months, for the problem is going to be worse this year than ever. Here was finally have a consortium willing to give a good price for our corn and manufactures, and you want us to drive them out unheard and untried?"

Aratel said nothing, simply looked away. "But at the same time," Mraal said, "no need to be incautious. Reswen, I should like your people to, ah, use the means at their disposal to look into what the size of these groups is likely to be. Oh, I know, at the formal meeting this afternoon

we'll ask them, and they'll tell us something which may be
the truth. But I'd like to make sure."

"I'll see to it, Lord," Reswen said. He said it a little
absently. He was still puzzling his way down through the
parchment, sorting out details of what things were to be
traded, in what amounts. "You don't have to give them an
answer right away, do you?"

"Even in the West," Mraal said slowly, with a touch of
amusement, "no need for that. No, we'll manage to keep
them here enjoying our hospitality until we know what
we need to. There should be no problem with that. . . .
Reswen, what ails you?"

For Reswen was still gazing at the parchment. "What's
this line at the bottom, Lord?" he said. " 'Stone and
water'?"

"Some ceremony," said another of the Arpekh, a middle-
aged councillor named Maiwi. "To seal the pact, we apparently give them a stone and a flask of water from the city.
Typical superstitious Eastern kind of thing."

Reswen looked up. There was a sort of tickle at the
back of his mind, and he had learned a long time ago to
pay attention to that tickle. "It seems strange, that's all. A
traditional thing, you would expect them to ask for it
informally. Hardly to specify it in the lead-up to the formal
agreement."

Another of the councillors, Kanesh, a big broad mrem
all splotches of orange and black on white, nodded vigorously. "It seemed strange way to me too. To no one else,
though."

"Kanesh," Mraal said, "you are probably one of the
best-read of us, and expert in the strangenesses of other
people. The Colleges would be lost without you. But I
can't see what difference this gesture would make, and I
think your book-learning is making you worry unnecessar-
ily here. Let the creatures have their rock and water, if
they like. The important thing is arriving at quotas for the
amount of grain and cloth we send them."

"Brother Lord," Kanesh said, "this sort of thing is
rarely just a gesture. In the stories it can often be a symbol
for something that one party or another is too wily to say
out loud. Once one city of the East sent another a bunch
of arrows—"

"Oh, for pity's sake, no more stories," Aratel said, grumpy. Reswen's tail twitched in momentary anger: The old fool was determined that, since no one had listened to him, no one was going to listen to Kanesh either. "Let's get on with it and meet with these dirty spies, since it seems some of us want to sell the city out as quickly as possible."

"I refuse to hear you, Aratel," Mraal said, "or your rudeness to a brother Lord, and if necessary, we will put you out of Council and refuse to hear you *that* way. The Arpekh assembled has decided to consider the Easterners' proposals, and if the decision was not unanimous, it rarely is. Meanwhile, whether they are friends or enemies-to-be, and the latter I much doubt, we must act like a united body to these mrem, not a bunch of squabbling dodderers fit only to lie in the sun. Hold your tongue, you were best, and act to these people as if you were gently bred, or I'll toss you out by the scruff like a kit that's been ripping up the furniture, I swear I will, uncle or no uncle!"

There was something of a shocked silence at that. Aratel stared, his tail bristling, and then very deliberately put his head down and set to washing one paw in a cool and reflective manner.

"Lord Arpakh," Kanesh said carefully into that silence, "I would still like to see this matter of the stone and water investigated thoroughly before we agree to it. As you said, no need to be incautious. . . ."

Mraal waved a paw, unhappy with the discomfort in the room. "Well enough. Perhaps you and Reswen should put your heads together on the subject; if there's anything clandestine about the matter, he'll find it out. We will hear your report when next we meet. Lords, let us rise and robe ourselves. Someone call for a runner and send him to the house in Dancer's Street. Sixth hour, let's meet with them. The day's heat will have a chance to pass off, and we should be done in time to let these mrem rest before the feast this evening. . . ."

The room emptied out. Reswen stood looking at the parchment a moment more before becoming aware of the clerk standing at his elbow: He rolled the document up and gave it to the mrem, then turned to look at Kanesh, who had not moved from his chair. Reswen waited for the door to shut.

"You know the story about the arrows?" Kanesh said.

"I do. And I have no desire to do something which an enemy might claim afterwards to have interpreted as unconditional surrender."

Kanesh leaned back in his chair. "I have more worries than that, Policemaster. I think this might be something rather worse."

"Such as?"

"Magic."

Reswen flicked one ear back, slightly annoyed. Magic had always struck him as an untidy, un-mremmish thing, more fit for beasts and prey than for people. Of course there were mrem wizards. Certainly the Easterners had them . . . had too many of them, to hear some of the stories that came out of the East. There were wizards in the West as well: They tended to keep secret—not that that helped them when Reswen had to hunt them down, as his job sometimes required. Mostly he considered magic and magicians an inconvenience. But he disliked the idea of them.

Not that that kept Reswen from keeping one on his payroll, of course.

"If you are truly concerned about that, Lord Arpakh," he said, "there are avenues through which such a suspicion could be investigated."

"Discreetly?"

"It had better be," Reswen said. Kanesh grinned, not altogether a pleasant look.

"I will leave the matter to you, then," Kanesh said. "You noted the exact wording from the proposal?"

" 'As a token of your good faith and to seal the bargain between us until time immemorial, and for the satisfaction of our Gods, a deal of the bones and a deal of the blood of your City, the same to be given over to us as a token of your City's endurance and greatness: in the form of a flask of pure water from well or river, and a stone of the City, of the wall or of the rock from which the City is hewn or on which it stands, to signify that our friendship shall be needful as water and enduring as stone—' "

Kanesh nodded. "Your, ah, 'consultant' will need those words."

"Very well," Reswen said. "If you would be so kind, have one of your scribes send over a transcript of the meeting with the Easterners when it's finished. I will be interested to hear what they say about your questions."

"So will I." And Kanesh went out after the others.

Reswen quirked his whiskers in sour resignation and went off to find Lorin.

He could have sent for him, of course, but it would have attracted attention; and it would also have meant he had to stay in his office. So Reswen got out of the second-best kit he had been wearing, and got into some of his worst—a harness of ragged, dirty, worn leather, the fittings not even honestly rusted, because they were base metal. He put his fur badly out of order with a wire comb, a process which took about twenty minutes and left him feeling very mean indeed, and then went out the back door of Constables' House, the door where they left the garbage to be taken away.

Lorin's hovel—there was no use dignifying it with any other name—was not too far from the town's marketplace. Reswen went straight through the market, as much for a perverse sort of pleasure as anything else. It was one of the great trouble spots of his city-wide beat, almost as bad as some of the upper-class gamers' and joy-houses. But it was alive and honest, in a filthy way, as none of those were. Here, in the heat of summer, on market day, the place had a horrible, cheerful, cutthroat vitality that drew Reswen even as it repelled him. All the houses around the market turned blind walls to its noise and smells, and any gates were triple-locked. The market square itself was cobbled, and the cobbles were worn, and here and there were great gaping holes where the setts had been stolen (or pried up to throw at someone, usually a policeman); boards covered the worst of these holes, but even some of the smaller ones could make shift to swallow you if you weren't careful. Above the cobbles was erected a little forest of tents and canopies and sunshades, tattered banners or banners of cloth-of-gold flapping in the hot breeze over them. The banners were figured with the devices of the merchants under them—fruits, vegetables, fish, meats, bolts of cloth, pots and pans, jewelry, clothes of various kinds, anything one could imagine.

Reswen walked through the heat, trying not to breathe, then giving it up. The Niauhu market was not kind to the fastidious nose: The smells simply got worse or better depending on where you were and how the wind was setting. He passed the butchers' tent and had to wave his paws in front of his face to ward off the shrilling clouds of flies. Great carcasses of uxen hung down here, the flies spinning about them, flashing blue and green in the fierce sun, diving in and out of the stink of meat and blood. Then came a smell of musty feather pillows, coming from a tent where a long horizontal pole was festooned with every kind of game fowl—brownwing, setch, lallafen, breastbird. Hung like an afterthought from the end of the pole was a string of hortolans, tiny and brown, like one of the bead-strings the Easterners played with . . . except that the beads rarely had tiny still feet sticking out of them. Reswen's mouth watered. It had been too long since he had had skewered hortolan. *I really must do something about that. A nice sweet-and-sour sauce . . .*

The assaults to the sense continued, but Reswen slowly began to be distracted from them. It was after all not the market itself that interested him: It was the people in it, *his* people, many of them the law-abiding mrem he was sworn to protect, many more of them not law-abiding at all, but most behaving themselves for the moment. Without turning aside to right or left, without even trying hard, Reswen could see four pickpockets, six sneak thieves, a suspected murderer *(and what is Thailh doing about that investigation? Must check—)*, a dealer in the *chash* drug, and a pretty little she-mrem who was in the business of distilling *vushein* without paying the city license fee. However, there were other of his people patrolling; it was all their business at the moment . . . and besides, the boot-legger and two of the pickpockets were merely doing their shopping, and being scrupulous about paying the shop-keepers. Reswen smiled to himself. When the nearest neighboring city was so far away, it did not do to get on bad terms with the grocers and fishmongers. A mrem could starve to death in short order.

Reswen went on through the yelling, laughing, arguing crowd, listening to bargains being hawked (and purported bargains), watching a stallkeeper caught giving short measure get hauled off to one of the constables, being bumped into by housewives with panniers of smelly fish. You could do the best you could to concentrate on the faces—bland, intent, angry, uncaring—but there was no escaping for long the market's assault on the senses. Over one ragged, striped canopy from which the sun had nearly bleached the stripes, a pole supported a banner with a faded red flower on it, and from that tent came smells almost more overpowering then the butchers' and knackers'. It was the perfumer's stall, and the wind seized a fistful of musk and nightbloom and day's-eye and thahla and almost every other perfume Reswen knew, and threw them at him all at once. The sweet reek almost undid him. He staggered away from it, muttering, refusing even to look at the jars of essences and dried flower petals, and kept on going through the marketplace. Next came the hide-sellers, and some of the hides were still raw; the mrem did wholesale business as well as retail, selling to those who liked to finish their own leathers, as well as those who preferred it done for them. Reswen almost turned and headed back for the perfumer's at the first whiff of old dung and ammonia . . . then he kept going. He was almost out the other side.

And then he was out: The crowd thinned suddenly, the dark cool tunnel-archway to the Lanes opened up before him. He dove into it, gratefully, as if into a cave. This had once been a city wall, before Niau outgrew it. There were houses built into it in places, and on a day like this Reswen imagined that the six-foot-thick walls would be a comfort.

At the end of the tunnel there was sunlight, but not nearly as much as there was in the market; it was blocked away by ricketies. These were buildings thrown up in a hurry a long time ago. Walking hurriedly under their leaning shadows, Reswen considered that "thrown up" might be the correct idiom.

Several centuries before, Niau had been the focus of a migration from several of the smaller cities to the north, whose crops had gone bad. To house the sudden influx of desperately willing labor, the ricketies had been built: hasty beam-and-clapboard buildings with barely any skeleton to keep them up, buildings that leaned on one another for support. Once, Reswen supposed, they might not have shown the leaning much, but these days one end of the long, twisting block leant against the wall, and all the others sagged toward that end and also sagged downward and inward into the street. Only the dry climate had preserved them this long . . . but worm and dry rot had set in long ago, and every now and then, one of the ricketies fell down. *Or more correctly, five or six of them*, Reswen thought, for the balance among buildings had become so precarious that knocking just one down was probably impossible. Sometimes he wished for a good fire to clean the whole area out; it was a notable nest of the worst kinds of crime. But that would have been cruel. Many mrem lived here who could not afford even the few coppers a month it would take to see them in cleaner, safer accommodation. They tended to stay there till they died, one way or another. The Arpekh occasionally threatened to tear the whole mess down, but there would usually be an enraged protest by the inhabitants, and the threat would go away. The inhabitants of the ricketies would make enough of a mob to burn any Arpakh's house around his ears.

It was in one of these edifices that Lorin lived, at the bottom of one no less. *No one but a wizard would have the nerve to live on the ground floor of one of these rattraps*, Reswen thought as Lorin's place loomed up over him, casting a shadow. It was one of the more wretched of the places, a three-story-high pockmarked facade with plaster gouged away by time, the beams showing bare. Between two of the beams on the ground level, a warped door hung awry, with some symbol marked on the door in chalk. Someone had used the dirt beside the doorstep as a sandbox.

Reswen sighed and knocked on the door. There was a rustling from inside, and a yellow eye appeared at the crack where the door failed to meet the doorjamb properly. "No betting today," a high-pitched voice said.

Reswen rolled his eyes. Lorin made his official living as a bookmaker, taking bets on the Games, and on some of the less savory sports that the mrem of the ricketies used

to while away their misery. "Look at me, idiot," Reswen
muttered.

There was a pause, then a sound of someone breathing
out. "Right," said the voice, and Lorin unlatched for him.

Reswen stepped in hurriedly. There were people in
this part of town who might recognize him, and it was not
entirely wise to be here alone. The door banged to behind
him as he stood looking around the place. It never failed:
When he came here, which he tried to have happen as
seldom as possible, he could always hear his dear dead
dam's voice saying, "You don't appreciate where you live,
Reswen. There are poor people in this world who would
kill to have as nice a place as we do." And Reswen would
think back to the wretched little cottage where he grew
up, and say to himself, *She was right after all*. The floor
of the—he stretched a term—flat was hard, sour, rammed
dirt, nothing better; Lorin usually managed to filch some
straw to hide the sheer awfulness of it. Almost all the
plaster had fallen away from the beams, leaving the barest
shell between the room and the street. "For all the gods'
sake," Reswen said, and his tone of voice reminded him of
his mother's, "Lorin, why don't you get someplace decent
to live? I'll give you a raise."

"I like it here," Lorin said, coming around to sit back
down at the rude bench and table where he had been
working when Reswen arrived. Lorin fairly well fit the
classic picture of a pauper: He was a sharply striped gray
tabby, mangy and lean, with big round eyes that looked
astonished at everything. Reswen sat down on the other
bench and kept quiet for a moment, because Lorin had
pushed up the sleeves of his ragged tunic and was counting what might have been the morning's takings. The table
was a welter of scraps of parchment and thick rough paper,
and money of all kinds held the scraps of paper down—
coppers and silvers, a gold coin here and there, elsewhere
a piece of paper scrip with a pebble to hold it down.

"Doing all right?" Reswen said after a moment, looking
around the single room. It looked more like a forgotten
storage space than anything else. There were boxes everywhere, piled up, old trunks and chests with rusted fittings,
the contents spilling out of them in places—mostly books.

If Lorin had more than one tunic, Reswen had never seen him in it. Nor were there any of the rumored trappings of magic to be seen, no crystals or rods or bizarre stuffed beasts, no potions bubbling. It was all very odd.

"Very well indeed," said Lorin after a moment, and pushed the money to one side. He looked sidewise at Reswen. "How are the guests?"

"News travels fast."

"Hnnh. Betting was five to one on an attack. I cleaned up."

Reswen's whiskers went forward. "I thought you weren't allowed to bet."

Lorin looked innocent, all big gray-green eyes as he reached out for a piece of parchment and turned it over and over, eyeing the brushstrokes on it. "Ah well, if someone else places a bet for me . . . well."

"But you knew it wasn't war. How?"

"Do you really want me to tell you?"

"Not particularly," Reswen said. "Our guests are a problem at the moment."

Lorin looked at Reswen with not quite the usual casualness. "Oh?"

Reswen recited the last part of the Easterners' document for Lorin's edification. When he was finished, Lorin looked at him with an expression composed of equal parts bemusement and suspicion. He said nothing.

"Well?"

Lorin shrugged. "The formula is very old," he said, "but it's usually a blessing. Harmless."

"I don't believe that," Reswen said. "Not in this case."

"Why not?" A pause. "You don't trust them? Devious Easterners?"

Reswen growled a little in his throat. "Don't lump me with fools like Aratel. There's just something about this that troubles me. I find it odd."

"Somethings else, as well," Lorin said, and paused again, staring at the table. He started to push a piece of stray silver money off to one side, then said, quite casually, "Who has blue eyes?"

Reswen stared at him.

"Silver fur. Blue eyes. Very pretty." Lorin pushed the

silver piece away, then looked up. "She had quite an impact on you."

"That's odd, too."

"Yes, it is," Lorin said, and chuckled a little. Reswen squirmed a bit. This kind of thing was always the problem with dealing with Lorin: the irrationality of it—the way he could pick truths out of the air, seemingly without trying, without reason or judgment, as if he could see some part or aspect of the world that others couldn't.

Reswen shuffled his paws. "That doesn't matter, for the moment. I'll handle it. What I want to find out about is that stone-and-water business. I'm sure it's more than some blessing, some nice formula for the gods to hear. Theirs, or ours. Find out. If you need money, it's yours. Make the usual connection and take whatever you need."

"All right," Lorin said. He got up and followed Reswen to the door.

Reswen looked out right and left through the crack, fiddled with the catch, managed to get it open. "And keep this business quiet," he said to Lorin.

Lorin laughed at him, just a breath of nervous amusement. "You think I want this"—he tapped his head—"to wind up over the city gate?"

"I wouldn't do that to you."

"Oh, yes you would," Lorin said, "if you had to. Go on. And Reswen?" His face went suddenly rather somber. "Mind the priest."

Reswen gratefully got out into clean hot daylight and set out for his office.

The door slammed hurriedly behind him.

▲

Chapter 5

▲————————————————————————————————————▲

Reswen counted himself lucky
that there was no need for him to be at the formal meeting. He spent the afternoon doing things that certainly
should have interested him more: looking over the daily
reports from the subconstabularies, for example.

Some people had been surprised, when he had first
been given the job, how much he relished what his predecessor had considered a burdensome bureaucratic chore.
But to Reswen the reports were lifeblood: the real news of
his city, not the sanitized stuff that one heard from criers
or saw in broadsides, not the grudging reports that he had
been given before by his superiors in the course of inves-
tigations, or that he had picked up via the rumor mill
around the constabulary. Now that he was Policemaster, he
was told the truth, all of it . . . most of the time. Much of
it was sordid, but that didn't bother him. Burglaries, murders, mugging, bribes, gambling, their incidence and the
patterns in which they moved and shifted—he looked at
them all and by them knew what was going on in his city's
mind as surely as a mother knows from the twitch of her
kit's hindquarters which way it's going to jump. Reswen
spent a happy couple of hours amidst the paperwork,
considering various arrests and failures to arrest, and decided that the criminal gangs on the west side of the city
were getting out of hand again; there had been many too
many robberies in the last week. Someone was trying to
finance something major. The whole place would need a
good cleaning out sometime quite soon . . . but not right
this minute. There were other things on his mind.

Blue eyes—

Damn.

Reswen then called in Thailh to see how the Shambles murder investigation was going. Thailh was one of those self-starting types who (in Reswen's opinion) did the best police work: a solid, stolid, slow-moving, careful officer who left nothing to chance and insisted on turning over every piece of evidence with his own paws, and going himself to find what others could not bring him. Only a few minutes after being sent for, Thailh came into Reswen's office with a thick stack of parchments and a restrained look on his broad gray-striped face. Reswen sighed a little; there was apparently no real news. Thailh would have been grinning like a mrem with a fresh fish if he had even the slightest cause.

They sat down together and went through the evidence again. No one knew who had been garroting the people down in the Shambles, a somewhat run-down part of town where the abattoirs had always been. Now there was only one slaughterhouse left there, buried in tenements and mean shops, but the place was earning its old name all over again. There were few new developments in the case, and the whole business was no less confusing now than it had been to start with. For one thing, the mrem who were dying were not being killed for money. One recent case had been a courtesan coming back from a late night out: the two claws'-weight of gold she had set out with were found on her body, untouched. Overlooked in haste? Thailh thought not, and Reswen agreed with him. Another killing had been of a sutler who had been out drinking with friends and had been walking home, again late, on the borders between the Shambles and the poor but respectable neighborhood where he lived. He had perhaps two coppers on him when he went home; those were left him, while his life was taken.

"We have a crazy on our paws," Thailh had said during their first conference on the case. Reswen had been inclined to agree with him, though he did so sourly, as there were enough crazy people loose in the poorer parts of town to fill Niau's gaols seven times over. And one could hardly arrest them all, or (as some of the angrier and less rational of the citizens' groups demanded) hunt them all

down and spike them up over the gates. Even if crazymrem
were not actively considered lucky in many circles, Reswen
would have refused to even consider anything of the kind.
It was inelegant to kill hundreds when killing one would
solve the problem . . . and it would be an admission of
helplessness and inadequacy. Not to mention that it would
simply be *wrong*.

But all the same, something would have to be done
soon. There was little the police could do at this point but
wait for the killer to strike again . . . while meantime the
people down in the Shambles got more and more upset,
and police patrols down there had to move in groups; the
people they protected were becoming inclined to stone
them when they saw them, and one constable too cocky
to patrol in company had had a knife put into him several
nights before.

"But at least we have this," Thailh said, and with great
satisfaction held up a plain cord of fine stuff, a sort of
beaten rope-weave. There were no stains on it, but it
needed none; it had been found around the neck of the
last victim. The murderer had apparently been frightened
in midact by the sound of an approaching foot patrol.
Reswen had been more than annoyed that his people had
been so close to catching the reprobate and had then lost
him, or her. But at least they had the garrote.

"And where does that leave us?"

"Further along than we were before," Thailh said,
"because now I know where it comes from."

Reswen looked up from the papers, mildly surprised.
"Is that a help to us? I thought it was just rope."

"Ah, but it's not," said Thailh, and at last his eyes
gleamed a little with that fresh-fish look. "This is hardly
something you'd just walk into a local shop and buy. See
the braid in it? That's lesh fiber, and the cord is draper's
cord. There are only two or three sources for it in the city;
it's difficult and expensive to make. And the two shops
that make it sell only to the drapers' trade. That narrows
things down a bit."

"So you're going to check all the people working for
drapers—and the people working in those shops that make
the cord."

"I've already started. Nothing significant yet, but I expect that to change."

"Very well. Keep me informed."

Thailh nodded and gathered up his parchments and tablets. Reswen glanced out the window, noting with some surprise that the sun was already quite low. "And Thailh? Do me a favor. Watch where you walk at night . . . and don't do it alone. This person may be crazy, but not stupid . . . and an investigator could wind up with some of that around his neck."

"I'll be careful."

"Good. Later, then."

Thailh bowed himself out, and Reswen stretched behind the desk, then fell to neatening up the piles of reports and stowing them away where they would come readily to hand over the next couple of days. Time to head home and freshen up for the formal reception for the Easterners. And then—

Blue eyes, he thought on purpose, so that he wouldn't think it inadvertently. Reswen was becoming angry . . . and was becoming determined to get some answers.

He got up and went out and down the stairs toward the street, purring an old Northern war chant.

The reception was held in the Councillory, in the Hunt Room, probably the most splendid formal hall in all Niau. Exactly how long ago it was built, no one was certain, but it went back to the first building of the city, and had never been changed or refurbished. It echoed the black stone which was the primary material of the rest of the building, but here the somberness was all turned to splendor. The city's first builders, it seemed, had decided that though the rest of the building might be spare and modest, it would contain at least one room that would completely astonish all comers. The architect had apparently been a mrem with a love of luxury and an unlimited budget.

It was all done in the polished black stone that faced the Councillory, at least as regarded the walls, but the floors were tiled in rough semiprecious stone—black onyx, black jade—with brass fittings between the stones, and here and there a carved plaque of white marble with the city's name-rune set in it in black inlay of onyx. The columns, a double row that ran the length of the room down its middle, from the massive doors to the throne dais, were also polished black marble, veined, but the veins were inlaid with gold and silver, and set here and there with gems where the normal cutting of the stone had originally revealed outcroppings of crystal. All this went up to a ceiling inlaid with gold and black patines; and below the ceiling, running right around the room, was a dado in old cream marble carved in hunting scenes. It was a hunt of the old gods, some of them so old their names were forgotten. Gemmed spears were brandished, arrows afire with gold were aimed, the quarry fell kicking; and the carving, in the old naturalistic style, was so real that when the room grew smoky from the braziers of spice burning between the black columns, you might stare at the carvings in the high dimness and wonder whether they moved a little, whether the old forgotten gods turned their heads a little, and smiled.

Reswen, standing in the doorway now, looked down the room at the splendor of the guests milling about there, and had little interest, for this once, in the carving. The Easterners had turned out in their best, no mistaking it, and the Niauhu nobles invited to the reception had done the same, considering it their business to outshine the guests . . . for the good of the city, of course. The torches, fixed to the pillars in holders resembling the hands and arms of mrem, glittered on gold and silver and rarer metals, glancing back smooth green gleams from breastplates of hammered shev, wine red ones from swordhilts or fillets of aretine. Jewels were all over the place, glittering against fur. Silks and velvets and point-laces beaded in seed diamond, tissues of all the precious metals, they brushed and swept away again in the haze-tangled light of the torches. Dancing was going on, a set piece in the Northern style; several couples moved toward and away from one another in swirls of rich fabric, stepping over the swords laid on the floor.

Reswen smiled a bit as the crier came back from leading some late-arriving Easterner down the floor. "Evening, Tarkh," he said. "How are the tips tonight?"

Tarkh, the Councillory's majordomo, sniffed softly. He was a tall lean mrem with cool green eyes and the shortest, plushiest blue-gray fur Reswen had ever seen; a mrem with an air about him that was far more aristocratic than most of the aristocrats he saw every day. "They tip too big," said Tarkh scornfully, and then nodded to a footmrem waiting by the door, with a gong. The gong was struck, and everybody in the place quite understandably stopped talking, since talking was impossible over the crashing, hissing clamor of the thing. When the noise of it had died away sufficiently, Tarkh filled his lungs and cried, "The Honorable Reswen *neh Kahhahlis-chir, Essh-vassheh ve Mhetlen*, that is to say, Chief Constable and Policemaster of the City Niau—"

Reswen started his walk down the hall, still smiling a bit, nodding to some of the nobles he knew, watching others' reactions to him and to his interest. The reactions were, he realized quite happily, not merely reactions to his clothes. Not that he wasn't well dressed. His best kit was impressive: chased breastplate and fittings all of polished red aretine or scarlet enamel and gold, a cloak of scarlet sendal, flowing out behind him like fire or blood from a wound; on the breastplate, the badges of his rank, various awards from the city for valour in battle or for aptitude at work, with the big gold-and-scarlet torque of his rank snug around his neck. Certainly there were a couple of hundred people here better dressed than he—not hard, considering the kind of money they had. But there was some small advantage, in any large group, of being the Chief of Police. Clothes, they knew, would not help them if they fell foul of you, and neither would money or power. Reswen walked down the hall, feeling on him the eyes of Easterners and city people alike, and enjoying it.

Meanwhile there was another set of eyes he was very interested in being introduced to, formally.

The Councillors were down at the thone dais end of the hall, mostly. Some of them were scattered around the room, but Mraal was there holding court with several of the others, including Aratel. *Keeping him under his paw,* Reswen thought, *where he can't get in trouble . . .* for

Aratel looked surly. The Councillors were as splendidly
dressed as anyone else, their own torques of office weighing them down as usual. Reswen smiled a bit more; his
torque might be gold, but it was also hollow. There were
Easterners with the Councillors' group as well; others
were scattered through the room, talking to the Niauhu
guests.

Reswen bowed and made the usual polite duties to the
council members, and then said, "Sirs, perhaps someone
would make me known to the notable guests?"

To Reswen's mild surprise, Mraal said, "I'll do that
office. Master Hiriv, here is our Chief Constable, who
makes the city safe for the people who live in it. Reswen-
vassheh, the eminent Master-Priest Hiriv, who cares for
the affairs of the grain-god Lakh in the Eastern cities."

"Reverence," Reswen said, and bowed slightly with his
paws covering his eyes, the usual greeting for a priest.
"You're very welcome," he said, straightening. And to his
surprise, this was a lie. Reswen was shocked to find such
instant dislike for the mrem welling up inside him. Usually he tried to stop such reactions in himself when they
occurred; they clouded the judgment. But this creature— As
Reswen had noticed that morning in the courtyard at
Haven, Hiriv was three times the size a mrem his age
should have been, a bloated, orange-and-white-splotched
mass of furry flab. Reswen would have been tempted to
think him eunuched, except that in the Eastern priest-
hoods as well as the Western ones, priests had to be
weaponed mrem. *Now, just being fat is hardly enough
excuse to dislike someone*, Reswen was thinking. But at the
same time the jolly expression that the priest wore—like
that of a favorite uncle who would sneak the children bits
of the best meat when they came to visit him—was nothing but cosmetic. Reswen could feel nothing at all behind
it, and over time he had come to trust his feelings about
these things. *Now, come then. Even that isn't reason enough;
there are many people who wear faces for their own
purposes, to keep themselves from fear or*— But this was
nothing of the kind. Reswen hated Hiriv, hated him on
the spot. It was very embarrassing.

And Lorin's words came to him then: "Watch out for the priest—"

Reswen held his face still by force. "Thank you, thank you," said the jolly priest, and chuckled, and Reswen hated him worse than ever. Someone whose intentions Reswen distrusted so shouldn't be able to wear such an expression. *But whatever,* Reswen thought, and applied as cheerful an expression to his own face. The priest's presence here, with the most senior of the council gathered around him, made Reswen suspect strongly that he was a major source, if not the only source, of the troublesome document of this afternoon. "I hope you are enjoying our hospitality," Reswen said, and hardly noted the answer, just made certain that he was answered with more benign platitudes while he glanced from councillor to councillor to assess their mood. Mraal was difficult to read, with his party face on, but Aratel was not bothering to hide his sulkiness, and the usually unrufflable Lawas and uncaring Harajh both looked somewhat unnerved for once. *Oh, bad, very bad; they heard nothing in the meeting with the Easterners that relieved their minds one bit. I am going to be called up to the Arpekh's House again in the morning, and my job is going to be no fun at all for the next few days. . . .*

As soon as it was possible, in politeness, Reswen bowed again, with his paws over his eyes. "Reverence, I would talk to you at more length—" *(Lies, all lies!)* "—but courtesy surely requires that I give my regards to the rest of your party. . . ."

"Of course, of course, Master Reswen, have a good time," purred the old reprobate, and somehow managed to make a slightly dirty joke out of it, while the council members around him chuckled in false good humor, and (Reswen suspected) wondered what was so funny. Only Reswen had caught the brief flash of eyes that told him the priest Hiriv had decided the Chief of Police was likely to be some kind of problem. He was covering as best he could: not very well. *Good. Let him worry a little.*

Reswen sauntered away off to one side to find himself a cup of wine and continue the introductions. One of the merchants, the tall gray-striped one Reswen had marked out that morning at Haven, was standing toward one end of the richly draped table that held the iced wines and herb drinks. The she-mrem standing over him—for she was taller than he—was talking insistently in the merchant's ear, and her expression and barely concealed hiss of voice did not suggest that she was inviting him out on the tiles, or indeed to anything but a frightful session of ear-biting once they were out of there—

"Honorable Rirhath," Reswen said kindly from one side, bowing, and the female broke off, flustered.

The merchant turned to him with an air of mingled relief and annoyance, bowed slightly. "You have the advantage of me, master," he said.

"My business, I'm afraid," Reswen said. "Reswen-*vassheh*, at your service."

"Oh, the softpaw," Rirhath said, and Reswen had to grin slightly in spite of himself; it was one of the more casual slang words for policemrem.

"Yes. Pleased to make your acquaintance, and welcome to Niau. But I have not had the honor to be introduced to your lady wife—"

"Kirshaet," Rirhath said, very shortly, making no great attempt to hide his bad humor, and took immediate refuge in the cup of wildflower wine he had been drinking.

Reswen ignored the merchant's shortness of manner, took the lady's paw, and pressed it to his forehead with the best grace he could manage—which was considerable, considering how many she-mrem he had practiced it on over the years. "Madam," he said, "your servant."

The ruffled lady put her soft brown fur down and broke out into a rather astonished purr—which did not last, somewhat to Reswen's chagrin. "Oh, Master Reswen, thank you so much, and if that is true, can you do something about this food?"

"Madam, if our food disagrees with you, I shall have every one of the catering staff from the scullions to the Artificer of Delicacies spiked up over the city gate." Out of the corner of his eye Reswen saw the poor wine-server fluff up from ears to tail in terror. It was too bad, for the moment, but Reswen had other thoughts on his mind besides reassuring the kitchen staff. From the report Krruth had given him, this creature was one of the gods' great gifts to an intelligence officer—a mouth on four legs—and Reswen for one was not going to let go of her until he had flattered and cajoled her into giving him her views on everyone in the room. "Meanwhile, tell me what the problem is so that it can be put right. Is it too cold? Too hot? Is there nothing here that appeals to you?"

He broke off for a moment, noticing Rirhath moving away from the wine table. "But I would not want to take you away from your noble husband. Perhaps I could have something sent for—"

Rirhath caught Reswen's look, and gruffly said, "No matter, sir," and walked off toward the group at the head of the room, looking entirely relieved to be shut of his wife.

Reswen filed the exchange away for later consideration, and then said, "Your husband is gracious, madam. Come away from here; these wines do not favor the best of the food. Try this red wine instead, it encourages the heart's humors, with which you are so well provided. Not everyone has the taste to understand the bouquet of it— yes, you are quite right, it is a soft stuff, it cries out for something to cut the sweetness. Here, see these hortolans, see the sauce they perch in. You will not find a more delicate tidbit anywhere. Ah, just a bite, my lady. No? Then I will. Ah, well then, here's one for you. Another? Indeed, madam, are you sure? Your girlish figure—"

Reswen spent no more than five minutes in such outrageous flattery, which was just as well; too much more of it would have turned his stomach. Between wine and fine food, and a bit of attention, the lady Kirshaet was shortly telling Reswen the history of her life and of the lives of everyone she knew, liberally intermingled with every thought about anything or anyone else that crossed her mind. Within twenty minutes Reswen knew quite well why her husband was so glad to be out of her company for a while. The she-mrem was a glutton, a minx, and a fool, endlessly hungry for attention and unable to realize that she was being given any, full of grievances against a world assumed to be in conscious conspiracy against her. Reswen had only to nod and smile to keep her going; his pleasant

looks were all she seemed to need to confirm to her that
he was in league with her against everything that was out
to do her harm or annoy her. She spilled out her complaints against her husband ("I cannot hear words against
him, he is a guest," said Reswen more than once, for the
benefit of any listening ears, but that did nothing to stop
her); against his business, which took him away from her
for interminable hours; against this errand to the West,
which kept him with her just as interminably; against her
children, her servants, the politicians of the East, the
weather, the gods. . . .

Reswen finally found himself in possession of more
information than even he needed, and he began wondering how to shut Kirshaet off; the sheer flow of delighted,
self-satisfied malice was beginning to wear him down.
There was also the small matter that someone else might
become suspicious of all the time he was spending with
her. She was going on about Rauji, the junior merchant
with the strange specialty in betting on uxen-breeding,
when Reswen first heard, then saw his excuse. A soft
purring peal of laughter, from behind one of the great
black pillars, and then the long-limbed, gray-furred shape,
and the flash of blue eyes peering out at someone else—

"And who might that be?" Reswen said, into the torrent of words.

Kirshaet looked, and broke off short. *"That* one," she
said. "The whore. Certainly you have no interest in *her*,
Master, everyone in the room must have guessed by now
where she spends her nights, she and the other one,
surely littered in a gutter somewhere, amazing that they're
allowed to consort with decent people, jewels or not, just
the commonest kind of—"

"Oh, certainly it's not true," said Reswen quite purposefully. *Though it's a bit perverse, since that's possibly
the first thing she's said in some time that* is *true.*

"How dare you contradict me, you—you civil servant,"
said Kirshaet without a moment's hesitation, and with
great relish. "Arrogant creature, contradicting your betters—"
And off she went across the room, doubtless to tell her
husband what a boor the policemrem was, not that it came

as a surprise, no matter how fine the airs he might put
on—

Reswen breathed out and surreptitiously stroked the
pads of his forepaws down his cloak; they were damp. He
felt actively sorry for Rirhath, no matter what the Easterner
might or might not be planning. But at least he was now in
possession of a great deal of information about the delegation. Heaven only knew how much of it was true. It would
all have to be correlated with the results that Krruth and
his people produced from the next week's listening to
matters in Haven. *But not bad, not bad at all for one
night's work. And meanwhile—*

He started to make his way to the far side of the room,
which took some time—there were more mrem standing
about and milling about than ever, a little boiling storm of
silks, shot through with jewelled lightning, the thunder of
much speculative small talk and gossip running under
everything. Few people fell aside for him, which suited
Reswen well. He came under the shadow of the right-
hand portico, eyed the crowd on the far side of it, very
carefully put his back against one of the massive pillars,
and waited.

It took only a second, and she was there, escorted past
him on the arm of Aiewa, one of the older Councillors.
Hard to make a better choice, thought Reswen rather
sardonically, for Aiewa was old and half blind, and (to put
it gently) of limited intelligence. Unfortunately he was
rich, perhaps the second richest mrem in Niau, and therefore his opinions (such as they were) counted for something in council. Aiewa's opinion of Deshahl was quite
plain: His hungry gaze clung to her, slipped down her and
up again like paws, trod her down, seized her neck—
Reswen held quite still, frozen by simple revulsion, with
annoyance at both prey and predator as they went by,
crossed in front of him, came to rest in the shadows by the
wall. Deshahl was in smoky blue again, silks so fine one
could see through them, a floating cloud of the stuff draped
from neck and arms and loins; a glittering blue stone as
long as Reswen's claw-joint hung low from her throat on a
chain like a golden thread. Another one rested against her

forehead, hung from a delicate golden webwork about her head and ears. She looked fragile, wanton, sweet, and fierce at the same time—and Reswen looked at her and felt nothing whatsoever.

He breathed out, confused. After the odd feelings of the morning, this was very peculiar indeed. What he had seen then had nothing to do with what he saw now: just a whore indeed, plying her trade and doing it well. *Going to have to find out just who she's working for,* he thought. *A pity Kirshaet didn't know anything about it . . . but if she had, she would have made a point to tell me about it right away. Something else for Krruth to look into.* But now here she stood teasing poor foolish Aiewa, stroking him not in any outwardly provocative way—and Aiewa was reacting to her like a mrem utterly besotted. Reswen felt like spitting. *Bad news. I am going to have to speak to Mraal about this. Aiewa has become a liability, not to be trusted with anything serious that the council enacts: she will know about it in a second, if this beginning's any indication of how she intends to continue. And then whoever she works for will know about it as well—*

"She is rather shameless, I'm afraid," said a soft voice at his elbow.

Reswen looked around and down, and found himself gazing into golden eyes in a dark face. The other one, the "less highly flavored sweetmeat," Krruth had called her. "Your pardon?" Reswen said, slightly at a loss for the moment.

"Laas," she said. It was two syllables, and she sang it more than said it.

"Reswen-*vassheh.*"

She laughed at him. It was a delightful, quiet sound, warm and intimate, as if they had a joke together. Reswen leaned back against the pillar again, rather bemused at being laughed at by such a pretty little creature, and one he'd not spoken to for more than a breath's time. "And is 'policemrem' part of your name, then?" she said.

"Not when I'm off duty."

"And does that ever happen?" she said. "Surely not now."

Reswen smiled ruefully and shook his head.

"No, I suppose not," she said, and settled back against the pillar next to him, with her arms folded. "Certainly not with that going on." She sounded faintly disapproving.

Reswen looked sidewise at her, trying not to be too obvious about it. She was dressed much more modestly than Deshahl, as she had been that morning. The material was similar—the gauze dark golden, instead of blue—but the cut was demure, not designed to point to certain parts of a she-mrem and indicate that one might get in there under certain circumstances. There was a touch of gold here and there on the dark, dappled fur, a bracelet or two, earrings of braided gold wire, but nothing like the ostentation that Deshahl was indulging. Looking up to the golden eyes again, Reswen found himself wondering what he had seen in Deshahl in the first place.

"No," Laas said, as if to herself, but just loudly enough for Reswen to hear, "subtlety was never one of her talents." She looked over at Reswen, and her eyes narrowed with barely restrained laughter, including him in the joke again. "Though I suspect it has been one of yours."

"Oh?"

"This morning. In the courtyard. I'm glad to see they let you wear better clothes to parties, at least. Hiriv thought you were something to do with the stables."

Reswen let his jaw drop in a smile, while inside his mind was racing with a mixture of bemusement and dismay. *This one is* sharp. *Just what I need . . . I think.* "And what does he think now?"

Laas looked at Reswen with something like resignation, but the humor was still very much to the fore. "Gods above, why would I be telling you a thing like that? You're a policemrem, anyway; surely you already know. . . ."

Reswen was conscious of being mocked, and found that he didn't mind it. "Well, I did have to try," he said.

There was a pause. "Yes," Laas said, "I know. So did I . . . ."

The companionable silence fell again, leaving Reswen feeling completely confused, and not minding that either. It was a peculiar feeling, for Reswen hated not understanding things . . . as a rule. *And now what do we say?*

he asked himself. *'How was your trip? Do you like the weather we're having?'*

"And did Kirshaet tell you everything you needed to know?" Laas said. "And everything else? The wretched gossip."

Reswen turned and looked at her with mild astonishment. "Was it that obvious?" he said.

"Oh, I don't think so. Not to any of our group, at least. We've been stuck with her for forty days across the desert, remember . . . I think anyone who notices her at this point is just relieved that she's talking to someone *else*."

"I believe that," Reswen said, and glanced over at Aiewa again. Deshahl was whispering something in his ear, and his tail was twitching. "But it was obvious to *you*."

"After a little while, yes."

"I think I'd like to talk to you, sometime," Reswen said quietly.

"So send for me," said Laas equably. "No one will be particularly surprised, especially since I'm supposed to be seducing you anyway."

That made Reswen's ears go forward. "Well," he said, with every indication of reluctance, "I guess we'd better make it look that way, hadn't we?"

"Not unless I choose," Laas said. Reswen considered her casual tone with bemusement. For a courtesan, she seemed fairly uninterested in the business.

They paused for a moment as Kanesh swept by. *Unfortunate creature*, thought Reswen, noticing that he had Kirshaet on his arm. She glared at Reswen and Laas as she went by, speaking small venomous nothings into Kanesh's ear. When she had passed, Reswen and Laas exchanged a look of incredulous humor.

"That's it for you," Laas said. "You've been seen talking to me. You're going to *have* to send for me now."

"Not unless *I* choose," Reswen said, thinking, *Two can play at this game*.

Laas shrugged her tail and smiled. "You haven't even fed me anything yet," she said. "And after all those little bird things you made her eat, to cover up how many of them *you* ate. You should be ashamed of yourself."

Reswen had to laugh out loud at that. His bemusement was becoming worse by the moment, but he was enjoying it, and there seemed no reason why he should not indulge in hand-feeding a courtesan in public. "Very well," he said. "Since I didn't have enough of them before, we'll start with them now."

"And don't get the gravy on my clothes," Laas said, "the way you did with Kirshaet. We're going to be hearing about that for days, I'm sure."

"Perish the thought," Reswen said. He led Laas across the room to the table where the hot foods lay smoking over their lamps.

Two hours later the party was still going strong, but Reswen was beginning to think he should leave, because the rumors about him and the pretty little dun-and-orange number were more than sufficiently started; the serving-mrem behind the tables had started winking at him every time he and Laas came back for another cup of wine or plate of hortolans. *That should make whoever she's working for quite happy,* Reswen thought calmly, as he finished one last cup of wine, and stifled a hiccup. *We'll see how long we can keep this going.*

He lowered the cup to see Laas looking at him over hers. She sipped, then put it down. "Don't tell me you have to leave so soon," she said.

Reswen blinked, then smiled. Laas had this gift for reacting to what he was thinking before he said it. "I'm afraid I must," he said. "Unlike some of the people here, I have to get up and work in the morning. And some of them are watching me with great care to see if you've got me tied to your tail yet, my dear. So better to keep them wondering."

"True enough," she said, "though I have to be seen to be arguing the point a little." She drew close to him. Reswen found himself being rather astonished by her nearness. All the evening so far, she had rarely come closer to him than a long arm's reach. He bent his head down so that she could reach better, and she stood on tiptoe and whispered, "Don't go. Or if you must, let me go with you. I've heard the rumors about your house."

"News travels fast, I see," Reswen whispered back. Her fur was most astonishingly perfumed: something fresh, something that made you want to lean in closer. . . . "But it's stories, mostly."

"I know. It was just the expected thing to say. I think you actually have just an ordinary couch."

He smiled. "True enough. And am I really expected to send for you very soon, or can this take a while to develop?"

"No rush. You're the police chief, after all. They expect you to be difficult."

The matter-of-fact information, delivered in the husky, sweet, purring whisper, made him want to chuckle a little. "All right," he said. "But bear in mind . . . if I can prove that you're doing all this for the detriment of Niau, I'll throw you ears over tail in gaol."

"You'll have to prove it," Laas purred, and nipped his ear. He reached out to catch her.

There was no one there.

Wine, Reswen thought; *it's death to the reflexes*. And indeed he felt pleasantly tiddly. He spent a few minutes making his good-evenings to the most senior Councillors present, and to various other notables, and to the Easterners, who were mostly much farther gone in wine than he was, and then he headed out into the cool dark air.

One of his people, an officer both of the police and the H'satei was standing outside the Councillory door; he came to attention as Reswen paused by him. "Oh, relax, Biuve," Reswen said to the young mrem. "You're not needed here. Do this for me: run to the Underhouse and tell Krruth's people that I'm not going to bother doing the first night's surveillance myself. I leave it in their capable paws. But tell them I want special attention paid to the blue-eyed party. Krruth will understand. Once you've done the errand, you're dismissed for the night."

"Yes, sir," Biuve said, and went off at a trot.

Reswen stood breathing the good cool air, then headed off home himself, away from the torches of the Councillory, out into the quiet streets and the darkness. He thought nothing more about blue eyes, and nothing at all about golden ones.

But golden eyes watched him walk away . . . and narrowed.

She never tired of inhabiting them, not really. It was one of the reasons she had been assigned this mission, and every now and then she had to admit it to herself.

The training for inhabitation usually took a long time, for her people. They tended to be unwilling to get into a skin; skins were what one got *out* of. And generally speaking, when someone mentioned to one of her people the concept of actually putting on one of *these* skins over one's own, the result was revulsion. Well, perhaps it was understandable.

She had certainly felt that way herself, the first time. One of her teachers had had the idea that she would have an aptitude for the inhabitation, and she had been quite young—though already old in magic—when they brought her the fur-thing and told her to put it on.

She had been shocked. Even then she had known that she was beautiful by her people's standards, and was somewhat vain about it. No one had tried to stop her, either; that beauty was a tool that she, or they, would use later. But now her teacher sat there in his great squalid bulk, at the other side of the small cave where they worked, and the fur-thing crouched huddled and terrified on the floor between them. Its fur was falling out in patches, and it looked as if it had been beaten.

Not that *that* particularly mattered, of course. The fur-things were their slaves, to do with as they pleased. They had no other purpose in the world, and no better one. But here was this verminous thing, with the queer stink of the fur-things about it, and her teacher wanted her to slip free of her "hard" skin into the ethereal one, a hundred times fairer—and then into *this*? It was worse than being asked to become a beast. Much worse, for *this* beast thought that it was a person.

"I will not," she had hissed, that first time, her tail lashing in disgust at the thought. Her teacher had clashed his jaws at her in annoyance—a sound she had grown used to, and learned to discount—and ordered her to. She had refused, and turned her back on him.

And that was when she received a surprise, for sud-

denly, without his even leaving his skin, his presence was
all around her, and the pressure of it on her mind was
something awful, a fire that crushed. "You will do it," he
said, and to her own astonishment and terror she watched
her body wheel around, slowly, watched her foreclaws
move, first one, then the other, drawing her closer to her
teacher. She found herself, after a moment, looking directly into his jaws. Suddenly the clash of them made
somewhat more of a threat than it had, as she crouched
there frozen before him, her body refusing to answer her.
Convulsively she tried to slip free of the hard skin, and
found that she could not—that her teacher was holding
her there against her will, something she had not thought
was possible. She was trapped in this body, trapped, as
the great jaws opened, as the teeth lowered to her, as the
maw delicately slipped around her long throat, as the jaws
closed, and she felt the soft pressure of the fangs, pushing
in, pushing—

She roared, or tried to. It came out as more of a squeal
than anything else. After a few seconds the pressure re-
leased, and the hold over her muscles went with it, and
she almost fell on her face before her teacher. It took her a
few moments to regain her composure. When she did, and
gathered the courage to look up at him again, his cool old
eyes were bent on her, full of an expression equally comprised of amusement and scorn. She hated him, right
then, as she had rarely hated anything in her life, but she
knew he scorned that too, for she had not nearly the
strength to even think of challenging him.

"You will do it," he rumbled, "or I shall force you. You
will not find it pleasant."

She held a hiss inside—surely for the moment it would
be wiser; but her chance would come. Sooner or later it
would be her jaws around *his* throat, and *she* would not let
him free.

She had turned away, then, and turned her attention
to the shaking, furred thing on the floor. She suppressed
the feeling of revulsion that rose in her, as she had suppressed the hiss. Slowly she lowered herself to the stony
floor, composed herself, slipped free of the skin.

The vermin lay there before her, panting with fear. There seemed another aspect to it, from this angle, in the overworld: she could see its own self-shadow burning in its muddy colors, and could see what to do. Through the cool fire that seemed to fill the cave in the overworld, she drifted toward the creature, leaned down toward its self-shadow, and put her teeth into the dim, dirty fire of it.

The scream that went up from it was bizarre music for her. There was a moment of crushing, cramping—and suddenly it was gone. She was inside the thing. Oh, it was horrible, there was no mistaking that. The hot stench of these things from inside—the reek of their thick blood, the hurried pound of their organs, the *itch* of it all, the caged feeling! But she was not alone in the cage . . . and that alone began to fill her with a rich and perverse delight.

It was terrified of her. It loathed her even more than she did it. But its fear shot down its veins like the cold blood of her own people, and filled her until she wanted to hiss with pleasure. It knew itself helpless, it knew she could kill it with a thought—but it knew that she was much more likely to do worse than kill it. She was much more likely to stay right where she was, inside its own head with it, unutterably alien and horrible . . . and enjoying its horror.

She did enjoy it. She was intoxicated with its fear. There was nothing she had ever tasted that was sweeter—no flesh, no blood. Drunk with it, she sought some way to make the fear more intense. She moved the thing's limbs, let it feel her do it, let it feel how helpless it was. She lifted one hand before its face, unsheathed the dirty, sharp claws one by one, made it stare at them. Fear rose in it, beat at its breastbone to get out, the heart fluttering like a trapped bird. She moved the claw closer to its face, drank the fear like wine.

She did not stop until she had made it put out both its own eyes. Then, with its own claws, she made it tear its own throat out, and stayed with it, almost staggered with evil bliss, as it leaked out its life on the floor, the fear never ebbing until abruptly there was none left.

It took her a while to find her way back to her body. Her teacher crouched there on the floor, waiting for her to find her senses again, and looked down at her with that same amused contempt. But now she didn't care. Now she knew why she had been forced to this. Her people's needs could be well served by inhabitations of this sort; the other vermin would never suspect what was going on, when she and others like her could control every move they made, every word they spoke, almost every thought.

"Crude," her teacher said. "You will learn more delicate control. More subtle satisfactions."

She had bowed her head to him, for the moment. She had applied herself. She learned that control, those satisfactions; she learned them perhaps better than many around her, in that sheltered little enclave, had suspected. When it came her teacher's time to die, however, she had cast subtlety away, remembering the first time. The bloody fragments of him that they later found were a source of terror and wonder to her other teachers, and simply of terror to her fellow students.

That was when she had been given this mission.

But now, as she lazed, out of the skin once more, she had to admit that subtlety had its uses, and this present business was one of them.

Her overself lay in the middle of the floor of one of the great rooms in the house the Niau-vermin had given to her people. She had not bothered to move this long time, not since the slave she had chosen for the day had come into the room to begin her preparations.

They were not entirely verminous, some of the slaves. She still could not bear that some of them had magic, and *this* one she would surely drink the blood, and fear, and soul of, when all this was done and her work complete. But in the meantime it was well within her power to increase the small abilities the she-vermin had. And there were other compensations.

How she had relished seeing the creature step through her, this afternoon, as it came upstairs to make ready. The slightest shudder; yes, on some unconscious level it knew she was there, lolling on the cool marble floor, watching it slip out of its so-fine garments, watching it throw itself prone on the huge opulent bed, and slowly, luxuriously, begin tonguing itself. Slowly its shudders died away; the creature began to writhe and purr with a small absurd pleasure at its own touch.

She lay there and watched it for a long time. The creature was supposed to be a she; that was part of its value on this mission, she was told. They had told her that these creatures actually were somewhat swayed by sexual attractions introduced to them in their business dealings. *That*, she had hissed with disbelief on first hearing, but now she had come to accept it as one more fang in her jaws, one more piece of information to use in her mission. She supposed that the creature was attractive enough even without the small help its talents lent it. Her tail twitched again at the thought. *Magic*—

But her magic was stronger. On impulse she rose, slipped over to that huge bed, leaned over the creature. It paused in its washing, discomfited, not knowing why.

She savored the sight, her tongue flickering in pleasure, tasting the fear on the air of the overworld. Then slowly she slipped in. No ripping of the muddy colors, this time. This time she seeped into them slowly as oil into water, silent but heavy, a presence, feelable. The creature shuddered as she leaned down onto its feeble, fragile soul, oppressed it with the feeling that something was watching it, something terrible, and that if she did not do exactly as her superior told her, something awful, *awful* would happen. A hint, an image, a flicker, there and gone, of teeth, closing, the pressure—

Then she let up the pressure, banished the image, and retired to the back of the creature's thoughts—watching them, letting its hurried little emotions wash over her. Fear, irrational fear leapt up instantly, followed by another fear that it somehow had *not* done right, followed by more fear of a petty theft that it had been contemplating—

She hissed with inward laughter, caring nothing about that. The creature could do its little stealings as it pleased. She would sooner or later have something from it that was much more worth stealing. And in the meantime, it would do her will, without question. She had only to make a suggestion at the right time.

She waited. Waiting had never been a problem for her. Even as her people counted it, she was patient—as her teacher had discovered, not so long ago. She lay there on the ghost of a marble floor, and watched the gathering start in that other building across the city. She had no need to go there. She had eyes there. Through the little vermin who was her mount at the moment, she saw them all—the other vermin, dressed in their ridiculous toy finery, flaunting their little pomp at one another, jabbering, trying to impress.

Her pet did this quite well. She was pleased. Out of its eyes she looked at them, gazed into the furry eyes, gauged (though dimly, as if looking through a gauze) which ones would be worth her attention at another time. She could not ride more than one of the vermin at a time; no one could, and it was a pity. She could have done miracles, brought this whole business to an early end, and been about the part she enjoyed—the blood, physical and psychic. But meantime, one was enough, and through her pet's eyes she marked the greedy, the fearful, the ambitious, the angry. One by one she would impress her will upon them.

One had to start somewhere, of course. She picked the one, one of the "councillors" of this wretched little place, and steered her pet toward him. Looking through her eyes at him, as her pet's talent reached out and made him susceptible, she could see things that would be of great use to her: vanity, an overblown sense of its own importance, and a stupidity colossal even for one of the vermin. Oh, this one would make a fine tool, and better yet, he was a great coward. How his soul would scream when her teeth closed on it at last! With relish she filled her pet with the desire to have *this* one want her as she liked to be wanted. Then she withdrew to watch.

It did not take long. Her pet was not much good for looking at anyone else for the rest of the evening. One odd glimpse she got, in passing, of one of the vermin who was *not* impressed by her pet, and that troubled her obscurely, so that she stored his face away to look at more closely later. Odd, for before she had thought he was as stricken by her pet as the rest.

But meantime there were more amusing things to watch, as she lay there on the cool marble, in the dark, and heard the thick movements in the bed, the rustlings, the cries, the whispered questions. The stink of verminous lust was in the overworld's air. She flickered her tongue at it every now and then, savoring the odd hot smell with a perverse pleasure. Disgusting it was, beastly, completely unlike the decorous joinings of her own people. But amusing to watch, at least.

She put her head down on her claws, lazy, and watched, and the hiss of her amusement was soft in the air. All was going as it should. Soon enough the time for waiting would be done. Then this bed, and many another, would be a welter of blood. No one would ever know what had happened.

But considering what was going to happen to this city, it was only a kindness. One had to look after one's own pets, after all. . . .

▲

Chapter 6

▲━━━━━━━━━━━━━━━━━━━━━━━━━━━━━━━━━━━━━━━▲

The one thing about being a wizard that Lorin had always hated most was the hours. You had to do so much of your business at night, just to avoid attracting the neighbors' attention. And Lorin was a day mrem at heart; as soon as it got dark, he started to yawn.

But when you had work to do, you had no choice. He had cursed a little over it, of course, when Reswen had shown up on his doorstep. Grateful as he was to the police in general and Reswen in particular for letting him live in peace, he still shuddered inwardly when any need for his services came up. And he was more nervous than usual, at the moment. The memory of his trip out of body—a kind of travel he tried to avoid whenever possible—was still filling him with dread. It was none of Reswen's business, that, of course; probably nothing that would interest him. But Lorin hated the thought of doing any sort of magic, at this point, or anything to do with magic, and possibly attracting the attention of something worse than the neighbors. That cold regard, the memory of the hissing, and of the priest, were still much with him.

Still—this stone-and-water thing needed looking into. It was certainly a spell of some kind, and a spell meant a magic-worker. He would need to find out which of the Easterners it was before talking to Reswen again, and though Lorin really didn't care much for the thought that he would have to do magic to that purpose, he had always taken a certain pride in making sure that the information he gave the Policemaster was as complete as he could make it. He might be a crook, in the eyes of the city's law, but he was an *honest* crook, and liked to give good value for his bribe money.

So Lorin did his usual business for the day, making his normal rounds of the seedier taverns at lunchtime, taking bets and paying them off—and then went home to count his takings, and hide what needed to be hidden. It was well into late afternoon when he finished, and much as he hated it, he took a nap then—being careful to lay wards around the bed, this time, drawing the appropriate circles and diagrams so that his sleep wouldn't be disturbed just now, when he needed it. Of course the presence of the wards themselves would alert anyone who was looking for evidence of a working wizard, but they would first have to be physically close to detect them—and it would take an active imagination to think that there would be a wizard working in *this* part of town.

Lorin sighed a little as he lay down, considering it. Truly, he could do as Reswen had been urging him, use some of his pay from the police—it was considerable—to take a better place in town. And indeed sometimes he walked by them, some of the snug little houses between the market and the hill, with their walled gardens, and thought seriously of having one himself. A garden, with flowers; a little warm sunbaked place, sheltered from the wind, and quiet, as this part of the city hardly ever was. . . . But then the truth of the way the world was would reassert itself. Someone would start wondering where he had gotten the money to afford a place like that—certainly not from bookmaking—and questions would start being asked. Questions were unhealthy for a wizard. People still had a tendency, remembering the depredations of the liskash in the old days, to burn a wizard first and ask questions when there was nothing left but the smell of singed fur. And even if that didn't happen, questions were just as unhealthy for a bookmaker . . . or a police informant. No, it was better that things stayed the way they were, and that he stayed snug in his hovel, and counted his money, and used it (however occasionally) for a small feast down at the local cookshop, or a she from one of the less filthy joy-houses.

He drifted off into dreams that were confused and

troubled; odd images of one of those sultry she-mrem from the joy-houses, turning into something that hissed. In the dreams he remembered thinking that this was faintly unfair . . . the wards should have protected him. When he woke up, well after dark, he sat up cursing softly, and rubbed his head. He hated sleeping in the daytime. It always made him feel weak and scattered when he woke up. And on top of that he now had to deal with feelings left over from the dreams, of being watched, of something portentous and terrible about to happen, of an odd smell. All this faint and distant, for he couldn't remember much of anything about the dreams themselves—but hanging over him nonetheless, like an old half-forgotten worry.

There was nothing to do about it, though, except consider himself warned. Lorin got dressed in his least disreputable clothes and headed off for the Councillory.

He went by a circuitous route and with several stops in several taverns, taking some bets, to give himself at least the beginnings of an alibi if he should prove to need one. This would also keep any questions from being asked as to why Lorin was out at night. The people who talked about such things—and there were many—would simply assume that his day had been bad, and so he was working late. There would be no further questions about that. It was generally understood that Lorin, like many another "tradesmrem" working on the edges of the law, was paying protection money to someone, either another criminal or some police official. Lorin smiled at the thought of that, thinking how it went much the other way. But he was hardly about to disabuse people of a misapprehension which could serve to protect him.

Quietly he slipped through the night, toward the parts of town that smelled better. The Councillory would be well guarded tonight, of course, but it was on one side of a very public square, a place full of traffic except in the dead of night, and the police or the city cohorts could hardly close the whole square down for what amounted to a party. There would be plenty of room to skulk about in, and plenty of places to watch from. And for the kind of watching he intended, Lorin did not have to be too close.

He found a shadowy doorway right across the square,

and settled into it. No one was likely to bother him; the constables were concentrated on the far side of the square, about the bright lights of the Councillory. Lorin suspected that most of their minds weren't too closely on their work, or their vigilance; they too were eager to catch a glimpse of the strangers, and the high doings going on inside. He pulled the dark cloak about him, watching them, and did a little preliminary feeling around.

This kind of "feeling" was always a tradeoff. Wizards, excepting the most powerful ones, had sharp limitations on how far they could "see" while still in the body, and how clearly. Each wizard's "range" was a constant. The closer a wizard was to a situation he desired to divine, the better he could perceive what was happening, but he might also be in more danger there. The further away the wizard was, the harder it was to clearly sense what was going on, but the safer he was, as a rule.

Lorin tonight was pushing his personal range as close as he dared, consonant with good results. He needed to sense if there was indeed magic happening, and what kind . . . but he also needed to walk away from the square afterwards. Reswen might be kindly disposed toward him, but Lorin seriously doubted he had ever told any of his staff that he had a tame wizard on the payroll . . . and whether any other policemrem knew or not, it seemed unlikely that they would connect the Policemaster's agent with the skulking mrem out in the square. At least not before morning—and annoying things could happen to one in a police cell between midnight and dawn, no matter how carefully Reswen worked to keep such things from happening. *No*, Lorin thought, *I'll watch out for myself first. If the information has to suffer a little, so be it. . . .*

He concentrated on being still, for a while. He suspected it would seem surprising to the untrained how hard it was to simply be perfectly motionless except for one's breathing, but that stillness was vital to the stillness of the mind that would follow, and allow him to "hear" and "see" while still in the body. It would also make it that much less likely that any passing constable would notice him; even a chance shift from foot to foot could be fatal—Reswen's constables were a sharp lot, by and large.

He did not close his eyes. That was for the rankest
kind of amateur—or a wizard not standing in a public
place where anyone might come up to him without warning. Lorin simply let his eyes go unfocused, let the view of
the great square blur, and did as his father had taught him
all that while ago. *Simply allow yourself to see something
else where the world is,* his father had said. *Most people
refuse; most people spend their whole lives refusing. Just
stop refusing, for this little while. Don't strain, don't
push. There's nothing you have to* do. *It's all* stopping
doing.

So he stopped, and did nothing. Presently the square
didn't seem quite so dark. Not that there was actually light
there: but he saw, or rather felt, the impression of light,
and movement, and talk, and laughter. It was rather like
peering in a lighted window from out of the dark. Everything was somewhat remote, but more immediate for the
contrast of its brightness against the dark he looked in
from.

Through the impression of light and riches, impressions of people moved. There were no images as such. But
a bundle of something like light would pass by him, and
Lorin would catch a brief burst of emotion from it, or a
slow steady drone of thought, or the muffled sound of
speech happening—less muffled if the person himself was
speaking, more so if he was listening. Sometimes a word
would come through clearly, as if a swathing, sound-
deadening curtain had briefly parted, then closed down
again. The curtain was never open for long, nor did the
"gauze" enwrapping his mind's eye clear for more than a
moment or so. Nor was this his fault. It was simply that
few minds could do anything with utter singlemindedness
for more than a second or so without slipping.

Lorin leaned there against the doorway, and seemed to
himself no longer to be outside. Rather, he was standing
against a doorway in the gilded richness of the Councillory.
The gilt had a vague bloom laid all over it, as if of age or
distance, and every light seemed to be seen through some
suddenly risen fog from off the river. The shifting shapes
of light drifted past him, and he watched them and looked
at their colors.

The colors were always indicative; they were among a wizard's first and most important studies. Sometimes, in mrem of powerful enough personality, they would show even about one's normal body, which in less emphatic mrem tended to drown the nonphysical body out as daylight drowns out stars. But when one was "unfocused" in this manner, they showed. There were endless different combinations, and even in any one given person the colors would shift with a rainbow's unpredictability from moment to moment as his perception of himself, or his mood, shifted. But there were always general tendencies visible in a person, ones that took no time to perceive, as their emotional counterparts and correspondences would have done. The muddy colors of hunger, greed, rage, pain, scaling up through the clearer hues of interest and determination, and from them through the brighter (and rarer) shades of delight, commitment, compassion, love—Lorin knew them all of old, and like many other wizards, preferred not to look for them too often. Fair seemings so often covered the bitter truth, and any given group of mrem perceived in this way tended to shade unhappily down toward the darker colors. Here or there might be a brief beacon of some bright emotion, but in all there was the tendency toward the darkness.

An important part of the art, though, was to keep one's own emotions and reactions out of the seeing; they could too often contaminate the perception of everything one was trying to discover. And the colors of magic, which were several, were delicate things in most mrem not actually doing magic at the moment. One's own emotions could drown them out. So Lorin kept his own feelings at bay, and looked around the room, his arms folded, as light and shadow swirled around him.

There were knots of avarice, several of them: The bilious yellow of it swirled and mingled with the various greens of jealousy, envy, and pride. *Merchants*, Lorin thought. Several of them bulked large—the width of one's bundle of light told something about one's bodily size, though the manifestation could on occasion be misleading— and there was little to choose between the Easterners and some few of them whom Lorin recognized as Niauhu by a snatch of dialogue here or the brief sight of their clothing somewhere else.

It was not all as bad as among the merchants, though—all busy at seeing how much information they could extort from one another while giving as little as possible back. There was much genuine merriment going around, and a great deal of curiosity, and the soft colors of sheer satisfaction as nearly everyone ate and drank happily of what was undoubtedly a noble spread. Even food had its colors when it was fresh, and the vegetables in particular lay there still glowing somewhat, pleased in their mindless way that they had been chosen to be eaten. The consciousness —if that was the word for it—was fading, but it would last them unbroken until they were in someone's stomach.

Lorin smiled a little at his own folly—he could rarely afford to have that innocent pleasure of a happy vegetable in the house, or rather, people in the market would have noticed that his budget was suddenly large enough to get a nonessential like vegetables, and so he eschewed them and stuck to plain dried meat, good enough for him and his neighbors. He turned his attention back to the mrem gathered in the room. There was someone he particularly wanted to look at: the priest.

He found him, immediately, exuding all the colors of good humor and none of those of magic. He was drunk— his colors had that sort of florid look that too much wine or drug tended to produce, an outsweeping tendency. Normally that should have made a tendency toward magic more visible, not less. Yet none of the normal shades evinced themselves, none at all, and Lorin wondered whether anything he had seen during his soulwalk had been correct at all.

He watched the priest for quite a while, and outside of various perceptions of cunning, false joviality, and mild irritation, nothing further was evident about him that made him interesting to Lorin at all. It was a puzzle. Finally he turned away to watch some of the others.

There were a couple of them exhibiting most clearly the colors of sheer lust: colors as hard to ignore as a fire set in the middle of one's living room rug. Lorin looked carefully at one of them, a slender shape, and concen-

trated briefly to see if he could get a glimpse of him or
her. Her, it turned out: a quick image of a slender shape
in silks, gone again. But an Easterner, and the other party
was Niauhu; his colors showed hunger of a kind that had
nothing to do with the body, and a huge pride—and
almost none of the clear upper-level colors that indicated
anything to be proud of, such as intelligence or virtue.
Some sodden old fool, probably . . . Lorin narrowed his
"eyes," looking more closely at the lust-ridden creature.
One of the Councillors, it was. The name eluded him, but
he had seen the hobbling old mrem at several public
functions before this. It would be easy enough to get a
name, if Reswen was interested in him.

Lorin glanced around at that thought and saw what he
thought he would. He had rarely looked at Reswen in this
manner, but he knew him well enough from having worked
with him this long to recognize him from his colors: a
methodical sort of arrangement of them, colors that held
unusually steadily in one hue or another—no flickering
from thought to thought, but a slow steady certainty on
one issue before moving to another. Yet all the same, a
lively intelligence, and a humor, glowing through the more
somber colors—someone who saw no reason not to enjoy
himself at his work. He was enjoying himself now. That
sheaf of colors stood close to another, by a pillar, and the
two of them lanced intertwining light at one another—
conversation, barbed, searching, and merry by turns. For
a while Lorin just gazed at this for the sheer pleasure of it.
The colors of wit were a treat to watch, as tendrils of
colored fire touched, interlaced, flinched back, knotted,
strove, twined. Lorin smiled to himself a little, there in
the shadows. *Another of the Policemaster's conquests,* he
thought. *Though not his blue-eyed problem—*

He thought about that for a second, then turned his
attention briefly back to the she who showed the colors of
lust so clearly. She was leading the poor Council-mrem on
visibly. Lorin could see it, as she strolled casually away
from him across the room, but her hunger for him trailed
hot pulsing blood-colored tendrils behind her, toward him;
they clung, caressed, drew, and he lurched tipsily after
her—

Lorin frowned, then smoothed his annoyance away.
There was something there he needed to find out about—
some taste, some tang— He bent his attention fully on the
she, concentrated on brushing the cobwebs away. Was she
the magic-worker he was looking for? There were magics
of that kind— Lorin "narrowed" his eyes, held her in the
center of his attention, paid no attention to the Councillor
who came bumbling after her. The colors of her grew
clearer, sharper. Lust, swirling. Other motivations, sub-
merged, hidden even from her. The pleasures of control. A
murky pleasure at the helplessness of the other's desire.
Anticipation, buried for the moment, of what would follow
later. Lorin looked deeper. Fear, fear that she would not
do well, that someone she worked for would be displeased.
Rebellion. The someone was—

And then he touched it, and Lorin flinched away as if
he had touched a stove. Heat, the odd smell, a sense of
watching, the leftovers from his dreams—all there. His
magic-worker was not this she-mrem after all; it was working *through* her, though. And doubtless it knew it had
been touched. He jerked his consciousness out of there,
wobbled out of his doorway, and headed for the nearest
street that led out of the square. He almost ran afoul of a
troop of constables on the way out, hurrying past them
like someone who had had a bad scare, not stopping to
answer their hail. *Oh, go away!* he willed them, and
finally they did, heading off toward the square.

Oh, bad, it was bad. His dreams, his soulwalk, these
Easterners, all connected. And he had not found out what
Reswen needed to know. But there were worse worries.
Almost he could feel the tendrils of disembodied attention
following him out of that room, across the square, down
the street, fastening to his shoulder blades, digging into
him like claws—

Lorin moaned and ran home, to the wards, and safety
. . . for the moment.

▲

Krruth was one of those mrem who had never really
given up being fully nocturnal, so that Reswen wasn't
particularly surprised to find him calling around to the

office first thing in the morning, looking fresh and pleased with himself. Reswen wished he could have said the same. He had had a little more wine than he had really needed, last night, and had forgotten to take the usual prehangover remedy before collapsing on his couch. As a result, his head and mouth felt rather as if they were suffering from a case of ingrown fur.

"Nice evening last night, sir," Krruth said after closing the office door, and standing down from attention. It was more a statement than a question.

"Yes," Reswen said, rubbing his head, "and I suspect the rumors are flying. Which is what I had in mind."

"Just as you say, sir." Was that the slightest flicker of humor? But it was hard to tell anything from Krruth's lean dark face.

"Yes, just as I say. What happened in there last night?"

"Well, sir, I suspect you know about Aiewa and Deshahl going off together."

"I doubt there's anyone in the city who doesn't. She didn't waste her time."

"No indeed. Straight back to Haven they went."

"And?"

Krruth smiled a little. "Apparently the rumors of Aiewa's senility are premature. Or the lady's skill is considerable."

"Yes, I'm sure the staff had a good time," Reswen said. He had no objection to his operatives enjoying the things they saw and heard, as long as they didn't get so interested in them that they forgot details, or why they were watching in the first place. "But I take it nothing else of note occurred."

"Aiewa told her nothing of import, and she asked him nothing," said Krruth. "We will of course keep watching the situation. We simply hope that Aiewa doesn't conceive the bright idea of taking her back to his house in future. It would be nerve-racking to have to try to set up the same kind of listening system, and his servants are unfortunately of the unbribable old-retainer sort."

Reswen flicked his ears back in annoyance. "Anyone can be bribed. Set the butler up somehow, if it comes to that and you have to. But I doubt he'll risk the public onus of such an open liason with a foreigner, and an Easterner at that."

"He made no attempt to hide it last night," Krruth said.

"True enough. But that was once, and he looked befuddled. He had been hitting the wine. . . ."

"He wasn't drunk when he came back, sir. Would have been hard to be drunk, in my opinion, and, ah, function the way he did."

"Well, keep an eye on him. What else?"

"Nothing of note. The priest was up later than anyone else . . . stayed till they closed the Councillory down, talking to all the councillors. Didn't miss a one. Stayed up late even after he got back to Haven, drinking and telling lewd jokes." Krruth looked slightly disapproving. "These priests of fertility cults," he said, "I tell you, sir, they have filthy mouths."

Reswen smiled gently. Krruth, as he had often told superiors and juniors alike, had been "raised old-fashioned," and considered many of the styles and habits of modern Niau to be downright decadent. "I don't mind a little dirt," Reswen said. "It's sedition that concerns me. That was all he talked about?"

"And food, sir. Not that that creature needs any more of it. Great gross thing that he is."

"Yes, well. What about the others? Rirhath and his uncongenial lady?"

"Rirhath went back to Haven early, cuffed the servants, drank himself stinking, and went to bed. Kirshaet stayed at the Councillory till the priest left, and went back with him and the underpriests. Same for her—drink, too much of it, and bed."

"With her husband?"

"Yes. They were in a fine state this morning, I tell you. On my life, sir, I wouldn't want a marriage like that."

"No argument there. The other merchants?"

"Went back not too long after you left, sir."

Reswen digested it all for a moment. "All right," he said, "keep watching them all closely. I want one of our people with each of them at every possible moment—manage it however you like. Especially watch that priest.

I'll make notes on everything that Kirshaet female told me, and you can set the lads to finding out how much of it was mere slander and how much might be used against one or more of these people if we needed to."

Krruth looked at Reswen a little oddly. "There was someone else, sir."

"Well?"

"Laas."

Reswen rolled his eyes slightly. He could see that his staff was going to be teasing him about this one for a while. "Yes?"

"She took Kanesh back to Haven with her, sir."

Reswen shrugged. "She's a courtesan, for pity's sake. I just want to find out whose orders she's taking . . . for she admitted to me last night that she was working for *someone*. Have her listened to wherever she goes that we can keep someone with her. Otherwise, I'll manage it."

"Very well, sir—"

Someone pounded on the door. Reswen put his paw to his head and moaned softly. "Why do my office help have to be so efficient? Come in, don't just stand there hammering!"

The door opened, and in burst young Second-Oct Recruit Creel, gasping like a bellows. "Ah, Creel," Reswen said on seeing him, "just what I needed to make my morning complete. Come in, young son, and sit down and tell me what's on your mind. How's the bunorshan-herding business?"

"Invaders, sir!" said Creel, and coughed, and fell more than sat in the chair that Reswen had indicated.

"No, no," Reswen said, massaging his temples gently, "that was yesterday."

"No, sir, today!"

Reswen glanced up from under his brows. "Not another caravan, surely. We're not due one for, oh, another couple of eightdays—"

"Bigger than the usual caravan, sir," Creel said as Krruth handed him a cup of water. He drank hastily and noisily, and then said, "They're wearing Northern colors. Lloahai."

"Are you certain? Gold and white?"

"Yes, sir. It's a big party, and there are twelve litters, and a lot of foot soldiery. More than anyone would need for an escort, no matter how far they'd come."

Why does everything have to happen at once? Reswen thought unhappily. "Well," he said, "I'm just glad the walls are still manned."

Krruth looked at Reswen with some discomfort. "They're not, sir."

"*What?*"

"The Arpekh canceled the alert at the end of the reception last night. The cohorts are at normal status."

Reswen briefly said things about the parentage and sanitary habits of the Arpekh, separately and collectively, then grabbed a wax tablet, scraped on it with savage speed, and dug his chop into the bottom of the page with unnecessary force. "Runner!" he shouted, and a slightly surprised-looking kit from one of the pool waiting around the constabulary offices poked his head in.

"This to the city cohorts, and right now. I'll be down at the gates shortly. If they have any questions, have Commander Sachath wait on me there." He was scribbling again as he spoke. After a pause, he jabbed the shorthand of his signature into the second tablet and looked up. "Then this one to the Lloahairi Embassy—hand it to one of your friends out there as you go out. My compliments to the ambassador. What are you waiting for?"

The messenger went out the door as if he'd been kicked. Reswen rubbed his head again and said, "Is there anything else I need to know about?"

"Nothing that won't wait, sir."

"All right. Back to work, both of you. Creel, well done. But for pity's sake, boy, do you have to run everywhere you go?"

"*You* do, sir," Creel said in tones of purest hero-worship.

Reswen made a sardonic face. "There should be a message there somewhere, Creel. Take your time now, because twenty years from now, when you have my job, you're going to have to run everywhere then *too*. Now get out of here."

Creel and Krruth went out, one at a run, one stalking thoughtfully. Reswen got up, stretched, picked up his cloak, and gazed out the window for a moment—then discarded the cloak and headed out at a trot.

So once again Reswen found himself waiting on the walls, with old Sachath standing beside him, the two of them looking down at the approaching entourage with some annoyance.

"Knew you were going to do this," Sachath said amiably, as soon as he set eyes on Reswen. "Can't let a man sleep after a good party, can you?"

Reswen grinned at him a little, for Sachath, as commander of the guard, had been much in evidence at the reception last night, and had done himself nobly over the wines there. "If I can't sleep, why should you?" Reswen said. "What I can't understand is why those idiots rescinded the alert. They knew its purpose."

"Hhuh," Sachath said, a disgusted noise. "They saw fat priests and traders, last night, and decided in their cups that maybe there was nothing to be afraid of. At least, that's one idea. Me, I think the sight of soldiers makes the Arpekh nervous, whether they're someone else's soldiers or our own. Silly old mams, they are. A city needs a standing force in evidence if it's to stay its own and not be swallowed by the first force to walk by. But gods only know what th'Easterners are thinking of such policy—panic like blind kittens one minute, throw caution out with the dirt the next—"

Reswen nodded morosely, watching the gold-and-white liveries of the Lloahai come closer in a long trailing line. There was this small mercy at least, that none of the Arpekh were present here this morning, and Reswen heartily wished that all their heads felt like his had a little earlier. *This too,* he thought, *there are none of them here to be explaining what was going on in their sodden brains last night, and that will make my position that much stronger when they come whining to me about what the city cohorts are doing on alert again. Here came a foreign force right up to our walls, and if not for my people, they could have walked right in here—*

The problem was that there was a little too much truth in that. Looking out at the approaching lines of soldiery, Reswen considered that Creel had been right: There were far too many armed men here for just another escorted caravan, and the great number of liveried personnel suggested that this entourage had little or nothing to do with trade.

"And they're well before time," Sachath said, having fallen into his own thoughts for a moment.

"They are that," Reswen said. It was something that was bothering him more and more as minutes went by. The relationship that Niau had with the little nation of Lloahai had been cordial enough of late, though they had had the occasional war in the past, usually over the trade route leading westward. Niau's lands sat just to the south of it, and Lloahai's to the north; the two tended to watch one another carefully, making sure that neither tried to strangle the other's precarious lifeline to the wealthy countries of the west.

Caravans were pretty carefully scheduled, according to treaty, so that neither sphere of influence would ruin the other's markets. This one should have been perhaps a hundred armed mrem, escorting a large trail of baggage beasts bearing northern fruits, the cloths made from the various native Lloahairi furs and fibers, and some of the grains, like yellowseed and oilberry, that would not grow in Niau's lands. It would have stayed about an eightday and a half, while the jobbers negotiated prices and divided up the goods. That was always a busy time for Reswen. Crime in the city rose somewhat as mrem with more money than usual to spend went out to spend it. He had been preparing for this, as usual, and for the normal cheerful excesses of the caravan people in taverns and whorehouses. Then toward the end of the second eightday, the selling and packing of Niau goods would begin—whitegrain and various beers and wines, the local silks, and bunorshan hide and wool—and the caravan would be off again. That someone had changed the schedule was not a good sign at all. The arrival of the caravans was vital to the Niauhu economy . . . and implied the status of relations with their near, uneasy neighbor to the north.

Now here came a small army instead of the fruits and grains, and all those Lloahairi liveries said that this was something political. *Damn*, thought Reswen. *What else is going to happen?*

He pushed away from the wall and headed for the stairs down to the courtyard. Sachath's people fell back to let him through, and at the bottom of the stairs he found Shalav waiting for him.

The Lloahairi ambassador was a tall, handsome creature, not as pretty as, say, Laas last night, but nevertheless a noble-looking she-mrem with a wily mind and a calm exterior that nothing ever seemed to trouble. Now she saw him coming and bowed a little in his direction, silver fur shifting under the Lloahairi gold-and-white ambassadorial robes.

"Madam," he said to her, and returned the bow. "Fair morning."

"Yes," she said, and they stood quietly together for a moment, watching the gates swing open to admit the approaching entourage. "A little too damn fair," she added under her breath, twitching.

Reswen smiled. It was not the kind of morning to be wearing more clothes than one had to, and the elaborate formal robes had to make one who wore them feel as if she was standing in a tent. For a few moments more he stood by her in companionable silence. He did not precisely trust Shalav; the Lloahairi embassy had its own spies around the city, and occasionally one of theirs would run afoul of one of his. Since Niau and Lloahai had very different priorities about most things, one of Reswen's jobs was to keep track of what the Lloahairi were up to in town . . . who they were bribing, what they were after. But though Shalav might not volunteer information to the H'satei about what was going on in her government's mind, neither did she hide bad news from Reswen when it might benefit them both, and she had done him and the H'satei the occasional good turn. They were friendly enough.

"What's this all about, Shalav?" he said under his breath.

"Damned if I know," she said, as the leading riders of the entourage came in.

With that he had to be content, for the moment. The first few riders, in white quilted cotton armor bound with bonetree, bore the traditional long straight swords of the

Lloahai, unsheathed; and one of them carried the Lloahairi banner with its white sun on yellow. Behind them came another mrem, a small rangy-looking white, in herald's robes, with a pouch slung over his shoulder. This he removed. He bowed to Shalav, and presented it to her with some ceremony.

She opened it, extricated a sealed parchment, and tossed the pouch back to the herald while she checked the seal. Then Shalav cracked the thing open and studied it. Reswen did his best to keep his eyes to himself . . . for the moment.

She hissed softly to herself. "Well, Reswen-*vassheh*," she said softly, "there goes an admirable business association. I am recalled."

"Why?" he said as quietly, astonished.

"Revolution," Shalav said. "If you would wait on me this afternoon or evening, at your convenience . . . I should be done with the Arpekh by then, and you will have to be formally introduced to my successor."

Reswen nodded and turned away, his mind in turmoil. He thought the Easterners had been a problem . . . but this was worse. One part of his job in Niau had always been overseeing the city's clandestine affairs with the embassies of the other nations there. It was a touchy business, at best, spying on one's permanent guests. But tradition made it easier for him in that, when a city had an organization like the H'satei, the embassies knew that an official interest would be taken in them, and it was traditional not to make more trouble about it then pride made absolutely necessary. The relationship, when it worked, as it had with the Lloahairi Embassy under Shalav, could be cordial enough. But when a new embassy came in, or an old one changed staff, there was inevitably a period of assessment, during which both sides felt one another out for weak spots. Reswen's forces were spread thin enough, at the moment, with half of them sitting either in or under Haven, watching and listening to the Easterners. Now this to handle as well—

Oh, for last night, he thought, *when life was simple and all I had to do was get drunk and talk to people. . . .*

Already it seemed about a year away, the half-wicked, half-cheerful banter with Laas. . . .

And then there was a police runner at his elbow, and Reswen turned to him in great annoyance at having his reverie disturbed, and almost spat at the poor innocent before thinking better of it. "What, then?" he said.

The runner held out a paper. Reswen unfolded it, only partly conscious, as he read it, of the Lloahairi entourage slipping past him, a great many mrem with long swords and a great many beasts loaded down with baggage. On the thick paper, brushed with incongruous grace (considering the source) were the words: *You have a problem. Marketplace. Lorin.*

"Shall I take an answer, sir?" said the runner. "It came from the offices."

Via Sithen, I suspect. "Go back and tell my secretary that I'll be back before noon. Tell him also that if the Arpekh are looking for me, I will wait on them when possible, and meantime they should consult the Lloahairi Embassy. I've got something to take care of. Have a runner waiting at the Nigh Gate to the market in half an hour."

▲

And off he went, feeling his pads begin to sweat.

It was second-to-last market day, but that in no way began to explain the noise the place was making as he approached it. . . . It was audible easily three blocks further away than usual. And there was something about the sound that made Reswen's fur begin to rise. Any policemrem comes to know certain crowd noises that mean very specific things: the hissing undertone of a mob about to attack something, the mutter of fear, the overstated noise of rage that will not be expressed in violence. But this was something in its way worse. It was not specific. Fear and anger and the attack-hiss were all mixed in it, and they shifted unpredictably. There was no telling *what* would happen, or what was causing it.

Reswen slipped into the market by the Nigh Gate, which had been the city gate once, and paused there, leaning in the shadow of the old, soot-crusted stones. No

one paid him the slightest notice, which was mildly unusual by itself, for he was in his everyday uniform and was
at least identifiable as a policemrem. Nearest him, there
was some kind of noisy argument going on over by the
butchers' stalls, twenty or thirty voices going on at once,
every now and then scaling into a yowl. And for as far as
he could see across the marketplace, there was precious
little buying or selling going on. Everywhere, little groups
of mrem—housefolk, servants, what-have-you—were standing and talking loud. The roar of all the voices almost
deafened him to the one that spoke in his ear.

"Fine fool you made of yourself last night," it said.

Reswen let himself be drawn back into the little niche
in the gateway. There was just enough room for a couple
of friendly mrem to stand there abreast—it had been a
guardhouse, once—and he and Lorin folded their arms
and faded back into its shadow in a companionable-looking
sort of way.

"And you were there, I suppose," Reswen said to
Lorin.

Lorin snorted. "I went past. Look, master, I had to tell
you. There are magic-workers there."

"Where?"

"Your precious Easterners. One or two of them. Maybe
more. I could tell, even outside the room."

"How?"

Lorin looked mildly uncomfortable. "It's like scent . . .
but you can't smell anything. . . . I can tell. But I couldn't
guess which ones they were, with all those bodies about."

Reswen held quite still and considered that. "I'll wager
I know who one of them is," he muttered, thinking of blue
eyes—thinking of how just one glance had affected him
for almost a day, thinking of Aiewa last night, utterly
besotted by the blue eyes. . . .

"Who?"

"No, I'm not going to tell you. Look, shortly there'll be
a runner here from the constabulary. I want you to go with
him and get into servant's clothes. He'll take you around
the house where the Easterners are staying. Can you tell if
you get close enough, and there aren't many other mrem
around?"

Lorin looked doubtful. "It depends. There are ways of hiding it."

"Will you try?"

Lorin nodded.

"Good fellow," Reswen said, looking out uncomfortably at the market. It was getting even louder out there. A crowd seemed to be gathering down at the far end. "Give the runner the word 'razor' and he'll know you're from me. And look you," he added, "tell him to send some extra constables down here. Tell him I said to pull our people off Northside for the morning, and get them into the market. Something's brewing. Meanwhile what about that stone-and-water business?"

Lorin shook his head. "You were right, Reswen-*vassheh*. It's a spell. I managed to find another one with almost the same wording. But that one uses fur as the ingredient."

"What for?"

"Curing the mange."

Reswen made a wry face. "And you don't know what this one's for?"

"No. And it's going to be hard to find out. It's not as if there are source works on magic lying all over town."

"Well, bribe who you have to. I'll see what I can do to help you." Reswen looked down at the end of the market; the crowd was getting thicker still, and the noise louder. "I'll see you later." And he slipped out of the niche and into the crowd.

The stench of the market seemed worse than usual this morning, and perhaps not just because there was no wind. The people crammed together, talking, shouting, may have had something to do with it, adding the stink of fear to the close, hot morning. They were crammed tightest at the end of the butchers' row, as Reswen had thought. Someone was standing on something, a box or chair, haranguing them. An old scarred, striped creature. There was something familiar about him, but Reswen could not place the face. Every now and then the crowd noise would sink away, and he would catch a few words.

"—selling us out, they're lettin' . . . here and soon we'll be . . ."

Another swell of angry sound drowned out the end of a

sentence. Reswen wanted very much to hear just what was being said, but it would be a mistake to work his way any deeper into that crowd; if they went off suddenly, there would be no way for him to get out and direct his people. *If they show up before it happens! There are surely no more than three constables in this place this morning. And gods only know where they are—*

He worked back out of the fringes of the crowd and went around the back of the butchers' stalls, holding his breath as he passed the pails of offal reeking in the sun. *Sanitation is a mess here, city ought to do something,* he thought for about the hundredth time as he came out the far side, and found another fringe of the crowd. But the press of people was not as deep here, and he was closer to the mrem standing on the bench—it was one of the benches from the hot-meat stall at the end of the butchers' row.

"—and they're lettin' in Easterners now, our high-and-mighty masters, think they can give the city away to those fine city folk, all silk and gold, when we fought for it and bled twenty years back, and now they're gonna sell us to them, sell them our meat and meal when there's little enough of it for *us*—"

The crowd growled. Reswen's fur stood up in earnest. He had heard *that* sound before, once, the time he got the rip in his ear. He wanted nothing to do with it now, but he could hardly just turn around and march back to his desk. On the other hand, there was not much he could do here, either, until his people arrived. He had heard legends about mrem with such innate authority that they could stop a crowd dead with just their voices . . . but Reswen unashamedly considered himself to belong to a less unusual but more dependable school, whose power was based on superior forces and coordination. If that runner would just show up, and take the message Lorin had for him, something could still be done about this. The crowd was angry, but not that angry, not yet—

"Lloahairi!" someone shouted from the gate by the Shambles, and Reswen moaned softly in his throat. *And me armed with nothing but my office,* he thought. He had nothing to hand but his baton, and that was just about

useless in a situation like this. "There's Lloahairi come,
Lloahairi soldiers, a couple hundred of them—"

That was all it needed. "Soldiers!" "An army!" "An
invasion!" "They're gonna—" "Foreigners!—" "Kill 'em,
kill 'em all!" "Let's burn the Councillory, they're—!" "No,
the foreigners! Let's—"

The crowd dissolved in the growl, stopped being people, became a mob. The roar went up and shook the walls.

It was right then that Reswen heard the one sound that
could have cut through the noise: the high clear jingle of
small bells. The sound spread right through the crowd, for
where it began, the people fell suddenly silent. Every
head turned to see what the noise was.

The fat priest Hiriv and his two assistants, having come
through the Nigh Gate to visit the famous Niau market,
were standing there in their belled robes, looking around
them with utter astonishment. And just in front of them,
looking just as amazed, were Laas and Deshahl.

The roar built back up again, turned to a scream, and
the crowd surged forward at them and surrounded them.

Reswen looked abstractedly to one side and realized
that there was a perfectly good-looking curved sword hanging in the belt of a mrem standing next to him. "Sorry,
police business," he said, and pulled the sword out of the
scabbard, and when the mrem turned, outraged, and tried
to stop him, Reswen cuffed the poor creature right to the
ground and went over him toward the Nigh Gate. Various
other mrem got in Reswen's way as he headed in that
direction; some of them did not get up again, though he
was using the flat of the blade. The cry went up behind
him, "A spy, a traitor—," but whoever started it apparently wasn't willing to close with Reswen himself. Mrem
fell away from him in all directions as he swatted his way
toward the screams and the jingling. They had managed to
get too far for his liking from the gate before being noticed; the pushing and shoving of the confused, angry,
frightened crowd was in fact pushing them toward him.

Someone rose up in front of Reswen and tried to take
the sword away from him. Other hands came in, claws
bared, to help. Reswen clawed with his free paw. It ran
into something, a feeling like dead flesh, then he realized

it *was* dead flesh. Without thinking he pulled the thing down off the hook it was hanging on, hefted it, and threw it full in the face of the mrem trying to take his sword. The mrem screamed and went down, understandable when one has just had half a prime loin of uxan lobbed at him. Reswen blessed the unfortunate beast and plunged on over the felled mrem, hit two or three more grabbing, screaming mrem out of his way with the flat of the sword, and there was Laas, right in front of him. In passing he kicked a tent pole and jumped toward her; the pole and the canopy it was supporting came down on top of those people in the crowd closest behind him. To one side, Hiriv and his fellow priests were cowering. Reswen jumped at Hiriv and pushed him with bruising force right through about two-thirds of the crowd that stood between him and the Nigh Gate. Reswen found this intensely satisfying, and also rather enjoyed the screams of the people that Hiriv fell down on. The priest scrambled to his feet somehow, and made it out the gate, followed by his two assistants.

Reswen shoved Deshahl in his wake, grabbed Laas by the wrist, and started backing toward the Nigh Gate. The mob was pressing in hard now, enraged; the screams were deafening. Reswen made a pass at someone's eyes who got too close, and several pairs of paws actually came in and grasped the sword blade and ripped the sword out of his fist, oblivious to their own blood being shed. He clawed, Laas clawed someone, another couple of screams rang right in their ears. Reswen pulled out his baton and cracked one last mrem across the face with it as the hands reached for them—

—And then gray, gray everywhere, a bluster of gray cloaks hit them from behind and rushed past them, pulled them out backwards through the gate and off to one side. Reswen sagged against the wall, panting and trembling, as at least fifty constables stormed past him and into the market through the Nigh Gate. Hiriv the priest was sitting on the ground, gasping. One of his two acolytes had fainted and the other was fanning his master desperately with his robes. Deshahl was leaning round-eyed against the wall.

Reswen looked over at Laas.

"Do you stage this kind of performance for all your ladies," Laas said, breathing fast, "or am I a special case?"

Reswen rolled his eyes. "Someone's been telling you my secrets," he said, smiling at her wryly. "Shocking." He beckoned over several of his staff.

It took an hour or so to sort everything out—to drive the crowd out of the market and pacify the parts of the Shambles and the neighboring Brick Quarter to which the rioters fled. There were various arrests, including the scarred striped mrem who had been agitating from the bench. Him in particular Reswen wanted to interrogate later on. Then Reswen saw to it that the criers were sent out to let people know the real reasons why the Easterners and Lloahairi were here . . . this being something that the Arpekh had seen fit to put off for a day or so. Reswen was already thinking of things he could say to the assembled lords when he saw them later, and they would be choice.

It took slightly less time to get the priest Hiriv and the rest of the Eastern party back on their feet and away. "You have saved my life," Hiriv said, repeatedly and with rather pitiful gratitude; for all that it was true, this got fairly boring for Reswen after what promised to be innumerable repetitions. He was glad to give the gross creature and the younger priests an escort out of there. To Deshahl and Laas, he detailed another escort, suggesting that they might like to see some more of the city, in a quieter mood. Deshahl agreed effusively, turning those startling blue eyes on Reswen full force. He braced himself for the clutch at the heart that he had felt the last time. But again, to his bemusement, there was nothing, though his younger officers were vying for the chance to be in the escort, and sucking up to Reswen in a most alarming manner. He glanced at Laas. She returned the gaze, but there was nothing in her eyes but golden fire and amusement.

"Ladies," he said at last, and they strolled off with their mooning escort. Reswen looked after them thoughtfully, determined to send word to Lorin to make sure he stayed in Haven until Deshahl returned.

The afternoon was a long and angry one. Reswen spent it in the Arpekh, and the only thing that could be said about the session afterwards was that he gave at least as

good as he got. Their shock on discovering how the Lloahairi
had arrived, their consternation at the news the entourage
had brought, and their horror at what might have happened to relations with the East if any harm had come to
the Easterners' party in the marketplace, were all overwhelming. When Reswen left for his meeting with Shalav,
he left behind him a very chastened group of Councillors.
Kanesh and Aiewa in particular looked very troubled, and
Reswen derived some satisfaction from that; they would
neither of them have inclination for Deshahl or Laas tonight, even if they had the time. The Arpekh would be in
session till late, trying to work out what the sudden
change in the Lloahairi situation would mean to their
trade and their security.

Evening fell at last, and though Reswen stayed later
than usual in his offices at the constabulary, no summons
came to him from Shalav. *It's probably been put off till
tomorrow*, he thought, and picked up his cloak to head
downstairs and homeward. *Just as well. I'm a tired mrem.*

As he passed the guard's desk downstairs, Chejiv, one
of the evening-shift oct leaders, called to him, "Sir? Someone's left a package for you."

"Oh?" He turned away from the doorway, went back to
the desk, and took the parcel from Chejiv. "Who left it?"

"One of the Easterners' servants, sir. Said to say it was
a thank-you gift."

"Huh," Reswen said, and put his cloak down over the
desk. With one claw he slit the wrappings open. Inside
was a hinged box of lasswood, very finely polished and
shining with red-gold highlights.

And inside the box, on a black felt pad, lay the knife,
the knife of rose and gold, that he had admired at the
cutler's on the way back from Haven. It gleamed at him
softly in the sunset light that came in the constabulary door.

Reswen shut the box carefully, tucked it under his arm,
said good night to Chejiv, and walked down the steps to
the street, carefully, like a mrem who expects the steady
world to suddenly give way under his paws, like a mrem
who smells magic. . . .

▲

Chapter 7

▲————————————————————————————————▲

So he sent for Laas.

Reswen was several days about it, for he was waiting for matters to quiet down somewhat. He had rarely had quite so busy a time in his career. The Arpekh was in disarray, the city was rumbling along the edge of further riots, the city cohorts were beginning to react unhappily to the unrest and the presence of what they considered too many foreigners. . . . None of these latter concerns were Reswen's fault, of course, but his now-daily meetings with the Arpekh gave him to understand that various of the less senior Councillors would have liked to blame him for the situation. Reswen kept his counsel and let them storm. *They'll quiet down soon enough,* he thought to himself again and again, that eightday, as he went home later and later from work or the Council chambers. *I have other fish to fry.*

He spent most of his evenings, as late as he dared, in the cellar underneath Haven, listening to matters going on upstairs. They were becoming a matter for some amusement among the H'satei staff, and there was some jockeying for the night shift. Krruth had become bored with it, but Reswen spent three nights listening to the goings-on in Deshahl's room and becoming increasingly impressed. He had found his magician . . . or rather, one of them.

"That's the one," Lorin had said to him, quite late on the first evening after the riot. It was another party—various of the city's merchants were feting the Easterners as a lubrication to trade. When first "eavesdropping" on the meeting at the Councillory, and then walking by the rooms in Haven, had both proven insufficient to give Lorin a

clear enough feel for where the magician among the group
was hiding, Reswen had availed himself of other options.
He had stuffed Lorin into constable's formal kit (much to
the wizard's annoyance) and had brought him along to the
next reception as a young adjutant being shown the ropes.
Reswen made a careful point of introducing Lorin one by
one to everyone, and when they came to Deshahl, Reswen
actually had to brace Lorin from behind to keep him from
falling over.

"Charmed," Deshahl had said. It was usually all she
had to say. Since the night of the formal reception, Deshahl
had been working her way through the Arpekh with the
kind of steady determination that one usually attributed to
bricklayers. She had only to look at a mrem, and for hours
afterward he would dote on her, follow her everywhere,
do anything she said. What she usually said was, "Will you
walk me back to the guest house?"—and afterwards,
walking was the least of what happened. It was all mildly
amusing, except when Reswen considered that he had no
idea why she was doing it, and possibly might not till the
damage was done.

This time, Reswen had let Lorin goggle at Deshahl a
little, then marched him away on a pretext. On the way
out, they passed Laas, who was chatting amiably with a
Niauhu merchant's wife. Laas flicked a friendly ear at him
and said, "Business taking you away again, Reswen-
vassheh?"

"Afraid so," Reswen said, smiling back, and pushed
Lorin ahead of him into the kitchen. There he gave him
first a few friendly cuffs, then a cup of wine to steady his
brains down. This process took a while, but finally Lorin
shook his head and said softly, "Oh, you have a problem.
A charismatic."

"Speak Niauhu, for pity's sake, not wizard-talk. I don't
want to hear it."

Lorin glowered at him, then rubbed one ear. "She can
make anyone who sees her, uh, want her. That way."

"I know. I wanted her too . . . but it seems to have
worn off me. And you don't seem particularly affected at
the moment."

"Don't be too sure." Lorin sighed, then fished around

under the collar of the constable's breastplate and came up with something that looked like a piece of dried fish on a string, and smelt vaguely like it. "After I did my 'eaves-dropping,'" he said, "I began to wonder whether some-thing of her sort was going on—so I took the liberty of preparing myself a nonspecific. It counteracts some of the attractive kinds of magic. This one isn't specifically for the sexual kind, but it works somewhat. . . ."

"It wouldn't have worked at all if I hadn't gotten you out of there," Reswen said, mildly annoyed, "and I can't go pulling the Lords Arpakh one by one out of her bed. Neither can I give them one of *these*, however specific you can make it, because they're going to want to know what I'm doing fooling around with magic, and then they're going to want to know my source, and shortly both of us are going to have a view of the city gate that we won't like much. What am I supposed to do about this?"

Lorin said nothing for a moment, only rubbed the cuffed ear thoughtfully. "And I'm still not sure why she's not affecting me any longer," Reswen said.

Lorin shook his head. "It could simply be that she's not interested in you."

"That won't help me if she *becomes* interested," Reswen said. "Can you make me one of these charms or whatever they are?"

"Of course," Lorin said.

"Then you'd better do it, right away."

Lorin nodded, then said, "With two of them, you're going to need it."

"Two of what?"

"Who was that we passed on the way out? The brown one with the gold eyes?"

Reswen stared at him. "*Laas?*"

Lorin nodded. "She's one too. Less powerful than the other one, I think. Or maybe just less obvious. I caught a clear whiff of it as we went by."

Reswen stood very still, caught somewhere between horror and embarrassment. "But why doesn't she—" He stopped himself. *Why doesn't she affect me the way Deshahl did?* Suddenly there was the memory of Laas leaning against the pillar, her arms folded, as they both gazed over at Deshahl, and her soft remark, "No, subtlety was never one of her talents. . . ." And the easy way they had fallen into conversation that evening. The way she had seemed almost able, sometimes, to hear him thinking. And the way when he saw her, in the marketplace, with the mob rushing at her, he went briefly out of his mind—

How do you know she hasn't affected you the way Deshahl did? "Less obvious," he said—

But . . . no. It can't be. She's charming, yes; I like her, yes; she has wit, and even though she's honest about working for some Eastern cause, she's cheerful about it, she—

But suppose that was the spell working? She was a spy; there was no reason for him to like her. He had dealt with female spies before, and no amount of liking had kept them from exile, or in severe cases, the spike—

Reswen went quite cold inside. The thought that he could be *made* to like someone—made to feel attracted toward her, emotionally, even sexually—for he *was* attracted to her, not that he would do anything about it, of course, but—

How did he *know* he wouldn't do anything about it?

The loss of control, even the potential loss of control, terrified him. An officer of the H'satei must, above all else, be trustworthy, not be vulnerable to manipulation by others for whatever reason—

And the problem was he *liked* liking her. Was that part of the spell too?

"Get me one of those things right away," he said. "Tomorrow morning. Do you need any special ingredients?"

Lorin shook his head. "I've got everything I need at home."

"All right."

"Listen, Reswen—"

Reswen looked curiously at Lorin. He had an odd tone to his voice. "What is it?"

"There's something else about her—" Lorin broke off, looking dubious.

"What?"

"I'm not sure yet." He shook his head. "There may be

another magic-worker, that's all—working through her. Someone a lot more dangerous."

"May be? You're not certain?"

"I was—at least, I thought I was. But I can't find any traces of the other wizard's workings now."

Reswen sighed. This was one of the things that annoyed him most about dealing with magic: There seemed to be nothing about it that could be depended upon . . . situations changed without notice, and seemingly without reason. "Well, look, never mind it for the moment. Just let me know if you find out anything further."

Lorin nodded, and Reswen saw him safely out of the place and went out himself, the back way, determined not to see the she-mrem again until he could be certain that his mind was clear and his own. But her laughter floated out one of the open windows after him. Without thinking, he turned to go back to the party.

Then Reswen cursed and headed for the office.

On the third day after the riot, he sent for the scarred mrem who had instigated it. Reswen had a philosophy about incitement to riot. If it was an impulsive thing, and the inciter had never done anything like it before, three days in the damp cellars under the constabulary would make sure he never did anything like it again. On the other hand, if the inciter were part of some plot, three days in that celler would render him that much more willing to talk about it. The cellars were not damp enough to have dripping water—the climate hereabouts was much too arid for that—but they did have absolute, tomblike silence, being dug far below the normal Niauhu cellar level. The rock was porous enough to admit air, but not enough so to transmit sound. The doors were solid; the constables who served the place were silent. Far from having other voices to rail at or harangue, the inciter would have an unsettling three days with his own heartbeat, and nothing else. Excepting, of course, his own waste. The sanitation down there in the cells was primitive, and Reswen intended that it stay that way. It led to serious thinking.

When they brought the gray-striped mrem up, Reswen kept him standing between a couple of constables for a couple of minutes, while fussing with papers and pretending to ignore him. It gave him a chance to look the creature over surreptitiously, and Reswen was annoyed to find the mrem neither abject nor frightened, but sullen, glowering around him. He said nothing, but he was tense in the constables' grasp, not resigned. He also smelled awful, which was not in itself diagnostic. Even innocent people tend to become loose of the bowels when thrown in a dungeon.

Reswen looked up, finally. "You can let him go," he said to the constables. "Wait outside."

They looked slightly reluctant, but obeyed him. When the door shut, Reswen picked up a paper and looked at it speculatively. "Nierod, your name is?"

No answer. "Sit down," said Reswen, indicating a chair.

Nierod stood and glowered.

"Stand, then, it's all one to me." Reswen looked again at the paper. "You're an assistant to one of the chandlers over in the Bricks, you have a room a few doors down from where you work, top floor rear over the Sun and Flag." It was one of the worse of the inns in the Brick Quarter, a regular problem for Reswen's people: Legal drugs like lash were sold in the back rooms, but no tax was paid on them—and over the past few years a few mrem had died there, overdoses mostly, or barroom brawls with doctored drink at the bottom of them. "Sometimes they pay you a copper or so to be bouncer when the usual one is off his feed, or drunk."

Nierod spat on the floor.

"You'll clean that up before you go," Reswen said matter-of-factly. He laid the paper face down, then, and met the sullen green eyes full on. "I know why you were standing down by Mud Cross at an hour past midnight four nights ago," he said. "I know who met you, and why you went into the Dicer's. I knew what he paid you, and I know how much he paid you."

He paused after saying that much, and saw what he had been hoping for: a flicker of fear, quickly covered over. Notwithstanding that the last sentence had been a lie, and the second partly one. The business about Mud

Cross had been true enough, and about the Dicer's; pieces of information brought to light by good police work and a bit of extra gold slipped into One-Eye's paw up on the Northside. The rest of it was a guess. But the parts that were public information were nothing that would cause anyone fear. Reswen was exultant, but he sat on it tightly.

Nierod, though, grinned: not a nice look. "If you know so much, then y'can find out the rest for yourself," he said.

"Oh, bold, bold," Reswen said, very softly. "That was what he told you, then—that the police would question you, but would let you go if you kept quiet. And then there would be more gold afterwards. Well, let me tell you a truth, my son, and it's this: Once you're through that door," he pointed at the way into the office, "you're mine. The Arpekh themselves can't touch you if I decide not. Oh, there are procedures for appeal, but no one in the Arpekh is going to start them for a mucky little heap of gutter scrapings like you. Do you seriously think one of your fine friends is going to come here with gold, and soil his paws and his reputation bailing you out? Poor fool."

He let that sink in for a moment. Nierod looked a little less certain, not so much a change in face as in posture, a bit of a sag, a bit of pulling in on himself, and the angry tail, which had been thrashing since he was brought in, had slowed down a great deal.

"What you need to know," Reswen said, quietly, "is that I don't approve of riots in my city. It spoils people's shopping, and that spoils the city's trade, and that spoils the amount of taxes the good townsmrem pay, and then I don't get my end-of-year bonus. That makes me most annoyed. So I make sure that riots don't happen—especially not to order, not to *anyone's* order." His voice began to get quieter and quieter. "To help me see to this, you are going to tell me exactly what you were told to do in the marketplace; and what else you were paid to do elsewhere as well, for the gold we found buried in the canister under your dirt-box was much more than anyone would pay for one riot, even in a seller's market. And you are going to tell me who hired the contact who came to you and gave you the money. And you are going to do this before tomorrow morning, for I have had a bad week and I would

love a chance to take my claws to such a cheap little piece
of lickspittle filth as you are, indeed I would." Reswen was
rising slowly behind his desk, feeling no need to act the
anger at all: it was real. "And you will never, *never* leave
this building until you tell me what I want to know," he
said, very softly, "bail or no bail, friends or no friends; you
can sit down there in the dark cellar and take root in your
own muck, and bleach like a whiteleaf till you go night-blind
and die of the cold shakes."

Nierod said nothing, but he was trembling.

Reswen came out from behind the desk. "And before
you do that," he said, "you are going to clean the mess you
made on my rug." And before the shocked Nierod could
so much as stir, Reswen caught him by the scruff of the
neck, hooked his hind paws out from under him, and
tipped the mrem forward so that he sprawled flat. Reswen
scrubbed the rug vigorously for a second or so with Nierod's
forehead, then scrambled to his feet, hauling the creature
up with him by the scruff, shook him, and flung him away.

"Until tomorrow," Reswen said in a whisper. "I do
hope you keep mum. My claws are itchy. Constables," he
added, in a normal tone.

They opened the door and came in. "Gellav, take him
downstairs," Reswen said. "He has one day to tell us what
we want to know. Otherwise, don't bother opening the
door till it's time to take the bones out."

Gellav hustled Nierod out the door. Reswen nudged it
closed and said to the other constable, "Shilai, have him
checked three times between now and tomorrow this time.
If he hasn't offered to talk, tell him I'm too busy to beat
him myself, and then have them leave him shut in for
another, oh, five days. Make sure he has plenty of water to
start with. This one may take more scaring than most, and
I don't want to lose him."

"Yes, sir," Shilai said. And added, "*Beat* him, sir? *You*?"

Reswen smiled. "I'm a frightful liar," he said. "My dam
always said it would get me in trouble. Meanwhile, have
the lads downstairs keep looking for his contact. We need
a name and some more information . . . I hope to heaven
we can get it from Nierod. Go on with you, now."

Shilai saluted and left. Reswen sat down behind his

desk again, reached in under his tunic absently, and fiddled with the thing that hung on a ginger-colored cord
there: something that felt and looked and smelt rather like
a bit of dried fish.. Then he turned over the piece of paper
from which he had been reading Nierod's "crimes." It
said, "Tonight, at the Play House, the Lord Arpakh's
Men, a Play of Merrie Contrasts and Humours, entitled
The Claw Unsheath'd. . . ."

Reswen smiled to himself, a touch grimly, and reached
for paper and brush to send a message to Laas.

There had of course been some teasing about it, since
it was a constabulary runner who took the message to the
house in Dancer's Street, and everyone knew whom it had
been addressed to within a few minutes of the runner
leaving Reswen's office. There was this to be said, at least:
Laas and Deshahl had been so busy working their way
through the Arpekh that the Chief of Police seemed like a
perfectly normal next step for at least one of them. The
gossip around the constabulary, Krruth told Reswen when
he came in to report, was that the two concubines had
been ordered to seduce every major official in Niau as a
goodwill gesture.

Reswen laughed at this, and Krruth looked wry. "It's
as good a theory as any, sir," he said. "Nothing we've
heard has given us any hints to the contrary. This is the
driest surveillance I've run in many a year. And I'm getting tired of that fat priest's jokes."

"If you prefer, I could move you over to some other
operation," said Reswen. "The Lloahairi business, perhaps."

"No, I'll stay with this, by your leave," Krruth said. "A
dull surveillance is usually one that's about to break open.
Is the business with the Lloahairi getting any clearer,
though?"

Reswen sighed. "Not. very. Oh, the new ambassador
has presented his credentials. He's a dull creature, I'm
afraid. Looks to be the type who'll be a real tail-biter to
work with—a letter-of-my-instructions type who won't find
a way to make his instructions flex, just because he *likes*
them inflexible."

"Wonderful," Krruth muttered.

"You don't know the half of it. He's told the Arpekh that he doesn't expect any 'interference' from the police."

Krruth considered that in silence. Everybody knew that the police kept an eye on all the embassies. "What are you going to do about it?"

"Interfere," Reswen said, "discreetly. I have *my* orders, and I don't take them from any half-gaited housecat."

"Half-gaited?"

"He has a 'war wound.' " Reswen sniffed. "Funny how the limp comes when he wants it noticed, and goes away when he forgets about it. At any rate, maybe Shalav will be able to talk some sense into them before she leaves. Some of our people are keeping an eye on the place, very quietly . . . we'll wait for things to calm down a little before moving in any more closely. There are enough other problems at the moment. All those Lloahairi troops quartered around town, the inns are full, some of them are in private houses— People are getting tense."

"Don't blame them," said Krruth, getting up. "Well, I'm for Haven."

"Have a good time," Reswen said.

"Not as good as *you* will," said Krruth. "Don't keep her out late."

Reswen's whiskers curled forward as he smiled.

▲

She stretched, lazily. All around her it was shadowy, the pale light of the overworld's evening as it shaded toward night. For the moment, her surroundings had no features: merely the pallid sourceless radiance, muted to gold and fading slightly as the light of the real world faded. It would never become entirely dark, of course. One of her kind would hardly permit that, for with the dark came the cold, and the cold she did not have to suffer, not *here*.

The hunger was on her. It had been growing for some time now. She had never been fond of doing nothing, of waiting and watching. True enough, her masters had commanded her to do so until all was certain here . . . but they were not *here*, and she was, and the situation was hardly as dangerous or fraught as they had told her it would be. None of the vermin here suspected anything

. . . at least, none of them who were in a position to do anything about her presence. And she was doing well—already her pets had discovered many things that she needed to know, things her masters had ordered her to discover before moving her mission into the active phase. Quite shortly now she would know much more.

But for the moment, she was hungry. Not in the bodily sense—she had spent a long time out of body now, and in such cases one's physical needs grew less, not more, with time. But her soul hungered. There had been no taste of blood for some time now, not even in dream, and something had to be done about that.

There were of course several possibilities. Rolling over in the soft warm light, she considered one of them that had occurred to her: the little wizard she had frightened. His soul had had a most satisfying feel to it, that time when she had so frightened him. Terror rose well in him; he panicked nicely, and maintained the emotion well, however involuntarily. And truly, no matter what her masters might say, he was no important part of what was going on here. No one would connect his sudden disappearance with her, that was certain.

But perhaps not, perhaps not. There was another thought. She turned time back briefly and looked through various of her pets' eyes at the golden-colored vermin with the stripes and the insouciant manner. The policemaster. It would be easy enough to manage him. Very easy indeed, since one of her pets was working on him at the moment. Very easy indeed, to catch him at an undefended moment—what moments of these creatures were *not* undefended, by her people's standards?—and then spend hours savoring the screams of his soul as her teeth tore it. He had been asking questions that she found inconvenient. Such inconvenience was not to be borne, not from something one step from a dumb beast, something that doubtless had vermin of its own.

She hissed softly to herself after a moment. No, it might not be wise, not just yet. The death of so prominent a member of this little community of vermin might create more difficulty than it would provide pleasure, and her masters might prove troublesome afterwards. No, better not to bother . . . just now. There would be time for that particular irritant later . . . all the time she liked. The only questions he would be asking then would concern why he had not died as yet. And ah, he would desire his death. And in vain.

Her tongue flickered in anticipation of the taste of fear. Not him. The little wizard, then? He had tasted her presence a time or two, now. His terror had had good time in which to mature. But it was always a temptation, to snatch such a choice meat before it was high enough. No, let him be as well, for the moment. Something fresh, this time, something that would not suspect her at all, something that would struggle most satisfactorily in her mind's gullet, protesting in anguish all the way down. But something impotent.

She thought about this for a time, then reached out to one of her pets.

It fought her, which always amused her. She had specific orders not to kill this one under any circumstances . . . which was a pity, since *its* terror was developed into something of rare bouquet indeed. It never remembered her after she left its tiny mind—she saw to that—but every time she returned to it, it remembered, and it struggled like a winged thing caught in mire, filling the overworld with its screams. Most gratifying, really. Yes, that one, for the moment. She reached out and filled it, and felt its pitiful little lurches and wrenches of soul as it screamed and struggled to get away from her. Shortly its struggles quieted, as it perceived her and froze in horror and awe. She lay there savoring its despair for a good while.

And as for the one to die . . . , she thought. This was always the best part. A feast lay before her: a warren of little undefended minds. No great subtlety about them, of course—there was none of the skill needed that would be required to destroy and kill one of her own kind, and none of that utter satisfaction of having consumed one of one's own kind against their will, against their best efforts. The efforts that the vermin could put up were pitiful indeed by comparison with the rich struggles of her own people when devoured. But the vermin were satisfying enough, if one got enough of them. And one would do for the moment. It was just a matter of picking which one.

She thought for a moment, and then smiled the terrible smile of her kind. She had been watching the little doings of the vermin for some days now, and there was certainly a way that she could have her pleasure and yet justify it to her masters as having been for nothing but the good of the mission she had been sent to enact. Oh yes, yes indeed. *That* one.

She turned her attention back to her pet and allowed herself a while more of its horror. Who knew how long it seemed to these creatures—minutes, hours—it hardly mattered. Her time was the only kind that counted, and she had all of it that she wanted in the world. It groveled before her in her mind, whimpering as it would have in the body, if it could have moved. Its body was still, held so by her power. She had learned some time ago that the creatures' terrors increased if they could not move—if (even in mind) they had to sit trapped in their bodies, unable to cry out as they perceived her coming and what she intended with them.

After a time she grew weary of this and turned to the business at hand. The overworld's light was dimmed to almost its darkest, a deep crimson-golden glow. She looked through her pet's eyes, made it get up, prepare itself, and take what it needed. Then she sent it out into the night.

The city looked strange through its eyes—bigger, grander than she actually knew it to be. A pitiful place it was, and pitiful it was that these creatures thought it so grand. It was merely another indication of their true nature, which was that of beasts without reason, deluding themselves to think that they did. They would find out the truth about that, soon enough. Their little mockery of reason was no match for the old subtlety of her people, come among them again at long last for their undoing. . . .

Her creature did not have to be kept waiting long, once it was near the place where she planned to assuage her hunger. Through its eyes, down the quiet street, she saw the great rich building with all its lights. She smiled again and reached out to the building, then felt about there, delicately, for one mind in question. She found it

swiftly. Its colors burned dark and angry almost all th
time; it was one of those minds most apt to control, an
control was not even what she needed here—just an apti
tude to suggestion. She suggested to it that the vermin
was conversing with had designs on its life, and should o
no account be dealt with. The conversation swiftly erupte
into outrage on one hand, plain rage on the other, a
accusations and denials flew. It was not very long befor
the vermin she desired turned its back on the one that sh
had prompted to make the accusation, and started to leav
the great house.

Her pet was ready. He followed the vermin, and h
caught her, and the cord went around her neck like a tail
clenched tight, choked the breath out. That was when *sh*
moved, when she positioned herself in the overworld i
such a way that the struggling soul should see her befor
anything else, before the underworld had even finishe
fading; should see her in her might, revealed, as she ha
not been able to reveal herself for too long now. Th
vermin's soul saw her, and screamed in fear—and her wi
laid hold of it and forced it to silence: even its soul, whic
under any other circumstances would have been untouch
able now.

But other circumstances had come to pass. *She* la
before it now. She opened her jaws. It could not even cr
out, now, and its terror filled her like wine, ran hot a
blood.

She made it drift closer to her, closer still. It cowere
inwardly, but had no choice. Her fangs gleamed in th
blood-colored light of the overworld, glittered with all th
shades of final severance. No afterlife for this one—a
least, none save one within her. The vermin's soul woul
become part of her, part of everything it loathed. It migh
fight and resist at first, but not for long. Eventually
would will as she willed, for the destruction of its kind
and it would rejoice in that.

All these things she allowed the vermin's soul to per
ceive, and then bathed, wallowed, in its terror. It went o
for a pleasant eternity, until she had had an elegar
sufficiency.

Then she moved, and her jaws closed, and the soul

blood ran, screaming. It always managed to do that, somehow. She could not bring herself to care. She let it, let it
swell out, then let it fade, savoring the sound like the
fading taste of the blood itself on her tongue.

Silence, then, and the blood-gold light.

She sent her pet home and dismissed it to wait her
next need, and then lay there for a long time, feeling the
subsiding struggle in her gullet.

Merely a foretaste, she thought sleepily, as the soul-
blood digested slowly and began to run thick in her veins.
*Only a sharpener for the palate. Soon enough, this whole
den of vermin, in a thousand different ways, at my pleasure.*

Soon enough . . .

▲

Reswen walked over to Dancer's Street. He rated a
litter, of course, if he had wanted one, but a day behind
the desk always left him jangly and wanting a good stretch,
and it was a pleasant walk over across town, into the
tree-lined avenues of the mercantile and noble quarters,
where the evening slipped in fragrantly under trees hung
with lamps burning scented oil, and the occasional soft
wind breathed in whispers through the branches. The
moons were up, one low and golden, one high and cool,
both at the half; shortly stars would be pricking through
the twilight.

How romantic, Reswen thought, in very ironic mood,
and his paw stole to the bit of "dried fish." What it really
was, he hadn't quite gotten up the nerve to ask Lorin, and
Lorin had been too busy, rushing off to pick up something
he would not specify from some*one* he would not specify.
"Just don't lose it," Lorin had said. "I'm out of lizards."
And off he had gone, leaving Reswen open-mouthed.

Reswen dropped the thing. *And what if it doesn't
work?* he wondered as he turned the corner of Dancer's
and strolled down toward the lanterns hanging in front of
Haven. *What happens to me then? Is she going to leave me
helpless, hanging on her every breath, like Aiewa and all
the rest of them, like Mraal . . .* For even the Senior
Lord had spent a night in her bed now, causing wild
merriment among Haven's H'satei staff. The report had

130					Guardians of The Three

been full of references to people being tied to couch legs and ridden around the room. Reswen had had to forbid the discussion of the report even in the constabulary, and had threatened to pull a few tails out by the roots if he found out who had leaked it outside the H'satei proper.

Well. Whatever, he had to find out as quickly as possible whether his own trustworthiness was still in danger of being compromised . . . if it was, then figure out something to do about it, for he could hardly simply resign from the force and the H'satei. There was a small matter of a promise made many years ago to a king now dead. Now that he had finally reached the position and power he needed to keep that promise, to protect Niau, and through it, the kingdoms of Ar, he could hardly just give up that power on a suspicion. And even without the promise, no one presently in any staff position whatever was capable of handling the situations going on at the moment; they were difficult enough to handle when one had had ten years' experience. *But what* am *I going to do?*

At Haven's gateway he sighed, paused, and brushed at himself. It was a pleasure, however nerve-racking the meeting itself might be, to get out of uniform and into something more informal, something with a little more dash. For Reswen that meant a kilt of crisp cool ivory-colored cloth that perfectly picked up his lighter points, and no jewelry but one perfect ivory ring in his ear, and his father's heavy gold signet, back in place where it belonged. A very understated effect, indicating someone somewhat conservative, but someone stylish . . . and if it also indicated someone well off, there was surely no harm in that. He took one moment to preen down the difficult fur behind his ears, then straightened himself and headed into the courtyard.

This entrance was a little different from the last one. This time people were watching for him. This time the Easterners' servants met him at the door, bowed to him, and censed him with smokes of sweet-smelling spices, and offered him wine. This time the Haven staff lingered in the background, bowing him honor, and otherwise acting as if they had never seen him before. He did the same with them, took a place on an offered couch, leaned back and sipped wine and ate dainties that were brought to him. Hortolans were much in evidence. He smiled a bit, and ate them without wondering too much who had noticed the preference.

She came down the white stairs at the end of the guest hall after a few minutes. At the sound of her footstep he looked up slowly, bracing himself, as he had with Deshahl before, for the inner seizure, the clutch at the heart. But there was nothing: only a she-mrem in silk velvet the color of peat water and as fine as air, draping softly about her and caught to the shoulder with a stone the same yellow as her eyes. She laughed at him, very gently, as she came down and sat on the couch beside him.

"I would offer you another cup," she said under her breath, putting her paw on his, "but Hiriv is threatening to come down here and start thanking you again for saving his life. If we hurry, we can miss him."

Reswen bowed over her paw and said as quietly, "Right. We're away."

They hastened out the front door, Laas chuckling softly as they went. It was a reaction that Reswen had not heard in some time: honest laughter from a she-mrem, not round eyes or nervous giggles or silent smiles. Behind them the cries of "Where did they go? Policemaster!—" faded away in the whisper of wind in the trees.

"So where are we going, and are we going to be followed there?" Laas said. "Or do the police consider that having the chief of police with the person being followed is enough of a tail?"

"One too many, perhaps," Reswen said, and chuckled himself. "As to where we're going—"

"Already you start evading," Laas said, her voice scolding but humorous. "A poor beginning. How do you expect me to do anything but evade back at you when you start asking me questions?"

"I'll give it all the consideration it's due," Reswen said. "Meanwhile, I'd thought perhaps we might take in a play."

She looked at him with an odd combination of surprise and delight. "Somehow I hadn't thought of you as a particularly religious mrem," she said.

He looked at her in some confusion. "Pardon?"

"Religion. A play—you don't have plays in your temples? Then where do you have them?"

It took them a few minutes' feeling their way around the subject for Reswen to realize that in the Eastern cities, at least, plays existed only as religious ritual, as solemn drama enacting the legends and desires of the gods. "Goodness," he said. "No comedy?"

"What's that?"

"Oh, heavens," Reswen said, and began to laugh uproariously, and Laas started to laugh too. "What's so funny?" he said, when he could get his breath.

"You, laughing for no reason!" Laas said, and started laughing again.

It took a few moments for both of them to get control of their laughter—though Reswen was a little sorry when it happened. *She has a lovely laugh. . . . Is this thing working? If it's not, I'm going to skin Lorin tomorrow. . . .* "I can see I have some explaining to do before we get to the theater. Would you like a drink of something?"

"Yes, but no wine, please," Laas said. "I've had so much of it in the past few nights that my head swims just thinking of it."

Yes, I'm sure, Kanesh for example is something of a lush—

"What's his name, Lord Kanesh," she added, after thinking for a moment, "he's a terrible drinker."

Reswen breathed out as they turned a corner onto one of the main streets leading down toward the finer shops in town and the theaters. "Well," he said softly, "we're speaking very plain. Since you mention it, I dare say he is. So are some of the other people you've been with nights, of late. I wonder that you mention it to me so freely."

Laas looked sidewise at him as they walked, not a sly look, but a confiding one; her paw on his arm tightened a little. "I have no desire to play games with you," she said.

"Because they wouldn't work?" he said.

"Hardly." She was silent for a moment, then said, "I simply saw that you were someone with whom deceit would be a mistake. You know what I am, and what I'm doing. Anyone with eyes would know it. But so few mrem have eyes. . . ."

"True," Reswen said, and smiled a little. It was one of the things about life that still astonished him. Since he had first started *seeing* things—occurrences, motivations—and realizing that other people could not see them, his life's course had been laid out for him. But at the same time he found it astonishing that people could *not* see the facts and images laid out right before their eyes, and in fact sometimes *would* not; and it also amazed him that it was necessary to have a job, an official position, for people who saw things, to report on them to people who did not. "But if you chose to play games with me," he said, "they would work?"

She glanced down, refusing to meet his eyes. And *this* time he felt it, the clutch, the almost painful realization that he would do anything for her, anything at all—

Then she met his eyes again, and the feeling passed off, leaving him shocked, breathing hard. "No," she said. "As you see."

He was silent for a moment.

"You are a magician," he said, quite baldly. "A charismatic, my adviser calls you. Don't you know we have laws against that, in Niau? I could have you put to death."

"And precipitate a pretty little diplomatic incident," she said, with kindly scorn. "I rather doubt it. Besides, you have no proof. All you could say in a chancery would be that everyone who sees me wants me. And since you want me too, and other people have noticed it, that would hardly be a charge that would be taken seriously. Besides, I'm a courtesan. Everyone is *supposed* to want me."

Was that a touch of bitterness, Reswen wondered? He opened his mouth to ask, then paused. There was something so fragile about her— "Should I start the interrogation now," he said, "or shall I wait until we eat? You would like dinner, wouldn't you? There's time before the play."

"Do wait, please," she said, and turned a look on him that was a mockery of the coquettishness he had seen her use on, say, Kanesh. "I daresay your patience will be rewarded."

He took her to the Green Square. They knew him there, but never made a performance of his arrivals. Their

discretion suited him; it was better that the head of the
H'satei should not become too well known, as he was
to the common lag of people. They waited in the doorway
for a moment for the host to come over, and Laas looked
around her with obvious delight. It was an eating-house
set in a walled garden, lush with big trees that had more
of the scented-oil lanterns hanging in their branches, and
there was a small fire in a brazier at the middle of the
seating area, burning sweetwood to take off any chill that
might set in later. In fact, calling the place an eating-house
was a misnomer, since everything was outdoors. There was
only a sort of rustic woven reed awning over the pits and
hearths where the cooking was done, to keep the rain and
the wind away. Chairs and tables were made of the same
reed, woven together with curiously carved wood, the
tables topped with wood highly polished. Off to one side,
against the wall, a tiny stream ran down over stones to a
pool, and there was the occasional glint of blue or silver
from the fish swimming in it.

Ishoa came over from a table when he saw them standing there: a big honey-colored mrem, pausing at another
table here, tossing a word over his shoulder to a patron
there, hurrying without making it obvious. "The owner,"
Reswen said in Laas' ear. "Discretion's own soul, wrapped
in fur. Sometimes I wish he worked for me."

"You mean there's someone in this town who doesn't?"
Laas said.

Reswen smiled as Ishoa finally got to them. "You should
have let me know you were coming tonight, sir," he said.
"I would have saved you the good table by the pool."

"I didn't know if I was going to be able to make it until
late, Ish," said Reswen. "There aren't any bad tables here.
Just give us the best you've got."

"Absolutely. If the charming lady will come this way?"

Several minutes later they were seated in what was
certainly the best table in the place, no matter what Ishoa
might say, under one of the wide-leaved lass trees, a silver
filigree lamp on the table to match the ones hanging above
them. The murmur of the other diners' voices mingled
with the rustle of leaves. Laas leaned on her elbows,

looked about her. "This is very lovely," she said. "The right neighborhood for a seduction."

"Or an interrogation?"

"That's what a seduction usually entails," said Laas. "I find out what you like . . . and then I give it to you."

Reswen made a wry face. "And then *I* find out what *you* like . . . and give it to *you*."

"Equable, don't you think?" she said. "What shall we drink? Interrogation is dry work."

"A sherbet, perhaps?"

"What's a sherbet?"

Reswen looked at her with mock astonishment. "How can you live next to a desert and not know what a sherbet is?"

"What makes you think I live next to a desert?"

"No fair your asking the questions," said Reswen. "Half a moment." One of the servingmrem came over to the table. Reswen ordered, then turned back to Laas. "You're in for a treat."

"That's what Deshahl said," Laas said.

"Oh, indeed!" Reswen had occasionally heard rumors about various of his lady friends comparing notes about him in private, and that favorably; but this meeting was something of a different business. "And how would she know? She's never been closer to me than arm's length."

"Neither have I," said Laas, "but I don't have to be. If one has the ability to . . . attract . . . one also knows when interest is returned. And to some extent how it would be returned, and in what coin."

Reswen flushed hot, opened his mouth and closed it.

"Yes," Laas said, "when she looked at you, she would have felt the response somewhat. One feels, do you see, what will *increase* the response . . . what kinds of things."

"You find out what I like . . . ," Reswen quoted.

"Yes. It's not hard. Sometimes it's as clear as if words had been spoken. Other times, more like pictures, or feelings."

"Wait, wait, I haven't begun the interrogation yet," Reswen said, only half in jest, as the sherbets arrived.

They drank, and Reswen had the pleasure of watching Laas's eyes go wide. Some bright creature had had the idea of making a sherbet, not from fruit and ice, but from

wine with the spiritous portion cooked off. The resulting
drink was like a frozen wine without any of the drawbacks.
"Why, this is like . . . I don't know what it's like," Laas
said after the first long drink, and then put her paw to her
head. "It makes my head ache."

"Snow," Reswen said. "It's like snow. Take it slowly."

"I've never seen snow," she said.

"I have once," Reswen said. "Some time ago, when I
was just a recruit in the city cohorts . . . all the police are
recruited from them, you see . . . some of us were sent
North to aid a city we had an alliance with. There are
whole mountains covered with it." He shivered at the
memory. "We marched in it, we slept in it . . . sometimes
we made houses out of it. We made balls out of it and hit
each other with them." Reswen sighed. "Some of us were
buried in it. It falls off the mountains all at once, sometimes, when the weather warms too suddenly. . . ."

"A bad memory," she said, watching him go grave.
"I'm sorry—"

"What for? It wasn't your fault."

"You should not be sad," she said. And then added
hurriedly, "Not during a seduction, at any rate."

"Yes, right," Reswen said, and waved for Ishoa again,
wondering a little at that last response. "And we can't have
a seduction without food. May I order for us? Is there
anything you don't like?"

"Being bored," Laas said, and the smile she gave him
was very wry.

Reswen thought about that, too, and when Ishoa came
over, he ordered several of the most unboring things he
had ever eaten there. Ishoa went off rubbing his paws, as
well he might, Reswen thought, considering how much he
was going to make off this dinner. It was just as well the
constabulary was paying. "Now," he said. "The interrogation—"

"Yes. Do you ever think of going back there, to those
snow mountains?"

Reswen shook his head. "No . . . there's too much to do
here, and besides, that old alliance is broken. . . ."

"They do seem to come and go, don't they?" Laas said.
"How do you get the snow here, then?"

"We still have some trade agreements. War may go on, but it doesn't necessarily have to stop trade. . . . We buy the snow a few times a year; it comes down to us buried in hay, and we store it in cellars full of sawdust. You'd be surprised how long it keeps." He paused then. "But this is *my* interrogation."

"All right," Laas said, putting down her sherbet and leaning toward him again. "Ask me some questions."

"What have you been up to?"

She raised her brow-whiskers at him. "What I hope to be up to with *you*, later. Shall I go into details?"

Reswen cleared his throat. "Very funny, madam. Why have you been doing it?"

"Why should I tell you?"

"Because if you don't, I'll throw you in gaol."

"No, you won't," she said. "We've been over that."

"It would be a very *nice* prison," said Reswen.

"It is already," Laas said. "Indeed, do you think I haven't noticed?"

He wondered briefly exactly how much she knew about the nature of that "prison" . . . but it would have to wait. Reswen sighed. "Very well. You should tell me because I don't trust your people, and if you should tell me why you're doing what you're doing, I might trust them more, and save us all a great deal of time."

She laughed gently at him. "I don't care if you don't trust them! Or me . . . and it doesn't matter whether you trust *me* or not, especially with that fishy-smelling thing around your neck."

"Goodness," he said, "is it that obvious?"

Laas shrugged. "I've smelt it before," she said. "It's fairly well known, back East, where there are more of us."

"And does it work?"

"Of course it does," she said.

Reswen sat back, then, and didn't care whether his relief showed or not.

She was looking at him oddly. "Has it occurred to you," she said, "that perhaps I would like not to—" And then she fell silent, for the first plates of food arrived: cold spiced yellowfruits in an innocent-looking golden sauce. She took a bite, then paused with the tongs in her hand, looked astonished, dropped the tongs, and took a long drink of sherbet. "My mouth!"

"Interesting, isn't it?" Reswen said. "Bored yet?"

The conversation went off onto the topic of why hot countries tended to have spicy foods, and by the time the next one arrived—minced bunorshan cooked on a steel plate, with steamed spiced grains and another hot sauce—Reswen had decided on another line of attack. "Let's try this—"

"What I'm doing," Laas said, while attacking the bunorshan with great pleasure, "is trying to get your high-and-mighty folk to tell me certain things that I have been ordered to find out. Isn't that what you were thinking?"

"It would be hard to think anything else."

"May I have some more sherbet? Oh, not yours, please, how can you eat this without something to drink at hand?"

"Habit. One gets used to this stuff. Take mine; Ishoa will bring me another. Do you suppose you might consider leaving off what you're doing with the 'high-and-mighty'?"

"For what reason?"

"Well," Reswen said, "I might pay you better."

Laas put the tongs down carefully on her plate and looked up at him, and there was such anger in those yellow eyes that Reswen had to restrain himself from pulling back as if he had been struck. "What makes you think I'm doing this for mere gold? You are utterly ignorant, and insulting as well."

"I'm sorry," Reswen said hastily. "You may be right. But the interrogation hasn't got far enough to tell what you were doing it for."

She eyed him, then the plate, and picked up her tongs again. "Do they pay *you* well?" she said. "As well as you think you deserve?"

"No," Reswen said.

"Then why do you keep this job of yours? Long hours, being on call day and night to your ridiculous Arpekh—well, I have not known them as long as you have, perhaps they are wiser than such short acquaintance would indicate—"

"No," Reswen said, rather resigned this time. It might be treasonous, but it was also obvious.

"Then why do you keep this job?"

"I like it." He thought for a moment. "And it does something important for Niau, something I can do better than anyone else presently senior enough to be in the position."

"An honest interrogator," Laas said, bowing a little to him where he sat. "So. Your reason is the same as mine, policemaster. *That* is why I do it."

Reswen was quiet for a moment, while Laas ate another couple of bites. "I have given my word," Laas said finally, "to do something that I feel will make my part of the East safer in the great world, where there are many interests that do not have *our* interests at heart. Ah, don't look askance at *me*. I know the thought: How can a mere courtesan possibly be knowledgeable about great matters of policy?" She looked at Reswen with scorn. "If she is *not* knowledgeable, how can she know what to listen for—and how can she direct her questions to matters of importance when she hears them? If your agents' schooling doesn't extend to such things, I must say I don't think much of them." She ate another bite. "In any case, my word is given, and *I* at least count it to be worth something. I will not stop doing what I'm doing until I've finished my job."

"Well. Will you tell me what these matters of importance are? What information you're looking for?"

"No," Laas said. She put the tongs down again, having made a clean sweep of her plate, and sighed. "There," she said. "Now you do not have to take me to this play, if you don't want to, and tomorrow you can send for me and throw me in gaol, and create a great deal of trouble for yourself. Or not. In either case, you don't need to trouble yourself with me any further."

Reswen turned his attentions to his plate for a little while, then put his own tongs down; his appetite was somewhat abated. "Tell me this, then," he said. "Can you give me some assurance that the things you have been directed to discover will do no harm to Niau?"

"Would you take me at my word, if I could?"

He took a long moment to consider it. "Actually, yes," he said. "You've been open with me so far. I doubt you'd bother to lie. In fact, I think you'd tell me the truth to spite me."

"I would," Laas said, and was silent a moment herself, seeming to consider. "Truly," she said, "the things I've been told to find out strike me as fairly useless. I can't imagine how they would hurt your city, or any other. But I won't tell you what they are. At least—"

Reswen waited.

"No," she said. "My word is my word. Well? Will you walk me back to the gilded prison?"

"One more thing," Reswen said. "What about Deshahl?"

Laas astonished him by bursting out in laughter. Around them Reswen saw various heads turn and smile in approval at the lovely she-mrem and the handsome young mrem, her lover perhaps, being so merry together. He flushed hot, then recovered somewhat as she whispered, "Surely you know she's my cover. She's a courtesan, yes, and one of the best in the East, I believe. But she hasn't a brain in her head. It's just that her . . . talent . . . is so overwhelming, and she turns every head that looks at her . . . she attracts much more attention than I do. She's a distraction."

"She is that," Reswen said, and was mildly relieved, because if this was true, it saved him the trouble of throwing Deshahl into one of the damp quiet rooms under the constabulary to try to get out of her the information that Laas was withholding. *Of course, I could always toss* her *in there*— But the thought was awful, and not just because of the political ramifications—

For about the tenth time, he wondered whether the charm against her "attractiveness" was working.

"Well?" Laas said. "Prison? Gilded or otherwise?"

Reswen looked at her. "I think we'll take in that play, if it's all the same to you."

She gazed at him, smiling, through lowered eyelids. "A spy who doesn't talk to you today," she said, "may talk to you tomorrow, if treated kindly . . . is that it?"

"Yes," Reswen aid.

She reached out and patted his paw gently. "Don't get your hopes up," she said. "But you're an honorable creature, and I'll remember you kindly when I'm gone. By the way . . . did you like the knife?"

He looked at her, astonished again. "That came from you?"

She smiled. "I have a little spending money."

"A little—! But Laas, how did you know? I never spoke of it to anyone—" He paused. "Then again—if you were able to feel what I—"

Laas chuckled. "I may be a bit of a magician, but I can't work miracles. When we were walking into the marketplace, that little cutlers' shop was on the way. We stopped to look, and the shopkeeper boasted to us that the knife had been admired by none less than Reswen-*vassheh* himself. Afterward—" She shrugged. "You didn't have to do what you did in the marketplace; I wasn't 'working' on you. I don't know—" And Laas looked away.

Embarrassment? Reswen thought. *Or something else?. . .*

It didn't matter. "Thank you," he said.

"You're more than welcome." She sat up straight. "Now, do we have to go right away, or is there something else you're going to burn my mouth out with?"

"There is, actually."

"Cruelty," Laas said, and laughed again. "Subtle punishments for not telling you everything you want to know. Give me another sherbet, you torturer."

They burnt their mouths out happily in company a while more, while Laas talked about life in her city in the East, which was on a mountainside some ways from the desert, and Reswen told her about the glories of Niau, all harmless banter. When the gong at one of the nearby temples struck the hour, they got up together, and waved good-bye to Ishoa—Reswen would get the bill in the morning, and probably have to do some fancy talking to the mrem who handled the constabulary's accounts. It seemed a natural thing to walk arm in arm, tails curling lazily together, friendly enemies if not lovers. Though it was true, the speculation had occurred to Reswen, *What if she feels she needs to keep up appearances for her masters, whoever they are? I might still get lucky. . . .*

But when they walked out of the gateway, out of the light of the lamps and the sound of the running water, there was a runner from the constabulary, waiting patiently.

"I thought I told everyone not to be able to find me,"

Reswen said, resigned, and took the paper that the runner
held out to him.

"Sorry, sir," said the runner, gazing longingly at Laas.
Reswen made a face and opened the paper.

It said, *Shalav dead. Draper's cord. K.*

Damn, Reswen thought, and "Damn!" Reswen said,
and turned to Laas. "Another night, lady," he said, and
bowed over her paw.

She stared at him and nodded. "When you have time."

"Escort the lady Laas back to Haven," he said to the
runner, and was off down the street, swearing all the way.

▲

Chapter 8

▲————————————————————————————————▲

They found her in a gutter, not far from Lloahairi Embassy: lying in the street, sprawled, the upper half of her body facing the sky, moonlight dancing through the leaves of the trees on her face. Her tongue was swollen, her eyes bulged, and they were completely brown-red except for the bloated pupils, blood vessels had broken in them with the pressure, and blood had leached into the iris, blotting out the calm green that Reswen remembered so well. The cord was found around her neck, embedded so deeply in the swollen throat that the strangler probably had simply not been able to pull it out. It was the same sort of cord as the previous strangling, but a different color this time.

Reswen went over the scene with his people. Krruth, as most senior on duty, had been called there first, and Thailh had come hotfoot after him, away from his wife and children and dinner: heaven only knew what *they* thought of it all. Reswen and Thailh and Krruth were there until well after moonset, while the shocked people who lived on the street peered out between drawn curtains at the torchlight and speculated. Their speculations, Reswen suspected, were no more informed than those of the frustrated police. Thailh had been investigating drapers since Reswen last spoke to him, but had not yet found anything of help.

Also not of much help were the Lloahairi Embassy officials. The worst of them was the new ambassador, Maikej. He turned up in the street making a nuisance of himself almost instantly: a small grey mrem without any markings or other distinguishments, and a colorless way about him, except when he railed. He did that very well,

and Reswen found himself entertaining suspicions that
that was what had gotten the creature this job. If that
was the case, it did not bode well for the Lloahairi's
opinion of the Niauhu.

"This is a scandal, an outrage, and I demand action!"
Maikej shouted.

Reswen looked wearily around the area, which was
crawling with policemrem, literally crawling, for Krruth
and Thailh had them face down on the ground, hunting
any slightest piece of evidence, any scrap of cloth or fur or
other stuff, any mark on the exposed earth beside the
street which might give them some hint as to where the
murderer had been or how he had come at Shalav. "Ambassador," he said, "look around you, if you would. If this
does not look like action to you, perhaps you would describe to me something that does."

"You know what I mean, *vassheh*," Maikej said. "I
want the creature who did this found and executed! Pub-
licly, so that the scum of this godsforsaken city can see
what happens to those who defy the immunity of diplomats and the rule of law! If there *is* law here! Such a thing
would never be allowed to happen in Lloahai, and we
don't intend to let it go unpunished! And I want to know
from the Arpekh why you allow common criminals, mur-
derers and worse, to walk your streets when important
people are about!"

"Ambassador—"

"And more," said the little mrem, panting. (Reswen
had a passing thought that if he was lucky, the new ambassador might expire of apoplexy, or some draper's cord. Ah,
shameful . . .) "I want to know what your policemrem are
doing wasting their time hanging about my country's embassy, asking impertinent questions which are none of
their business, when they should be out supposedly protecting your none-too-innocent citizens and—"

"Ambassador Maikej," Reswen said as quietly as possible, "those officers whom you complain of are part of the
force detailed to you to see that this kind of thing does no
happen—"

"They're doing a fine job of it, aren't they? If you—"

"If *you*," Reswen said, much more loudly, "had not

already complained to the Arpekh and the constabulary
about the 'overstaffing' of the embassy compound area
with police, and the 'shadowing' of your staff by my staff,
and thereby caused a significant reduction in the number
of policemrem assigned to you and your suite, this perhaps
would not have happened, because the honorable former
ambassador would have had an appropriate escort with her
when she left the embassy, so don't use that tone with me,
you—"

Reswen caught himself just short of saying something
that might have proved actionable in chancery. It did not
stop the ambassador's outrage. Maikej waved his claws in
Reswen's face. "Be still! You're nothing but a gate-guard
with delusions of importance, my man, and I'll see you
broken if I hear another word from you! I want to know
who killed the honorable Shalav, and I want to know the
first thing in the morning, and I want to see the miscreant's head off and its liver and lights nailed to the city wall
before I have my lunch! Now be about your business!"
And Maikej stalked off with his tail lashing, and several of
his attachés close behind. His police escort hung back a
moment, looking to Reswen. He sighed, and waved them
after the ambassador.

Krruth came up quietly behind him. "A night down in
the quiet rooms in the cellar might do him good," he said.

Reswen shook his head. "A temptation."

"Interfering with police work," Thailh suggested as he
came to stand with them. "Breach of the peace."

"Being a pain in the tail," Reswen said. "No, that's not
actionable yet, alas. Is there anything at all to show for all
this but the cord?"

"A pawprint. But no way to tell whether it's anything
significant."

"Take a cast of it," Reswen said. "Look carefully for
another, too. I'm for home."

They looked at him in something like shock. "Not back
to dinner?"

Reswen looked at them wryly. "Maybe there's something to what Maikej was saying after all. Who was tailing
us?"

Krruth and Thailh both looked innocently at one another, then at Reswen.

Reswen laughed at them. "Oh, come now. I know there were bets on when I would bite her neck, and how, and where. How *anyone* in the constabulary would have bet on it happening in Haven, I don't know, but you can tell them they've lost their money. I like the beds there, but not *that* much. You two get back to work now, do what you can here, and then early to bed. That's what I'm doing, for tomorrow is going to be a *horrible* day."

They saluted him as he walked off. Reswen twitched his ears back.

"Tomorrow night?" he heard Krruth say softly as the two of them turned back to the strangled body and the crawling constables. "The play, and then—"

"You're on," said Thailh.

Reswen smiled sourly and went home.

But Reswen was surprised to find himself wrong about the next day. He went into the office expecting an angry summons from the Arpekh, but there was no runner waiting for him, and nothing of the sort happened all day. Reswen became mildly unsettled.

He turned instead toward other concerns as the day trailed towards its end, sending off a message to Laas asking for another date. Then he sent for the young constable Shilai. "It's almost a day now since we locked our friend from the marketplace in the root cellar," he said. "Any revelations?"

Shilai shook his head. "Nothing yet, sir. He's doing a pretty fair imitation of a groundroot himself."

Reswen leaned his head on one paw. "Someone must have threatened him with something that still seems worse than being starved to death by the police," he mused. "Shilai, how long has it been since you did any undercover work?"

The young constable practically trembled with excitement. "Sir, I've had the training, but no one ever asked me to do any."

"That may be to your advantage," Reswen said, "since no one will know you. . . . Do this for me. My compliments to your section commander, and tell him that I'm relieving you of your usual duties for a few days. I want you to do some small-selling in the market, with a push-cart or a tray, starting tomorrow. You might go into scents, possibly. There are enough apothecaries and others working out of home who come to the market on a sporadic basis, and you shouldn't have any trouble passing for such. Check with the quartermaster; he has to order these things every now and then, and can put you onto a discreet source. Once you have what you need, get busy selling, and move around the market, and *listen*. I want to hear anything about the riot that you hear. Report to me once daily, but don't come here to do it. The intelligence officer downstairs will tell you how to set up a drop or a meeting with one of the other undercover people."

"Yes, sir!"

"You trained with Krruth," Reswen said. "I don't want you to drop a word you hear, understand? I want to know *everything* you can pick up. Can you do that?"

"Sir," Shilai said, earnest, "try me."

"I will. And if you mess this up, you're going in the root cellar to keep the other vegetables company." Shilai grinned a little. "Now get out of here."

The youngster got, and Reswen had to smile a little at the sight of him, full of the excitement of dressing up and doing something mysterious and important. "Runner, please," he said to the open door, which Shilai had left ajar in his hurry.

A runner poked his head in. "Go find Investigator Thailh for me, if you'd be so kind," Reswen said, "and tell him I want to see him as soon as he's free."

"Yes, sir," said the runner, and no sooner was he gone than another one put his head in. "Well, what message?" Reswen said.

"Sir, the lady Laas wasn't there, and the mrem I spoke to said she was out and wouldn't be back till late tonight. Should I take back some other message and leave it for her?"

And read it on the way, more than likely, Reswen thought, wry. "Don't bother," he said, and started going through the paperwork on his desk. It was turning into a shocking pile. "No, wait," he added then. "Go over to

Underhouse and tell Krruth that I would like his report on
the movements of the Easterners over the past couple of
days. I also want to know what's going on over at the
Lloahairi Embassy."

The runner nodded and was gone. Reswen sat there,
staring at the papers and tablets, but not really seeing
them. He was seeing the golden eyes across the table from
him, and hearing that soft voice say, a little angrily, *Has it
occurred to you that perhaps I would like not to—* He
folded his paws together, put his head on them. *Not to*
what? And then later, *You didn't have to do what you did,
I wasn't 'working' on you—* It certainly implied that, as
Reswen had thought, the talent was controllable; it wasn't
just a matter of whomever a charismatic looked at, simply
falling in love with her. There was intent, and lack of it
would turn the enchantment off. But the words also seemed
to imply that Laas might possibly wish that she was rid of
the talent. *Why, though?* Reswen thought. He had seen
enough people who would have killed for power, *had*
killed for power, sometimes very mediocre kinds compared to this. Wanting to give up such an incredible
advantage over people hardly made sense—

He fingered the charm Lorin had given him. He had
nothing but Lorin's word, and incidentally Laas's, that it
was working. Certainly he was not head over heels with
her, not doting, the way other mrem had been with
Deshahl. But he couldn't shake that memory of her with
folded arms, that first night, and the calm voice: *Subtlety
was never her style. . . .* Was it Laas's? Was he being
used after all?

There was only one way to find out, but he couldn't do
it tonight. . . .

Later the runner came in with the report from Krruth.
It was quite specific, quite dry. Reswen ran down it quickly,
seeing nothing particularly surprising about any of it. The
various priests had been touring the town, seeing the
temples; they had been to the market and the shops several
times now, buying such things as tourists might buy . . .
wools, local delicacies, and so forth. They had also been
shopping pretty aggressviely for local meat and produce,
and wines, since they had started holding receptions for

the local merchantry, to make connections with the whole-salers and show off their wares. The chief merchant, Rirhath, had been heavily involved for a couple of days now with setting up these receptions and researching whom to invite, and had hardly left Haven except to go confer with the herald Tehenn about the town's notables and their businesses. Tehenn, with his usual courtesy, had let the constabulary know that he was being given handsome presents for this service, but that he had not been asked by the Easterner to do anything out of the ordinary. Krruth noted as well, in an aside, that there were no indications that Tehenn had been bribed by any of the town merchants to give them an unfair advantage with the Easterners. "That is," he said, "they have *tried* to bribe him, but he has refused."

Meanwhile the lady Kirshaet had been attempting to amuse herself by attending the theater, the public sessions of the Arpekh, and doing other culturally oriented things, "possibly," Krruth noted, "to annoy her husband, who detests everything about being here except the business." She had found the theater substandard and the state of art and entertainment in the city "provincial." Nevertheless she continued going out, in an attempt to find something worthy of her attentions, and made enemies wherever she went. This morning she had attempted to have a jeweler flogged in the marketplace for not displaying clearly marked prices on his wares. *Easterners*, Reswen thought in annoy-ance; it was a problem with them that they expected flat rates on everything sold retail, and were ignorant of the finer points of bargaining. The report indicated money spent in the market, among other things, and Reswen noted that they were being marvelously overcharged for almost everything because they did not think to question the prices. He shrugged his tail. *If they won't take the time to find out the customs of a place they want to trade with, they're going to have to find out the hard way. . . .*

But Kirshaet was hardly his major concern, nor her children, who had been continuing their effort to wreck the rooms given them. Reswen was much tempted to bill their parents for the torn tapestries and the damage to the plumbing, which they had gone to great pains to stop up.

But thoughts of the Arpekh's comments restrained him. Deshahl, now— She had been out and about today: lunch with Bachua, a merchant in the wool trade. Laas, meanwhile, had been discreetly followed to the corn-factors' guildhall, and after that, to lunch with about twelve of them. "The merchants seem uncommonly taken with both these ladies," Krruth's report commented dryly, "as indeed is almost every other male mrem in the area; and the lady Deshahl in particular. . . ." *She's my cover*, the laughing voice insisted. But what Reswen found himself paying more attention to was the laughter. . . .

I must find out who she's reporting to, somehow, Reswen thought, and turned to the next report.

It was sparse. Since the Lloahairi ambassador had formally requested that the police withdraw their presence from around the embassy, that was what they had seemed to do, but Reswen had had no intention of leaving the matter there. The street-sweepers on the Old Wall Road had been replaced by plainclothed policemrem, and a servant who had fallen ill was replaced with a scullery-mrem who was one of Reswen's best undercover operatives. *Though*, Reswen thought, *Thabe is probably going to want overtime for having to scrub pots. Well, she'll get it. I need to know what's going on in there*. So far his agents had nothing significant to tell, and he was not surprised. Not even Reswen's best people could produce results instantly. What *did* disturb him was that there had been no answer to the note he had sent to the Lloahairi first thing that morning, requesting interviews with the embassy staff regarding Shalav's actions in the hours before her death. *What's the matter with Maikej? One minute he's howling for blood, the next minute, nothing—*

One of the runners Reswen had sent out poked his head in Reswen's office door. "Sir," he said, "Investigator Thailh is with one of the Lords Arpekh at the moment. He sent to say he doesn't know when they'll be done."

Reswen's ears went forward. *What are they doing consulting my people directly, instead of through me?* "Which lord is it?"

"Mraal, sir."

"All right. Thank you." The runner went off, leaving

Reswen feeling uneasy indeed, but there was nothing else he could do today, not without some agreement from the Lloahairi or some word from the Arpekh. *Oh, well,* he thought, getting up to go home, *things will straighten themselves out tomorrow—*

He found out otherwise.

The messenger came for him, not at the office the next morning, but at his house, when he was barely off his couch, still grooming himself, and had put no more down him as yet than a beaker of hot herbmix. "The Lords Arpekh summon you, sir," the runner said, and stood there politely but pointedly waiting at the door.

"I'll be right along," Reswen said irritably.

"Sorry, sir, but I was told to wait and bring you," said the runner. Reswen growled softly under his breath, threw his good uniform kit on, and went out.

The atmosphere in the Arpekh's meeting room was unfriendly, to put it mildly. When Reswen came in and saluted, the Lords Arpekh looked at him with an uncomfortable assortment of expressions ranging from resignation to annoyance to embarrassment to outrage and anger. That it was Mraal who looked angriest bothered Reswen; he was usually the most even-tempered of the lot.

"Reswen-*vassheh*," he said, too formally for Reswen's liking, "we have been receiving some complaints about you."

Reswen restrained himself from saying what he thought of the source, and merely assumed a look of extreme receptivity. "Lord Arpakh, if you will describe the complaints to me, I will do my best to satisfy you regarding the problems involved and what actions are being taken."

Mraal blinked a little. That was apparently not the reaction he had been expecting. He harrumphed a little, trying to recover his stern and angry mien. "I spent most of yesterday morning," he said, "with the honorable Maikej, who has replaced the late and much-lamented Shalav as Ambassador to Niau from Lloahai—"

"And is the honorable Maikej ready to assist the constabulary with inquiries about the late Shalav's death?" said Reswen. "I sent him a note inquiring about that yesterday morning, but received no response."

"You received no response because he does not desire you to conduct the inquiry," said Mraal.

Reswen allowed himself an astonished smile. "Lords, whom are you suggesting should conduct it if not the constabulary?"

"Investigator Thailh has been—"

"The investigator is on the constabulary staff," Reswen said, "unless someone has moved him to the Department of Public Works overnight."

"Reswen," said Mraal, and the anger was not being concealed now, "the Lords Arpekh are *requesting* that you keep well away from this investigation. It is in the hands of the officer to whom you yourself gave it. With the murder of Shalav, it has become a very sensitive matter—"

"Since when have I not been trusted with sensitive material?" Reswen said. "Lords."

"Since you insulted the new Lloahairi Ambassador, and practically caused a war by yourself with your rudeness—" Aratel said. "There have been changes of extraordinary delicacy in the government of Lloahai, and until we have the matter well in hand, we don't want some crude young fire-eater making matters any worse—!"

Reswen kept quiet. Kanesh looked up at him sympathetically from across the room, and said, "It seems that the new government has had most of the old one executed—"

"Kanesh, that is a gross misstatement," Mraal said. "There has been an uprising, a change of personnel among the Council of Lloahai. Unfortunately there was some regrettable violence, and most of the old seats have been—"

"I understand," Reswen said. "And there have been policy changes. All our treaties with the Lloahairi are going to have to be renegotiated. And since this changeover in the council occurred with, as you say, violence, we may assume that most of the changes are going to be hostile, or at least difficult for us to deal with and unpleasant to accept. Cuts in trade, I would imagine . . . less capital moving out of Lloahai into places like, say, Niau. Our intelligence had been hinting for some time that the new coalition moving into power in Lloahai was extremely isolationist. Naturally the new ambassador would welcome the discrediting of your primary source of intelligence. Your primary non-Lloahairi source, I should say."

There was a silence, during which the Lords looked at one another uneasily. "Your intelligence-gathering has always been superior, Reswen-*vassheh*," said Mraal, "but of late, some of your behavior has been very questionable. Calling out the city cohorts twice in one eightday without consulting the council—"

"Of the first time, Lord, we have already spoken, and the second time there would have been no need to call them out if the Lords Arpekh had not themselves dismissed the cohorts before it was clear whether they were needed on the walls any longer. Had one of my staff on scouting duty not discovered them coming, the Lloahairi would have arrived unexpected and unannounced, and would have walked up to our walls and found them unmanned."

"As if it matters," Aiewi muttered. "Easy enough to send someone to open a gate when you see there are people outside—"

"Lord Aiewi," Reswen said, very gently, as if to an idiot, "which city would you rather think about invading? One with walls full of soldiers pointing spears and arrows at you, or one where you can walk right up to the gates and knock before anyone notices you want to come in? Our relationship with Lloahai has not always been peaceful. It has been a lot *more* peaceful since we warred them down, all those years ago, and now we greet them with spears every time they arrive. Spears held at attention, but spears nonetheless. They have been very polite. I cannot help but think that there is a connection."

Some of the lords pulled long faces at that. Kanesh stared at the floor with one paw to his mouth, hiding a smile, and not well. "In any case," Mraal said, "the precaution we took with the Easterners turns out to have been unnecessary. They are of peaceful intent and are negotiating treaties with us that are very positive in terms of trade, and we intend to give them everything they ask for, one way or another—"

Reswen was shocked. He had seen the text of the main treaty: one of the "cleaning staff" in Haven had carefully copied for him the draft treaty left in Rirhath's room. It was another of the things he had wanted to talk to the Arpekh about. But something more immediate was on his mind. "Lord," he said, "about the stone and water—"

"Bosh on the stone and water," said Aiewi. "Let them have it and welcome."

"But, Lords, we have not completed inquiries—"

"If you would spend less time with courtesans, perhaps you would have completed them," said Aratel. "This kind of dilatory and inappropriate behavior is exactly what we are finding intolerable. But in view of your long and faithful service—"

What have you *all been doing of late then?* Reswen thought about saying, and decided against it. It would make things worse. There was more to think about, for he knew what the phrase Aratel had used would mean: a dismissal or a raise . . . and he didn't think it was the latter. "Lords—"

"The matter needs no more discussion," said Mraal. "We are in the process of working out other details of the trading treaty, and that particular detail is sufficiently minor that it will be handled immediately. Tomorrow, in fact, in the main square, to please our guests."

Reswen's heart turned right over in him. With that decision he could feel something bad starting to come toward him, toward the whole city, and there was nothing he could do to stop it. "And what else are we going to do to please our guests?" Reswen said, his anger beginning to show in good earnest now. "Lords, have you given thought to the caravan scheduling they are proposing? The numbers of visitors during the peak periods in the spring and fall are in the *hundreds*, not the tens that one expects of a caravan—and those are exactly the times when an attack is most viable because of the easy desert crossing and the favorable weather. The treaty sets no limits on how they may be armed, and no limits for how many large carts over a certain size may be allowed—carts that could transport siege engines or other devices for attacking a city's walls—"

"You are overconcerned," Aiewi said mildly. "They intend us no harm."

"Perhaps not *these* people, Lord. But who knows when

their governments may change? And when they do, if this treaty remains unchanged as it stands at the moment, someone who *did* intend us harm could do no end of it. An army at your gates, instead of traders." Then Reswen saw the closed faces, and understood. He schooled himself to keep his voice level, for he needed to convince them more than he needed to salve his own annoyance. "But you've become concerned about our trade with the Lloahairi, have you not? You see in worsening relationships with an unreasonable Lloahairi government the end of all the old agreements, and so you are determined to make another, more lucrative deal with the Easterners while the buyers are so fortuitously at hand in your market. Then you will let the Lloahairi go to their preferred hell in their own way. And anything I could think of to say, no matter how reasonable, would be vain at this point."

Some of the lords looked at him, and away. Some would not look at all.

"Lords," Reswen said, suddenly thoroughly disgusted, "my position requires me to give you my advice. I have done so. Having so done, may I have your leave to depart? I have a police force to run, and various other business to attend to."

"Not the murder investigation," said Mraal.

"I will make no move to interfere with Investigator Thailh, or even to contact him," Reswen said.

"Go then," said Mraal. "Fair day."

Reswen bowed and went out.

When he got to the office, still fuming, he opened the door and found Thailh sitting there waiting for him. "I don't see you," Reswen said, tossing his cloak over a chair.

"That's good," Thailh said, "because I'm not here."

Reswen smiled, and the motion of his whiskers going forward felt as if it might crack his face. "Those idiots," he said softly. "Those chop-licking, tail-waving, lie-by-the-fire—"

Thailh's resigned and humorous expression as he folded his arms and sat back to listen made Reswen laugh out loud. "All right," he said. "It was pretty annoying. But I'll live. What have you found?"

Thailh shrugged his tail a bit. "Not much. But this I'm

sure of: if our strangler hadn't killed Shalav, the ambassador would have done it himself."

Reswen sat down, his ears forward. "Tell me," he said,
and bent down to rummage in the drawer for a bit of dried
meat. "And be quick about it. You can't be seen here."

"One of our people stumbled across some of Maikej's
briefs from the Lloahairi government," Thailh said. "Thanks,
don't mind if I do. There were some pretty letters, I can
tell you that. Notes from the party now in power that this
bitch-mrem has to be gotten rid of by whatever means.
And Maikej apparently has a good motive to see to it, for
the two of them have apparently been enemies, in the
political sense, for about ten years. She got him dismissed
from some other post, a minor one, for incompetence."
Thailh paused a moment to chew. "According to the embassy's own staff, there were some horrendous arguments
between Maikej's arrival and the last night Shalav was
alive. Shalav had had a change of mind, and was refusing
to be relieved of her post; she and Maikej almost came to
blows." Thailh smiled wanly. "The staff were rather hoping they would fight; no one can stand Maikej but the
people he brought with him. The feeling was that Shalav
would have ripped his ears and tail off and shoved them
where the moons don't shine."

"Pity she didn't," Reswen said.

"We agree on that. Anyway, she was last seen after
another argument with Maikej, a real fur-puller—seems
he accused her of planning to have him assassinated."

"Shalav? The mrem's a fool. That's not her style at all."

"I agree, but that's what he accused her of, and she
wouldn't stand for it. The new embassy staff say she left in
a huff. The old staff either won't talk, or say that Maikej
ordered her out and told the staff to lock the gates behind
her. The porter refuses to say anything at all . . . someone's thrown the fear into him."

Reswen thought about it for a moment. "In either case,
she goes out . . . and fortuitously runs into the strangler."
He looked at Thailh. "Does that strike you as a little
strange?"

Thailh broke out laughing. "To put it mildly."

"What are you going to do now?"

"Set my assistants to asking some more questions of these people," Thailh said, "and in the meantime, go back to the drapers' and keep asking questions. At least now I have *two* pieces of evidence."

"May they be of use. Keep in touch, if you can."

"There shouldn't be any problem." Thailh laughed again. "I mean, we're the secret police, for gods' sake! We'll manage something."

Reswen smiled a bit as Thailh slipped out of his office, and began making a new list of things he wanted his people in Haven to start listening for. When it was done, he brushed another message to Laas, and sent it out after Thailh, with certain instructions. And then he set to work looking very busy . . . while he waited.

▲

Chapter 9

▲——————————————————————————▲

He waited a couple of days. It wasn't easy; but fortunately he had enough matters to keep him busy in reality and not just in seeming.

"Sir?" the runner said, poking his head into Reswen's office on the second day. "Constable Gellav says to tell you that the mrem you had put in the quiet cell a few days back is shouting for you. Says he has something to tell you."

Reswen smiled and got up. "Tell him I'll be right there."

Outside the cell, nothing could be heard, but young Gellav was standing there in a state of great excitement. "I've been sitting over the listening-pipe for about a year, it seems like, sir," he said. "When he started to shout, I was so surprised I almost strangled myself with my tail. What do you want to do with him?"

"*You're* going to do it," Reswen said. "He's had a bad few days in there, and we don't want to remind him of who put him there, not just now; it might make him sullen again. Take a lamp in with you, and a couple of stools, so he doesn't have to sit on the floor while you talk. Get another constable to stand outside the door, and get a flask of wine. Don't water it; if it goes to his head, no harm done, especially if it makes him talky. Give him some dried meat as well—that makes a hungry mrem even more talky than wine. And be kind about it all. You're going to be the good constable, as opposed to the nasty wicked policemaster who threatened poor Nierod and put him through all this. If he reviles me, you help him at it, and never care who's listening. You remember the questions I asked him?"

"Indeed yes, sir."

"Well enough. I'll listen to you, and if I want information about anything when you're done, I'll scratch on the other end of the listening pipe so that you can check with me and then finish. You know the sound I mean?"

"Oh yes, sir, we use it as a signal sometimes ourselves, to let each other know when another cell's ready for someone being moved."

"Fine. And when you're done asking the questions, if he's answered what we want to know, put him in one of the upstairs cells. Tell him if he remembers anything else, we might—*might*—find a way to let him out and let him work for us. But no guarantees. Can you hold that hope low enough to make him jump for it?"

"I think so, sir."

"So do I. You manage it, my lad, and I'll see about getting *you* something worth jumping for. Now off with you."

Then Reswen went upstairs one level, to the regular cell blocks, and positioned himself over the listening tube to Nierod's cell. There was a sort of low moaning going on in there, a hollow noise, like a mourning ghost. Reswen nodded, satisfied.

Gellav gathered his props and went in, and for a little while Reswen heard nothing but frantic thank-yous, and the sounds of sloppy and hurried eating and drinking. Then Gellav began asking his questions, and it was as Reswen had thought: The wretched Nierod had some thought of trying to suborn the young officer first, and offered him a bribe. Someone else would pay the good constable well if he could only be got out of here, everybody knew constables didn't make much money, hey, what about some money— Gellav was firm, though, quite firm. And he didn't have to be firm for long, for the sudden food and wine after deprivation turned Nierod giddy. His mood swung from momentary craftiness to miserable, weeping despair at not being able to bribe the constable, and from that to pathetically desperate desire to tell Gellav anything he wanted to know. And now Reswen leaned close to the listening-pipe, as Gellav said, "Who was it hired your contact, man? Tell me, then, and it may be I can do something for you."

Nierod's voice dropped as if afraid that someone else might overhear him. "He said it was a foreigner, he said, a great mrem, a great mrem, with gold, gold enough for a lot of jobs. He wouldn't tell me what foreign parts the mrem came from, he said he didn't know all the names of the places. He said he thought the foreigner had been here a few tens of days, maybe more, he started to see the mrem around the market and the shops, always buying, always asking where things came from. He said, 'I went to sell him some lash, I thought he was one of those foreigners who wants forbidden things, drugs, stolen things, you know—and I thought right. He has business, a lot of business, and there's enough for us too.' "

"Where would he meet this foreigner? There's a lot of them in town."

"Don't I know it, dirty things, what do we want with them? The Whites, he came from the Whites somewhere, one of the big guesting-houses." Reswen breathed out softly. "The Whites" was slang for the well-to-do area between the mercantile quarter and the embassies and good marble houses of the Eastside: The houses there tended to be finished in white stucco. He made a mental note to have someone go around and make inquiries at all the better guesting-houses for travelers who might have come in during the last thirty or forty days. There would be a lot of them, but he didn't care.

"All right, then. What was it that this foreigner told your contact to have you do?"

A noisy slurp at the wine. "He says, 'People are riled up about the strangers coming in, the Arpekh doesn't tell anymrem anything, their own people, let's show 'em that they have to tell mrem what's going on. Get people mad in the marketplace, tell 'em about an army coming, an army of stranger mrem, these Easterners coming to take over the city, 'cause that's all they want to do really, they'll try and trick us and buy the Arpekh to get 'em to do the strangers' will.' And I did that, I did it, nothing wrong with it, you can't have foreigners coming in and doing stuff like that, we fought 'em and beat 'em so they couldn't!" There was a real sense of outrage in the dulled, thickening voice.

"Well enough. So you did that. What else were you supposed to do?"

"Unnngh . . . My head hurts."

"I know, poor creature. Come, tell me what I need to know, so we can put you upstairs where there's a bed and a warm place for you to get clean. Come, now. Maybe even better than that. Maybe out of here entirely."

"Out, yes, just let me out and I'll never—"

"Ah now, make no promises you can't keep, nor I'll make you none." Reswen smiled to himself a little at the slangy, country accent working its way back into Gellav's speech, from who knew how many years back. The recruits tended to lose it in academy, and some of them swore at that loss much later when they could have used their milk accent for undercover work. "What else were you after doing, then?"

Nierod's voice dropped again. "It was a worse thing, a worse thing than just making people mad. But there was more gold for it. He gave me a string."

Reswen's whiskers stood straight out.

"A string?" said Gellav.

"Like this, a smooth shiny string. This long." The voice dropped even further. "My friend, he said, 'There's someone who's cheated the great mrem, cheated him in the market. We'll tell you who it is when he's ready. You need to watch them and when they go for a walk in the dark one night, come up behind 'em and use this string on 'em. Choke 'em dead, and leave the string there.' A lot of gold he gave me, and there would be more when it was done. A lot more, even. And the foreigner said, wouldn't nomrem ever find out about it, because the police, they thought they knew who was doing it, somemrem else, and that other mrem would answer for it, he'd get the spike. And I'd have my gold." The voice suddenly broke out in weeping. "My gold . . . my gold . . ."

There was a pause. "Let me think if there are any other questions I need answered," Gellav said, and fell

silent. Reswen grinned silently at the listening-pipe and
did nothing.

"Come on, then," Gellav said. "Come on with you,
mrem. Puli, give me a hand with him." And the noises of
scuffed straw and weeping faded away.

Now then, Reswen thought with immense satisfaction.
Now *then*!

He left the cramped little listening-room and loped off
upstairs.

▲

She rolled over in the golden warmth of the overworld
at a sudden feeling of chill. There was nothing that caused
such a feeling but trouble or danger, and she had no idea
what could be going on here that could possibly endanger
her. The vermin were quite blind to her doings.

She blinked, trying to trace the feeling, but it was
gone. The merest chill . . . Still, even the occurrence of
such a tiny thing, such a minuscule breach in the walls of
her peace of mind, was intolerable to her. She could allow
nothing to interfere with her work here; her masters would
be furious, and more to the point, her status—her *potential*
status—as one of them would be endangered. *I must look
into this. . . .*

She willed the overworld under her into solidity, and
around her the brightness of day increased with her interest. There were ways to keep track of what one was doing
with magic, a way to track the effect of chance and event
on one's plans. They were slightly strenuous, but they
were worth it.

She began the spell. It was not one that could be done
offhand, even for her, even out of the hardest skin. The
careful, subtle pattern of hissing was one of the last things
her old master had taught her before she had reduced
him, in an unguarded moment, to bloody fragments. She
performed the Nine Circlings, making very sure of the
usual ritual movements with the tail, and then began the
chant, with great care for the intonation of the sounds.
Pride rose in her as she recited: pride in her own ability,
in the flawless way she wove and hissed the spell, pride in
the magic itself, a sort of magic endlessly more delicate,

complex, and involved than the crude shout-and-wave stuff
that the vermin did. This was the great art of her people,
which truly had set them apart from the beasts since time
was young, and continued to do so, though the vermin
might prance and shrill their little cantrips and mock the
majesty and power of the Eldest People. Let them prance
as they liked; they were no match for the Eldest, as they
would find now, and continue to find.

She paced and hissed her way through the spell. Light
gathered around her, the many-colored light of the
overworld, hot like fire, but the heat was not hurtful. It
exalted, it clarified the mind. The light, in all its colors,
swirled, parted, knotted about itself, parted again in strands
and tendrils, seeking a shape, experimenting with junc-
tures, breaking them when they did not work, trying
others. She paced and hissed, and slowly the light knitted
itself into a webwork around her, a frame of throbbing
connections. Slowly she brought the first part of the spell
to conclusion, stood in the center of it all, and looked
about.

The spell had wrought a representation of what she
had done with her magics since she began her work here.
Pressure on a mind here, a death there, everything showed:
and each mind she had touched or influenced or controlled showed here, with its connections and conversa-
tions with other minds all indicated as well. She looked
around at it all with some slight haste, for the spell drew
on all the live minds to which it referred, and even she
could not hold it there for long.

There were no overt indications of trouble. She turned
slowly, gazing at the lines of light as they burned and
faded, burned and faded again. They all led to her, of
course, through numerous primary connections—her pets.
One by one she examined them. There seemed to be
nothing out of place—

But wait. There, along that thread that had been most
recently touched—the pet who had killed the ambassador-
vermin's body for her—a thread led from that one, and a
second thread from the first, and the second thread pulsed
faintly with a color that meant danger. It had made a
secondary connection to another thread, and *that* thread

to yet another one—the policemaster who was in turn connected, at the moment, to one of her pets.

Perhaps this aspect of the game was in fact becoming too dangerous. Perhaps she should do something about it.

At first she scorned the thought. *They are only vermin, after all,* she thought. *What harm in letting them do their little worst?* . . .

But then it occurred to her that this course of action, in her masters' view, might be perceived as laziness on her part—or greed. There was no use letting them get any ideas about *that.* Supposing they should demand she be removed from this mission? She could not bear the thought of the splendid feast that awaited her going to any other of her kind. *Hers* was the work so far, all this careful groundwork laid down. *Hers* should be the reward. *She* would become one of the masters herself.

And once she had done that—

No, there was no use being anything less than conscientious about all this. Let something be done about that new connection, and right away, before it should have a chance to mature into something dangerous. *Still,* she thought, *I need not be hasty about it . . . I may still draw this business out considerably for my pleasure. As long as I am seen to be doing something useful, if suddenly I am investigated, that is sufficient. And there will be satisfaction enough indeed, when I bring the matter to the conclusion that I wish . . . yet another interlude, before the grand climax.*

She smiled with all her teeth at the thought of the taste of the policemaster's blood . . . and reached out into the spell to the mind and eyes of one of her pets.

▲

When young Gellav had finished his report, Reswen sent him off to tell Thailh what had transpired, and when a runner came in and handed Reswen a message with the Easterners' peculiar wax seal on it, he smiled all over his face. It was definitely his day. He broke the seal. *Tonight,* it said, just one word, but the one was enough. Getting the message was almost enough to distract him from the distasteful spectacle he had to watch from his office window an hour later. His office view was normally one of the glories of the place: It looked out onto the main square and across at the Law Courts on one side and the Arpekh's House on the other. Today, though, rather than being able to gaze out the window and let his eyes rest in their classically perfect contours while thinking about things, he had to watch the white stone square fill up with curious townspeople, and his own men on crowd duty; and finally, to not too large a turnout, the Eastern priest Hiriv and the merchant Rirhath received "the bones and blood of the city Niau" from the hands of the Arpekh, in the person of Mraal. Reswen watched it all, watched the priest sweat and smile and bow, rather diffidently, watched Rirhath stand there as if he would much rather be somewhere else. *And so he would,* Reswen thought, knowing from the listeners at Haven that the man was off for another meeting with the corn-factors, as they played with what the price of Niau's grain was going to be in the Eastern markets.

Reswen craned his neck a little to see what Mraal held out: a glass bottle in one paw, in the other a stone, sharp-edged, doubtless chipped out of the wall—Mraal had a keen eye for symbolism in some ways. Hiriv took them and spoke some words that Reswen couldn't hear, something ceremonial that he sounded bored with. And then all went down from the steps of the Arpekh's house together, probably off to Haven to continue the negotiations.

Idiot, Reswen thought, and picked up a sheaf of parchments he had been waiting to see. It was young constable Shilai's report of his first day in the marketplace, and there was a lot of it; he had dictated it to one of Krruth's people last night, and a note at the top of the report stated that the dictation had taken almost two hours. Reswen was pleased; Krruth had told him that Shilai was another one with "the gift," the ability to remember everything heard. And here it all was, gossip, backbiting, news useful and useless, or seemingly useless; faces remembered and described, sometimes in almost lyrical detail, sometimes in hasty abbreviations that suggested that the talk going on had fascinated Shilai into not caring about the face. Reswen plunged into it, feeling exhilarated ahead of time. Since listening to the interview in the cell, he had a feeling that the annoyances and halts and stumbles of the last couple of days were suddenly beginning to dissolve in front of him. Things were suddenly beginning to connect, to make sense. It was not a sense he particularly liked. *The city is in danger,* he thought, *worse danger than anyone thinks.* But it didn't matter whether he liked the sense or not. At least it was there. He began reading, expecting to find gold.

It was there, though well buried in dirt, as gold tends to be. *Nitchash (tanner's assistant) talking to Kolu (meatcake-seller). N: There goes that one again. K: Which one? Oh, him. The big spender. N: He was over at the skin-seller's this morning— K: Oh, old Vunun. N: Not him, he's off today, his wife's kittening. K: Again? At his age? The mrem's amazing. N: Oh aye, the only way he'll stop is if someone cuts them off. I meant Pihai. K: Oh, right. What was that mrem after this time? N: Not skins, that's all I know. Talked to him for almost an hour. Every time customers came near him Pihai would shoo them off. Finally the mrem points at one skin and gives him a claw of gold and doesn't take change back, just walks off! K: Gods, wish he'd do that for me. N: You and me both, brother, from your mouth to their ears, you know what I'd do with a change of a claw? I'd—*

Reswen skipped past some intriguing and humorous plans for what might be done with one of the joy-shes from one of the uptown pleasure-houses. He made a note to himself that if one really *could* get such services, the place probably needed raiding again, then passed on to Shilai's description of the alleged "big spender." *Large mrem, burly, brown-striped, cream front and paws, cream patch beside nose, kink in tail, green eyes. Well-dressed, brown kilt, brown/cream cezhe*—(that was the half cape, half throw that Niauhu of both sexes sometimes wore in summer or winter for warmth or to keep the sun off, depending: in summer it would be made of something light and usually bound around the head)—*clothing of good quality, no jewelry, no other identifying characteristics*—

Reswen scanned down through the rest of the document, finding nothing further of interest except a prim little note at the bottom: *Sold: three bottles essence of sparkflower, one large bottle decocted washing-herb, one small bottle white lotion of heal-leaf, two bottles of electuary of furweed, one boil simple, one small bottle lose-scab, seventeen bottles oil of mangebane, one claw-buffer.*

Reswen smiled at that and wondered whether there was another strain of mange going around all of a sudden. *Really must ask the Chief Physic about that. There's always a rise in the crime rate when a new strain hits—* Purring, he pulled over a tablet and scratched on it a copy of the Shilai's description of the "big spender." Beneath that he added a note to Krruth: *Find out where this mrem lives. I want information on dates of arrival, stated business, all social and business contacts. Frequents marketplace, makes large purchases or small ones with large payments for information. In light of interview with prisoner Nierod (see attached), I suspect subject is agent for foreign government. Query: which one? Query: source of subject's funds? Reply soonest. When subject is located, start level two surveillance but do not otherwise approach. Notify me immediately on location and identification. Coordinate with Thailh re: nature and provenance of murder weapon in the case he's working on. Connection? R.*

Reswen called in a runner to take the messages away, and then stretched luxuriously. There was nothing else but routine business to keep him occupied for the rest of the day . . . so he went about it with a good heart. But the thought kept intruding, the thought of the one word:

Tonight . . .

He spent more time than usual over his grooming, that evening, and left home early for Haven. This was not entirely a matter of eagerness to see Laas (or so he told himself). There was another small matter that was bothering him.

He walked in and found things much as they should have been, the staff, both the Easterners' and his own, bowing and scraping as usual. Reswen accepted wine, and more hortolans—with something of a smile—and reclined and made small talk with two of the Eastern merchants while he waited for Laas.

Shortly he heard what he had been hoping to: the light, rather astonished voice from upstairs. "Oh, he has finally come to grace the house—" And down the stairs, in a small storm of bells and robes, came Hiriv the priest. Reswen, looking at him, still found him rather pitiful: his earlier extreme dislike seemed to have passed off a bit. Perhaps it was a result of the aftermath of the riot, having seen Hiriv's glossy calm broken by something genuine.

Reswen started to stand to greet him, but— "Oh no, please, I beg you," said the priest, and took both his paws and sat down beside him, clasping them both enthusiastically. *This is embarrassing*, Reswen thought, but he managed not to pull away; there was no point in offending the mrem. "Reswen-*vassheh*, I have been waiting for a chance to thank you again for some time. The last time you were here, you left so suddenly—"

"It had been a bad day, Hiriv-*chagoi*. I had had nothing to eat all day . . . I confess my stomach was rather on my mind. And then that night, the murder, you'll remember. I was unable to bring the lady Laas back as I would have liked, when I would have had a chance to talk to you at more leisure; and naturally my time since has been very circumscribed. But I trust you've taken no hurt from that afternoon."

"No indeed, nothing at all, but what a fright! Nothing of the sort ever happened to me before." The priest fanned himself with one of the many objects hanging from his robe's belt, a fan of folded parchment. "Such things do not happen in the East, I'm afraid. Why, the last person to try to create such a public disturbance had his—" And Reswen had to listen to an energetic description of an old-fashioned execution, and had to nod politely all through it. "I trust," Hiriv said, "that something similar will happen to the miscreant who incited the mob against us."

"Something similar," Reswen said, feeling a positive pleasure in lying. If there were some way that Nierod could be turned to his benefit in this whole business, he would much sooner do that than hang the poor creature up to feed the winged scavengers that waited patiently around the spikes and hooks on the Punishment Wall.

"You will invite us, I do hope," Hiriv said.

"Infallibly," Reswen said, "if our justices are through with him before you leave for home."

"Justices?" Hiriv said, somewhat surprised. "Certainly justice is too precious to spend on scum like that. They would never appreciate it; they haven't the education."

"Perhaps our criminal classes are better educated," Reswen said, in a moment's sarcasm, and was vastly relieved when Hiriv laughed heartily, thinking Reswen had made a joke.

"Oh, very good, very good indeed," said the priest, and laughed harder. "It is true what we hear of you, that you're a wit as well as a clever officer."

Reswen shrugged genteelly. "Rather than clever," he said, "perhaps say thorough. As in, 'I am thoroughly enjoying this wine.' Will you take some?"

"Always," Hiriv said, laughing again as Reswen poured him a cup. The priest made some small sign over the cup and drank it straight off with a speed that astonished Reswen.

"You bless your wine before you drink it?" Reswen said.

"Oh no," said Hiriv, "the sign merely drives away the influence of Enuib the False, the bad genius of wine. Excuse me, our religion probably bores you, and certainly you have your own. I don't mean to proselytize."

"Oh no, indeed, it's not boring," said Reswen, for this was what he had been trying to think of a way to get Hiriv to talk about. He poured another cup. "I had thought, though, that you served a grain-god."

"Ssamos the Fair, yes, but wine is part of his business as well, one might say," Hiriv said, and he went off on a rather roundabout explanation of the Eastern pantheon. Reswen filed it for later use, but privately thought it was a pretty confused situation: a party of "good" gods and another of "evil" gods eternally arguing over the domination of the world, and none of them totally controlling anything.

"So let me get this straight," Reswen said, when there was a pause in the flow of exotic names and tales of bizarre attributes and, to put it gently, peculiar relationships. "Ssamos rules the grain and the wine, their good aspects at least—"

"That's right. And Enuib rules their bad aspects, and the two of them fight in the nature of each. As, wine may make a mrem merry, but it may also make him brutal. Or bread may satisfy, but too much of it may also lead to gluttony, or make one discontented with his lot."

Reswen nodded, thinking privately, *Aha: the starve-your-poor-and-keep-them-in-their-place school of thought.* "Very wisely put. What I'm curious about is exactly what a priest of Ssamos does."

Hiriv fanned himself with a pleased air, obviously flattered by the interest. "Well, he conducts the rites of Ssamos, of course, the usual seasonal observations, and sees to it that grain and wine are not misused, or used to excess, and counsels the merchants on how this may be done—"

"I see," said Reswen. *I do indeed. Helps control the prices paid and the amounts bought, so that the nobles and priests get enough of the grain and wine, but the lower classes don't have enough made available to get out of place. . . . Yet they're arranging to buy more from us: a great deal more than we had thought they needed, considering our intelligence about their buying habits in other markets closer to the East. Is their population expanding suddenly? Or are they preparing to have it expand suddenly? . . .*

Hiriv went on for some time, and Reswen didn't try to stop him, just let him rattle. Ssamos was apparently another of those gods who got themselves killed once a year, and then came back again, to the astonishment or annoyance of other gods and the delight of their worshippers . . . who overindulged in bread and got very drunk on wine to celebrate. "—And of course since the wine and the bread are blessed, it's a very holy occasion," Hiriv said, describing one of these festivals, but Reswen considered that the fees the priests charged for officially blessing bread and wine probably contributed a great deal to the atmosphere of rejoicing in the temples, at least on the priests' part. There were also fasting periods during the year, during which one was not supposed to use grain or wine, because Ssamos was buried under the weight of the world, struggling to rise again, having been killed by Enuib the False . . . though Hiriv mentioned that those who for health or other reasons could not refrain (say, mrem too poor to afford meat more than once in an oct of days) could still buy an exception to the rule at the temples.

"Very compassionate," Reswen said.

"Oh indeed, for the people must not suffer. At least, not more than necessary."

"Indeed not," Reswen said, thinking, This *is what Lorin told me to beware of? This petty hypocrite, this businessman in priest's clothes?* Reswen had never considered himself particularly religious, but what religion he had was better than *this*. At the same moment he heard a sound he had been waiting for, a light, laughing voice saying something to someone upstairs, and he was intensely relieved.

"But I've been doing all the talking," Hiriv said, as if just noticing it. "You haven't told me which gods *you* worship, Reswen-*vassheh*."

"Our expensive friend Justice, mostly," Reswen said, restraining himself from telling the priest that it was none of his business, and he wasn't going to get a chance to sell *him* anything, thank you very much— "And most definitely Truth."

"Right you are, very right indeed," said Hiriv, but Reswen paid no attention to him as he rose to greet Laas and bowed over her paw.

"I didn't keep you waiting too long, I hope," she s as he straightened up.

"Oh, no indeed, the good Hiriv and I have been having a fascinating discussion," Reswen said, and was inwardly amused to see the quirky look in Laas's eye, an expression that said, *Oh really?* and was gone again. They turned together to the priest, and Reswen said, "And Justice requires that a lady not be kept waiting, though Justice herself, being a lady, takes as long as she pleases. Please excuse us, Hiriv-*chagoi*."

"Of course," Hiriv said. "You two have a good time."

Reswen and Laas went away together, Reswen with some relief; Hiriv's pseudofatherly manner annoyed him. "Is he going to wait up for you?" Reswen said in an undertone to Laas, as they slipped out the front door together.

"I doubt it," she said. "You know his habits, I suspect.

He worships Ssamos pretty enthusiastically before he goes to bed."

"Now how should I know his habits?" Reswen said as they swung out of the courtyard and down Dancer's street together.

"Oh come," Laas said, and laughed at him, a sweet sound but a wicked one, and the conspiratorial note made Reswen laugh too. "Do you really expect me to believe that you don't own everyone in that place? Or some of our own people, at this point? I have ears—" And she flicked one of them at him most charmingly; the jewel in it, deep red like blood, flashed at him in the lamplight from a nearby tree.

"So I see," Reswen said. "Tell me: He obviously takes his religion no more seriously than he feels necessary. Are all your people that way? What do *you* believe in?"

Laas shrugged her tail gracefully. "We're no different from your people, I would say. I've met some here who believe in nothing but money, and some who worship and sacrifice as if they were afraid the gods would notice if they didn't, and stop them breathing, and many in between, who honor the gods when they think to, and honor the ones they like and ignore the others. And what about you?" she said, close to his ear. "You sitting there taunting poor Hiriv, whose brains are in his purse, or other mrem's purses, rather. And he not smart enough to hear you doing it. What do *you* believe in, scornful one? You with your fine talk of Truth and Justice."

Reswen thought about that, then smiled slightly. "I'll show you, later," he said. "Meanwhile, what shall we do tonight?"

"I thought you had made plans?"

"Various possibilities, no decisions. We could go see the Games. There's a session tonight."

"What games are these?"

He paused for a moment, wondering how to explain it. Niauhu shared the delight and fascination of mrem everywhere with dance: the flow of it, the expression possible in bodies perfectly married with minds, dancing rage, delight, lust, pain, joy, in language that could not be mistaken for anything else. But the Niauhu, left somewhat to themselves, martial by habit and necessity, and eventually by habit and preference; they had evolved dance into forms that some of their Western kin would probably have found barbaric. *Let them*, Reswen thought; they were not sitting on the edge of the world with only the sword's edge between them and invasion, with only a pocket of kindly weather and a few precious wells between them and the pitiless desert.

Fumblingly, he tried to explain how in the Games, dance had become the expression of the spirit of war, with all its daring, danger, grace, power, and sudden death. The dancers who danced the Game were wagered on, mobbed in the streets, almost revered; the beasts who fell to them were honorably buried when they lost, had honorable revenge visited on them when they killed a Game-dancer. There were mrem who bet their whole incomes on the Games, lived for nothing else; some were ruined, and counted it worth it. Some made great fortunes, and were almost as revered as the Game-dancers for their skill—for indeed the betting pools were labyrinthine in their complexity, and a rightly placed scrap-of-claw bet could become a thousand claws'-weight of gold . . . always assuming that the Game-dancers put their paws right, and the gods were kind. The Gods were always invoked by the Game-dancers, and sometimes even remembered afterwards, if one survived. But the important question, in many parts of the city, was "Do you follow the Games?" Reswen followed them as a hobby, not a passion; but as a hobbyist, when he had time to spare for it, it interested him intensely, and he could discuss the Game-dancers' statistics and habits in depth that might have surprised some who accounted themselves specialists.

Laas listened to all this as they strolled into the city, and when Reswen trailed off after a while, she walked gazing quietly at the flagstones for a little ways before answering. "I have had so much lately," she said softly, "of life-or-death matters, and great wagers. . . ." She looked up again. "Perhaps something lighter?"

Reswen shrugged. "There's always the play."

"Tell me about it again."

He reached into his belt pouch and brought out the

broadside for her to see. The printing on it was rough and
smudged in places, speaking of printing done hastily from
a rudely carved ironwood board, on one of the cheap
presses belonging to a small criers' firm. It said, in great
fat letters,

TONIGHT
at the Play House

the Lord Arpekh's Mrem
playing a Play of Merrie Contrasts and Humours
a Pretty Fine new Fantasticall Satire
entitled THE CLAW UNSHEATH'D
(—and here there was a rough woodcut picture of a claw,
with a drop of blood pendant at the end of it—)
with Marvellous new Masks & Costumes,
Never Before seen
alsoe Musick Songs and Dances
wrought for this Play and No other.

The Play to begin
about the Ninth Stroke on Tezhrue's Bell
ground Level 1 minim Galleries 2
chairs 1 minim ea.

wine ½ minim the Stoup
and small Beere ¼

No Passes for this Engagement

Laas laughed again. "I think we should go see that,"
she said. "Besides, you intrigued me. I've never seen
anything at a play but something like The Passion of Lord
Ssamos, His Betrayal By the Wicked Enuib the False,
and Ssamos His Rising." She chuckled a bit.

"Sounds like rather heavy theater," Reswen said.

"I wouldn't know," Laas said, thoughtful. "I've never
seen any that was light. But surely I could use some
lightness . . . it would be a pleasure."

Reswen was afire with curiosity, but for the moment

he said nothing. "What shall we do, then?" he said. "Walk till time for the play? Or eat first?"

"Food, please," Laas said. "Can we go where we went the last time?"

"Heavens, yes," Reswen said. "You don't have to talk me into that! But Ishoa will be cross with me for not letting him know to expect us."

So off they went to the Green Square, and Ishoa did indeed scold Reswen at the sight of him, but bowed to Laas as he might have bowed to a queen with a misbehaving courtier, with an air of cheerful complicity. She smiled and played the part, and Ishoa put them at the same table as before, and sent them wine. It was early yet; there were few diners, few heads to turn at the sight of the policemaster. Reswen thought that just as well.

Laas laughed again, looking around. "What's funny?" Reswen said.

She gestured slightly with her head in a direction behind Reswen. He turned, casually, and saw two of the table-waiting staff, who had been looking at them, turn suddenly away. "So?"

Laas looked at him with a wry expression. "I don't think they're used to seeing you bring the same lady in here twice," she said.

Reswen went a touch hot, then cooled down again. "You may have a point," he said. "Bear in mind: When one's policemaster, it doesn't do to become too well known . . . it can be used against you, or by others, against your partner. . . ."

"But when your companion's a criminal . . . well." Laas watched him, then smiled, letting him off. "No matter. How's your bit of 'fish,' my friend?"

Reswen patted it under his tunic. "Intact."

"Would you believe me," Laas said, "if I told you I would not use . . ." She trailed off. "That I wouldn't use it on you?"

"I would be very curious why," Reswen said. "But I might just believe you. Convince me."

She looked at him, and sighed. "No," she said. "Tell me now: What are we going to eat tonight?"

They went off into the inconsequentials of deciding

about food. Reswen called Ishoa over, and Ishoa and Laas
promptly got into a most animated discussion about spices,
Eastern and Western, and how hot one could make meat if
one tried. Reswen began to suspect that he had created a
monster. When Ishoa threatened Laas with the prospect
of baby bunorshan in firespice and verjuice, Laas tossed
her head and dared him to go ahead and do it. Off went
Ishoa, rubbing his paws together, and Reswen began to
wonder whether he was going to survive dinner or not.

"You really like that, don't you?" he said.

She beamed at him. "The meat tastes of something,
here. It's not bland. One can get weary of blandness. A
little spice makes a lot of difference. . . ."

Reswen laughed out loud, and then choked stopping
himself. "What's funny?" Laas said.

He made a rueful face. "One of my . . . never mind.
Someone I know described you, at first sight, as 'a less
highly spiced sweetmeat.'"

Laas looked a touch rueful too, for a moment, and then
chuckled. "Than Deshahl? Heaven, yes; but that was the
point. No one looks twice at the second-class courtesan,
not really. That makes her much the more effective of the
two."

"Does it indeed?" Reswen said. He sipped at his wine.
"You've been busy with the corn-factors," he said. "A
boring lot, most people would think . . . but apparently
you found them otherwise. They certainly found *you* so."

"Your eyes and ears are everywhere, I'm sure," Laas
said, and drank her own wine with an abstracted look.
After a moment she put the cup down and said, "Why
should I tell you anything? Convince me."

Part of Reswen's mind began shouting, *This is it, she's
about to talk!* but he pushed that part of him away for the
moment. "I can't, I suppose," he said at last.

She smiled at him a little. "I could have sworn you
were about to say, 'Because I could throw you in gaol.'"

"I was," he said to his surprise, "but I decided that
would be a silly thing to say. What about the corn-factors?"

"I could be killed, you know," she said, "for telling you
anything at all. They would make it look like an accident,
I'm sure."

"I'd investigate your murder, though," Reswen said, trying to make it sound light.

"That wouldn't be much consolation to *me* at the time," Laas said.

"Well, I suppose not. . . ." He pretended interest in his wine for a moment, then said, "But how would they ever find out?"

She gazed at him over the rim of the winecup. "You think you're the only one who has hired ears?" she said. "We have our own . . . or so I've been warned."

Reswen considered that. He had long suspected it, and now found himself wondering about the big spender in the marketplace, and other such matters. "Well," he said. "I can't convince you. I won't try. I'm doing my job as best I can, protecting what matters to me."

"So am I," said Laas.

Reswen drank his wine and was still. Something hung in the air, balancing like a winged thing in an updraft, wavering, pushed up on a wind, pushing against it.

"Reswen," she said. She had never called him by his name before, or at least not without the title. Now, at the sound, something like a shock ran down through him, up again, rooted in his spine, and lifted the hairs all along it. His tail bristled in alarm. "Reswen," she said, and all the hairs that had begun to lie down stood up again. "I don't know what to do, truly I don't. There are odd things going on. I don't understand them."

He held still and concentrated on breathing until his fur calmed down somewhat. "Tell me what your honor permits," he said, "and maybe I can help."

She drank wine, then looked up and smiled brightly. Ishoa had arrived, carrying a tray with bowls of something steaming on it; some sort of broth. Both of them made anticipatory noises as the broth was put down in front of them. It was aromatic, and quite clear, except for slices of some tiny green pod floating in it. For a few minutes, while Ishoa hung about waiting for a reaction, they made appreciative small talk, and then Reswen made the mistake of biting into one of the little green pods instead of merely swallowing it. His mouth went up in flames like some tenement in the Shambles after an arsonist had gone by, and Ishoa went away in satisfaction, rubbing his paws again. Laas gave Reswen bread and otherwise made compassionate conversation while he recovered himself.

"I am never coming back here again," Reswen said finally. "The mrem's a sadist."

"Reswen," Laas said again, and Reswen swore softly, for there went the fur again.

"You said you weren't doing it," he said, aggrieved.

"I'm *not*," she said, just as aggrieved, and then they both looked at one another and fell abruptly silent.

"All right," he said, "go ahead. I'm sorry."

"The corn-factors," she said.

"Yes, right." He was still eating bread, trying to kill the fire.

"Why should I be asking them if they would like *not* to have a crop next year?"

He looked at her, bemused. "That's no great mystery," Reswen said. "I have an idea that one of the main responsibilities of our friend Hiriv's priesthood is to limit the grain available to your cities, so that—well. He limits the available supply, and the price goes up as a result. Didn't you know that?"

"Surely," she said, and drank some more broth. This time she was the one who bit down on a little green pod by accident. "*Oh, gods!!*" she said. Reswen looked resigned and handed her bread.

A few minutes later she said, "It still seems very odd to me. We came all this weary way to set up quotas for grain shipment. Now I'm told to see who would be willing to have an 'accident' happen to their crop. Fire, drought, blight, just crop failure, explainable in any way one likes. They get paid, almost as well as they would for growing the crop."

Reswen thought about that. "Another way to force your grain prices up," he said. "The priests get even more for their bread at festivals—extort more from those they allow to grow it or sell it successfully, for the privilege of doing so. It's dirty, but not all that strange."

Laas shook her head. "I think there's more to it."

They both played with their soup for a couple of moments more until it was gone, both of them staying very clear of the little green pods. A server came to take the dishes away, and for the moment they touched paws, while they sipped their wine, to confuse anyone who might be watching.

Reswen, after a moment, said, "I was going to ask you: Why are you telling me this now? You said, not until your job was done—"

"It is," she said, "or so I'm told."

Reswen considered that. "Who *are* you reporting to?" he said.

Laas eyed him. "I really think I should leave you *some* things to find out." There was a warning glint in her eye, though; no anger about it, just caution.

Reswen nodded, sipped at his wine again. "Apparently the trade treaties are about to be signed," he said. "Your merchants and ours seem to have reached agreement on just about everything."

"That's what I hear," Laas said. But she still looked faintly troubled.

Reswen said nothing, and was rescued from having to by the arrival of the bunorshan on a platter full of grain, first toasted, then boiled. Ishoa stood nearby while the servers put the food on the plates, left small grain-scoops next to clean tongs, and retired. Reswen tried the bunorshan, then ate grain, very fast, for several minutes, while Laas laughed at him. Ishoa very genially brought over a flask of iced wine. It helped . . . just barely.

For a while Reswen and Laas ate and suffered happily, the tears running down their faces from the sheer heat of the spice. "I'm going to make that mrem the city torturer," Reswen said between cups of wine. "How I never noticed this hidden aptitude . . ."

"You're an innocent," Laas said, "that's the problem."

Reswen gazed at her in astonishment. "Pardon?"

She waved the tongs at him, fighting to get down a particularly violent mouthful, and then said, "You do look for the good in people, Reswen. I've noticed. It's rather unusual in a chief of secret police." Reswen, astonished, took another mouthful of the bunorshan and once more spared himself having to do anything but fight the food down. It put up a valiant struggle and made him pay

dearly. "Your younger officers worship you because of the
way you deal with them. You may make them work their
tails off, but you give them chances—"

"I am a bundle of suspicions and fears, most of them
well-founded," Reswen said in an I-deny-everything voice,
"and I beat my junior officers every day. But they're all
masochists, that's the problem."

"You are full of fur balls," Laas said. "Talk truth to me!
You just like excitement and disguises and doing secret
things, that's all. So by hard work and careful planning,
you've gotten yourself into a position where that's all you
have to do: dress up in rags and sneak around, or hide
behind curtains and eavesdrop—yourself, or others working for you—" She chuckled at his discomfiture. "Reswen,
I told you . . . one with my brand of, ah, talent, can feel
the response. Something underneath the basement at Haven responds very well to me. . . ."

Reswen covered his eyes. No wonder the reconnaissance
had been, as Krruth said, "so dry." "Who else knows?"

That cautious glint again. "Those who needed to."
Then the glint died away, and Laas looked slightly somber. "At least, those whom I thought needed to. I'm
beginning to wish I hadn't told them."

There was a little silence, and they went back to the
bunorshan and fought the last scraps of it down them. "If
all bunorshan tasted like that," Reswen said at last, wiping
away the last of the tears, "they'd be safe from mrem
forever. At least from mrem without your fondness for hot
food . . ."

Laas poured out a last cup of iced wine for them from
the flask Ishoa had left. "Look there," she said, "you've
drunk it all."

"*I've* drunk it all? Look at you, you could teach a fish!"
They laughed crazily, perhaps a little more crazily than
necessary. "No harm in it," Reswen said, "as long as
whoever may be watching us thinks we're drunk. Not that
we are, of course." He hiccuped decorously.

Laas looked cheerful mockery at him. "When is this
play we're going to, O sober one?"

"Oh heavens," Reswen said, "when did you last hear a
gong?"

"Some time ago. An hour, perhaps."

"Late again," he said with resignation. "I've never been on time for a play in my life. No reason to start now, I suppose. You didn't want a sweet, did you? No, of course you didn't. Come on, we're going to be late!" He got up hastily from the table, caught her by the paw.

"If we're going to be late anyway, why shouldn't I have a sweet?" Laas said, laughing, but there was no point in it, they were halfway out the garden gate already. Ishoa waved a tolerant good-bye to them.

They ran. Reswen had forgotten how out of breath one could get, running; it was something he didn't do much these days. But Laas kept up with him with no problem, and shortly it turned into sort of a race, each of them grimly determined not to have to stop before the other one did. They laughed a great deal, and mrem in the streets stared at them with some surprise as they went by. Reswen was relieved that it was night; at least he was spared being widely recognized.

They took shortcuts Reswen knew, dodged through alleys where the reek made them both laugh and spit in disgust. Then suddenly they were there, and both of them stopped and put their clothes to rights and strolled into the crowd outside the Play House as if a litter had just let them out. Only their gasping gave them away, making the mrem standing about turn to stare at them again. Reswen glanced at Laas, who was playing the high-society she-mrem for the moment, her head high and haughty for all that her chest was heaving like a sprinter's.

"Very fine," Reswen said, under his breath, in her ear.

"If these good people want to think—" she said, smoothing her soft robes, "that my handsome escort—has been pawing me in a—back alley somewhere—then let them—" She gave him another of those wicked smiles.

He gave her one back, and said, more softly if possible, "Do you think we made it here quickly enough to have lost whoever was following us?"

"Entirely possible," she said. "Why? Do you mean us to go somewhere else before they arrive?"

"Only if you want. But I thought you wanted to see the play—"

"Of course I do!"

"Then in we go."

They went up to the ticket kiosk together. The Play House was a rude old joint, originally a travelers' tavern. It had been expanded when plays had begun to be performed there, a couple of hundred years earlier. Galleries had been built onto the tavern and around the big courtyard, and the stables for the burden-beasts had been turned into dressing rooms for those more interesting beasts, actors. A big stage had been built in the middle of the courtyard, more or less backed up against the main tavern building. People staying in the tavern sometimes got to see the plays whether they wanted to or not; some of the windows had players' galleries running right outside them. The mrem staying on the second or third floors might look out from an early nap to see Girul and Oviah from the old story falling into one another's arms, half mad with passion, or Lishawi and Neahan of *The Poor Mrem's Tragedie* raging up and down the balcony with swords drawn, trying to cut one another into collops. Occasionally, particularly dozy or drunken patrons got into the play themselves, hollering in surprise or outrage at the lovers or fighters, sometimes climbing out the windows to try their own hands at loving or fighting. The crowds took it all in good part, and the management of the tavern usually remitted a little of the patrons' lodging-fee, especially if the actors had had to beat them up.

Reswen bought them tickets and also a couple of billets for chairs. "You needn't go to the expense," Laas said, at that: "I don't need to sit, really."

"Sit? We may want them to stand on. Or hide under. The crowds can get pretty rough."

She chuckled as he ushered her past the barrier which was lifted for them to enter the courtyard. There were about three hundred mrem jostling about in there, drinking, laughing, and shouting excerpts from the play at one another. Reswen found a good spot far enough away from the stage to make sure that they would see all the action, took possession of it by standing on it, then waved for one of the courtyard's servers and gave the seat-billets to the mrem when he came over.

"And two wines," he said, and the mrem nodded and hurried off. To Laas, Reswen said, "You've got to try this wine."

"Is it that good?"

"Good's not exactly the word, I suspect," Reswen said, "but you have to try it anyway. Your experience of this place would be incomplete without it."

"Oh dear," Laas said, and looked around her with fascination. She glanced up at the galleries on either side of the courtyard, where numerous fashionably dressed mrem were sitting and chattering to one another.

"You wouldn't want to sit up there," Reswen said. "It's all rich mrem, slumming; they don't want to mingle with us groundlings. They're going to sit up there and gossip all night about who's biting whose neck and whose clothes cost more. You can hear what's happening much better down here, believe me."

"And besides that," Laas said, "someone up there might recognize you."

Reswen smiled. "The odds are actually about the same down here as they are up there," he said. "But I have more on the mrem down here . . . so that if they do recognize me, they're more likely to keep their mouths shut."

Laas looked around her with renewed interest. "There are really criminals in here?"

"I'm standing next to one. Oof! I could have you arrested for that, you know."

"Go ahead. Brute. Oh look, here are the chairs—"

The name was more a courtesy than anything else; they were actually stools, and desperately well-worn ones, in Reswen's opinion long overdue to be fuel for someone's fire. The stools were made of hard woven reed, rather than wood, on the principle that it was harder to do someone serious damage with a reed-and-cane chair during a brawl than with a wooden one. Laas sat down on one; it creaked ominously. "Wonderful," she said, as a second server arrived with two wooden cups of wine.

Reswen sat down beside her and drank, surreptitiously watching her expression. Her eyes went wide. She lowered the cup and actually stared into it. "Oh come now," she said, "you said this was wine."

Reswen smiled gently. "That's what they call it," he said. "Rather a lot of water, though. Oh, they don't want their patrons getting too drunk. Disturbances start that way."

"I wonder that there aren't disturbances over the way the wine tastes!"

"Yes, there are," Reswen said a bit ruefully, having policed some of them in his time, "but mostly the groundlings avoid that problem by bringing their own. It's illegal, of course." There was a sudden burst of noise, of clapping and mrem shouting unlikely suggestions. "Look there," he said.

He pointed toward the back of the stage. Something could dimly be seen moving upwards through the roped-together beams of a somewhat rickety-looking tower. "What is it?" Laas said. "Looks like a pulley—they're hauling something up—"

"They're arming the thunder," Reswen said. "What? Don't you have stage thunder at your plays?"

She looked at him with cockeyed bemusement. "Usually we leave that to the gods."

"That's the Niauhu for you," said Reswen. "Wait for gods to send thunder during a play, and you'll be sitting and waiting for weeks. And who wants to wait for the rainy season to have plays? Not that we have much rain at the best of times."

Laas nodded at that, looking briefly thoughtful. Then a gong sounded: Tezhrue's Bell, in the old temple down the road from the Play House. The audience in the courtyard got louder, if anything, with more clapping and yowling and cups being thrown. A group of cheerfully drunken mrem in front of the stage began reciting, rather raggedly, and at the top of their lungs:

"Come all good Mrem who seek to hear a Tale
of citties in the West, for bliss or bale,
Of how the land of Ythun lost its weal,
for lack of anymrem who knew to steal;
And how a mrem by gold did set great store,
and how his ladie made him so no moare—"

Laas laughed softly. "They seem to know the play pretty well already," she said. "Why do they come then?"

"Because they know it well, I think," Reswen said. "I don't know. Why do people in the East go to the plays? Since they're religious, they must know the stories."

"They go because they have to," Laas said, with a wry look. "The 'donation' to the temple is required."

"And what if you don't go?"

"There's a fine." She looked resigned. "They get you one way or another, I'm afraid."

Reswen had his own thoughts about that kind of religion, but for the moment he kept them to himself. A lone mrem, impressively dressed in clothing of a hundred years before, stepped up onto the stage and began reciting the same prologue that the overeager groundlings had been. "Who's he?" said Laas.

"The Chorus."

"But there's only one of him."

Reswen shrugged and grinned. "You *did* want to see a comedy. . . ."

Laas eyed him with mild perplexity, then shrugged too and drank her wine, and listened. It had been a long time since Reswen had seen the *Claw:* probably one of the silliest plays in the Niauhu repertoire, full of sly village "idiots," ludicrously mercenary merchants, amorous serving-mrem, clever thieves, philandering ladies, a Hero-Thief who robbed "according to his conscience" (which changed hourly), wastrel lords gaming their livings away, crooked gamblers only too willing to help them do it, country bumpkins, drunks, fools, raunch-dancers, and a Chief of Police who Reswen was secretly delighted to find had been patterned on him, and who was portrayed as a buffoon in fancy clothes with an overfondness for the table and the couch.

He settled back to enjoy himself, and tried hard not to stare at Laas and wonder when she would start laughing. She started soon enough, around the time the two Village Idiots find the burden-beast and dress it up as the Lady of the Castle, intending to put it in the rich Lord's bed, "for sure he'll never know the difference," and their efforts to

get the two actors dressed as the uxan up into the second
level of the proscenium left her weak with laughter.
Reswen was no good for much of anything himself, for the
Police Chief had been on stage just before, lying in a
welter of splendid overindulgence on his couch, being fed
choice tidbits by fawning raunch-dancers, while pontificating about the Public Good—he was nervous that someone
might try to steal it, like other kinds of goods. . . . The
play itself was in the commonest kind of rhyme, but it was
fiercely topical, and had been rewritten, as usual (probably
that day), to include themes involving unwelcome visitors
with spears, and more welcome ones, with money that the
alert and honest citizens of a city might inveigle or steal,
and never get caught. Laas fell sideways onto Reswen,
snorting with laughter at something that looked dangerously like Hiriv wearing a cross between a priest's robes
and an uxan-harness with bells all over it.

Reswen put an arm around her, purely to keep her
from falling down and being trampled by one of the wine-
servers, and glanced up, then down again, quickly. He
had had a flash-image of someone in the galleries: a large
mrem, burly, brown-striped, cream front and paws—

He put his head down beside Laas's. "It is funny, isn't
it?" he said, having to raise his voice a bit over the happy
yowls all around them, as the She-Thief made her overly
sultry entrance. "Laas, we have company."

She was still gasping with laughter, but she managed
to get it under control, or at least reduce it to shaking
shoulders and a grin. "What? Who?"

"Someone in the galleries. I'm not sure who it is, or
who he works for, but I don't think he means us well. We
have to get out of here when the act is over, and lose
him."

She kept laughing, more for effect than anything else,
Reswen suspected. "All right. How long do we have?"

"About another twenty minutes."

"I'll manage to enjoy myself somehow," she said, turned
her attention back to the stage, and went off into more
peals of laughter at the She-Thief's attempts to pretend to
be a courtesan.

Reswen had a little more trouble relaxing, but another

glance upward, stolen during the general hysteria atten-
dant on the line "You mean she's *not* your sister?" showed
him the mrem leaning on a railing, scanning the crowd
with the air of someone who has not seen what they're
looking for. *He might not have seen us,* Reswen thought,
*but I don't want to take the chance. Who knows whom he
may have paid to do a little murder tonight*— It was
annoying; Reswen's chances of finding a constable to follow the man home seemed slight, at least combined with
the problem of needing to get out of the Play House
without being seen.

He breathed out, then; there was nothing to be done
about it. He would just have to trust Krruth and his
people to be on the mrem's trail already. Meanwhile,
there was at least the happy sight of Laas enjoying herself,
laughing so hard the tears were rolling down her face.
Reswen smiled a bit at the sight, then heard someone say,
"But you dropped your—," and looking up, lost himself in
the action as someone dropped an uxan out of the second
level onto a bag of gold and the Priest bent over to
pick it up. *I don't remember* that *being in there,* he
thought, wiping his own tears of laughter away a few
moments later.

And then the Chorus came out, and the groundlings
started to get restless at the prospect of getting out to the
tavern across the street during intermission, for some better drink than they had been getting, and Reswen glanced
up and saw the mrem in the gallery watching the crowd
with great care. "Here we go," he said, not bending his
head down, for fear it might attract attention when everyone else was looking up. "You ready?"

"Yes."

The Chorus spoke his last words. The crowd got up
before they were done, and there was the usual rough-and-
tumble rush for the gates out to the street. Reswen and
Laas ducked low and let it take them, Reswen being
careful to keep the tallest people he could between them
and the keen-eyed figure in the gallery. He dared not look
up again to see whether they had been seen or not, but
once out the barrier, he put an arm around Laas and
hustled her off to one side of the Play House and down a

small, ill-lit street on which the back of the original tavern gave.

Laas was still laughing; Reswen joined her, and they made something of a play of being drunk together, swaggering down the little street, swaying, half-supporting one another. " 'You mean she's not your sister—'!" Laas gasped, and laughed again.

Reswen chuckled, and in the spirit of the thing, began to sing the song about the mrem with the crooked tail, and what the gods left him in his watering-trough. The choruses were simple enough that Laas was able to join in after the first one, and together they staggered out of the alley behind the tavern and back up toward the high town, the exclusive district where Haven and the various embassies lay.

After several blocks Reswen thought it was safe to stop staggering, and besides, he was running out of verses for the song. He guided Laas over to a sheltered spot, a wall of someone's garden, and they paused there to get their breath back.

"Oh, oh my," Laas said, leaning against the wall. "I never saw anything like that. You mrem are mad. How often do you do that?"

"Every night."

"Oh, surely not!"

"Sometimes twice a day, on market days and feasts when people come in from the townlands."

Laas was speechless for a moment. Then she said, "How do they manage it, the actors? Where do they get the energy?"

"From the other mrem appreciating them, I suppose. You can do a lot if you're appreciated."

She looked at him quietly. "They don't, much, do they?"

"Don't what? Appreciate me?" Reswen shrugged his tail. They stepped away from the wall and began to walk down the quiet street, into a neighborhood where lamps hung from the trees again and not everything smelt of sweat and spilt beer. "I'm the establishment, after all," he said. "Enemy to many of them who feel that the only way to succeed is to cheat. I'm the one who catches them . . .

the symbol of all the people who stand in their way. No reason I should be popular."

Laas nodded reflectively as they went. After a moment she looked up. "Now what?" she said.

Reswen looked at her. "I was going to show you something," he said. "Come on."

It was a longish walk, but a peaceful one, and pleasant this time of night. The moons were up again, and their light slipped silverly onto the paving through trees and past the surrounding buildings. More moonlight began to fall on the paving, after a bit, as they started to climb, and buildings got less in the way, being fewer. The city had only one hill; it was mostly left as parkland, with some few prey-beasts in it, living reminders of the earlier days of Niauhu history, when anymrem might have needed to catch one with his own claws rather than let the paid hunters do it for him, rather than buy it in the market. Reswen pointed and showed Laas, as they climbed, the old places where the wall had been built out, and built out again, as the city grew too large for it: a set of lopsided circles, one offset this way, one that, and scattered within the circles, lamplight, torches, here and there a single burning oil-soaked reed in a window in its little iron holder—a scatter of mellow lights, as if stars tired from too much rising and setting had come to rest.

Before them the hill bulked black, and on top of it, something rose up that refused the moonlight and lay under it obstinately darker than the night overhead. "No one comes here any more," Reswen said, "at least I don't think so. Tourists, perhaps, in the daytime. Not that we have that many tourists. But I thought I would show the one that I have with me what the best thing in the city is."

"Not the Green Square?"

Reswen laughed softly. "Much better than that." They walked up a path so rough it wasn't even paved, merely a scatter of gravel winding around the top of the hill. "I used to come here a lot," Reswen said, "when I first got to Niau and was trying to understand this place. . . . Sometimes I got in trouble with my superiors for being late on post . . . when I had been here and had forgotten the time."

Laas looked up at the darkness in silence. "I saw this

from a long way off," she said, "as we were coming in. I
wondered what it was, but no one could tell me. And from
the city, I kept forgetting to ask people—this can't be seen
from most places."

"Yes," Reswen said softly. "That's a problem." They
turned the last curve on the path. The building stood up
before them, huge, dark, ruinous. Where a door or gate
had once been, now there was an empty maw of somewhat
paler darkness. "Watch your footing," Reswen said. "There
are loose stones."

They went in. There were crumbling steps leading up
onto the walls of the place. It was a fort of some sort, very
old, long abandoned. Grass and bushes grew in the middle
of it. Some small creature of the night lairing there squeaked
at the sight of them, a disgruntled sound, finally settled
down to muttering, then to silence. Reswen led Laas over
to one side, toward one of the flights of steps. Together,
carefully, they made their way up. The silence was total,
except for the occasional clatter of a dislodged pebble
falling down the steps, or into the shattered, overgrown
courtyard. Finally they came up to the wall, and started to
walk around it—and Laas froze, seeing someone standing
on the old battlement before them, someone with an arm
raised—no, a sword raised—poised, dangerous, still—

Reswen patted her arm. "Yes," he said, "she looks that
way, sometimes. Come on."

They walked toward the waiting figure. She did not
move. A she-mrem in middle years, she was a little thick
about the middle, nothing special as regarded muscles or
grace, but there was a danger about her that no amount of
mere physical training or prowess could have given her.
Reswen stopped a few yards from her, leaning against the
waist-high battlement.

"It was the original fort," he said. "When they built the
first city, they abandoned it, left it outside the walls. Now
it's inside again. But this was the first Niau. And Sorimoh
there," he gestured with his head, "she saved it. She died,
of course. But here she stands."

Laas leaned beside him. "Tell me."

Reswen gazed at the statue reflectively. "She was one
of the first settlers who came from down North, wanting a

place to live that was a little less safe than the kind of place that the housecats lived in, up there." A smile in the darkness. "Nothing special: she was a weaver, with a few kits. They grew up down here—it was nothing but grassland then—they grew wild, as kits will. Everyone grew wild down here, until someone suggested that they should build a city of their own. There was argument among the people who had made the trip. But she said"— he nodded at the statue—"that there was no reason we couldn't live in a city and be hunters too. 'Others can forget,' she said. 'But some of us can remember. They, and I, will remind you.' "

Reswen shifted position a little. He saw the moons glance cold fire in Laas's eyes as she shifted to watch him. "So they built this place. They had to drag the stones a long way, from the south. Word of it got around, I suppose; word always gets around." He breathed out. "The liskash, the lizards, came to raid the place. That's how long ago this was. There weren't many of them, but there didn't have to be, since they were sorcerers. One of them was greater than the rest. He threatened to throw the fort down stone by stone and kill everyone in it unless they left it to the lizards for their own." A breath of laughter. "They would all have been killed, they knew that. A lot of the settlers were tired and afraid, and wanted to do what the lizards said. But Sorimoh there, she told them to buy time, to bargain. She still knew how to hunt, she said, and how to hunt for her kits. And she stole out by night, and she went into their camp, at the cold time before dawn, when they were slowest, and she killed them one after another, with their own swords, and when the chief of their sorcerers woke up, the one who was protected against any wound any sword or spear or knife might give, Sorimoh went for him and tore his throat out. He killed her too, of course," Reswen said softly. "How not, with those claws they had? But it did him no good. Not one of those lizards ever went home again to tell the tale. And it used to be said that that was why they never came back— that they had a legend after that about how this part of the world is protected by demons, and will never fall to their kind."

Laas nodded, said nothing.

"So here she is, where they put her, a long time afterwards," Reswen said, "with one of the lizards' swords; see how big it is? No one of our people could manage such a thing normally, with that strange grip. But Sorimoh could manage anything she said. And what she had said was, 'I will take care of my own.' And so she did."

He hunkered down on his forearms next to Laas. "I would come here," he said, after a while, "and be with her, and I would say to myself, 'Here is the heart of it all. Here is what being a mrem is all about.'" He felt Laas's soft breath near his ear. "Silly, I suppose. But she is the best thing in the city."

He looked at her for a little while, and then out at the city, under the moonlight, with all its mellow, fallen stars, and then he held quite still, as something touched him.

Very gently, Laas began to wash his ear.

He did not move. He held quite still, feeling the warmth move about his head, and after some time he shut his eyes and bent his head sideways and simply sank into the warmth, the sweet touch, and the way his own warmth began to answer it. All the night held its breath. There was nothing but the gentle stroking and the warmth of her breath and the subtle scent of her, nothing else at all.

Finally he said, "Shall we go home?"

Her purr in his ear was his answer.

How long the walk home took, he never knew. He had never cared less whether he had left his clothes all over the furniture, what state the couch was in, that there was no fire in the grate. They lit no lamp. The moons' light came in the windows and lay warm on the floor; that was enough. The warmth built in him was heat, was blood; he felt fur between his teeth, he clutched with claws, was fought, was welcomed, both at once. Ferocity and desire, mingled, rose up and clutched at him in turn, pulling him down to the couch. She offered herself to him and he took what was offered as it was offered, roughly, needing it now, taking it now, abrupt, hungry, as she was abrupt and hungry. They rolled, they fought; claws were bared, claws drew blood. And then there was her cry, and his, again and again; and then the panting, the rush of breath, the sinking down, both spent.

Later there was time for gentleness; later her tongue touched him everywhere, and his did the same for her. Later they slept tangled, later they woke again to wash, and love, and love, and wash again, and sleep. But even in dreams, there were claws, sometimes unsheathed, sometimes hidden.

Reswen awoke from one such dream to feel the claw digging into him, hard, just above his heart. He felt of his chest and found something there, something on a cord, smelling vaguely like fish.

He tore it off his neck and threw it across the room, into the cold grate, and went back to sleep in Laas's arms.

▲

Chapter 10

▲————————————————————————▲

Laas slept late. For Reswen, it was impossible; he woke with the sun, as always, and lay there blinking, rather astonished that there was someone else in his couch and he was at the same time so calm about it. Normally Reswen liked to be more in control of a situation than he had been last night; now he lay there curled around her, gazing about him at the morning light on everything—the clothing dropped or laid neatly over furniture, the paperwork that he had brought home with him last week and which now lay on the floor in the corner, gathering dust and looking at him accusingly—and wondered how he had gotten himself into this, and discovered to his astonishment that he had no desire to get himself out of it.

Very quietly he extricated himself, got up, got dressed in his ordinary uniform kit, and picked up a note tablet from a dusty table. *This place is a mess,* he thought regretfully, as on the tablet he scratched in the dusty wax, *Stay. Back shortly.* He left it on the low table by the couch, and paused there to look down at her as she slept. Laas lay curled like a kitten, her mouth a bit open, breathing softly, a sound that rested on the borderline of a snore but never quite became one. *I wonder if I snore?* Reswen thought. It had never occurred to him before to wonder if he did, or to care what anyone else would think of it.

He glanced briefly at the shriveled-looking little fish-smelling thing lying in the grate, its thong trailing half out onto the floor.

Reswen left it there. He went out, locking the door behind him, and walked sedately to Constables' House, heading up to his office. Krruth was waiting for him there, looking rather disturbed; he jumped up from a seat as Reswen came in.

"We have your mrem," he said, and held out a sheaf of papers.

"I thought so," Reswen said, leaning over his desk and rummaging through some other parchments as he looked for a note he had made for himself. "I saw him last night; he looked nervous. Where is he now?"

"Goldsmiths' Street, in the Whites," Krruth said. "That's where his rented lodging is. His name is Choikea; he's a traveler, a merchant's agent, supposedly, from the Western cities . . . the last one he was in was Raihok, according to his papers. He's been here about two months on this trip. That's all we've had time to find out so far."

Reswen found the piece of parchment he was looking for, scribbled on it, and folded it up. "All right," he said, "get on him. Be cautious. What kind of place is he staying in?"

"A house, rented. He paid cash up front for four months' rental. In that neighborhood, that's quite a bit."

"Find out how he paid it," Reswen said. "I want to know where his money comes from. I want to know everyone he talks to, everyone he sees." He waved in a runner who was peering in the door, handed the mrem the scrap of parchment, shooed him out. "How is Thailh doing?"

"He's at the drapers' again."

"When our friend Choikea is out of his place," Reswen said, "bribe the landlord or the housekeeper or whoever and get in there. I want it searched, but have the lads and lasses keep their claws in when they do it. I don't want them to leave any sign we've been there. Make sure Thailh is with them."

"Yes, sir," Krruth said.

"One more thing. Anything from Haven?"

Krruth shrugged. "Nothing but the continuing adventures of Deshahl."

Reswen grinned a little. "Getting bored with her, are you?"

"Bored isn't exactly the word, sir. . . ."

"Ah," Reswen said, "we're losing staff through exhaustion, eh? They can't keep up with her? Or rather, with the effect she has on them. . . ."

Krruth looked a little nettled. "They're doing the best they can, sir."

"Better than they need to, I suspect. Take her off the watch list, Krruth; I'm convinced she's a waste of our time."

Reswen thought Krruth looked faintly relieved at that. "As you say, sir. But begging your pardon—who do you think *isn't* a waste?"

I don't have to tell him, Reswen thought, and then breathed out a little. There was no point in playing the great mrem detective with his senior staff. "Old jingle-bells Hiriv, for one," he said, "and master Rirhath, our closemouthed merchant prince. I only have hints as to the whys, though. I'm working on it all; I'll let you know as soon as things start to fit together closely enough to hold an accusation."

"And the lady Laas . . . ?"

Reswen looked sidelong at Krruth, then smiled slightly. "The lady Laas is assisting the police with their inquiries," he said.

Krruth's face didn't move, not by a whisker, and Reswen had to admire his restraint. *Gods, with control like that, the mrem ought to be promoted. Except that the only place to promote him to would be* my *job.* "I'm taking today off," Reswen said, "and possibly tomorrow. You and Sithen can handle the office between you, yes? Or is Haven keeping you too busy?"

"Indeed not," Krruth said. "They're having parties every night, but the staff have their ears open as usual. They'll send for me if anything of interest comes up."

"Very well, then. See you tomorrow, or the next day, it might be."

"If we need to reach you—"

"*Don't*," Reswen said, waved, and hurried out the door. He could feel Krruth staring after him.

He didn't care.

▲

Lorin sat in his house, bent over the books, muttering

to himself. He had always had difficulty with books; that was another reason why he had never made more than an indifferent wizard. There was nothing wrong with his scholarship—in fact, he was better with languages than most—but his eyes hurt him when he tried to read in any light but daylight. And he was not about to take *these* books out in the street and read them—indeed not.

He groped sideways for the damp cloth that he had been using to wipe his tearing eyes, dabbed at them, tossed it aside again. The paraphernalia of his bookmaking business had been pushed off to one side of his rough table, and a heap of books lay atop the ledgers and the little piles of cash money wrapped in notes that told for whom they were intended. The books were for the most part not as old-looking as wizards' books were usually thought to be. That was protective coloration, and a very purposeful thing. People tended to suspect ancient tomes at first sight, or at least to be interested in them. But books in a modern hand, that looked like accounting ledgers—no one cared particularly about those, especially when they were labeled as accounts for the past ten years, and the first ten or fifteen pages of them seemed to bear out the labeling. It was a wizard's business, Lorin's father had told him, to copy out all the reference works that had been left to him, and destroy the old ones. Lorin and his sore eyes had rebelled at this, but Lorin's father had not been interested in the complaints, and Lorin's ears had ached from much cuffing when he started the long business of copying his father's books.

Later he had begun to wonder whether the "protective coloration" explanation was all of the story, for copying the spells and stories and legends out was certainly a good way to learn them. His father had not had that many books, but Lorin had begun to pester him for more books to copy after the first ones were done, and as discreetly as possible, his father had gotten him more.

That was what had gotten him and Lorin's mother executed, at last, in that other city a long way from here. Lorin's first reaction had been to decide to burn the books, all of them. But then he realized that that would have made everything his father had gone through count for nothing. So he had loaded up the books, taken them elsewhere, finished the copying, and burned the last ones that had not been in his own hand.

Lorin suppressed the old inward gripe of pain that the memory still brought him, and went on turning pages. Nowadays these books had a slightly different form of protective coloration: Lorin's handwriting, which was almost illegible even to him. He squinted at a paragraph in which he had paused to doodle in the margins: There was a picture of a mrem with a long tail, badly out of proportion and definitely female. *Who was I thinking of?* he wondered, and scratched idly at the parchment as he tried to read what it said. *Hmm. "An infallible cure for Themm that hath a suppuration of the fur, or Mange—"*

He swore softly to himself—there were more spells in this book purporting to cure the mange than there were for anything else. And everything was all jumbled together out of order: tales of the older days, legends, and (supposed) natural history about the animals of the world; old stories, in which the usages of magic were rooted; the actual spells which grew out of the stories (or the actual events of which the stories were age-corrupted remnants); chants, discussions on the theory of magic, discussions of the discussions, commentaries, jokes, the occasional piece of poetry. It made fascinating browsing. It also made it impossible to find anything quickly. Lorin's father had often said that "one of these days" he was going to do all his copying over and this time add an index and cross-referencing, but all Lorin's father's days had abruptly come to an end on the walls of that other city, and Lorin had never had the heart, or the time, to do the job himself. Now, as usual, he was wishing that he had.

He went past two more mange cures, muttering. He was not satisfied with his results for Reswen on the stone-and-water front. He kept having a nagging feeling that there was something about the business that he was missing. And worse, there was the matter of that brooding presence that he had sensed in dream and soulwalk: that slow, cruel, subtle presence that had been eyeing the city with increasing bloodlust. The sense of it had broken into his dreams twice more recently, and there was no sense that it was even aware of him at that point. That meant that it was somehow exercising its power. But the kind of power that would indicate meant a wizard of great talent, far greater than any wizard Lorin had ever heard of— certainly far greater than himself. And far greater than the Eastern priest, if he even was a magic-worker—for he had shown no sign of it when Lorin had looked him over. That, though, by itself, was not diagnostic. So either there was another wizard—or there was something else. Lorin was looking for the "something else," having had (as with the stone and water) a feeling that he had missed something in his hurry the first time around.

He turned more pages, skipping past a dissertation on the teeth of the akoos and the uses to which a wizard could put them. Lorin clucked his tongue in annoyance; he had no time for love potions. There was too much of that kind of thing going around at the moment anyway, without potions even being involved. Those two at the police house—Lorin shuddered a little, wondering whether Reswen knew what he was getting himself into, having anything to do with one of *those* at all. A charismatic in a bad temper could drive a mrem to his death without even trying, and their tempers, supposedly, were variable and unpredictable things. No, indeed, Reswen would be well away from the situation, but he seemed to be getting deeper into it instead. Lorin simply hoped that he wouldn't get his paws burnt off.

Lorin turned another page and sighed. It was tiring work, this, and he was getting hungry, and he had no guarantees that he was getting closer to anything. Copying these books out had *not* given him immediate memories of where everything was. There was a chapter on sympathetic magic that he was hunting that could have been in any one of fourteen different volumes. This was the sixth. *Of the purported History of the Old Goddes of the East*, said the paragraph on which his eyes fixed. Lorin grunted with vague disgust. *Eastern gods,* he thought, *filthy things can't keep their hands off each other, always rutting around—*

He turned several more pages, stopping once or twice to indulge his disgust: The stuff really was pornographic, and it rather astonished him that anyone seriously worshiped gods who did anything like *that*. Then again, heaven only knew whether they did, any more. This might all be ancient history, for all he knew. There might have been war in heaven, and all the old Eastern gods might have been replaced by a cleaner-living bunch who married out of their families occasionally and let the resulting children live past the age of reason, whatever that was for gods.

Disgusting, Lorin thought, turning over another page, past several chants intended to draw game closer. *Wonder if these even work—*

Of the great Terorr caused by Them that worke Wizardryes from the distance,

said a paragraph halfway down the page. Lorin glanced at it, started to turn the page, then on a whim stopped, and looked at it more closely, scanning down it.

—yet truly it be said that no wizard nor Worker of magic may work to death or other great effect from any distance greater than one thousand times theyr Bodie's length, and it takyth great Power and Puissancie to overpass this Limitt: yet such hath been done, it is said, though not since the ancient times when ye Devills from beyond Desert came often to plague the Mremm of the Common Lands, and walked about the Lands and threw down all who opposed them with their subtile Sorceryes, and with Fires: yet this is long Ago, as the Tale telleth, and whether there be truth in the Telling, it bee not now known. It is said that the Devills, that bee also called Lishkesh in the tales, did go gretely and easily about in the Next World and wreak mickle spells upon them that suspected them not, being in Dreme or otherwise Unsuspecking: and they might Dwell in folke's Minds in their Dremes, and turn them to theyr Will, and cause them to do Evil: so that Mremm who were under the Glamour of the Devills did betray their towns and cities, and other Mremm who were Slaves and Servitors unto the Lizardes did take those towns, and enslave those withyn them, or kill all they did

finde and take all things for their own. And Mremm
who knew Magic said, Surely these Lizardes need not
be soe Close as our wisdom hath heretofore tell'd us,
but are yet far away, and by theyr great and Wicked
Sorceryes do do theyr will uponn us, to our woe. And it
was thought that there was no defence against their
Wreaking, so that Mremm speered there was neither
hope nor help for them, and many a Prowd city fell to
the Devills that were Lizardes to beholde, and great
and fell. . . . Yet on a time did a Wizard come uponn
one of the Lishkesh at its Sorceries, when his City
was besieged by Mremm of the East: and all thought
that the City was lost, for great Magics were done by
day and night, and yet it could not be so, for these
Mremm had not the Power to do such works: and all
said, It is the Devills, that doe kill us so. Yet that
could not be so, for no Liskesh were with the Armie,
and all that kind of Devill were far away. And Night
and Day mremm in that City did die. But this Wizard
by chance did one night putt Wardes about his bed,
to keep off the dremes that had troubled him: and
that night there were none that died. And the Wizard
did come to know that the Devill did Use him, and
therefore he Layd a trap for the Lishkesh, and it
Came to possess him, and he Gripped it to him with
magic, and together they died in soul: and that war
went awry, and the Mremm that did besiege his city
fell away thereat and were beaten off with great Slaugh-
ter. And when that Wizard's friends did seek him,
the body of that Wizard was founde empty of him,
and lived a while without his soule within, and right
so died. And Where the Devill's body was, none did
know. . . .

Lorin sat very still.
This is crazy.
But there was no arguing what he had felt. Something
slow, and cruel. Something different. Not mrem—not mrem
at all, *never* mrem, from the very beginning of his sensing
of it. It was only his refusal to consider any other possibility that had been blinding him until now.

But there are no more liskash. They died out hundreds of years ago.

Didn't they? . . .

All his common sense rose up in him to take that position. Of course they had. If there were still lizards, surely they would still be overrunning the world, as they had been all those years ago. But the mrem had been victorious over them, at the end of the great wars of which the legends all spoke, and the last lizards had been exterminated off the face of the world. Their bones whitened the deserts for miles, the stories said.

But those are stories.

What's in your dreams, then? Are those stories?

Something slow and cruel and subtle. Something hot. Something with an odd smell. Metallic. Something that smells like claws. Like dry skin. Like fire.

Lorin shuddered all over. This was worse than any mere mremmish wizard, if it was true. And it would explain why sometimes he felt magic-workers around, and sometimes didn't. If there was a liskash somewhere about, and it was controlling mrem in the area, then sometimes the magic would be obvious . . . and sometimes there would seem to be nothing there at all.

Which was exactly what had been happening.

Oh, this is worse than anything I could have thought up. Reswen is going to pull his fur out—if he even believes me—

And how can he? Everyone knows there are no such things as liskash any more—

. . . except me . . .

Yet if liskash *were* involved somehow, then perhaps there was some hope of finding out what was going on around here . . . for the sorcery in question would not be merely an Eastern one, as Lorin had thought. Some little was known about the sorceries of the liskash—or rather, some little was reported of their styles of sorcery, in the records of the old wars that had been fought against the "Devills" in the ancient times.

Hurriedly he grabbed for a piece of parchment, found none, picked up one of the piles of money, shook the cash out of it, stuck the parchment into the book at that spot, tossed it aside, and went burrowing among the boxes for another. *I know it's here somewhere, I saw it before. . . .* Dust clouds rose up; Lorin sneezed heartily, getting excited. For the moment, the excitement was drowning out the fear. Now he knew what he was looking for. Later, when he stopped to think about it all, then he would start shaking in earnest.

But at least now he had a clue. . . .

▲

"This place," said the sleepy voice from the couch as he came in, "is a mess."

Reswen sighed and sat down on the couch, brushing Laas's whiskers gently. "I know," he said. "I was cherishing some sort of faint hope that you might clean it up while I was gone."

"Dream on," Laas said, laughing, and stretched long and lazily. "I'm a courtesan, not a servingmrem. And from the looks of the place," she said, sitting up on the couch, "you're not likely to keep yours long, if you keep leaving it like this."

"I don't have a servant," Reswen said.

Laas looked at him mildly. "Well," she said, "I guess I can believe that. Why not? Too many private papers laying around?" She glanced at the pile in the corner. "But anyone who wanted to read those would have to work their way through the dust first." She wrinkled her nose, then sneezed at the thought.

Reswen laughed softly. "I took the day off," he said. "There were just some things to check into first."

Laas sat up, then, and looked at him. It was a cool sort of look, a weighing, assessing expression, and Reswen found himself trying to understand it and failing. "What kind of things?"

"Business," he said. And then thought, *Gods, why shouldn't she know?* "You know about the Lloahairi ambassador?"

"The old one was killed the other night, wasn't she? Strangled. I heard it from a crier."

Reswen nodded. "I have reason to believe that the killing wasn't just another random murder," he said. "I believe the mrem we were avoiding last night has something to do with it."

"I didn't see him well," Laas said. "In fact, I didn't see him at all. Him? Her?"

"Him. His description matches information given me by the mrem who started the riot the other day. Nierod, that's the loud lad in the marketplace, said that this other mrem put him up to it. He was certainly well enough paid for it. I want to find out who was paying, and why. For that riot, and for the murders. This other mrem is someone's agent, I'm certain of it."

Laas shook her head, and then shivered a little. Reswen put an arm around her. "Are you cold?"

"No," she said, and looked thoughtful for a moment.

"Hungry?"

"No, no." The thoughtfulness was turning somber. "Reswen, I've been sheltered, I suppose. . . . I've seen enough nastiness, but rarely the kind that causes mrem to strangle each other. At least, it's never come near me before. . . ."

He looked at her quizzically. "Somehow it seems strange to hear a courtesan describing herself as 'sheltered.' "

She leaned back against his arm. "But we are," she said. "Cosseted, I suppose. Polished like a weapon . . . kept away from the wet and the paws of people who might smudge it. Used, then put away safe. . . ." She looked up at him. "But I've never been in a crowd of drunks, until last night. Well, richer drunks. But I've never almost been trampled, or had cheap wine like that, or heard people say what they really think about something to each other, and laugh. . . ."

"I bet you've never almost been killed in a riot, either."

"No," she said, thoughtful, "you have a point there. . . ."

He looked down into her face, and lost thought. Everything went away but the clear sense of the warmth building in him again. "This can wait," he said. "Can't it?"

Laas looked at him.

"Unless you don't want to," he said.

"I've rarely had anyone ask me that, either," she said. "They tend to assume that because *they* want to, I must want to as well."

"And so you said," Reswen said, " 'If only they wouldn't all react to me that way—' "

"I never said that," she said, looking shocked.

"You started to," Reswen said.

She was silent. "Are there times," Reswen said, "when you *can't* stop 'working' on someone?"

Laas said nothing.

Reswen put his other arm around her and simply held her for a moment, then let her go. "Are you hungry?" he said, getting up.

"I could eat something," she said softly.

"All right." He got busy with the grate. It was one of those that was split between the two main ground-floor rooms, the kitchen and the sleeping and entertaining room. Hooks were positioned in the chimney walls at various heights to hold pots and pans, and a large flat plate on a semicircular handle hung down from a long swinging hook to sizzle meats on. Some said the thing was descended from times when only rich mrem were allowed to eat meat, and the poor had to grill it in the fields, in secret, on plowshares, if they wanted it.

Reswen pulled out dried sods from the basket by the grate, and kindled a splinter form the fire pot to get them started. Lorin's charm he left conspicuously in among the sods, though later he was going to wish he had just buried it instead; it burnt with a fearful stink. He saw Laas react to the smell, turning to see the last flames run along the burning thong. She glanced at him, a look of concern on her face, another expression he couldn't understand. He ignored it, rummaging in cupboards and among sideboards in the kitchen for the one decent knife in the place.

"Reswen—"

The name made his fur stand up again. *Damn,* he thought, *but I'm beginning to like it. . . .*

"Something to drink?"

"Yes, please. Reswen, who gave you that?"

"A friend."

She looked a little nonplussed. "Then there are—I mean, we heard—"

"The official position," he said, "is that there are no magicians in this city. Magicians of whatever kind are evil,

perverse, and bent on our city's destruction and that of all
mremkind. If someone was found to be a magician, I
would be hard put to confine their execution to the spike.
There would certainly be a drawing and quartering, with
the victim shown his heart after it was cut out. You follow
me?"

"I'm afraid so," she said, and her laugh was a touch
shaky.

"So. The Chief of Police can hardly be seen to openly
employ a magic-worker. All the same, there have been
times when he's come in handy. . . ."

He found the knife, and went back to the meat safe at
the back of the house, a cool-box with an ornate bronze
screen portraying the creation of the uxan by the god of
herd-beasts. It was a ridiculous antique, overblown in
style and hard to keep clean; he wondered for the thou-
sandth time why he'd bought it, but he could not imagine
the kitchen without it any more. He pulled down the leg
of uxan he'd been hanging from its hook, and sniffed it. By
a miracle, it was perfect.

"It's just that I have a feeling," Laas said, "that you
might need him."

Reswen put the meat down on the chopping block and
began the usual argument with himself about how to cut it
up properly. "Tell me your thought, if you will," he said,
"and if you feel it's something you can tell me without
your honor giving you trouble."

She looked at him with a slightly confused expression
from the couch, then got up and strolled over to the other
side of the counter to watch him. Reswen caught his
breath at the sight of her moving, the grace, the way that
sweet body moved—then took a couple of more deep
breaths to try to get back to acting normally. "I have to
explain," she said. "It was really the grain that did it."

Reswen looked up, confused. "Did what?"

She breathed out, folded her arms on the counter, and
rested her weight on her elbows, watching him. "This
business with asking people to sabotage their grain crops,"
she said, and was silent a moment. "I grew up poor, did
you know that?"

Reswen shook his head.

"Very poor," she said. "My mother, five brothers, four sisters. Mother was a weaver . . . there was never enough food. If so much as a measure of grain came our way in an eightday, we counted the *kernels*, Reswen, we boiled the husks and made soup of the water. Meat . . ." She looked at the leg of uxan, which Reswen was attempting to dissect in something like the traditional manner. "We would have . . . I don't know *what* we would have done for meat. But it wasn't just us. There were a lot of poor people. To hear that one of the neighbors had starved to death was a common thing. You shrugged at it, it was too bad, but what could anyone do?" Laas breathed out angrily. "Sometimes rich people would come down to the poor parts of town and give us grain, 'of their charity' . . . it never tasted as good as what we bought ourselves, somehow, but my mother said, 'You take it, you take it and don't you ask.' And we would . . . but I remember one of these high-and-mighty people saying to another one, 'What's the use of this anyway? They breed like dunghill worms. The ones who survive will just kitten as fast as their sires and dams, and more of 'em will die. Why bother?' " Her voice cracked with rage and pain. "Did it ever occur to the pretty housecat that it wasn't *our* fault that we were there, that we didn't enjoy the fact that our bellies screamed at us at night so that we couldn't even lie still? That we didn't want to bother the rich people, that all we wanted was a chance to live and be happy, and not just lie down and die and be out of their way? . . ."

Reswen chopped meat and shook his head. "Fools," he said, "are in no shortage in the world. It would be nice to believe it's otherwise elsewhere."

Laas brooded a moment, then lifted her eyes to Reswen's, and the gold of them shocked him afresh, not with its beauty, but with its anger. "That's what this is, again," Laas said. "There are still hungry people, still poor. In our cities, and in yours. I see them in the street. I can smell it through the curtains of the litters, no matter how they're perfumed—that stink of hungry mrem. And here are people willing to burn their crops, lose them, for money. While there are mrem lying around their doorsteps who would crawl to the rich mrem's paws and weep on them for enough grain to keep their kits alive. And believe me, there are plenty of rich mrem don't care. Either they've never been without food for more than a half day in their lives . . . or else they have, and they don't care who else is, just as long as *they* aren't any more."

Reswen cut the meat and said nothing.

"I can't bear it any more," Laas said. "Intrigue is my meat and drink, but not starving people for gold, no indeed. I did my job . . . but I didn't like it, and I haven't done it as well as I could have, and if they don't like that—"

She broke off, her anger choking off her words for the moment. The fire snapped and sparked to itself under the broiling pan.

"Where does the magician come in?" Reswen said, severing the shinbone from the leg, and looking at it ruefully. The job was not exactly neat.

She glanced up at him again, the anger ebbing. "I'm not sure," she said. "Only, someone said something that I overheard—"

Reswen looked up, waited; when she mentioned no name, he nodded at her. "I can find out one way or another," he said. "Said what to you?"

"The discussion was about the shortages of grain that there would be here, if all the merchants shorted their crops," Laas said. "One mrem said, 'But if they change their minds about doing it, all this planning and paying we'll have been doing will be useless.' And—someone—said to me, 'They won't be able to change their minds; natural means won't make a difference to what will happen, and they don't believe in the other. And it's happening already.' "

"Where did this conversation happen?"

"In the back garden, in Haven."

Reswen swore softly; it was the one area of the place that could not be covered completely. "They had sent the servants away, I take it."

"Yes."

"Damn." This was for the meat, not the situation: Reswen was cutting steaks out of the upper leg, and one of them had cut poorly. "Well. What would they be doing that wasn't 'natural'— "

And the thought of the stone and water came back to him, and he froze.

"I wonder," he said.

"What?"

He looked at her speculatively. "You'll find out later," he said. "But tell me one thing. Has anyone mentioned anything to you about the 'blood and bones of the city' that was asked for?"

She looked at him blankly. "No."

It's happening already.

Oh gods, gods . . .

But the gods helped those who helped themselves. He finished his cutting, and thought. "I told them I was taking today off," he said. "Quite frankly, I wanted to lie around here and . . . well." He glanced up at Laas; her gaze rested on him for a few moments, unreadable, and then she slowly smiled.

"Maybe later . . . if you like. But today I'd like to go around the city and see about some things. Would you come with me? Maybe help me?"

Laas nodded. "If I can."

Reswen put aside two of the steaks, thought a moment, and sawed off another one. "I'll never make a butcher," he said. "No matter. Tell me the truth, first. Is this going to get you in trouble—that you're missing for a day without reporting?"

Laas cocked her head and thought. "I doubt it, really. They'll assume I'm doing what I was supposed to do: seducing you, finally. They may even be pleased—you were scheduled before the corn-factors."

Reswen smiled. "My wounded pride and I thank you. Then after we're done, we can amuse ourselves. I can get us into the Games tonight. Would you like that?"

"From what you've told me, I think so. All right."

"Well enough." He carried the meat out to the grate, swung the grill-plate out to load it up, then swung it back over the fire. "How do you like your meat?"

"A little rare."

Reswen pulled over a chair and sat down to keep an

eye on the meat, poking it occasionally with a two-pronged meat prod that hung by the fire. In the middle of turning over one of the steaks, he paused, and his heart began to hammer. Someone was breathing in his ear.

"You were really much better than the corn-factors," Laas whispered. "I'm sorry it took so long."

He glanced at her, sidewise, then shut his eyes as very softly she began washing him again.

Reswen burned breakfast.

▲

Early in the afternoon two mrem were seen strolling into the market: one veiled in the manner of a Winui she-mrem from the far west, head to hind toes, only the eyes showing; the other, her companion, a fine bold swaggering young bravo, black as night, in silken kilts and jacket and an eye patch, with a fine slim sword belted at his side. Together they ambled among the stalls, pointing at fine wares, pricing things, often buying. The Winui never spoke, only signed to her companion, as the she-mrem of that city do when traveling abroad. Her bravo was expansive with his gold, a cheerful, laughing sort, and she had only to point but he would buy something for her. The shopkeepers didn't even bother sending their apprentices around to beseech them to buy, for the couple had hired one of the market urchins to carry their goods for them, and it seemed likely that every stall in the place was going to sell them something sooner or later.

Therefore no one found it strange when the two happy buyers stopped a roving seller, one of the people who go about with trays or baskets rather than working from a stall, and asked what he sold, and on finding that it was scents, asked him to stop and show them what he had. The young scent-seller propped his tray on a broken half wall near one side of the market, and the three of them pored a long time over the scent jars, the she-mrem pointing at one, then another, and signing quickly with her fingers, while her companion asked questions about the ones she pointed at.

Naturally no one expected to hear speech coming from under that veil, Winui mrem being the way they were, so no one *did* hear it, or if they did, they attributed the murmurs they heard to the handsome young bravo. Which was just as well, considering what was being said. "You're sure about that, Shilai? This will be a life-or-death matter for some of our people."

"That's mangebane," Shilai said to the handsome young black. "More expensive than the hair-grow oil, but in my opinion it works better, sir." And then he whispered: "I'm sure, sir. He bought at least five bottles of the goldwater—you know, that liquor with the gold leaves floating in it?—and had them sent to the Lloahairi Embassy. I heard him say something about a party there tonight, after the Games, and another one tomorrow night, in honor of the new ambassador."

"Do you have anything for the itch?" said the young black, poking among the bottles on the tray with one claw. Very softly he added, "This dye is enough to make you want to climb out of your skin."

"You think *you're* suffering," Reswen whispered, "it's like a tent in here."

Reswen paused for a moment. "So," he said then, "our mystery mrem has made an appointment, and we know about it. This is good news. And the Games, indeed. Look, Shilai, get word to Krruth by your usual drop. Tell him to send the reports from the Lloahairi Embassy situation over to my house tonight, before the Games. I want to see what the inside crew has to say for themselves. And I want that mrem's house searched tonight, if it hasn't been already." He pointed at another bottle.

"Yes, sir. Oil of dayflower, madam, good for the aches and for open scratches. Smells good on a wood fire, as well, and the smoke drives away insects."

"You've really been studying this," Reswen said, impressed. "Good for you. We'll take a bottle of that, and—what is it with the mangebane this eightday?"

"I don't know, sir. It's still selling well."

Reswen chuckled a bit. "Keep this up, and you'll be a commander by the end of the moon," he whispered. "Or an auncient at least. Pay him, Laas."

Coin changed hands, and the two of them straightened

up and strolled away; behind them, the scent-seller picked
up his tray again and went off, crying his wares.

"So now we're on our own. What shall we do?" said
Reswen, very softly.

Laas scratched herself absently, then swore, a word
that Reswen hadn't thought a courtesan would know. "Home
to get this dye out of my fur. And then—"

There was a silence, as of a smile, from under the veil.

"Shall I burn lunch?" Reswen said.

▲

He held her. He held her. He could not let go of her.
It was an astonishing thing, how suddenly his body seemed
incomplete without her, without the touch of her, at arm's
length at least, and preferably much closer. If she left his
embrace, it was only temporary; that was the best part of
it. She would be back. Now teeth closed on the back of his
neck, and he lay there and loved it, the reversal of roles,
the surrender, the brief pain sweet with anticipation. He
knew the reversal wouldn't last. It hadn't lasted before.

Why was I so worried? he thought. *What was I afraid
of?*

The teeth let him go. "Ah, don't stop," he said.

"I have to, for a few moments anyway," she said, and
lay down beside him again, panting a bit. They had closed
all the blinds, and pulled all the coverlets and pillows off
the couch, and lolled in front of the low-burning fire like a
couple of kits just discovering the delights of rut. There
was wine, and some meat not quite so overdone as breakfast.

He stroked her side, from shoulder down to breasts,
reflective, astonished all over again at the softness of her
fur. He had always prided himself on his own fur's softness, but Laas's was so soft that you couldn't quite tell
when you started to feel it. "Tired?" he said.

"A little."

"Rest then," he said, and pulled her close, stroking
her. She lay against him, her head on his chest, and
purred.

"Why was I afraid?" he said.

"Of what?"

"You."

She lay silent for a moment. "Lack of control," she said. "At least, I suppose that's what it is. We see it a lot, when we're not using the talent. One day a mrem wants you . . . the next day, unless you're sure to use the talent on him, he's terrified of you. He doesn't know why he wanted you, he doesn't want you now . . . and he doesn't want to want you. So you must use the talent, again and again, on so many people. . . ." She opened her eyes; there was a weary look in them. "A curse," she said. "Sometimes it's a curse. I never wanted to frighten anymrem. I just wanted to live. . . ."

"How did you find out about it?" Reswen said. And then added, "Maybe I shouldn't ask."

"It's not a problem." She closed her eyes again, content to lie there and tell it in a faraway voice, as if it was a story. "I didn't know until I was ready to have kits. That first week the bleeding came . . . with it came the he-mrem. At the door, in the market . . . My mother was scandalized." Laas stretched a little. "None of them came offering marriage . . . they just wanted *me*. My mother beat me. She thought I was leading them on. But after a while it became clear to her that I had nothing to do with it . . . or rather, it was me, but nothing I was *doing*."

She sighed. "Then later it began slowly to change. If I worked hard at it, the he-mrem would only want to do what *I* wanted, though of course they wanted me physi- cally too . . . and the situation got a little easier to control. The worst offenders, I could tell them that what would make me happy would be for them to stay away. But sometimes it worked too well." Her eyes opened, grew cool. "One or two of them killed themselves for want of me, while I was youngest and the power was strong."

Reswen was still, and held her close.

"I grew into it with time," Laas said. "I began to get a sense of the ways that it could be controlled. . . . I had no choice; if I didn't control it, there was no peace for me. Then a minor lord of the city saw me in the street. He 'loved' me at first sight, of course. . . ." A slightly bitter laugh. "I had thought life was too complicated. . . . I'd never seen anything. Barely ready to kitten, and suddenly plunged into the intrigues of a court, and suddenly being the one that everyone wanted . . . everyone male, at least. While the jilted she-mrem plotted and schemed, and thought of ways to poison me. My control slipped again and again. I was still so young. . . . It was a bad time. Duels fought over me, and lovers killed, and me passed from paw to paw like a war prize. I had little money of my own then, and no way to control what was going on."

Reswen shuddered at the thought of it. "Didn't you ever think of running away?"

Laas laughed softly. "When half the lords of a court would think one of their rivals had stolen you, and thus insulted them? I didn't dare. I had seen the insult fall on the she-mrem in question once or twice, seen her staked out or spiked up, or taken down into the Undercastle in Cithiv city, where no one and nothing came out but cries, once someone had gone in. No indeed," she said. "I did all I could: I controlled it. I learned. I found a wizard—or rather, he found me—and he taught me something about how to handle myself. In return for favors at court, of course."

There was something about the way Laas said "favors" that made Reswen shudder. "I see," he said. "I think I see. But I don't see how a wizard prospered openly in a city, unless your people do things differently from ours."

"Oh no," Laas said. "He wasn't *openly* a wizard. But there are always things, you know, that the rich want done for them that aren't quite legal. But they find their ways . . . and Usiel was one of them. If you wanted someone to come to grief, in some way that couldn't be attributed to some specific person, you went to Usiel. He would manage it for you. Your enemy would die of a fever, or fall from some wall or balcony when no one else was near, and no one would think anything odd about it. Except those who knew . . . and a lot of mrem knew. Usiel had a lot of business in the court at Cithiv. And some of it got to be mine. He would want to get someone under his claw . . . so he would send me after them, and they would want me, and the price would be some little favor they could do for Usiel. He had long since taught me how to not be a playing-piece for the lords any more, how to turn them against one another and make them strive to grant me

favors." She said it with the utmost matter-of-factness, as
one might talk of making a bed or washing a dish. "I was a
fairly rich mrem, then, and I got richer . . . from their
gifts, from other gifts that various lords or ladies would pay
Usiel for his services."

Reswen thought of the gold-and-rose-colored knife and
said nothing for a moment. "Yes," he said finally, "I can
see where you would be something of a commodity, in a
place like a noble court."

Laas was still, and after a few moments, rolled away
from Reswen and lay on her stomach, her head pillowed
on her arms, gazing into the fire. "A commodity," she
said. "Yes."

"But you stopped doing it," Reswen said.

"No," Laas said, "I'm still doing it."

Reswen was quiet.

"But free-lance," she said. "I moved out of Cithiv to
Hazik and settled down there. There was no use trying not
to be what I was. I did the only thing I knew how . . . I
turned it to advantage. Finally various people in Hazik got
wind of my talent and approached me about this trip. I
took the opportunity. I've seen enough of the East. I
thought the West might be different."

He had to say it, no matter how the possible answer
frightened him. "And has it been?"

She rolled over on her back, stretched her arms above
her head, stretched that sleek and lovely body before him.
Reswen's mouth dried with desire. "Mrem are the same
here," she said in that cool voice that upset him so. "Your
Arpekh, the corn-factors, all gluttons, gorging themselves
on a dainty, never noticing that the dainty has a mind.
They are fools, and their folly may be the end of them. I
don't know. I can't bring myself to greatly care about
them."

And then she looked up at him. "You are the only
one," she said, slipping her arms around him, drawing
him down, "the only one not to look at me as a perquisite of
your office, as some kind of prize that you have a right to,
or some kind of business bribe that you expect and don't
give a second thought to. The only one."

Reswen had to hold off, despite the fact that the heat

was rising in him again, threatening to sweep him away. "I looked at you as a job," he said. "It's not much better."

"At least you saw someone there when you looked," Laas said, "instead of some*thing* . . . instead of a complimentary gift." She smiled at him, a small smile that gradually grew broad. " 'An honest interrogator.' You were never less than that, with me."

The heat rose, but he held. "I think," he said, "I think I'm falling in love with you. And you're not doing anything. Are you?"

She shook her head slowly; the smile faded, leaving something better behind it, a sweet somberness. "No," she said.

"It may be a stupid thing to do," he said. "Almost certainly."

She gazed at him. "Yes," she said.

Reswen buried his face in her fur.

"Let us be stupid together, then," Laas said.

He raised his head in astonishment. She looked at him silently . . . then bit his neck, made the heat rise out of bounds, made him take her.

I am lost, Reswen thought, as they moved together. *But at least I'm not afraid any more. . . .*

▲

That evening they went to the Games. It was all too rarely that Reswen had an excuse to take a night off and indulge himself; he was wallowing in the delight of it. *I'm wallowing in everything,* he said to himself as they walked over to the Hills, the high ground just inside the main city wall where the Enclosure lay. *And I don't want it to stop. . . .*

Before the Games had developed, the place had been the site of the rudest kinds of entertainments—the baiting of wild beasts, predators like kofomo and tarleth that made the grainlands unsafe for mrem and uxen alike. There had been gladiatorial combats, too, until such things went out of style as being barbaric, neither aesthetically pleasant nor a preparation for war and combat, as some of its proponents claimed. What had supplanted the beast-baiting and the gladiators was something that combined elements

of both of them: the hunt, confined in a small area where
mrem could watch; a warrior, pitted against the beasts,
who could not leave the Enclosure without winning; and
the dance. Perhaps that obsession with movement and
grace had come a little later to the martial-minded Niauhu
of earlier times than it had come to mrem elsewhere, but
when it arrived, it did so with a vengeance. The Games
became the primary obsession of the city for days, months
at a time.

They waited outside the gates of the Enclosure with
the rest of the crowd. It was a rowdy gathering, drinking
having already begun in earnest. Wine-sellers and beer-
sellers and mrem carrying sacks of stronger spirits were
going among the crowd, each with his single cup from
which a drinker would swig if he hadn't brought his own.
Sanitation was rather left to the gods in these cases: the
better wine-sellers had a cloth to wipe the cups with
afterwards, but Reswen saw one simply picking up the end
of his tail and using that. He rolled his eyes a bit. Laas
laughed.

"And I thought the other crowd, at the Play House,
was rough," she said softly, watching a brawl start a ways
across the crowd. "Half these mrem look like they want to
be in a fight . . . the other half look like they want to bet
on it." For betting had indeed started on the fringes of the
crowd, mrem circling in for a better view, exchanging
odds and small money on the two mrem who were scrap-
ping. The fight had not yet got to claws-out; the two were
only boxing, but Reswen saw two of the constables rou-
tinely assigned to gate work at the Games watching the
situation closely. Claws-out fighting, or fighting with weapons, was theoretically forbidden in the city streets, but
false arrest was also a problem, and Reswen had more than
once cautioned his people to be careful about how they
broke up fights.

Then suddenly blood flowed, and the constables moved
in, and so did the crowd, yelling at the sight, changing the
odds, passing more money back and forth. Reswen was
grimly amused to hear odds being laid on his constables,
and better ones than on the two who had originally started
the fight. But abruptly the gong went off that signified the

opening of the gates, and the mob dissolved away as quickly as it had appeared, except for the two mrem who had started the fight. Reswen turned from his place in the ticket line to see that the constables were already taking them away, ignored by the rest of the crowd, many of whom were hurrying in past the gate-guards in the usual rush for the cheapest viewing areas. Others, able to afford better, headed in more slowly.

Laas looked around her with interest as they got their tickets and went in. "Do we have to ask for chairs this time?" she said as they went up the stairs to the first level.

"No, they come with, for once," Reswen said. They came out on the landing. The place was a short oval, with tiered seats close to the "field" at the bottom, and fences between the seats and the much larger standing areas behind them. "Standing" was filling up rapidly, as usual; the seats tended to take their time, since they were expensive enough to be mostly affordable by the slumming wealthy, or by middle-class mrem who didn't care to mix much with the brawling unders "up among the gods."

They seated themselves in one of the better areas, along the wide side of the oval. "Not quite the best," Reswen said, a bit apologetically, "but then I can't afford those." He indicated the boxes at the ends of the oval, large cordoned-off areas that contained actual chairs rather than benches, and tables on which food and wine were being laid out in preparation for the arrival of guests.

"Is that where you think the Lloahairi will be?" Laas said quietly.

"More than likely. Those boxes are mostly the Arpekh's, and some of the richer families. They've probably lent them out to our friends." Reswen grinned a little. "A 'business bribe,' as you say."

Laas glanced at him, bemused. "If this—sport—is as plebeian a thing as you make it sound, I wonder that such people have seats here at all."

Reswen smiled. "A consortium of them owns the place," he said, "and they also own some of the better players' contracts. Oveuw, for example, and Aele. They like to see that their investment is making money as it should. And believe me, this place makes money. Some of the worst corruption in the city has centered around it, at one time or another. Mostly before my time, of course, but every now and then some merchant lord gets it into his head to fix a Game, or to try to get control of someone else's interest by way of blackmail or some such. Very nasty."

Laas nodded. "Yes, I would expect that. Gold always draws such, sooner or later. . . ."

"But as for plebeian," Reswen said, "it's nothing of the kind. Some of the original players were noble. But that alone has nothing to do with its nobility. This isn't just a game; it's an art in itself. It's a matter of great strategy and skill, of nicety in judgment. One must kill the beast, but one must also dance it. And the beast doesn't care about the dance, of course. That's one of the things that makes it a beast. The player must mind his weapons, and not kill too soon, or too late, or too brutally, or with too much ease; he's not a butcher, or a torturer. The beast has its own priorities, its own tactics and graces, that have to be respected and properly exhibited before it dies. Otherwise the marks are bad."

Reswen looked across the oval. "See there, the judges are here already." Six or seven of them were seated behind their long table; several others were conferring off to one side, holding open parchments, rolled ones tucked under their arms. "They have to make sure that the players are properly matched to the available beasts," Reswen said. "If a beast hasn't been sufficiently evaluated, it's not played at all—"

" 'Evaluated'?"

"Oh yes, they test them carefully for skill and strength and ferocity and so forth," Reswen said. "There's a whole list of qualities, and a point system for rating them. Apprentice players dance the beasts in rehearsal time, during the day, so that the judges who manage evaluations can see how they perform. Those dances aren't to the death, naturally. Except sometimes for the apprentices . . . but it's rare that we lose one. They've gotten very clever with padding and armor and so forth for the players who haven't had sufficient experience in the Enclosure."

Laas looked at him with mild amusement. "I see," she said, "that I have made the mistake of going to see a sport with an enthusiast. I knew I should have let you be; you looked like trouble from the start, but orders were orders—"

"Hush, my kitten. I'm pontificating."

"You certainly are. Get me some of that cheap wine, please. I have a feeling I'm going to need it."

"Certainly.—Over here, youngster! A wine for the lady, and one for me. And a clean cup. —But there's a reason for all this. You couldn't put, say, Aele, up against some poor nosuk that when turned into the Enclosure would try to run back down the tunnel, or dig a hole and hide in it. You want one fearless and wily, as they properly are in the wild, one that knows to some extent what it's up against, and can deal with it. An educated beast, if you like. Then when Aele comes in to dance it, there'll be some competition for both of them. A nosuk is faster on its feet than almost any beast alive, but Aele specializes in nosuk and knows how they tend to react, knows how they move in the attack. She would want one that would properly stretch her, make her work a little—no player wants it easy, or at least no good player does. An easy dance makes for low marks, and low marks pull down your yearly average, do you see, and then at the end of the year your point bonus is lower than it should be. Not to mention the matter of honors and so forth, which are all based on score averages, with suitable handicaps—"

The young mrem selling wine came hustling over. "All right, two wines," he said, "and which of you gets the clean cup?" He snickered.

"Son," Reswen said, "that joke was old when Sorimoh's eyes were still closed, and if anything is living in either one of these cups, you're in trouble. Get out of here. And here, take this. Get yourself something to drink, and I hope whatever's at the bottom of *your* cup bites your nose." The lad hastened off, still snickering. Laas laughed herself.

"Cheeky kit," Reswen said. "But never mind. Now, if someone like Aele is dancing, as she is today—"

"Oh? How do you know?"

"Oh, a crier comes around in the morning and lets everymrem know."

"Don't tell me," she said, "that you were paying attention to anything some crier said this morning!"

He smiled at her. "Would it ruin your day to think
so?" he said.

Laas pummeled him, claws in, but just barely.

"Peace, peace," he said. "I heard it last eightday. They
do a summary as well."

"And you remembered it all this time? You must be
very fond of all this."

"Very," Reswen said. "And besides, a policemrem never
forgets."

"I'll make a note."

"Anyway, about Aele. She has a handicap of nearly
eighteen points, these days, which means she's considered
too good to handle anything less than a prime bull nosuk,
or maybe a chieshih older than, say, five years—"

"Your hunters," Laas said, "must have decimated the
countryside. Where do you find all these beasts?"

"Hunters? Heavens no, we breed them. There are
several breeding farms outside the city. It's very lucrative
. . . some of the Arpekh own shares in them as well."

"Is there anything your Arpekh don't have their
claws in here?"

"Precious little," Reswen said, and made a snide remark about where else their claws might be in between
times.

"Tsk. If we're being watched again, or listened to,
you're going to get in trouble."

"I'm in trouble already," he said, "or didn't I mention?
But never mind that. Look, they're ready—"

There was a stirring and exchange of papers among the
judges, and then one of them stood up and signed to
someone high up on the Enclosure walls. The gong rang
out again. It was almost immediately drowned out by the
shouts and yowls of the eager crowd. Onto the bare sand
of the "field" came walking one lone figure, a tall, slender,
white-and-patchwork mrem wearing a light leather apron,
nothing else; and the roar that went up to greet him was
considerable.

"It's Ogov," Reswen said. "Not a bad player, even
though this is only his second season. Probably the last

year he'll be starting; he's getting too good to go on first, these days. Lovely hand with the sword. But he hasn't got one today. Can you see a sword, or a knife?"

"No," Laas said, sounding rather distressed. "Surely he's not going to take something on with just his teeth and claws—"

Her question was answered by a creaking of machinery, and Ogov turned to face in the direction from which the sound came. All eyes turned to a small door in the wall of the Enclosure, and there was a muffled *grumph* noise from inside it. Slowly, cautiously, something came out.

It was dun-colored, about half as tall as the mrem it faced; it went on four legs, and its tail lashed behind it like a whip. "Akoos," Reswen said. "Do you have them back East?"

"No, and I'm glad of it." Laas said, sounding relieved. Reswen could understand why. He had never quite believed in the way an akoos looked—that huge head, all those teeth, the saggy skin all around. This one was apparently youngish; when it opened its mouth to roar, he could just barely make out that its second and third rows of teeth hadn't grown in yet. But the hungry little eyes, buried in their rolls of flesh, were looking around it with a sullen anger that suggested that it was willing to work fairly hard to make up for the lack of them.

It saw Ogov and gave tongue again, that curious cutoff grunt-cum-roar. He moved cautiously closer to the akoos, and the crowd roared.

"It's an interesting match," Reswen said, having to raise his voice a bit to be heard. "If he manages it, it'll drive his season's average up considerably. Akoos score fairly high on maneuverability, but that's Ogov's strong suit as it stands. If he can—"

Reswen forgot what he was saying as Ogov moved closer and leapt at the beast. Beside him, Laas watched, but more with curiosity than interest, and Reswen felt a quick stroke of sadness. He couldn't explain to her, not quickly, what the Game meant to one expert in it—how the combination of grace and ferocity and danger always moved him. He got the sense, too, that it bored her; not the combat itself, but the business of it, all the surrounding

statistics and jostling among players for rank, the things
that were meat and drink to him. But there was nothing
he could do about it. Besides, things were getting excit-
ing. The akoos had a weak spot, the vertebrae in its neck
were partially fused, and to attack by biting, it had to go
straight ahead. Ogov was feinting at it again and again with
a dancer's grace, almost indolently, then spinning around
to get behind it. The akoos had avoided him the first two
times; this time it missed, and Ogov was behind it in one
move, half leap, half roll, and clinging to its back, biting at
the neck. The akoos shook him, screaming, trying to dis-
lodge him; but Ogov was not letting go. With such a
young beast, there was nothing to be gained by another
pass with it. It had done all it knew how to do—there
were no other tricks to be coerced from it. He clung, he
bit. No clawing: A clean kill scored more points than
merely ripping a beast inelegantly to ribbons—

"Reswen, look," Laas hissed from beside him. Reswen
tore himself away, feeling something of a pang as the
crowd's shout went up for something he had missed. But
there was movement down in the empty boxes, a line of
bright-colored robes filing in from one of the private gates
on the lower level. It was the Lloahairi. Reswen could
make out Maikej's color from here. Then, "Indeed," he
said softly, for the mrem who had been watching them at
the Play House, the "big spender," was seating himself
several seats behind Maikej. "Laas," Reswen said, "that
one. See him? The green kilt."

"Gods," she said, and stared.

Reswen looked at her in surprise. " 'Gods' what?"

"Masejih," she said. She sounded utterly shocked.

"Who? What? Do you recognize him from somewhere?"

"Yes! No, no, not the one in the green. Behind him, a
couple of rows. Blue robes, with the striped *cezhe.*"

Reswen searched the box for the mrem she meant,
then found him: a big mrem with gray-blue fur of a kind
he'd seen a few times before, though it was rare in Niau.
He had seen the description of this mrem in the summary
that Krruth had sent him of the names and descriptions of
the new Lloahairi Embassy. "I see him. Who is it again?"

"Masejih. He's a wizard. He's fairly well known, though not as a wizard. Something of a court fixture."

Reswen looked at her. "I didn't know you'd been to Lloahai."

"I have been," she said, "but that's not the point. He's not Lloahai, Reswen. He's from Cithiv, from one of the cities in the East. Another one like Usiel. Occasionally one of his cronies, in fact."

Reswen was shocked. "Then what's he doing pretending to be a Lloahairi?"

"How should I know? But Reswen, he makes his living the same way Usiel did. 'Quiet work' for the nobility. And he's nothing to be toyed with. Many mrem are dead because of him, and no one could lay it at his doorstep at all. Those who tried—" She shuddered.

Reswen sat there, having lost all taste for the Games . . . a most unusual occurrence.

"Let's head out of here when intermission comes," he said. "We've got real problems now, and we've got to start doing something about them. . . ."

Beside him, Laas hugged herself as if she was cold. Reswen put an arm around her . . . and was troubled to see that it didn't seem to help.

▲

Chapter 11

▲————————————————————————▲

There was little that could be done, though, as Reswen soon discovered. Most of his constabulary staff were out about the various businesses he had set them; there were no messages waiting for him when they got back from the Games. There was really only one thing left to do. . . .

Someone hammered at the door. Reswen cursed.

"Such words, darling one," Laas said softly, biting his ear. "Who taught you language like that?"

"You're a fine one to be talking. I heard you this afternoon. Give you a sword and you turn into a ruffian." He got up and threw a kilt on for the looks of things, then went to the door and shouted, "Who is it?"

No answer. Reswen reached behind the door for the gold-and-rose knife, hanging on one of the clothes hooks in the wall. Then he threw the door open.

Lorin stood there, looking small and hunched in his poor tattered robes.

"Get in here, you idiot, why didn't you say who it was?" Reswen said, pulling Lorin in and slamming the door to behind him.

"Do you really want me shouting my name so the whole street can hear?" Lorin said, putting his shabby hood back. "Are you busy?"

"Rather," Reswen said, "but I know you well enough that you wouldn't be troubling me unless it was something important. Come in."

Lorin walked past the screen into the sitting room, which looked rather more like a lying room at the moment, especially with Laas lying in the middle of it, propped on an indolent elbow, drinking Reswen's dark sweet wine and looking at Lorin with interest.

"The lady Laas," Reswen said, as Lorin goggled.

"We've met," Laas said, "that day at the party, when you brought this young gentleman by to have a look at Deshahl. And he sniffed me out, too: most perceptive." She looked at Reswen for a name.

"Lorin neh Thibaha-chir," Reswen said. "An honest bookmaker of this city. And other things as well."

"*Erath ivilhih ren ssahmeith,*" Laas said, inclining her head to Lorin gravely.

If possible, Lorin goggled at her harder than before, then clutched at something under his robe—his own fishy-smelling charm, Reswen supposed—and said to her, bowing a little, "*Na erath ssahmeith usaj lel-ivilh.*"

Reswen raised his eyebrows at Laas. " 'Workers' sometimes have ways of recognizing one another," she said, "that have nothing to do with feeling one another from across a crowded room. Though that was certainly how Lorin recognized me. You are trained, then," she said to Lorin, "in at least one of the Eastern disciplines."

"At least one," Lorin said nervously, "a very little, and right now, I wish I was trained better." He looked at Reswen, a rather helpless expression. "Policemaster, how much—"

"—can you say? Anything necessary. This lady is in my confidence, and anything she hears will be used in honor." He glanced sidewise at her; Laas shut her eyes in agreement.

"All right." Lorin flung off his cloak, one-handed. Under it he had a tight roll of parchment, and what appeared to be a potted plant.

"What in the world—" Reswen said.

"I found the spell you were curious about," Lorin said. "I wish I hadn't. Look."

He put the pot with the plant in it on the floor, and sat down beside it. From one of the pockets of his tunic he removed a little flask, and a rock. Reswen's fur began to stand up at the sight of them, and the memory of the other day in the square. "What's in the pot?" he said. "Just grass?"

"It's enough," said Lorin. "The formula you gave me *was* a blessing, once. But it depends on your turn of mind exactly what results are produced when you use it." He put the water and the stone down. "I was outside the city walls this morning," he said. "This grass comes from out by the river. This stone was under it. This water is from the rivulet that fed it."

Reswen sat down on a pillow beside Laas and watched as Lorin opened up the tightly-rolled parchment he was carrying, then glanced around him. "All the windows are shut," Reswen said. "Go ahead."

Lorin said, rather weakly, "Can I have something to drink, please?"

Laas handed him over her cup. Lorin was apparently so shaken that he took it from her without hesitation of any kind, and drank it straight off. Then his eyes goggled again.

"It's good wine," Reswen said. "I'll have you sent a skin. For pity's sake, Lorin, get on with it."

The little mrem's fur was standing up all over him. He put the cup down—it fell over, his paws were shaking so badly—and unrolled the parchment, and began to read. *"Irheh ne beino ral pagoh' dichhev lel losheh echin . . ."*

It sounded like nonsense, as the greeting—if it was one—that Laas and Lorin had exchanged had sounded to be. But there was an uncomfortable rhythm about the words; and then Reswen turned his attention to the fire, which seemed to be drawing poorly. It looked dim, and was giving little heat. Indeed, there seemed to be a frightful draft in the place. Was there a window open? And what was such a cold draft doing this time of year anyway, when it was just cool enough at night to make a fire pleasant—

Lorin kept reading. Reswen put his paw out to Laas, found her shaking slightly. He gathered her close. The soft, insistent rhythm of the words continued. It got colder; even the light from the fire seemed to be less warm . . . what there was of it. The rhythm of the words kept thudding harder and harder, shutting away sound as ringing in the ears does, getting louder and louder, and the light throbbed dimmer with every beat. Soon there would be nothing but the dark, the cold, everything gone, everything dead—

The words stopped.

The air instantly seemed clearer. The warmth of the fire and the clarity of the air flooded back, until a second later Reswen wondered whether they had ever really been gone. Laas was shuddering in his arms; he cuddled her closer, if he could. Lorin had dropped the parchment and was hiding his face in his hands and moaning.

That, when Reswen looked up from comforting Laas for a few moments, was when he noticed that the grass in the pot was dead. Blasted dead, wilted and withered; some of it was rotting where it lay, as he watched.

"Oh no," he said.

"That's what you wanted to know about," Lorin said, and actually wept. "Filthy stuff." He sagged where he sat, as if exhausted, and scrubbed at his eyes with his ragged sleeves.

Reswen was stricken still. "Oh no," he said again.

Laas looked stricken too, but rather confused. "It's just *grass*, though."

Reswen turned to look at her in miserable realization. "But *grain* is grass, Laas. That's all it is, really."

Lorin was recovering himself a little. He sat up straight, sniffling. "It wouldn't do *you* any good to say any of that," he said. "You could say it a hundred times a day, but you don't have the power and you couldn't fuel it. Magic is the fuel . . . the spell directs. Nothing happens without both. And to do any larger harm, you'd need a lot more power than I have, a lot more talent, more training. And more ceremony—"

"But they have the magic," Reswen said. "The talent. *Someone* has it." He turned to Laas. "Our friend, there. Masejih."

Lorin looked blank. Laas nodded, looking very shaken indeed. "So that was what they meant."

" 'It's happening already,' " Reswen quoted, getting up and beginning to pace. "Lorin, if you had the stone and water from a city, and did this—what would happen?"

He looked shocked. "You'd need such power—"

"What if you had it?"

Lorin blinked. "Everything that grows could die," he said. "For miles around."

"And it would look like this," Reswen said, pausing to look down at the pot. "Anyone who saw that would mistake it for blight, rust, rot, half a dozen other things. But not magic, because who thinks of magic?" He looked at Laas. " 'They don't believe in the other,' he said. Whoever 'he' was."

She nodded.

And, "Hiriv," she said after a moment, gazing down and refusing to meet Reswen's eyes.

"I thought so. But thank you, dear one. Thank you for making me sure." *That jolly bastard*, Reswen thought. *Now I know why I didn't like him on sight. "Trust your instincts," they always said to me, but I always had to reason things out, I could never let them simply be true—* "You warned me," he said to Lorin. "And you were quite right. But I had too little evidence—"

"At least, about this." Lorin shuddered again.

Reswen looked at him uncomfortably. "What's the problem now? What else have you found?"

"I haven't . . . I mean, I've been having . . . encounters. In dream and out of the body. With something—" Another convulsive shudder. "Something that isn't mremkind."

Reswen's fur began to stand up. He stared at Lorin.

"There's just nothing else it could be." Lorin was starting to babble. "I didn't want to mention anything until I was certain. I didn't think you'd believe me—"

"Lorin—"

"—it has to be, the affect and the aura are too typical, the power is too great—"

"Will you please speak Niauhu and tell me what you've found!"

"*Liskash!*" Lorin said, almost moaning, and fell silent.

"Impossible," Reswen whispered.

"No, you've got to believe me, it's *real*—"

"I don't mean impossible *that* way, shut up, of *course* there are liskash!" He became aware of Laas's eyes on him, and added, a little absently, "Unofficially, of course. Officially, there's no such thing any more. . . ." He turned to Lorin again. "I meant, where *is* the thing?"

Lorin shook his head. "I don't know."

Reswen began to pace. "So now we have a wizard, *and* a liskash somewhere—and a spell that can destroy every green thing that grows outside the city. At least it sounds like it. What would have to be done?" he said to Lorin.

Lorin looked bemused. "To do so much damage—there would have to be considerable preparation. You couldn't just do it like that." He gestured at the pot. "There would have to be circles drawn, the right influences . . . called." He shivered all over, as if that cold draft had come back into the room and run right up under his fur.

"How long would it take?"

"Days, at least."

Reswen paced. *Two days, since they got the damn stone and water. Damn the Arpekh, damn the whole lot of them!*

Lorin was still shaking like a frightened kitten. Reswen paused by the table, leaned down to pick up the overturned cup, refilled it, then handed it to Lorin. "Drink," Reswen said. "You're a wreck, and I need you functioning. Tell me this," he said, and paused while Lorin drank the wine with what looked like desperate haste. "Without the stone and water, can they do that?"

"No, of course not! The stone and the water are the bones and the blood of the city. That's the point. Without them, willingly given, no wizard could do anything."

"But you just took that stone, that water."

"Different situation. I went beyond the city's boundaries, where the land owns itself, and anything taken is given willingly."

Reswen considered the implications of that for a moment, then shook his head. "All right. But if trickery was used—"

"It doesn't matter," Lorin said. "The stone and water were given willingly. It's too late now. And you say they've got a wizard? Oh woe—" He started to weep again, then stopped with comical abruptness. "Wait a moment. They couldn't do it with just one wizard."

"Are you sure?"

"Of course I am. There would have to be more than one."

Reswen went to stand over Lorin, and glared down at

him. "How sure are you? Come on, Lorin, look me in the eye. This is important."

Lorin looked up at Reswen indignantly. "One of them might die in the middle of it," Lorin said. "Or do something else, even just slip, just say the wrong words and break the circle. There has to be another one, to back up the principal worker. Otherwise the backlash—" Lorin shuddered. "Don't even ask."

"Wonderful," Reswen said, pacing again. "Another wizard. Can you smell that one out too?"

"No," Lorin said, sounding aggrieved. "She's—begging your pardon, lady—"

"No offense taken," Laas said.

"She's a charismatic. You can smell them without much trouble if you're close enough," Lorin said. "The talent just boils off them. Other kinds of workers, they need to be working for you to notice. You have to have a fire to have smoke to smell. I've been trying for days . . . but I haven't found out a thing."

"All right," Reswen said. "Lorin, as far as the liskash goes—if there is one . . ." He sighed. "I wouldn't order any mrem alive at one of those things. Find out what you can. But keep your skin in one piece; you have other business. Especially other business than taking bets, just now. I want you to drop whatever else you might be doing, until you hear otherwise from me. I want you to do nothing else but 'smell,' you understand me? Nothing else whatever. You smell smoke—I want you to get word to me, wherever I am. I'll show you how to do it: there are runners in various places in the city, available for mrem who need to contact me quickly."

"All right," Lorin said.

"I'm going to give you a *lot* of money," Reswen said. "So keep your nose open. And by the gods," he added, "I'm going to buy you some new clothes. Now go home. And thank you, old friend."

Lorin seemed glad to go. He pulled his robes about him and bowed to Laas and was gone, slamming the door behind him. Reswen watched him through the slightly parted curtain, a shabby, hurrying figure, bright as he passed the torchlight of one of the neighboring houses, then shadow, a shape in shadow, gone.

"And then what are you going to do?" Laas said quietly.

"I'm going to take back the stone and water," said Reswen.

Laas looked concerned. "But the Arpekh—"

"Let them try to stop me," Reswen said.

"They'll fire you," Laas said.

"Fire me? They'll spike me up as a traitor," Reswen said. "But only if they can catch me doing what I'm doing. There are *some* advantages to being the chief of the secret police, you know."

Laas smiled at him. It was a small, slowly growing smile, but it heartened Reswen nonetheless. And that was good, for the word "traitor" rang in his mind like a bell, a leaden stroke, one that lingered; and he could use heartening.

Laas stood up and put her arm around him as he stood in front of the fire. "And how much of this are you going to tell our friend Hiriv, when you see him tomorrow?" Reswen said. "For surely you've got to go back. They're going to get suspicious."

Those golden eyes gleamed at him. "I can be quite circumspect when I choose," she said. "I can tell him a great deal of the truth . . . but nothing that will do him any good."

"Oh? Such as what?"

"Such as the fact that the chief of police likes his pleasures, likes his food, and his Games, and his plays." She chuckled. "And his she-mrem, especially."

Reswen gathered her close. " 'Likes'?" he said.

"And is an outrageous lover," she said, nestling her head into his shoulder.

" 'Likes'?"

Laas laughed softly. "Loves," she said. "Loves."

Reswen bit her gently.

"Loves," she said, and this time, and for some time thereafter, Reswen knew she was speaking for herself.

▲

She lay in the midst of the gleaming webwork and hissed.

She had not left it for some time now—not since she

found that things were no longer running as smoothly as
they had been. The situation could not be permitted to
continue . . . but it had continued, despite her attempts to
stop it.

The problem, as usual, was subtlety. She dared do
nothing that was too obvious. Obvious actions attracted
attention, and could ruin a well-laid plan. But on the other
hand, some of the vermin were coming too close to her
plan, and were beginning to perceive the general drift of
it.

The little wizard, for example. That was a bad one, but
if she killed him outright, or had him killed, she would
perhaps betray more than she wanted to to the policemaster.
At the thought of him she hissed again. The wretched
meddler! He was entirely too intelligent for a beast.

Now perhaps *he* might be killed. But no—that might
do damage to the group which she had been using and
guiding since their arrival here. And it was not subtle. She
rebelled against any action so obvious.

Control?

Possibly. Possibly. But with all her other pets, she had
had time to practice first. It was just as well, for some of
them had struggled mightily when she first took them—
and though she had swiftly recovered them, even a moment's escape, in circumstances as perilous as these, could
be fatal. Not only to the plan, either. Her masters' opinion
of her must not be allowed to suffer.

That was another thing. Who knew if, even now, they
were watching her from some more hidden part of the
overworld, as she was watching the vermin? It was entirely possible. There were some things they could do that
not even her power showed her how to manage. If they
saw her taking unsubtle action, there would be no reward
for her at the end of all this . . . no sweet flow of blood.
There might even be recall—shame, and possibly worse,
would befall her. No indeed . . . she must conduct herself
as if she were being watched every moment, for possibly
she was. She must make no unwise or precipitate move.
Killing the policemaster, therefore, would have to wait. It
was a pity.

The little wizard, though . . . the policemaster could do

nothing without him, at least nothing that would seriously
threaten her. And perhaps there were other ways to strike
at the policemaster. She would have to consider these.

Her pet, for instance. The policemaster was too close to
it to perceive that it might be a danger. It would be simple
enough to use that pet to put a knife into him, some
night. . . . But no: That was just as unsubtle as anything
else she had been considering before her annoyance steadied down.

Certainly her pet could feed him misinformation; that
would be simple enough to arrange. Or perhaps decoy
him into danger that he might have avoided . . . except for
her. She hissed softly, a pleased sound. That was not a bad
idea at all. Her humor rose at the thought of the ridiculous
little relationships that arose between these creatures with
so little trouble. They were certainly no match for the
relationships of her own people, with their complexity and
their splendid cruelty. "Worm grows not to dragon till
worm eats worm," the saying was, and though it applied to
one of the lesser kinds, it was true as far as it went. One
could not truly grow without devouring others. She watched
the vermin try to pretend otherwise, and watched too with
amusement as they so often proved it true no matter what
they did.

So then—her pet. But first she must call out another of
them: the only one she ever deigned to use words with. It
knew how honored it was, she thought. It always groveled
most satisfactorily when she became apparent to it . . .
and that was quite as it should be. That other pet must be
apprised of some of the things that were going on. In its
small way it could be quite efficient, and it had handled
most of the business it had been sent to the city for,
anyway. It might as well have something else to do now.

She glanced at the webwork for the strand that led
from her to that particular pet. It burnt low at the moment; he was asleep. So much the better, for messages
passed on in sleep were that much more effective.

She reached out with her will and touched the strand—
sent a line of fire down it swift and hard, to communicate
her impatient and perilous mood. The glow of the overworld
dimmed somewhat to show her the pet's perception of it

in dream—a shadowy realm, full of places to hide, silences, protecting darks. Her intention flared through that darkness like heat lightning, and the creature perceived her and very prudently fell at her feet.

She simply loomed over it for a few moments, enjoying its terror. Because she deigned to speak to it, it had an idea that it was somehow favored among its kind, because it was her slave willingly. It *was* favored, in a pitiful, crawling sort of way, but it little suspected what result wooing her favor might have. It would find out, some day, when she had trained a pet that could better do her will. Its inflated little ego would crush wonderfully in her teeth.

But for the moment it lay there on the floor of the realms of dream, face down, quaking, its colors shading through all the vividest tones of fear, with here and there the slightest thread of pride or ambition showing. *Priest*, she said at last, when she began to weary a little of watching its fear.

Great one, command me, it said.

I have a task for you.

Ah, great one, you honor me beyond my worth—

Yes, I do. Be silent and listen. You have the stone and water I commanded you to seek.

Yes, great one.

The time has come to turn them to our advantage. Call out your colleague and tell him to begin preparations for the spell itself. In the meantime, we will use the "bones and blood" to produce some results which will aid what you must do. Here she instructed the pet at large in what had to be done, and it agreed fulsomely with everything she suggested. That was just as well; certainly it suspected what she would do if it had dared to disagree.

Have you all the other ingredients you will need for the spell? she said.

Yes, great one, everything is prepared.

Then see to it. I will be watching you . . . and it will be the worse for you if anything is done improperly. Death will be the first and least of the things that will happen. Do you understand?

It blubbered on the floor of its dream. That was most satisfactory. This one had few fears except of its own death, or of an unnatural one . . . and she loved to inflame that. The pet little knew what she had planned for it some day . . . and there was no point in its finding out just yet; that would jeopardize its effectiveness.

Go, then, and do my will. Remember that I see and know your every thought.

It blubbered more, and she withdrew, her tongue flickering in amusement at its tiny horror of her. Well, it was the best the creature could do. It would never achieve the great fear, the complex and terrible terror that one of her kind could have of another that was stronger or greater than itself. That was another thing that set her people apart from these slightly-more-than-beasts. She smiled slightly as she lay down again in the webwork, glancing about it.

Was this web drawing tighter? It looked as if it was.

No, surely. I am growing, that is all.

She settled down in the golden silence to watch the flickering fire of her power run along the tendrils of the plan . . . about to come to fruition at last.

▲

He swung into the office the next morning rather early, having made his good-byes around dawn, knowing that work would be piled up, and it would be as well if he was there to start handling it before too many questions were asked. In the aftermath, it turned out to be just as well; for at least he was there when Mraal came rushing into the office, at a most unusual hour for an Arpakh, and cranky to boot. Behind him came Krruth, looking most disturbed.

"Your useless policemrem," Mraal shouted. "What's the point of them if even they can't defend themselves against what's going on in this city? What are you doing, Reswen? How are we supposed to guarantee protection to the embassies and this city's guests if even the police can't take care of themselves—"

"Lord Arpakh," Reswen said, restraining his temper with some difficulty. Being shouted at, especially in front of his staff, had never been one of his favorite things. Mraal fell silent, looking at him with surprise. "Please start at the beginning of what you have to tell me, rather than in the middle."

"Don't you get smart with me, my mrem," Mraal said with heat. "If you had better control of your folk, we wouldn't have these problems—"

Reswen controlled himself again, then turned to Krruth. "Two of our plainclothes people were very badly beaten early this morning," Krruth said. "They were dumped down the road from the Lloahairi Embassy."

"I see," Reswen said. *Damn them. Damn the Lloahairi! How am I going to get at those people to see what they're up to with that wretched Easterner?* "Lord Arpakh," Reswen said, "it is entirely possible that if you had not ordered me off the investigation of Ambassador Shalav's murder, and had not ordered me to withdraw the normal surveillance of the Lloahairi, this would not have happened. They alone of all the embassies in the city have chosen to protest against the surveillance that everyone understands goes on when another country has an embassy in a city not allied to them. And now, as a result, their people have *their* spies out among our own, and we have none to keep an eye on what *they* are doing." He carefully neglected to mention Thabe and the others posing as servants inside the Lloahairi Embassy at the moment, without the Arpekh's knowledge.

"You have allowed the Arpekh to be browbeaten into his stance, out of a desire for the Lloahairi's goodwill while you renegotiate all your precious trade treaties, but no good will come of it, nor is coming of it, as we see already. Those people outside were doing the Lloahairi no harm: they were on security duty to make sure nothing such as happened to Shalav happened again without our knowing about it. And you come complaining to *me* about the effect this assault has among the embassies? Who do you think *did* it, my lord? The Lloahairi are telling you loudly of their contempt for you, even while they extort new settlements from you ten times better than any present circumstances deserve, even while they wait to see whether they can extort yet *better* ones from you over this ugly little matter, which I have no doubt they engineered themselves. Oh yes, my lord," Reswen said, seeing the unnerved look replace the look of anger in Mraal's face, "I know about the negotiations, and how they have been proceeding. The chief of the H'satei would be rather a poor mrem about his work if he didn't; knowing such things as make this city safe are my responsibility. So don't come laying the blame for these poor mrems' beatings at *my* door, master Mraal, or theirs either. *You* and your spineless brethren are at fault, and you are welcome to tell those poor mrems' families as much, not that you will. And if you want my resignation," Reswen said, getting into the heat of things and actively enjoying the storm and confusion of rage and unease and other emotions chasing themselves over Mraal's face, "you may have it on the spot, for I'm tired of trying to keep this city out of the worst danger it's been in in a century, while lapcats and dilettantes and sit-by-the-fire milk-lappers tell me how to do my job and then prevent my doing it!"

Mraal stared at Reswen, speechless, for several breaths, and then turned and went out in a furious rush, slamming Reswen's door behind him. "Well," Reswen said, "that's that, Krruth; I'm either in a great deal of trouble, not that that's unusual, or else I'm not Chief of H'satei any more. Either way, you had better tell me your news in a hurry. I can see it's no better than Mraal's."

"Thabe," Krruth said. "We found her down in the ricketies, with her paws cut off and her tongue torn out."

Reswen had to sit right down on his desk at that. Little gingery Thabe with her merry ways? Sweet-voiced Thabe of the wicked dirty jokes, and the wit that could leave a whole room rolling and gasping, helpless with laughter? "Ah, no," he said. "Oh, Krruth, that's cruel."

Krruth nodded, expressionless. He had trained Thabe himself, had worked with her often. "I would imagine they found her 'meddling,'" he said. "Careful creature that she is, even in that plight she apparently took herself straight off to the ricketies after they dumped her, to try to make it look unrelated. We traced her blood trail, but she had purposely defaced it from the spot where they dumped her."

"How is she? Where is she?"

"She lives," Krruth said, "and she's hanging on. More

than that the physician can't say. She's down in the infirmary."

"I'll go there," Reswen said, and swung down off the desk; but as he did, Krruth put a paw to his forearm and stopped him. "What, then?"

"She's resting at the moment. They've got her full of snoreweed, and if she should wake up enough to notice you, she'd be in great distress that she couldn't report. Let her be, Reswen. I think you have other concerns."

"I have indeed. Sit down, Krruth," he said. "This may take a while." And for the next hour or so he filled Krruth in on the things that Laas had told him, and that he had discovered, over the past day or so. Krruth nodded and listened and committed it all to memory, looking more and more disturbed as the account continued. When it was done, Krruth sighed—a pained sound; he preferred his world orderly, but it never obliged him. "So," he said, "what are you going to do, sir?"

"Get back our stone and water, somehow," Reswen said, "before the rite involved has a chance to take place. This is complicated by the fact that we know nothing about where it now is, though Hiriv was given it. I know it was taken to Haven originally, but the odds that it's still there now strike me as very low. Nevertheless, I want all our people to look for it. If they find it, it's to vanish. They are not to wait, not to try to make other arrangements. They are to risk discovery if necessary. Nothing is as important as getting that stone and water back."

"Very well, sir."

"What's the status of our other people in the embassy?"

"Lying very low."

"Keep them so. But one way or another I want someone in there tonight who can snoop around a bit; there's that party, you remember. It's impossible to keep proper security during a party, and I mean to take advantage of that. Meanwhile, what have you found out about the source of the Big Spender's money? Our friend Choikea, I mean."

"Several fat letters of credit," Krruth said, smiling slightly, "from one of the merchant banking houses in Cithiv."

Reswen pounded his desk in angry delight. "Arrest the

mrem," he said, and then immediately added, "No, forget
that. Leave him loose. Loose, he can run about his business. He'll think he hasn't been detected, and he may lead
us to someone else we want. I want proof he's deeply into
this. Have him watched, Krruth; I don't want him to so
much as go to dirt without our knowing when he did it and
what he did. And meanwhile, I've got to do something
about that party."

Krruth got an alarmed expression on his face. "Sir," he
said, "I know that look. You can't possibly go yourself.
You're well out of favor with them. Nor even in disguise,
sir, begging your pardon. I trained you, but someone else
who was trained could see through your best without too
much trouble if they knew to expect you. And they would,
for certain."

"You are a pain in the tail, Krruth, and I'm minded to
fire you."

Krruth laughed softly. "Do it quickly," he said. "But
even if worse comes to worst, I guess there must be work
out there somewhere for two old toms like us. Private
work, maybe, skulking around watching rich mrem's mis-
tresses in the middle of the night. Or plainclothes, maybe,
with one of the private companies. The pay's not what it
used to be, but—"

Reswen laughed too. "Get out of here," he said.

Krruth was just turning to go when someone knocked
at the door. "In," Reswen said, certain it was news of his
firing. A constabulary runner came in, handed Reswen a
note, and waited.

Reswen opened the note and read it. When he looked
up at Krruth again, most of his teeth were showing in an
expression very little like a smile. "From Thailh," he said.
"They searched our friend's house last night while he was
at the Games with the Lloahairi. Thailh says, 'Choikea's
house has had its drapes replaced lately. Old drapes found.
Some of the cord is missing.' "

Krruth grinned, and began to purr; but it was the
purr one hears when a hunter sees prey.

"*Now* then," Reswen said. "Bless our good old Thailh,
and there's *his* case solved. There's only one problem.
Motive."

"Easy. A hired agent. Hired by the Eastern cities."

"Yes, but why, Krruth? To have a few paupers and whores killed, and then an ambassador? Certainly the other killings make a good cover for the last one. Or would, if we hadn't discovered as much about this situation as we have. But why the Easterners?"

Krruth thought for a moment. "To ruin the city's relations with the Lloahairi?"

"I think it's a good guess," Reswen said. "But we can't go on guesswork at this point. We're going to need a confession, and we can't get that for a bit yet, not till our friend Choikea has had a little time to show us some more of his contacts. And anyway, why would the Easterners care about our relations with the Lloahairi one way or the other? And what in the eight hells is this Eastern wizard doing among the Lloahairi?"

They looked at each other for a few moments. Finally Reswen shook his head. "We need to have someone at that party tonight," he said. "Several someones. That place has got to be thoroughly searched and listened to. Find me a way, Krruth."

Krruth nodded slowly. "I'll do what I can."

"Do it."

Krruth sketched a small salute and headed out.

Another runner knocked, then, and came to hand a folded bit of paper to Reswen. "This just came by a runner from one of the private firms, sir."

It was a scrap of the cheapest paper there was, the kind of stuff that the public runners' companies provided for their customers.

Reswen unfolded it and read, *Suspect some attention is being paid to me after yesterday—some questions were asked—so am trying to be circumspect. The objects you were asking about seem not to be at home, but no one is complaining of their being missing, so assume they are hidden away somewhere safe until needed.* Reswen nodded to himself. That helped a little, if it was true; the Haven staff would start searching immediately. *As regards the matter we discussed of mrem being requested not to do certain things in return for payment, a great deal of money has apparently changed hands over the past couple of days to this purpose. Wonder whether the demonstra-*

tion we saw last night could be performed so as not to take effect immediately? On this sentence the firm clear handwriting broke down somewhat, as if the writer were upset or angry. Reswen swallowed, well understanding why she would be. Pay the grain merchants not to bother raising enough crops to have a surplus, then work the spell now, but not for immediate effect; work it in such a way that next year, when the responsible parties would be well out of reach, the crops would fail. *All* the crops. No grain anywhere, no surplus stored up, famine, a whole city gone to ruin as the food beasts die, too—more than one city, perhaps—

He growled deep in his throat and returned his attention to the note. *On other matters, our group has been invited to gathering you were concerned about. Will look into matters for you.* There was no signature.

Reswen's fur stood up all over him. *No, oh no!* He sat down hurriedly at his desk, scribbled a note that said simply, *Do not. Under any circumstances, do not. Have to see you. Name your time and place. R.* "Take this to the lady Laas at Haven," he said. "Wait for an answer. If she's not there, find out where she's gone, and see that she gets it. No one else is to see the message, you understand?"

"Yes, sir," said the runner, and went off in a rush, probably to let the other runners know on the sly that Old Ginger was in a right lather about this Eastern lady, just as everymrem else was who saw her. There would probably be snickering as his mrem let one another know that Reswen wasn't as invulnerable and take-it-or-leave-it about the shes as he liked to let on.

Reswen smiled a bit, a wry look; better that mild confusion than that they should have any hint whatever of what was really on his mind. Then he sat back in his chair to consider the Lloahairi business in detail, while waiting to see if he was going to be fired.

But he was not fired, and the day dragged by without any word from Laas. The runner had not found her at Haven. No one knew where she was, or perhaps they knew and would not tell. And there was nothing else Reswen could do about the matter but wait, and be afraid that Laas would not do the same. . . .

▲

Chapter 12

▲————————————————————————————▲

She was not prepared to do any such thing.

Laas spent the day walking through Niau. She had taken some care to dress herself as she had seen some of the quietly well-to-do she-mrem dress in the city: kilt and *cezhe* in subdued colors, the long loose end of the *cezhe* drawn over head and ears, ostensibly for protection from the sun. That her face was hidden suited her well. She had a knife tucked through her underbelt, a slender wicked blacked-steel one that she had picked up at the same place where she had bought Reswen's present, the knife of rose and gold. Indeed she had tried to find another like his, but the cutler had shaken her head. "We see those only rarely," she said; "it's not steel, it's some other metal that takes that hard edge, and can take color like that. It comes from one craftsmrem up north, and he won't tell the secret, and he sends, maybe, four a year. You were lucky to find it at all last time, lady. We rarely manage to keep one in stock for more than an eightday. Did your friend like it?"

Laas had smiled and nodded, and taken the little knife, long and straight like a fang; had paid in silver and gold, and thanked the cutler, and gone away. The knife's cool, sharp presence against her middle comforted her. Not that her talent left her feeling undefended, but it was hard to kill with it, at least swiftly. Not that she had any desire to, of course. . . .

She walked. She walked the marketplace, listening to the brawling noise of the place, the cries and the bustle of mrem buying and selling, intimidating one another in the friendliest fashion, trying to get the better of bargains, as if

life depended on it. She walked the Whites, among the
high houses and the green trees, where song floated down
from the small wind creatures in the branches, sweet,
undecipherable, unconcerned with her or anything else,
and (as far as she could tell) completely ignored by the
passersby, for all its sweetness. That astonished her, but
she let it pass, as she was letting everything pass, this
morning, letting it all pass over her to be felt. She was the
stone at the bottom of the river, silent, seeming cold and
still; it seems not to think or act, but in time it knows the
water better than anything else.

She walked away from the Whites, into the middle-
class quarters, listening to the calmer business and bustle
of home life—swill pails being emptied in the street, stoops
being energetically brushed clean by small kits wielding
oversized bundles of twig, small herd-beasts bleating from
tiny backyards as they were milked. She walked down
narrow, crazily twisted streets where laundry was hung in
elegant swags from the windows of one building to the
windows of another across the road, and the housemrem
leaned their elbows on the windowsills and gossiped sex
and love and frustration through the baking afternoon,
across the little gap of air. Strolling sellers went by hawk-
ing water to drink, or lumps of soap or wax, or crying pots
to sell or to mend; little mrem hardly up to her haunch
went running in shrilling, delighted crowds down the streets,
playing games with rules that might seem strange, but
were rigidly enforced for all that. Old gap-toothed mrem
sat on stoops and watched her go by, and made lewd
suggestions and praised her looks with affection well flavored of the gutter; others, older still, watched her go by
but said nothing, only leaned their backs against cool
shady walls or little flights of steps leading up toward
ramshackle houses, and their eyes moved and glittered,
but nothing else. Laas made no sign, made no answer,
only walked.

She walked, and tried to think.

Reswen.

Nothing had touched her this way before. Oh, she had
had longings, had had crushes, even, but nothing like this.
How is it, she thought, *that in a matter of two days—or a*

little more, actually—this mrem can become the most im-
portant thing in my life? How is it that so much can
change, and against my will? This was never my idea.
Another flirtation, no more. If he must desire me, no harm
in my enjoying myself—

That had been the rationalization for so long, with so
many. She knew it for a rationalization; she had known it
for one for a long time. Until now, it had never bothered
her. *They made my life hard enough when I was young,*
she would think. *Now it's my turn to enjoy what's happen-*
ing. I've paid enough price of pain and trouble in my time.
Let them do what I desire, and let me enjoy it.

But suddenly that coin was no longer current. Suddenly it mattered more whether someone else was enjoying himself than whether she was.

It frightened her. In the background, while her body
walked the streets, out of the poor but respectable neighborhoods and into the ricketies, her heart and mind de-
bated one another and found no common ground. *This is*
not safe, said the mind, pragmatic, practical. *You're never*
going to be trusted with this kind of work again.

Fine, said her heart. *I don't want it. Nor would he*
want me doing it, really. He has been restraining himself
from saying as much, but he'd much rather his lady wasn't
a whore and a spy.

There, you see, said the mind, scornful. *What does he*
know, after all? You're neither.

Oh? said her heart.

She walked, and the sun shone on the muck in the
streets, except where the buildings leant so close together
that the sun missed the dung-clotted gutter entirely and
fell only in a single lean strip of light on a mud-daubed
wall. *Never mind that*, said her mind, retreating in slight
confusion, *what matters is that you won't be able to live*
the way you have been. No more travel, no more rich folk
hanging on your every word. You will have to be his only,
if you follow through with this foolishness. No more money
of the kind you've been used to. Others will desire you—
you know you'll slip, every now and then, and let the
talent work—but the desire will do you no good; certainly
none of the only kind of good it's ever done you—

There's better "good" than that, said her heart, as she sidestepped just in time to miss the contents of someone's sandbox as they hissed down out of a window into the street. *His love is given freely. He cares* without *being made to— Oh miracle, however it happened! Let the money and the attention of the stupid rich take itself elsewhere. He's here now—and oh, the thought of losing him by not acting, not taking what he offers—*

She walked, and the argument went back and forth, the mind steadily and desperately being pushed back against a wall of fear. That was what it came down to, at the last. *The way it has always been is going to change. And you will not be in control.* In the hot sunlight, when she chanced to walk where it fell, she shivered. The fear had not been so terrible since the first time it happened, since a he-mrem looked at her in a way no one else ever had, and she knew somehow that it was her fault, and that the peace of all her life before that was at an end.

She walked. She headed upwards, helpless hostess to the argument, the desperate plea that things should stay the way they were. It was not until the shadow fell over her, not until she looked up at the old dark walls and the still shape standing on top of them, that Laas knew her choice was already made, and her doom sealed, and all the arguing vain. Sorimoh stood there with her sword outstretched over her city; but more real to Laas, just then, was the image of Reswen standing between her and the statue, dreamy, amicable, his eyes resting on Niau with calm love—letting Laas know that his choices were made too, and letting her know what they were. She could not bear any more than he could the thought of all this raucous life starving to death. Nor could she bear the thought of his exuberance, his fierce passion, his gentleness, withering away in the aridity of her own fear. It should not be allowed.

Would not be.

Gods help me, she thought, *I am his, and his city's, and a traitor to my own people.*

She stood under the cool shadow, gazing up at the dark shape silhouetted against the bright noon sky. A breath of

wind, the first she had felt that day, slipped through her
fur.

Well, she thought, *if I'm a traitor, best I get on with it.*
She headed down into the city.

▲

Lorin was in a great quandary.

He was thinking that perhaps he should be brave . . .
and he had no idea where to start. He had never been
brave. Not when he ran away and hid after his father and
mother were killed; not when he left that city, sick of the
look of it, fearful of some later pursuit; not when he first
came to Niau and went to ground as quickly as possible.
He had not been brave all that time ago when Reswen had
found him out, and bought him . . . relatively painless
though that process had been, once he had been reassured
that Reswen was not going to have him spiked up. And all
the time since, he had stayed small and quiet, slunk
about, done his business in darkness and as much silence
as possible. . . .

It was looking as if it was time to stop. *That* was what
was troubling him.

There was no doubt in his mind now. Oh, perhaps the
tail-twitch reaction continued. *There's no such thing as a
liskash any more!*—over and over, a desperate denial. But
the denial wouldn't change the facts. Something was doing
a liskash's kind of magic, with deadly results.

There was only one problem. *There are no liskash in
Niau!*

Lorin had been thinking about that one for a while,
and unfortunately, the answers that kept coming up made
him shake like a distempered kit. The books might say
what they liked about the supposedly increased effective
range of liskash when doing sorcery, but that *still* meant
that a liskash had to be somewhere in the general neighborhood to do its spells. Even miles away would be too
far; it could not be hidden, say, up in the hills. Nor could
it be in the town lands—certainly it would consider that
too dangerous, even with all its power. And besides that,
someone would have found it and raised the alarm by
now.

Wouldn't they?

Lorin sat in his house with his head in his hands, in the dark. There were wards all around, now. They showed no fire, in the real world, but in the next he knew they would be blazing. He did not mind attracting the attention, at this point, if any was being attracted. He wanted no one inside his mind just now.

If I were a liskash, he thought, *and I wanted to get into Niau, how would I manage it?*

Tunneling under the city walls seemed ridiculous, though the legends seemed rather vague about a liskash's ability in this direction. He thought it rather unlikely, however. All the stories seemed to describe the liskash of old as too proud a race to do anything so demeaning as dig holes in the ground. Holes might be dug *for* them, but Lorin couldn't think of any way to do that without attracting attention . . . and certainly not from anywhere outside Niau which would enable a tunnel to be made in anything like a decent time. The town lands, on the hillside of the city, were notoriously open, and tunneling through the desert sand seemed silly too.

What, then? Tunneling by magic? But it would have been noticed. Simply appearing out of nothing? Lorin thought about it for a moment, and then snorted at himself derisively. Not even magic could move air out of the way quietly when something appeared out of "nowhere." No indeed, the explosion of air that would have accompanied the appearance of a liskash would have raised more than mere questions. Roofs would have come off for blocks around.

The simplest way, he thought, *would be to sneak the liskash in with something else . . . preferably something that won't be investigated. Your personal effects, let's say. If it came in through the front door . . .*

He had heard descriptions of the arrival of the Easterners. There seemed little to go on there; most of their baggage had been slung over the backs of burden-beasts. But there had been some big carts, draped—cages, for beasts from the Eastern countries. Some of them were in the city beast garden even now.

All of them?

Lorin shook. What a thought: that possibly there was something down in the beast pits that was a lineal descendant of the old lizards, the ancient master-species of the world, whom the mrem had supplanted; an angry liskash, biding its time and smiling while mrem-kits threw buns and feedroots at it, and keepers, all unknowing, pushed fresh meat to it once a day on billhooks.

In any case, it had to be looked into. And there was no use telling Reswen anything about it, not just yet. His constables would be helpless. If they stirred up the liskash, there would be death and destruction past belief. Of that Lorin was sure.

Yet someone had to go find out if the thing *was* in fact here—and if so, where it was, and in what condition, and what could be done about it.

There was no one but Lorin to handle that.

He couldn't seem to stop shaking. *It would be wonderful,* he thought, *if there were someone else I could give this job to—!*

But there was no one.

He started to go over the whole thing in his head again—then stopped, swearing. He had done this five times already. It was not getting any better.

He got up and moved fast, to minimize the shaking, and got on his cloak. No matter that he would swelter inside it, this time of year; the concealment would be of use. It would be dark very soon. And with any kind of luck, there would not be too many people around Haven tonight. . . .

Now that was a thought.

He flopped down at the bench again and fumbled over the books piled up on the table for one in particular. *I must be crazy,* he thought, as he riffled through the pages. He had certainly never tried anything quite this daft before. But it was necessary . . . or might prove to be. He doubted he would have the courage, or the opportunity, to pull off twice what he intended to try at least once.

He found another scrap of parchment from a paid bet, turned it over, hunted across the table for quill and gall-ink, dabbed at the inkwell, and swore some more. It was almost dry. He scrabbled the pen around at the bottom of the well and tried to get a glob of ink onto the point of the pen, then scribbled hastily, with much blotting and smearing. *Damn. Damn, damn . . .*

Normally Lorin took more time about his copying than this, but the fear was rattling his bones so that he had no desire to spend any more time about it than usual. The wording was straightforward enough, after all, and the symbology was not of the more difficult kind. He had been tempted, at first, to try the Eastern version of the spell; it was quicker and more effective. But on the other hand, his enemy would more likely be familiar with that one. Better stick to the West. . . .

His enemy. Oh, this was bad, very bad indeed. The whole thing had gone far past earning a bonus now. He was involved.

Lorin had sworn himself oaths, before, that he would never become involved. His father had become involved, and look what had happened to *him.*

But what could he do? There was Reswen, and that pretty lady, so obviously in love, and here was something lying up somewhere in the city—or so he thought—that was going to bring all the loves, and hates, and lives, to a very abrupt end. Whatever other emotions and reactions one might suspect from a liskash, mercy had never been one of them. Either there would not be one stone left upon another, after the thing was through with them . . . or something much worse would be happening. The legends were obliquely horrific about certain of the lizards' eating habits . . . in and out of the body.

He shuddered all over and finished his copying, tossing the miserable blunted quill aside and rolling up the parchment carefully, ink side in, to blot the wet bits on the dry back. Lorin stowed the thing in a pocket and then slipped out his door, locking it behind him, cursing his shaking hands.

He made his way through town unnoticed, as far as he could tell. No passing constable paid any attention to him, which was just as well, since if by bad luck he stumbled across one who could read, the little writing he carried in his pocket would be sufficient to see him sitting on top of the wall in a most uncomfortable manner . . . not that

Reswen would let that happen, but Reswen could hardly be everywhere.

There were a few torches outside Haven, but otherwise the place was mostly dark; the constabulary presence was minimal. Lorin breathed a sigh of relief at that. He had little enough idea what he was looking for—he hardly needed the constables breathing down his neck.

He slipped through the gates and made himself familiar with the shrubbery for a few minutes, watching the courtyard. There were only two constables there, one of them leaning in great boredom against a pillar of the house's portico, another standing to one side of the door. That was just as well, from Lorin's point of view. He had no immediate plans to go into the house—in fact, he was hoping to avoid it.

The constable by the pillar turned to say something to the one by the door. Lorin slipped out from between the friendly bushes and stole softly back along the left side of the walled property, down the passage beside the house that led to the stabling quarters. A few lighted windows threw pools of light on the flagging and the grass. Lorin avoided them, once or twice having unhappy disagreements with the thornbushes along the way.

Down at the end of the flagged passageway lay the stable block, concealed from the house by various ornamental plantings and a low wall over which various vines and down-trained trees sprawled and scrambled. Lorin paused there among the plants, trying to get his bearings. A light breeze sprang up, and Lorin got a whiff of the dark rich stable smell; there were soft shufflings and lowings from the beasts in their byres.

He slipped quietly around the plantings and headed toward the stable block, more for cover than because there was anything there that he wanted to see. To the best of his knowledge, all the beasts the Easterners had brought with them had been disposed of. It was their carriers that he was interested in . . . the big ornamented boxes. They had to be here somewhere. . . .

They were. He spotted one of them at the end of the stable block, its pull-bar lying on the ground in front of it with a large rock placed on top of the crossbar to keep the wagon from rolling. It was really a rather large box. It looked larger the closer he got to it. . . .

Lorin stepped softly down toward it past the doors of the stables. There was some snorting and snuffling as the beasts winded him, then settled down again. His footsteps sounded incredibly loud to him, but there was no sign of any notice being taken of him from the house; its backside was almost completely dark except for one window, high up.

He stopped about his own height's distance from the box. It had big doors on one side, which would certainly make hell's own noise if he tried to shift them. But there were also air slits higher up, and it would be possible, with some climbing, to get at them. Fortunately Lorin was a good climber, even as mrem reckoned it.

Less fortunately, Lorin was shaking like a leaf in a high wind. He paused there for a few seconds, thinking to try to calm himself down—but this was so patently absurd, and he was so terrified that one of the constables in front might take it into his head to come around, that he immediately grabbed a loop of rope hanging down from a canvas bound over the top of the cart, and began clambering up as quietly as he could. It seemed to him that the scratching noises he was making should have waked up the world, and most particularly the creature he suspected of being inside the box. But if he was correct in his surmise, that creature would not be awake at the moment. It would be out of the body, the better to keep an eye on things.

The better to keep an eye on things like you, his mind screamed at him, but Lorin simply gulped and kept climbing. That other's attention should be far away from him at the moment . . . otherwise he would never have gotten this far, surely. No, it had its mind on business.

If it's here, his mind remarked, sardonic and afraid.

He came to the top of the box and paused there a moment, panting a little; it had been too long since he had done any climbing. When he had recovered slightly, he looked around. The canvas did not cover the entire top of the box. There was another air slit showing down at the far end of it, where the canvas had slipped aside. Slowly and quietly he crawled down toward it.

There was a deep groaning sound, and the box moved. Lorin froze.

The sound stopped.

Idiot, idiot, he thought, and inched forward. The box groaned again, more softly this time. It was only settling on its springs.

If only the sound doesn't bring the damned constables, Lorin thought, and inched forward again, and again, to get the noises over with. Then the air slit was just under his hands.

He held quite still to make sure that there would be no more noises, then put one eye down to the slit with the greatest caution and looked inside.

Darkness, nothing but dark. He held his position. Slowly that eye got used to the dark; he closed his other eye to help it. The merest trickle of light came in through other air slits.

Nothing. Nothing but foul straw.

He swore at himself inwardly, all the parts of his mind which had thought this was a bad idea now hollering all together, *Stupid, let's get out of here, this is ridiculous, there's nothing here*— He ignored them and for the next few moments made it his business to climb down as quietly as possible.

There was the crunch of a footstep on the flagged path. Lorin froze in the shadow of the box, watching another shadow move toward him. *It knows,* he thought. *It knows I'm here. It's sent someone*—

But the constable passed him by without even a second look. Evidently this part of the house and garden was considered secure, and the constables were none too concerned about it.

Lorin breathed again when he had gone, and looked around him. The stable blocks ended here, but the exercise yard went on for a ways, and there was a part of it that he could not see off to the left, shielded by more plantings and trees. Lorin stole toward it softly.

Here the ground was just gravel, dotted here and there with beast droppings. Some beast-harness was hung out here on roofed racks, and there was another of the boxes. It stood all by itself, its pull-bar held down like the other's with a big rock. There was no canvas drape over this one, but in all other ways it was identical.

Lorin stepped along as softly as he could . . . a difficult business on gravel, but he managed. This time he walked up the pull-bar, scrambling up the front of the box by the pawholds built into it for a driver or inspector to use.

Panting again, he paused, then looked down through one of the air slits. His heart sank. Nothing. Nothing but more foul straw. *Idiot, idiot*, his brain began singing—

There was a movement . . . and the eye was gazing up at him. It was a dull eye, slitted . . . and about as big as Lorin's head.

His breath got caught somewhere south of his ribs.

There was the sound of a whuff of breath—then another, and another one, quicker than the second.

It's waking up!! he thought, and snatched the piece of parchment out of his cloak, and held it up . . . and then realized that it was too dark to read the spell.

Oh gods! he thought, shoving the parchment back into his cloak—no good dropping it where it might cause questions, or worse, get someone to look inside this box. Hurriedly he recited the rune. It was a short one, thank heaven, and he got the intonation right. He dared not look down into that air slit again to see what was happening inside. But he could hear the sound of breathing getting faster in there—

He felt the spell's effect settle down over him, dulling everything, all sight and sound. Lorin didn't waste any further time. He jumped down off the box and began to run. And yet he couldn't help himself; he paused to look—

He was sorry for that. He was sorry for the sight of the great towering shape of fire that leapt up out of the box. The fire was not real, as most people in Niau would understand real, but it would kill if it once touched him. The only advantage he had was that he was invisible for the moment, even to the sight and senses of another magic-worker. The question was how long it would last. . . .

He ran, ran out of there as fast as he could. He heard the step of the constable coming, veered to miss him— then changed his mind and ran full tilt into the poor creature. Better that he shouldn't go back there until things had become quiet again . . . until whatever wards the creature had to keep the nonwizardly away from there had been reestablished. Lorin and the constable went down together in a heap; Lorin scrambled to his feet and was off again. Behind him he heard the constable start shouting. He heard his partner call curiously from the front of the house, then head around after him. Lorin ran into him, too, on general principles, and knocked the poor creature to the cobblestones of the front courtyard . . . then loped out the front gates without stopping.

He did not stop till he was nearly a mile away, and there he sagged against the garden wall of some house in the Whites and moaned softly to himself. All his worst fears were true . . . and now he was going to have to do something about them.

Liskash. Oh gods, a liskash.

He was going to have to do something.

But *what*?

▲

The Lloahairi embassy, by comparison to Haven, was a rather drab place. It was as big, and well enough furnished, but there was an air of the furnishings being old and not well tended; *genteel decay,* Laas thought, glancing around her at the door, *soon not to be so genteel, if they don't get someone in here to do something about the upholstery.* . . .

She was ignored for the first little while. Hiriv and Rirhath and the other merchants got most of the attention, and of course there was Deshahl, turning her talent indiscriminately on whatever hapless creature happened into range. Most of the Lloahairi males in the room were already gathered around her, paying her compliments or looking unsheathed claws and messy death at one another behind her back. She never noticed; but then that was her way, to walk into a room and leave wreckage behind, tempers and relationships shattered.

But Deshahl's thoughtlessness suited Laas for the moment; she had other business. She paused by the sideboard to eat and drink while sizing the place up. One large downstairs hall; toward the back of the hall, a stair down, a

stair up. She was not used to houses that had cellars—
none of them did in Cithiv, possibly due to the little earth
tremors that were so common. Indeed all Niau seemed
inordinately solid to her. It was strange to see so much
building in stone rather than timber.

By Reswen's description she recognized Maikej: a
wretched little sour fruit of a mrem. Laas sighed. For
some reason, about half the mrem she had ever been told
to work on matched his description: self-important, full of
themselves, humorless, busy about things that there was
no need to be quite so busy about. *But it's probably just
as well*, she thought. *Full of themselves, they are, indeed;
so full that they never bother turning inward to find if
there's any more. And since they never do, they never
have the strength to resist me, or the wit to know what's
happening to them. Poor fools.*

She took a cup of wine and drifted over in that general
direction. She had told Deshahl earlier in the day that she
had business with this little creature; she was to stay away
from Maikej. This was a lie, since Hiriv had given her no
such directions, but Deshahl had long since learned not to
question Laas, and for the moment she was busily holding
rapt as many of the junior embassy staff at once as she
could, savoring the aggregate of their small crude lusts like
a plate of cheap sweetmeats. *Glutton*, Laas thought
scornfully.

There. He turned. He saw her. *Now*, Laas thought.
She hardly had to do anything consciously any more. Their
eyes met, she reached out without moving, reached in
with the mind, fastened claws deep in the tender places,
tugged. Tugged. And the hot blood of the mind flowed.
Maikej, a number of strides away, froze still, and the slits
of his eyes dilated round in a breath's time from the
backlash of the force with which she hit him. Laas smiled,
a demure smile, and set the claws in deeper, set them
heart-deep, tugged. *Come here. Come here, little mrem,
little slave.*

For that was it, with this one. She felt his response,
felt instantly his desire to be made small and helpless by
anyone, but especially by her. Laas kept the rising revulsion off her face. This would certainly explain the way he

behaved, as Reswen had described it to her: he went about antagonizing everyone in hopes that some one of them would see through him, strike back at him, reduce him to helplessness and expose the small frightened groveling mrem he really was to the world. And that would certainly be reason enough for him to have hated Shalav so, for she *had* so exposed him; just because he desired humiliation didn't mean he enjoyed it. *A dangerous one to deal with for long,* Laas thought, as she drew him closer, *but fortunately, I needn't; and while he's under my eye, he's safe enough. He won't be long out of it, tonight, if all goes well.*

He walked over to her. It looked very casual, that walk, but Laas could feel his muscles trembling with the sudden desire to cast himself at her feet. He was bewildered, dazed, he wanted nothing but to please her, to do whatever would please her enough that she would somehow do this one secret thing that would make him dissolve in a glory and ecstasy of abasement. *So the key,* Laas thought, *is to humiliate him, and inveigle him into letting me have my way by promising perhaps to do what he wants later. And then later, when I refuse . . . that itself will be humiliation of exactly the kind he wants.*

So she set about it. She wanted permission to move about the embassy freely; she made him give it to her, luring him into it, suggesting that she would possibly see his room, later, but not escorted, oh no; mrem would talk. She would find her way there herself. Surely he understood, surely he would speak to his staff and make it all right. And so he would. She felt his muscles jerk to go instantly to do it, and she murmured the suggestion to him, and he took the request as a command. She felt his brief spurt of ecstasy as he did something against his better judgment, did it because this beautiful mrem told him to and she had to have her whims gratified if she were to maybe, maybe, do what he wanted. . . . She steeled herself against it, bowed a little thanks to him, swayed against him, let her perfume fill his nostrils, flicked a wicked tongue against his ear, felt the heat fill him and fill him and leave him helpless—felt him wallow in the helplessness, in anguish and desire—

She detached herself gracefully from him, and went off to get another cup of wine to wash the taste of him from her mouth, and indirectly from her mind. That was always the worst of it. The flavor would fade as the creature's arousal did; but for the moment, wine worked very well to mask the flavor, to drown it briefly in her own giddiness. Laas had been conscious for some time now that wine was getting to be too good a friend. It was marvelous, by contrast, to be able to be with Reswen and not need the anodyne; to drink something innocuous like sherbet, and rest against a mind that did not smell of the sewer, that even in its heat burned clean. Endlessly better than the sweaty, reeking stews she found herself in sometimes. She desperately hoped that the wizard, later on, was not going to be one of those.

The wizard, now. There would be her great problem. There was of course no guarantee that he would be here at all; but if he was. . . . Laas sipped her wine and wondered. *Will he recognize me?* She had seen Masejih only a few times, when he was with Usiel, conferring on the details of some spell in the loft of the little house in Cithiv. Usiel had introduced her as "his ward," but as far as she knew hadn't bothered to explain any further, and for all she knew, Masejih thought she had been a servingmrem or some such. *And if he did, so much the better. I don't think he would even remember my name, if he thought me a slave or a drab; and even if he did remember it, I doubt he would believe that the same mrem would now be a high-class courtesan. So perhaps I'm worry for nothing—*

But more pressing was the question of whether he would be susceptible to her. Oh, such things as lacknot root, such as Reswen had been given by Lorin, were common enough in the East: but one would have to know that one was going to run into a charismatic, to be prepared for the eventuality. What would make him prepare for such a thing? *Unless someone had told him. Spies are everywhere. . . .* But there seemed to be few spies here who knew or suspected what she was. It was as Hiriv had said: The Western people did not much believe in magic, and so were helpless against it.

Except for one of them, Laas thought, *who believes in*

*it enough to use it to protect his city. The prudent, care-
ful, frightened creature—*

Laas leaned against the sideboard, and shook a little. It
was still much with her, the memory of Reswen holding
her as if to protect her against magic, and how the terror
of it burned in his bones until she could feel it without
even the benefit of her talent. *How can he care for me,
really,* she wondered, *when he holds magic in such terror,
such loathing?* But there was no question of it; he did. It
was most unsettling.

Then she shook her head, ruefully, and smiled and
drank wine. *I can't seem to get him out of my thoughts. . . .
Maybe there are more kinds of magic than the kind done
in dark places, with circles and mutterings. . . .*

And then she saw him, and her mind cleared, with her
own fear this time. Masejih came strolling down the stairs
from the gallery level, splendidly dressed in a sky-blue kilt
that set off that gray-blue fur most strikingly, and around
his wrists were bound bands of silver with smooth blue
stones in them, and around his neck a collar to match,
heavy and ornate. The green-blue eyes, like gems themselves, surveyed the place, lazy, cool, untroubled, opaque.

Laas held quite still, working to calm himself, as Masejih
surveyed the room. She looked elsewhere, drank her wine,
did her best to make sure she was part of the background
at this point, nothing more. Masejih walked lazily over to
another sideboard, took a drink, and strolled over to where
Maikej stood talking to one of the Easterners, slowly re-
gaining his composure.

She watched him from behind for a little while. His
stance and manner were those of complete ease, perhaps
even contempt for most of the company. Certainly there
was some contempt for Maikej, and Laas had to admit to
herself that the contrast between the two was striking, and
not at all in Maikej's favor. Placed next to the cool and
elegant ease of Masejih, and the size and solidity of him,
the puny, light-voiced, pompous Maikej dwindled to a
small thing, an insect shrilling under the shadow of the
foot that could crush it if it liked, but disdained doing so.
They were talking, Maikej a little hurried and nervous,
trying to sound important; Masejih nodding, sipping his

drink, murmuring occasional comments that always brought
Maikej up short and made him stammer hurried answers.
*I can't think what made them choose this little bug as an
ambassador*, Laas thought; *he can't say anything without
looking as if he's hunting excuses every time he opens his
mouth. He must have paid someone off.*

But there were more important things to think about.
Laas glanced idly around the room, avoiding looking at
Masejih for the moment, considering how she might manage to get herself most innocuously introduced to him.
She had learned long before that for a seduction to be
most successful, the other party must think that it was
their idea. Laas glanced casually around her. There were
various Lloahairi, some of her own people—but she disliked mixing with them while she was working; there was
a danger of their eyes or manner giving her away. *Let's
see. . . .*

But Laas found then that, all unwittingly, she had laid
just the right groundwork for what she needed to do. Out
of the corner of her eye she saw Maikej murmur something in Masejih's ear, saw them both glance her way.
Then, even through the noise and merriment of the
crowd, she heard Maikej laugh—that particular laugh that
makes she-mrem everywhere roll their eyes and want
to leave the room. Laas, though, turned to the mrem
standing near her at the sideboard, some Lloahairi cultural
attaché, and made brilliant but essentially meaningless
conversation for a few moments, while the situation between Maikej and Masejih sorted itself out.

The young attaché, a stocky young black-and-silver
tabby, was flattered beyond belief that such a beautiful
she-mrem should even look at him, much less speak to
him and begin asking him intelligent questions about his
work. Laas put forth her talent; she did not set the claw
deep in this one, just more or less drew it down the skin of
his mind, a hint and promise of something that might
happen later, if time allowed and the gods were kind.
Dazzled, though not sure by what, the youngster stam-
mered compliments, offered service in the old courteous
manner, and otherwise became visibly far gone in ador-
able yearning. Laas smiled at him kindly—he really was a

nice young mrem, another one who, like Reswen, burned clean when he burned hot—though he was not properly burning at the moment, merely in the early stages of smolder.

Laas let this continue for a moment or so, then turned as if to get herself another cup of wine. The young attaché naturally would not let her do any such thing, and laughing gently at his cheerful abjectness, she acquiesced and followed him to the nearby sideboard, using the movement to allow her a glance past Maikej and Masejih. They were still standing together, and still both watching her, Maikej with a poorly concealed leer on his face, Masejih with a small secret smile. Laas read that smile, and Masejih's stance, and needed no confirmation from her talent to know what had happened. Maikej had made a serious mistake in drawing her to Masejih's attention. Masejih had just decided that Maikej was not going to taste this little sweetmeat; oh no. He was going to find a way to steal her from under Maikej's nose.

She allowed her eye to be caught by Masejih's; she held it for a fraction of a moment, as she walked, then let it go, with no change of expression but the slightest cooling, a look that would say to Masejih, *Oh indeed; you think so, do you? I am not interested.*

With a he-mrem who meant well, the look would have cooled him instantly. It did no such thing with Masejih, which relieved Laas a great deal. She was also relieved that, at least for that fraction of a moment when their eyes met, there was no least sign of recognition. He did not know who she was; he did not know what she was doing to do to him.

Unless, of course, he has already sensed my power, and dismissed it. . . .

There was no way to tell. Lorin seemed to think that one properly trained could tell a charismatic quickly, and defend himself against her, but Laas had no idea whether Masejih had the right kind of training. She knew him primarily as a spell-worker, not one for deep thinking, but for using magic like a hammer or a knife, as a tool, not as a philosophy. So perhaps she was safe. Or perhaps not. It was a gamble, but at worst, she would use her talent to no

effect, and have a night's lovemaking with no result. Inwardly she shrugged; that had happened often enough
before and it had never bothered her.

Until now, that is, when what the other person felt had
begun to matter. At least, when it was Reswen. *And how
will I bear to lie down in this mrem's arms and find that
he is not Reswen, and never will be?*

She pushed the thought aside, and looked up and
spoke brightly to the attaché, even as she felt the blue-
green eyes fasten on her with purpose, as she felt the tall
strong shape approaching her from behind. "But these
parties tend to be so boring," she said to the attaché, and
felt the presence pause behind her, the heat beginning
already, though she had done nothing yet. And she read-
ied the claw. . . .

▲

The dispensary and infirmary in Constables' House had
once been a library, and was ridiculously ornate, considering its present purpose. The place was paneled and shelved
in some old wood, now rare and expensive; that was the
only reason why Teloi the police physician had not long
since had much of it ripped out—the carvings, at least, all
along the ceiling and floor, which made him furious. They
gathered dust, Teloi claimed, and were impossible to keep
clean, and besides, he hated the fussy carvings, the leer-
ing mrem-faces, and ornamental plant life. Teloi thought
things should be simple, clean, plain; so he told Reswen
every time he saw him, and every time Reswen would
have to apologize for the carvings.

But Reswen was in no mood for it today, and when
Teloi started, he was brusque with him. "I don't want to
know about it," he said. "I need to talk to Thabe."

Teloi scowled at him. " 'Talk' is something she won't
be doing any more," he growled. "The devils! Have you
caught who did it?"

"Not yet. How is she?"

"Awake. I wish she weren't, either, but I daren't give
her any more sedative at this point. It might interfere with
her breathing. But the pain woke her up, and she keeps
waving her stumps at me and grunting. It's you she wants.

The grunting gets louder when your name is mentioned
than it does for anything else. Get in there, for pity's sake,
don't stand out here talking to me and keeping her waiting."

Reswen nodded and went in, refusing to rise to the
bait of Teloi's well-known temper. He went into the little
curtained cubicle that had been set aside for her, and
pulled the curtain closed after him. Thabe lay there on a
soft couch, quite still, until she opened her eyes and saw
him. Her paws, or the places where they had been, were
great swathes of bandage. Her face was drawn with pain—
there was nothing to be done about *that* wound but to let
the place where her tongue had been heal naturally. Here
and there the ginger of her fur was still dyed brown with
blood—not all just hers, Reswen suspected; in a fight,
Thabe was a terror. *Had* been a terror . . . for what was a
mrem without claws? She was struggling to sit up. "Don't,"
Reswen said. "Thabe, lie still!—" but it was useless; sit up
she would. Reswen helped prop her up with some pillows
against the raised end of the couch. She rested there for a
moment, reeling a little, perhaps an aftereffect of the
sedative.

"Thabe," Reswen said, "I'm so sorry."

She hissed at him. *That* she could still do, and her eyes
flashed scorn. Apparently Thabe thought there were more
important things to be tended to than apologies for what
was done. At least that was what Reswen suspected, for
Thabe had much of the so-called "ginger" temperament—
quick-tempered, clever, impatient with idiocy.

"You got too close," Reswen said. "You got too close to
what we were looking for, and they caught you."

She nodded.

Reswen put his face in his paws for a moment. *If only
she could tell us what it was, what she saw—*

Thabe hissed again, annoyed. Reswen looked up at
her, at her anger, her tail lashing, and wanted to weep.
This was his fault—

Her tail lashed so hard, thumping the bed, that Reswen
was startled. He was more startled when he realized that
he was hearing a pattern. *Thump. Thump thump. Thump
thump thump—*

Reswen stared at her. "*Aszh,*" he said, "*veh, raih—*"

Thabe nodded violently, and grinned, then winced; the movement stretched too hard at the place where her tongue had been. She settled for showing her teeth in a smug snarl.

"Right," Reswen said. He put his head out the curtain and said to Teloi, "Send your runner upstairs and tell him to get one of my office people down here. Tell them to bring wax pads and parchment. Move it."

He turned back to Thabe. "How you can even think of something like this," he said, "when you've got such injuries—"

She hissed at him again, but it was a softer sound.

"Yes," he said softly, "I suppose. Before they come in: Magic, Thabe—was it magic?"

She nodded hard, and hissed again, and bristled.

"Right." They were quiet for a moment, and then one of Reswen's scribes came in, with Teloi behind, in full cry. "I won't have you bothering her," he said. 'What idiotic thing are you up to—"

"Teloi, be still," Reswen said. To the scribe, who was putting down an armload of tablets, he said, "Cunnek, Thabe is going to give you some transcription, but it's going to take a while. She can't talk, but she can use the standard tap code, with her tail. One thump for *aszh*, two for *veh*, and so forth. If it gets tiring, make a chart and let her use her tail to point. Does that sound all right?" he said to Thabe. She nodded.

"All right, then. Get on with it. Cunnek," he added, and the young black-furred mrem looked up at him apprehensively. "This material is extremely sensitive. If *anymrem* but you and Teloi sees it, I'm going to sit you on a spike on the walls and leave you there to enjoy the view. Are you clear about that? When Thabe is done telling you what she has to tell you, those tablets go straight up to my desk, and you stay there with them until I come and take them from you."

"Yes, sir," said Cunnek, sounding slightly nervous.

"All right, then. This material is time-sensitive—get on it. I'll be in the building for a while yet—if you need me for something that you or Thabe judge important, send a runner for me. I'll be along."

"Very well, sir."

Reswen stepped outside the curtain and listened to the thumping begin. Thabe was apparently in an impatient mood, and he could hardly blame her. Teloi came out of the cubicle and growled, "I don't want her tired. She gets tired, he goes out."

"Teloi," Reswen said with some patience, "she may just have to get tired, since what she has to tell us may make the difference between this city standing where it stands, next year, or being reduced to an empty pile of stones set in a patch of naked dirt. You let her go on as long as she feels the need. She's no fool. She won't jeopardize herself—she understands her own importance in this matter too well. You give me trouble on this one, and by the gods, you're going to have one of those pointy seats on the wall yourself."

Teloi snarled and walked off, which Reswen took, as usual, for agreement. Slowly Reswen headed out of the infirmary, back for his office, trying to calm his mind. *Laas.* She had to be in the Lloahairi Embassy at this point; the fool mrem, the brave creature, she was going to risk herself for what he felt was important. *Oh, don't,* he implored her silently, as if she could hear him. *Don't, please. There's no need. My mrem are there, they'll find a way. And these foreign mrem aren't playing games any more.* The thought of her suffering something like Thabe's fate— He shuddered. *Stay away from them, be cautious, don't get caught in this, oh love, don't—*

No answer came, not that he had been expecting one. He went up to his office, went in, and shut the door.

▲

"Madam," the voice said in Laas's ear, "surely you won't do it."

"Do what?" she said, all innocence, turning around. His eyes met hers. She struck, struck the claw deep.

For one moment his face lost all expression, his eyes lost their mocking bite, as his desire rose up and blinded him, drowned him, choked him. She felt it rise, felt the prospect of long slow lovemaking, a little cruel, a little sweet, now personified for him in her. She breathed out

a little as she tightened her hold on his passion, bound it
to her. At least this one was not a sickly welter of desired
shame like Maikej. It would be an enjoyable evening, at
the very worst. She could sense skill and a pride in his
ability at lovemaking, but again, that shade of cruelty on
the edge of everything, like the bright edge of a knife.
Laas didn't mind. She could be cruel too, and by the end
of the evening would doubtless feel like it. *For he isn't
Reswen.* . . .

"Decamp with sour old Maikej," he said, finally. The
words did not come out in the casual tone they would have
originally, before she set the claw in his heart.

"Why, who told you such a thing?" she said, demure.
"Even were I about to do it, I would hardly advertise the
fact. Nor would a mrem of gentle breeding inquire about
it, were he gently bred at all, or even simply gentle. I
think you weary me," she said. "Your pardon." And she
turned away.

He turned with her, as she expected. She could feel
his excitement rising at the little stab. There was no hint
of anything else, though; if he knew she was a charismatic,
he didn't care. And he was wearing no protection against
her talent—that at least she could tell from this close. He
stepped in front of her and bowed, a most insolently
apologetic bow, saying with a flourish of arms and tail that
she was quite right, he was a boor—as long as he got what
he wanted from her, and not a moment longer. Laas
smiled a little. "Madam," he said, "forgive me."

"Possibly," she said, "but one needs a name to know
whom to forgive."

"Masejih," he said. "A traveler and merchant of Lloahai,
for now attached to the embassy as an adviser on matters
of trade."

Does he then truly not recognize me, Laas found herself wondering, *or is he merely keeping up the pretense for
those who would be listening?* . . . *We'll soon enough find
out.* Aloud she said, "Ah, now you seek to impress me
with wealth and status. If I liked the look of you well
enough," she said, shooting him a sidewise glance as she
turned away, "I wouldn't care *that*"—she flicked one ear

elegantly—"for your salary on your connections. A brisk young mrem should be able to make his way without such crutches." She yawned sweetly as she paced away, and he followed. "I think you are too young for me, sir. Or perhaps I should rather say too old. Catch a mrem young enough, and one can train him out of these habits and into ones better suited to please a lady."

The seductive twist of tone she applied to the word "please" provoked an instant response in Masejih, so that he had to force himself to keep his paws down and not seize this saucy she-mrem to teach her how much he knew about how to please . . . if indeed he chose to do so. The response washed over her as well, and almost kindled her own body's heat, but Laas pushed that down and away as she had long been able to do even in the most tempting situations. There were, after all, few things more pitiful in the world than a seduction that boiled over too early, before the things one needed had been accomplished.

He followed after her making courtly protestations, apologies, trying to entice her as she had enticed him. Laas smiled and let him do it, let him follow her right around the room to let him realize how utterly he wanted her. Skillful, she stopped just before it would have made him angry, just at the point where he still found it humorous, and was still thinking ahead to what he was going to do to this infuriating, wicked, delightful creature when he got her where he wanted her. She gave him just enough of her eyes, just enough of her smile, to let him get a sense that she was weakening. She stopped by a sideboard, allowed him to serve her with food and drink, allowed him to drive himself wilder and wilder with anticipation.

Finally they were standing in a corner together, he between her and the rest of the room, towering over her. He leaned in close and said, "Well then? What about old Maikej?"

She gazed up at him, and smiled. "Who?" she said, and drove the claw in as deep as it could go.

His whole body shouted at him, *Take her, take her!* She could feel it. "Come with me," Masijeh said. "Now.

Oh, Laas, come, come, please come, I will do anything you ask of me—"

Very softly she slipped her tail around behind him and stroked his with it. All his fur stood on end. "But what about the party? What about your duties, the people you must meet—"

He was shaking so with desire that he couldn't even make the rude suggestion about those other people that would have been the natural response. "Laas—"

"Yes," she said very quietly. "Yes. Yes. Go. I will follow you."

He went, in something of a rush, storming off up the steps. A few people noticed him, particularly Maikej; the little mrem saw that rush and mistook its hurry for fury. He smiled at Laas across the room, an expression that was a bizarre mix of sheer malice toward Masijeh and desire for her. Laas smiled back, setting the claw deep in him too, for there was no telling when she might need it. He started to come toward her, but she wagged an admonitory claw at him, a "not yet, mrem will talk" gesture. Reluctant but obedient, he turned away, still smiling an awful smile of delight that the young upstart Masijeh had been sent about his business.

Some while later, feeling that the anticipation upstairs had reached that delicate point between rabid desire and rage, Laas moved softly toward the steps, went up them unchallenged, and was gone. She thought of the expression on Maikej's face when he turned, in a little while, looking for her, and found her gone. It made her smile.

But then she thought of Reswen . . . and it took many moments to get the smile back against before she opened the door behind which Masijeh waited.

"Laas," he said. For so softly spoken a word, it was almost a cry of triumph.

Reswen, she thought, and smiled, and went in, and closed the door.

▲

Reswen sat with his paws folded, and he twitched a bit while he waited. He was trying to keep a rein on his patience, but finding it difficult. *It's just so annoying*, he thought. *The place is full of our people right now. There are any number of places we could be prying into. But until Thabe tells us what we should be looking for, I don't dare spoil our chances, if we should get caught looking for something else, something of lesser importance. And Laas, oh, Laas, what are you doing, please stay out of it!*

The knock on his door almost made him jump out of his fur. It was the scribe, come back up to his office. The burdened-down youngster put down most of the pile of tablets he was carrying, and handed Reswen just two of them.

"Good work," he said to Cunnek. It had to have been wearying work, counting thumps and making sure they belonged to the right letter, scratching one letter at a time, starting all over again.

"She fell asleep, sir," Cunnek said. "She was hurting a lot."

Reswen looked at Cunnek suspiciously. Were his eyes red? And from what? "All right," he said. "Get out of here . . . you've put in enough overtime for one day. Take tomorrow off, if you like. And find me a runner on the way out."

"Yes, sir. Good night, sir."

"I seriously hope so," Reswen said, letting his eyes fall again to the tablet. The report was terse, but then Thabe's reporting usually was, even when she wasn't having to spell it out letter by letter. *Oh, poor kit, what can we do for you now. . . ?* He sighed and read the thing.

Investigated most of embassy and was unable to find anything of interest except in subbasement. This area usually guarded, door almost always locked except when subbasement is occupied. Persons seen to enter it: once, Maikej; more than once, Masejih (alleged trade attaché). All entries take place at night. Took advantage of slack guard to pick lock and enter. Room is large and square, walls rough, appears to be a late addition. Lacks supports, probably not dug by licensed workmen, looks liable to collapse. Possible building code violation? Contents: bookshelves: small

> *box of roll-books on one shelf, written in numerous*
> *languages, some locked, most seeming quite old. Draw-*
> *ing on floor, large circle with various letters and*
> *numbers inscribed in it, along with numerous geo-*
> *metrical figures. Some bottles, large and small, most*
> *contents unidentifiable, but one with scentless clear*
> *liquid (water?).*

At that, Reswen's whiskers stood out in a mixture
of alarm and pleasure.

> *Three braziers, ashes in them indicating coals no*
> *older than two days. Narrow sticks leaning against*
> *wall. May be more smaller objects in small boxes*
> *against wall, but uncertain since operative was dis-*
> *covered at this point by alleged attaché Masejih: sur-*
> *prised from behind, knocked unconscious, bound.*
> *Guards were not called in, but subject Masejih de-*
> *clared that operative "would not tell anyone about*
> *this" and removed paws and tongue.*

Reswen shivered at the dryness of the account.

> *Guards were then called and instructed to "dump*
> *this refuse somewhere. Maybe she'll save us some*
> *trouble and bleed to death." Was dumped somewhere*
> *outside the Whites in the neighborhood of Clock Lane.*
> *Left area, waited for pickup.*

Reswen rubbed his forehead with one paw. A little
removed from this, dug into the wax with more than
necessary force, were the words,

> *Kill the motherless bastards, sir. In some legally*
> *permitted manner, of course. Thabe.*

Reswen clenched his fists and thought. *Water, then.*
But no stone. Where is it? In one of those boxes she didn't
have time to check? Gods, the place stinks of magic. Lorin
has got to see this . . . I need advice. I need more than
that. Oh Laas, stay out of there—

He moaned softly to himself. No one had ever told him that love was such a terrifying thing. . . .

Reswen got up to find out where that damned runner was—and then found out, as the youngster hammered on his door. Reswen flung it open.

The runner was gasping. Reswen recognized her, with an awful sinking feeling, as one of the ones he had attached to the Easterners at Haven for their use. "Sir," she gasped, "the priest Hiriv says to tell you to come right away, the stone and water they were given have been stolen!"

She turned and ran out again.

Reswen went out right behind her, swearing.

▲

Chapter 13

▲————————————————————————▲

She had been about her business, away from her body, watching all things develop as she had ordered—and then it happened. Something violated her wards.

Her body had its instructions in such cases: immediate return, painful though it was. The tenuous cord that connected her overself to the hardest skin yanked her back and out of the golden warmth of the overworld, into the cold harsh unyielding shell that was all she had to wear in the physical realms. It was at times like this that she hated physicality, hated the rough edges of it, the crassness and indelicacy of it, its lack of subtlety. But pulled back like this, tumbled over and over, dragging protesting through the aether, to slam down into the hard-skinned shell—this made her curse with her people's curses, and the sound was terrible to hear.

She had not been back for a long time. The body was sluggish in responding. Her outrage lent it no impetus toward its awakening. There was something still here, something using magic, *vermin's* magic, pitiful little art that it was, and she could not immediately reach up and hook it down from its perch and slay it—

Scrambling noises, scratching sounds. It had seen her. Or perhaps not, perhaps something else had frightened it. No matter. She would give it something to be frightened of—

Her body still would not answer her. No matter; in it, she commanded other levels of magic. Her semblance rose up in fire to swirl about her hiding-place and look about her for the intruder, to strike it dead.

But there was nothing to be seen—

She swore again, in a torrent of hissing. She knew the spell, and also knew that there was nothing that could be done about it. No doubt now; the vermin-wizard had come prepared, had suspected her presence. It never occurred to her, at any point, to accuse herself of her own folly in having taunted the creature, sleeping and waking—for this was certainly the same one she had taken such pleasure in tormenting. But she would make it pay, soon or late. Sooner or later the creature would sleep, and warded or not, she would have her way with it. It would take a long time dying, the creature would, and she would relish its screams, every one.

Meanwhile, there were other concerns. She recalled the fire-form, then reached out in mind to the one pet she deigned to speak to. *Hasten*, she said, and ran fire down its bones to impress it with the need to hurry. *Be about the spell, or it will be the worse for you. Find the other and begin. I am watching.* Indeed, she had to be; without her assistance, the two could never manage to bring through the power whose assistance her masters desired. That was one of the things about this mission that had angered her, that her people's own magic was in this one area insufficient. It took vermin to do it—so her masters had insisted. She had not argued with them . . . not then, at least . . . and she would not, now. But after the spell was done, she was minded to take matters into her own claws, and show her masters and these vermin alike what *real* destruction was. . . .

Go! she cried to the vermin, who still abased itself, listening to her. It fled, moaning in pain and fear. She settled down into herself again, half of a mind to leave her body again. She was coming to loathe it, the immobile, ungraceful hulk. But no. She would remain it in just long enough to see her will done. And then . . .

Fire everywhere, and blood in rivers.

▲

Reswen went to Haven and was greeted, if that was the word, by Hiriv. The priest was far gone, wailing and moaning in a way guaranteed to wake up the immediate neighborhood at such an awful hour, well past middle night. Reswen found all the noise and anguish hard to understand, though he said nothing out loud. *He ought to be reasoning that the city could always give him another stone and another bottle of water,* Reswen thought. *Or is he thinking that someone might be urging the Arpekh otherwise? Or more to the point, would it simply take too long? Is something going to happen for which he requires the stuff right away?*

Or, he thought then, *is this actually a blind to distract us? Has he already passed the stone and water on to someone at the Lloahairi Embassy—our friend Masejih, perhaps?*

And if not, then whose was that water that Thabe saw there? If it was water at all—

There were too many questions going around in his head, and not nearly enough data to begin answering them. Reswen put them all to rest for the moment by beginning to conduct a standard investigation for theft, having all the rooms checked by the constables he had brought with him, touring the rooms with Hiriv to make sure of where the stone and water had been, verifying that they had not merely been misplaced. Hiriv showed him a cupboard and told him that things had been locked in there when he left for the party. He always, he said, kept the key around his neck. Reswen knew this was true—the key was a courtesy to visitors who had goods they wanted to keep locked up. But he also knew that Hiriv was lying about the stone and water having been in there, since his staff had a duplicate of the key, and the cupboard had been checked several times in the past couple of days by the "cleaning staff."

At the end of the check, they found nothing. "Good priest," Reswen said, thinking privately that in Hiriv's case the terms were antithetical, "I will need a list of everyone who came here today, and of all of your staff who left for whatever reason, and where they went." It would make interesting reading, Reswen thought, checking it against the one the Haven staff and the people down in the cellar would be compiling for him under Krruth's guidance.

"You shall have anything you want," Hiriv said, sounding very desperate indeed. "Only find them again for me. My head will answer for it, back East, if you don't."

Reswen bowed, his best bow of reassurance, and Hiriv swept off, still more or less tearing his fur.

Then Reswen called his people together out front in the courtyard and gave them their instructions, well away from the Easterners' ears. "I want you all to be very busy here," he said. "Do what you like, but keep this place a-bustle as late as you can. They want an investigation; investigate them. Ask every stupid question you can think of, practice your interrogation technique—no knives, Gishitha, you wipe that look off your face. Turn the place inside out and upside down. I want them to think we're running mad for their sakes. I want you to seem like a hundred constables instead of twenty. While you're at it, keep your eyes on these people. I want to know where they go, what they do. One exception: Should the lady Laas turn up, give her this *immediately*"—he handed one of them a folded note—"and give her whatever assistance she requires. She's working inside for us, my dears, so stop looking at Old Ginger as if he's gone into his dotage at last." There was some much-subdued snickering at this. "All right? Be about it, then."

They went about it, leaving Reswen in the lamplight by the front gates. He grinned to himself, and it was not a pleasant expression. *It'll be awhile before anyone leaves the place*, he thought. *Time enough to go home and change. Then I want to find Lorin. And then. . .*

Reswen went off, smiling still, and melted into the darkness. It had been awhile since he'd had a good night's field work, and this one promised to be more interesting than most.

▲

It was late when Laas awoke. Everything was very still with the quiet of late night in a sleeping house. The party was apparently over, the guests all gone. She turned over sleepily, and found the other side of the couch empty.

She yawned, stretched, sat up in the darkened room. Her evening with what's his name, Masejih, had been enjoyable enough, as she'd thought it would be; otherwise, nothing spectacular. *Certainly not, in comparison with Reswen . . .*

Laas glanced around the room, splendidly but rather shabbily furnished, like the rest of the place. *Now what would he be doing, so late at night? Relieving himself, perhaps*— But she put out her paw and touched his side of the couch, and found it quite cold. *Not that. Well then, I will find out. That's what all this is about, anyway. . . .*

She shut her eyes for a moment and felt for him. This was not always easy; after sex, the attachment of the "claw" of her mind in a subject's sometimes weakened. But more usually there was a trace of a bond remaining, enough to lure the subject back if she wanted him again. The bond could serve as a directional sense, in a vague way. It did so now. He was somewhere in the area, thought not close. Not on this floor, certainly.

Laas got up, dressed—easier to explain that she was going home, if someone should come upon her—and slipped to the door, eased it open, peered out into the dark corridor. Nothing. Faintly, intruding of her sense of Masejih, she could get a less intrusive sense of Maikej, across the hall, perhaps, very much awake, very much frustrated. She shrugged her tail gently and padded out into the hall, shutting the door silently behind her.

At the head of the stairs she paused. *Down,* the sense said, so down she went. The feeling of lazy, blurred fulfillment got stronger. The hall was silent, dark, the drapes all pulled. Only the faintest light streamed up into it from a torch fixed somewhere down the second flight of stairs, the one to the basement. Laas turned and went down that flight. The torch was not actually fastened there, but somewhere further down yet. Its reflected light shone on the wall as she went down.

Cellars, she thought. *I'll never get used to them. Especially at night.*

At the bottom of the second flight she paused and looked around her. Where there should have been a flat wall, there was a doorway, and it stood ajar. Laas peered through it. The torch was fastened inside, by an iron bracket, to a wall that looked to be of rough stones embedded in smaller stones and dirt. Steps of slate went further down. A cool damp air breathed up them, slipped past her hind paws, and chilled them.

Laas hesitated.

But then, she thought, *this is what I came to do . . . and what Reswen needs to find out.*

In utter silence she eased the door open enough to take her body, pulled it back as it had been, and slipped down the stairs, around a corner from the torch, and into shadow . . . .

▲

The only advantage to the reduced police force around the Lloahairi embassy was that they were forced to use their own people for security, and their own people were not very good. They didn't like staying up late at night, and their watch slacked off considerably then. They also seemed to have that regrettable tendency of temporary security people to believe that they are really unnecessary, that they're being paid for someone's paranoia, and that no one would *really* try to come in that window.

Reswen found this a delightful tendency, and one he intended to exploit to its fullest. He crouched under the far side of the blank back wall of the Lloahairi Embassy's garden, breathing the sweet cool night air and thinking cheerfully wicked thoughts. No one was patrolling outside this wall; an oversight, but an understandable one, since the Lloahairi in general were uncertain about their welcome in town, and some of their forces posted here some days back had been set upon by townmrem and beaten up fairly severely. Reswen would not have admitted to encouraging such behavior, of course, but he had had a small conversation with the division-level constable who handled this area, and both of them together, in making up the duty patrol rosters, had forgotten to post any policemrem at all in the area. *Careless of us . . .*

He was perfectly in his element, as happy as he could remember being for a long time. Reswen had first achieved his reputation in the constabulary by inspired "lurking and skulking," as his commanding auncient had called it. He hadn't lost the talent. He could still move like a shadow when he wanted to, and the black hair dye he had used on Laas had more than one use. Now, instead of ginger fur, no torch would find anything of him but darkness. He was all in dark street clothes, an overcloak and tunic that looked unassuming enough at first glance, but would reflect no light whatsoever. At Reswen's belt, the bottom of the sheath tied round his leg with a thong, hung the rose-and-gold knife, for luck, and also because it had one of the wickedest edges he had ever seen on a piece of cutlery.

Behind him crouched Lorin, in his own ragged dark cloak, muttering softly to himself. "Oh, be still," Reswen said for about the tenth time. "We'll be fine."

"This is illegal," Lorin muttered.

"You're with the chief of police," Reswen whispered. "It'll be fine."

"Not as far as the Arpekh are concerned. And we have other problems."

Reswen breathed out and put the thought of the Arpekh far from him. It was a good thing the old mrem hated to be waked up for what they considered insufficient cause; otherwise, he would probably have to be with them now, in late session, answering stupid questions, rather than ready to go over a wall and break into diplomatically protected ground. But then again, he was the one who usually decided whether the cause was sufficient. . . .

At least, I am for the moment. Who knows whether I still will be in the morning? Mraal's last meeting with him came up for consideration, and Reswen had to push *that* unsettling memory away too. *Never mind that.* As for Lorin's "other problems," about which he had babbled when Reswen first picked him up, they would have to wait. He had a lot of trouble believing that Lorin had seen anything that wasn't a product of his own nerves. *Anyway, one thing at a time—*

"You ready?" he said softly to Lorin.

"Of course not, what a stupid—"

Reswen ignored him, half rose from his crouch in shadow, and threw the clawhook over the wall. There was the softest *chunk* as it fell against the wall's opposite side, then a soft ratchety noise as he pulled on the cord to snug it in place under the wall's top course. Reswen tested it, gently at first, then with a good hard pull, and there was no slippage. "Come on," he said, and went up the rope.

For all that Lorin was a good climber, this was another matter. It was apparently a deal too far from the ground for him. Finally Reswen, perched on top of the wall, had had to reach down and pull him up by the arms. Lorin clutched the top of the wall, wild-eyed, like a kit afraid of falling from a height. "Come on, come on," Reswen said, ready to jump down, and realized from Lorin's frozen posture that the poor mrem *was* afraid of heights. And at a moment when delay could be fatal, with the two of them perhaps silhouetted against some chance light. Under the circumstances he did the kindest thing possible: He pushed Lorin off. It all happened so suddenly that Lorin had no time to do anything but grunt when he hit the ground. *It's not as if it was more than twice my height*, Reswen thought, a little guiltily, and jumped after.

When he landed, Lorin was saying astonishing things under his breath. "Oh, shut up," Reswen said, and glanced around them.

The garden was as deserted as it ought to be, this time of night. They had come down in a mercifully concealing patch of spikeweed, some parts of which had speared them in passing: Lorin was pulling one particularly impressive sliver of the stuff out of his right haunch. Reswen looked out between the wide leaves. Nothing but a perfectly mowed sward, a small formal herb garden, some tables set about on a paved belvedere, and then the house itself, its galleries dark. A few windows were open, probably due to the heat. Reswen smiled.

"There," he whispered, pointing to one of them that was fairly easy of access, up a trellis heavily covered with vines.

"You want me to climb up there??"

"Anymrem old enough to have his eyes open could manage it. And besides, from what you were telling me, you've had a nice warmup for your climbing already tonight. Come on, we can't sit here forever!"

They slipped across the empty garden, Lorin limping slightly from where the spikeweed had caught him in the pad of one hind paw. Under the trellis Reswen paused, looked up, and then said to Lorin, "You first."

Lorin snorted very softly. "You're just afraid I'll come to my senses halfway up and go off and leave you."

"You'd never do a thing like that. Especially with me to catch you if you fall."

Lorin growled softly in his throat and began to climb.

To do him justice, Reswen thought, he was better with vines than with ropes, and he resolutely refused to look down . . . which was probably wise. Once Lorin was almost level with the floor of the gallery that ran past the rooms, Reswen yanked on Lorin's leg to make him stop, then clambered up beside him as quietly as he could.

The window that was open was actually a large glassed door, about halfway ajar. Inside, hangings stirred in a slight flow of air out of the room. Reswen hoisted himself up with utmost care between two of the balusters, then came to his hind paws and balanced there silently, out of direct sight of whoever might be in the room. He glanced down. Lorin was hanging on grimly, nothing but eyes and ears showing over the massed foliage. He gestured him up, made a "But softly!" gesture, and turned toward the door.

Reswen listened hard. No sound. No, wait: sound, but very slight. Snoring?

Lorin came up behind him with only a slight thump.

There was a catch in the snoring. Reswen froze, glancing at Lorin. Lorin's eyes were wide with fear.

The sound steadied again. Reswen leaned around the open door to peer in. There was nothing to be seen but the dark shapes of furniture, clothes thrown over a chair or two, a huge bed with a canopy. In the middle of the bed, amid a welter of the bedclothes, lay the source of the sound. A particularly loud snore rose up, caught on itself, expired in a wheeze.

Come on, Reswen motioned, and stepped into the room.

Once in, he paused just long enough to let his eyes get used to the deeper darkness. There was a faint scent of nightflower in the air. *Now let's see . . . where's the door . . . ?*

Lorin stepped in quietly behind him and held still too. The form in the bed turned over, snored, paused, snored again—

And woke up, looking straight at them. All Reswen got was a glimpse of terrified eyes—

He threw himself at the bed, snatched for a pillow, and stuffed it down over the wide-mouthed face just a breath before the yowl of terror came out. It came out muffled, if at all.

"Sorry," Reswen breathed. He felt around for the vase full of nightflowers on the bedside table with one paw, took the pillow away with the other, and smashed the delicate vase on the mrem's head. Water and flowers went everywhere, but the unfortunate snorer was unconscious a second later.

Reswen tossed the pillow away and looked at the mrem with resignation. It was Maikej.

"We'd better find something down there," he said softly, "that's all I can say. Get me one or two of those tunics on the chair. I'll tie him and gag him."

Reswen worked quickly, ripping the expensive cloth with a sort of bizarre cheerfulness. *After all,* he thought, *if he's going to get me executed, at least I'll have destroyed a couple of his best shirts. . . .*

He finished. Together he and Lorin padded out of the bedroom of the ambassador's suite, toward the door into the hallway. There they paused and looked around them. Everything was darkness and quiet; nothing else. Reswen knew the layout of the place, and led the way toward the stairs. Coming to them, they looked down and saw a hint of light, uncertain, wavering, somewhere below.

"Come on," Reswen said, "and let's see what we can see."

▲

Laas held very, very still, holding a rough wooden door shut almost against her nose, and trembling. The corridor of rough stones had some rude storage rooms cut into it, tiny places perhaps meant for wine at one time. Now they seemed to have nothing in them but old moldy rags and ancient broken scullery tools that hadn't been used for years. And one of them had Laas in it. She was not a brave mrem, no matter what other people might think, and the sound of a voice seemingly repeating something over and over, in angrier and angrier tones, frightened her badly enough to make her jump into one of the filthy little cupboards as if it were lined with silks.

Slowly, slowly her thudding heart began to stop trying to shake its way out of her chest. Laas breathed in and out very softly, very purposefully, trying to find her calm again. The voice down the hall seemed to be getting angrier and angrier. Or was it just increasing in volume? The way the corridor carried echoes made it hard to tell. And what was it saying, that voice? Laas leaned a little against the door, pushing it ever so slightly further open—

The sound of footsteps shook her as violently as if she had been stepped on herself. But she had enough presence of mind not to move the door any further, to stay perfectly still. It was possible she hadn't been noticed. Laas held her breath, and wasn't even aware of it. Not three inches from her nose, a large shape walked hurriedly past the door and off down the hall to where the other voice chanted. She felt the air of the mrem's passing brush against her eyes. Laas closed those eyes, just for a moment, breathed, gasped air in again, and tried to recover.

But there's no use in my being here unless I find out what's going on, for Reswen, she thought, and ventured to push the door just the slightest bit open. It made no sound. She took courage, slipped out of the little cupboard, and went stealthily down the hall in the path of the mrem that had walked past her. There were other cupboards to hide in if she needed one, and besides, the bend at the end of the corridor would hide her—

"About time you got here."

"You're a fine one to talk." Laas drew shocked breath at the sound of the voice, for it seemed to her that it was someone she knew— She came to another cupboard much nearer to the bend in the corridor, tried the door to make sure it wouldn't squeak, and secreted herself in it. She could hear much better here.

"Ah, leave off. I was with someone."

"Our little Laas, hey? That heat-crazed little piece, I should have her—well, never mind. She had no idea we two had business, and I suppose she's due a little skarking on her own time. No matter. I just wish you'd been where you were supposed to be when I wanted you there. I had to start the idiots looking before you even actually *had* the things. Here, take them. Let's be on with it."

"Are you sure they're distracted?"

There was a laugh, and no mistaking it. *Oh gods, Hiriv*—"Distracted? They're crazed. All Haven is astir with their spies and constables. And just as well, since that way, no one will be bothering us here. Come along, let's finish the business. I want to get out of this foul place, and the sooner the better. We have other work to do."

There was a pause, some shuffling around, the sound of something heavy being pushed somewhere. Laas was burning with confusion, and terror, and an odd sort of rage. *What in the world is Hiriv doing here? With Masejih, for pity's sake? Hiriv isn't a*—

"Have you got the book—"

"Yes, here. Come on, come on, this makes me nervous."

—*at least I didn't think he was a magic-worker*—

A laugh, loud and self-assured and insulting. "You? I thought you were older in power than *that*, priest. Can't you deal with what we're doing, even now? It's not as if we've never done it before."

The anger was building in Laas, and for which cause, she could hardly make up her mind. *That little heat-crazed piece, hm?* she thought. This from the mrem she had served well and faithfully? And now who knew what filthy work he was about. She wanted to find out—not just for Reswen: for herself. She pushed this second cupboard door carefully open—and gratefully, for the place was reeking with a smell of vegetables dead of extreme old age—and stepped out, silent-footed. There was one more, very near the bend. In fact, she could look around the bend itself for a moment, perhaps. Torchlight fell there from the room around the corner, where Hiriv and Masejih worked, but it was very faint. Perhaps she wouldn't be seen if she kept quite still. *Light blinds those who're standing in it, after all*—

The sounds of some kind of preparation went on down in the room, as Laas stepped softly closer. "By the way, I talked to our friend this evening. The police were around his place, it seems. Snooping around after something."

"Sent them on their way, I hope."

"He wasn't there at the time. Found out about it later."

A snort. "Not that it matters. By the time they figure out what's been going on, we'll be long gone on our way to Vezoi . . . and *they* won't give us so much trouble about the same trick, I'll warrant. No police there. 'A peaceful city.' "

There was laughter from both the voices: not particularly cruel, just as if they found the thought of peace rather a funny thing. Laas paused in shadow, held her breath, and looked around the corner.

The room was rather bare, except that she could see a couple of upstanding braziers, full of some sort of sticks or twigs ready to be ignited. A rushlight burned on the floor, its little yellow star of light seeming bright and steadfast despite the draftiness of the place. Hiriv was there, in his robes, but they were tied up out of the way, and he appeared to be sprinkling colored chalks on the bare rammed dirt of the floor, in a very steady and businesslike manner. Laas shook her head to herself. She had seen Hiriv all kinds of ways—drunkenly jolly, hilariously pious, serious when he was being made fun of and couldn't tell—but "businesslike" was no word she had ever thought to apply to him. Masejih was there too, in his nightgown, but stepped out of sight almost as Laas got a clear glimpse of him. He was working with another jar of powder, in another corner. "Looking forward to this one," he said. "I always prefer to work with two. The results are a lot better."

"Mmmf," said Hiriv, and straightened up for a moment from his sprinkling to rub his back. He had always had trouble with it. *And how many times have I rubbed that back, for kindness' sake*, Laas thought, now for the first time feeling angry about it. *What's going on—*

"It does work better," Hiriv said, as he bent to his work again. "You get more than twice the reaction: You get about four times, for some reason. And it's going to be more fun than usual, watching it happen. These damned pagans, anyway. And these two deserve each other. Damned posturing, noisy Niauhu with their little toy army, and the

blowhard Lloahai—" There was a pause. "Damn. Out of
yellow. Do we have another one?"

Laas saw some small objects in one of the two corners
of the room that were within her view. There were two
little bottles of water, and two rocks. *I had to start the
idiots looking before you even had the things—"*

Laas repressed a growl. *Did that mean that he's told
the police that the stone and water were stolen? When all
the time he had them himself, in fact brought them here to
Masejih? And that means Reswen is with all those people
he mentioned at Haven—oh no!—*

She breathed deeply again, calming herself. *And where
did this other stone and water come from? Lloahai? What
are they doing??*

"All right," Masejih said, from out of sight, "that should
do it for the physicals. Shall we start the verbal preparation?"

"Right. Where's the book? I had the place marked,
what happened?"

"Right there, the mark fell into the roll. Come on, old
mrem, I want to get this over with and get back to the
'piece.' "

"Enjoy her while you can," Hiriv said, sounding unconcerned, and then began to read. He sounded as if he
was conducting some particularly boring service. "Hear
then, all Powers and Principalities with power to hear and
to wreak for good or ill; by the Elements here concate-
nated and with their will we call your might to hear or to
speak, to do or to let be as we command, and we declare
ourselves for this time your goodly and lawful masters,
saving always the eye and paw of the Name beyond Names,
which hears you not and knows you not;"—a long breath
here—"wherefore it is good and proper that you own us
your one only and most excellent masters till that we let
cease this binding upon you, which we bind in the names
Diqid, Otej, Elov Nenepu the Flail of the Dark Gods,
Chigue and Puzoth and Shacifa Fewchance, Amuej and
Chil Thettig, Eshehkegi and Fazmad—"

The list went on for quite a while. It was a spell, no
doubt of it, and something about the cadence and the
bizarre names made Laas's nape-hairs stand up. But at the
same time there was an odd silliness to it, coming perhaps

of the way Hiriv read the spell as if it were a grocery list. Laas inched a little closer, to see what else she could see.

"—and thereby we request, require, and command that you present yourselves in such form as shall do us no harm but shall be proper and fitting to carry out your deeds of power, invulnerable to iron and fire and the holy things of the world, and having so manifested yourself and done service, you shall be well thanked in the ancient ways, and honor be done to you before you be sent to your own place; therefore for your weal and the swift fulfillment of our desires, hear our bidding, and obey. *Aratha, aratha, aratha*—"

There was a rustle as the book rolled shut, and Hiriv tossed it to the floor. "Fine," he said then. "Get inside the circle."

Masejih moved into sight to pick up something from beside the wall: some kind of black wooden stick. "All right, light them—"

Hiriv bent down to pick up the stones and flasks of water, carried them out of sight, then returned and bent down for something else, a common clay fire pot. He opened it and dumped its coals into one of the braziers, blew on them to help them catch, then picked up a burning twig and walked almost out of sight to the other one. Laas waited, almost bursting with impatience. She had seen Usiel do enough magic that she was no longer crippled by the simple irrational fear of it, but she wanted to know what they were *doing*—

The twigs and wood caught, and there was a smell of scorching, and then a stronger one, the scent of spices burning, a sweet-sharp reek that provoked one to sneeze. Laas restrained herself.

Some shuffling sounds ensued, and a clunk. "Dammit," Hiriv said, "don't be knocking things over while I'm spelling, or—"

"Don't say it. Not now. It's unwise even to joke about it."

Hiriv snorted again. "Afraid, are you? Never mind. Just pay attention now, we have to be finished before the burning stops. —Now we call upon you, great Nufiw, master of devourings, ruler and acceptor of all midnight murders, first singer of the song of loss; lord of waste places and despiser of the rank growth that mars the sweet barrenness of the face of the world; be called by us, great Lord Nufiw, Lord of the emptiness before life and the dry sterility after it; who looks forward to the day when all worlds shall be bare stone under the deadly fires of heaven, and the insult of life be gone; hear us now as we cry out upon you. Hear our offer of these fair stones, once yours, now to be yours again; this water, once trapped forever in the ice of the longest night, now soon to be boiled away in the rage of your fires—"

It was getting dark, and cold. Laas thought of what Lorin had done the other night, that petty sorcery, that had still been so overwhelming. *If I'm not going to miss anything,* she thought, *I had better get closer. They won't be in any condition to notice me while they're right in the middle of it, and the darkness will hide me—*

"—take now, we beg you, these offerings, and devour them, and by their joint devouring, devour also the fruit of the lands of these places, to the least blade of grass, to the last drop of water, save where we beg you spare; blast and destroy the livelihood of the fields, and the beasts of the land, and the trees and herbs, and all things that fly and creep and run and move, save only the mrem thereof. And when this is done, let the mrem of these cities be bound by your devouring of their stone and water together, and let them refuse not to fall upon one another in red war such as is pleasing to you, and leave these lands clean for your faithful servants who shall come into them to worship you in after times, after your revenge is fulfilled—"

The darkness grew. The torches in the room quarreled weakly with it, and slowly began to lose the argument. Laas shook like a leaf in a storm of black wind, in the feeling that some other presence was leaning over all these undertakings. *So. No wonder they wanted to know who was willing to lose part of their grain crop. Everything will be destroyed, everything in Niau and Lloahai alike, except those small crops necessary to keep the barest few people alive. And then the two will go to war. Easy enough to set it up; probably evidence is being provided right now that the Lloahai are responsible for it. Surely the Niahu*

*will think so, since this is happening in their embassy. I
daresay the same evidence will be provided for the Lloahairi,
against the Niauhu. The two cities will destroy each other.
And the Easterners will move in as they always wanted to,
and take these cities for their own . . . without having
been seen to have done anything but behave properly. In
the aftermath of the wars, they'll move to "protect the
interests" of their allies on Niau's and Lloahai's borders.
After almost everyone in them has died to glut this half-
dead god, of course. And if they happen to annex one
land, or both, or more . . . well, these things happen. . . .*

Laas was indignant. There would be no more starving,
no more dying *that* way, not if *she* could help it, not for
gods or for anyone else. But what could she do?

She inched closer—

The whole circle was visible now, as much as anything
was visible through the darkness settling into the room
like some dark, heavy liquid stirred into water. The torches
gave up. Only the braziers glowed unchoked, and the
lines of chalk sprinkled on the floor glowed too, a smolder-
ing chilly light pale as corpse fire. Hiriv stood reading
from the book with Masejih looking over his shoulder,
most concerned. It was a standard practice, Laas knew: In
the more dangerous sorceries, a fellow sorcerer could act
to say a word properly or turn a page when his fellow
celebrant failed, and so save their lives.

"Therefore come, come, O come, master of the bar-
ren places; come accept these offerings, and make our
desires truth; O come!—"

Darkness swirled in the circle. The two wizards backed
away from it, staying carefully inside the circle's confines.
Hiriv resolutely refused to look up. Masejih looked up as if
he enjoyed it, but shaded his eyes as if gazing into something blinding bright. The swirl of darkness tightened,
gathered, the way a dust-swirl gathers and tightens in a
closed courtyard, only half seen, but there enough to feel
if one walks through it and dares the stinging dust in one's
eyes. And then there *was* something there, slowing from
its spinning. Eyes Laas saw, the same corpselight color of
the lines of the circle, but horribly piercing, as if light did
not have to be bright to do harm. A shape formed around

it, something that stood upright, but crookedly so. Great
long arms hung to the ground, gestured vaguely, with slow
malice; hunched shoulders, crooked spine, long thin limbs,
head fastened to the body by a neck that looked like it
should snap under the head's weight; all these spoke of
starvation, but something that enjoyed suffering hunger,
with a horrible vitality, and felt all others should too. The
eyes looked around. They looked at Hiriv, who stood with
eyes downcast, and at Masejih, who bowed as if over-
whelmed by majesty.

And they looked at Laas, and her heart froze, and her
breath froze in her lungs, and every muscle froze, unable
to move. She could not even cry out.

A voice spoke. It did not speak in any mrem language,
but Laas understood its meaning. It was all hunger, and
pleasure at the sight of a dainty, a treat.

Hiriv and Masejih looked up in astonishment and saw
her.

I'm undone. Ah, Reswen!! Where are you?

She could not even cry out. No satisfaction, that, whether
or not she had considered herself past crying out for
anyone's help, male or female. Now she would have cried
to anyone who passed, but could not so much as grunt.

Masejih waved with the black stick he was holding. A
swirl of corpse light went up from the circle, parted like a
gateway to let him out. He walked toward her, slowly,
reaching into the pocket of his bathrobe for something.

He came close, came out with it. Laas could not even
move her eyes, could only just make out what it was. It
was a cord, a cord of something silken, such as one might
find hanging from drapes.

"These ceremonies," he said softly, as he put a paw
under her arm, "commonly work better with a death. You
are *most* welcome."

▲

Reswen and Lorin went down the steps as softly as
they might. It wasn't easy, especially for Lorin. He was
never the most courageous of mrem; now that he felt
certain he was implicated in the death of the Lloahai
ambassador, he shuddered like a fish out of water all the

way down to the main floor, and one step before it, he stumbled and fell flat on his face.

"Come on, come on," Reswen whispered, picking up Lorin in the darkness and dusting him off with inaccuracy but good intentions. "Don't give out on me now."

Lorin said things under his breath as they turned the corner of the stairway and headed down another flight. Then he stopped, simply stopped like a statue and refused to move.

Reswen heard the footsteps behind him cease. He stopped, turned, shook Lorin. It did nothing. From down the stairs he could hear some sort of speech, a garbled sound. "Come on," he said. "Come on!—" And he refused to pay any attention to Lorin's rigidity, simply dragged him down the stairs like a board of wood. At that, some of the rigidity wore off. Lorin, perhaps, had not been prepared for the possibility of being dragged like baggage. At any rate, he began gasping. "No," he said, "Reswen, you don't—"

"Don't bet on it," said Reswen. He was certain, now, that Laas was down there. Reason had nothing to do with it. He had more or less given reason up for the evening. Besides, considering her stubborn, well-intentioned ways, where else would she be? She had doubtless tried to seduce the wizard—and whether she had failed or succeeded, this was the result: lights and chanting in a cellar—

Reswen plunged on down the stairs with Lorin in tow. "Reswen," he hissed, "don't you get it? They're right in the middle of some kind of binding. If you disturb it you'll get caught in it—"

"*She's* caught in it," Reswen fairly snarled, and down they went together, past the rude door Thabe had mentioned, down the rude corridor, past the cupboards— At the corridor's end, where it bent, caution hit even Reswen. There was a darkness in the air that came of more than lack of torches, and that dark air throbbed, faster and faster, as if with an expiring pulse. He gave Lorin a last wake-up shake, let go of him, and peered carefully around the corner.

And saw it—and yowled, a mrem's battlecry, spitting; and with his knife drawn, ran straight into the heart of the darkness—

▲

Laas could not move of her own will, could barely breathe, could hardly think with terror, but one thing she could still do. As Masejih took her by the arm to lead her away, she set the claw deep in him and pulled, pulled harder than she ever had before. *Want me,* she cried inwardly, *want me, you poor creature. Melt where you stand, go limp with desire, be able to do nothing but stand and look at me—*

Masejih's paw on her trembled. Just freshly come from her embraces, he was easy prey, and she felt the claw settle deep and turn his blood hot. He stared at her, only her, and shook all over; the murderous look on his face had for the moment slacked into vacuous lust. *But how long can I hold it?* Laas thought, shaken. She still couldn't move. And she needed to run, to get away from there—

Another flicker of pale fire from that circle. Out of the corner of her eye she could see Hiriv coming. And Masejih twitched too; just from that tiny break in concentration, her hold on him failed somewhat. He gripped her arm harder, began to pull her toward the circle. *No,* she commanded again, setting the claw in as deep as she ever had with anyone, until the force of it made her head ache. *Be still, just stand there and worship me—*

Masejih subsided again. Laas turned her attention to Hiriv—too late; her head rang with the slap from behind, her concentration fell apart, and there was another paw on her. "Meddling little bitch," Hiriv snarled. "You want to know about magic, we'll show you—small loss to us—"

Then he reeled as Laas drove the claw into him. She felt utter satisfaction. How many poor mrem had she done this to, on his orders? Let *him* see how he liked it now. Hiriv sagged, a great bloated bag of desire, and looked at her with moon eyes. Laas thought longingly of the way Reswen looked at her, all directness and merriment, and gulped back a sob, and concentrated on holding both Hiriv and Masejih still at once. It could be done. She had done it before—

—But before, that horrid dark presence had not been

lowering at her, beating at the walls of its confining circle, as eager to get hold of her as she was to be out of there. It was more eager for her by far than these were, for all the hold she had on them at the moment. A little movement came back to her. She glanced up at the thing, in the process of turning her head to look down at the hallway—but then she froze again as those eyes rested on her, swallowed her, drowned her in cold pale light, willed her into nothingness, hungered for her as it hungered for the stones and the little flasks of water bound at its feet in the circle—

She fought it. It was a losing fight, and she knew it, as first Hiriv and then Masejih came free of her spell, and they dragged her toward the circle. They went across the floor in a strange halting sort of parade, as she would strike first one of them, then the other with desire for her, and one or the other would halt, would gaze into her eyes or start to take her into his arms. There would be a struggle as the first one tried to pull the other and Laas along. And then she would feel that awful dark regard pressing, pressing on her, and she would lose her hold, and both of them would become their own mrem again, and pull her onward again—

And then they crossed through into the circle, and her talent left her entirely. Laas collapsed to her knees, freezing cold, frozen stiff, at the feet of the dark thing. Claws reached down toward her; she could do nothing to prevent it, could not even scream. She could only stare in ultimate horror into those pale cold eyes as the cord came around her neck from behind and squeezed, squeezed, squeezed everything black—

▲

Reswen saw her: saw the hideous dark shape bending over her; saw Masejih behind her with the strangling cord, choking her life out; saw Hiriv with his arms raised, chanting almost in an ecstasy of evil; and he saw the stones, and the bottles of water, and understood what was happening. But worse, he understood what was happening with Laas, and that was much more important. He leapt out of hiding and raced for the circle.

The priest and the wizard paused, stared at him expectantly, with what might have been incipient laughter on their faces. Reswen drew the knife and ran at them—and bounced away from nothingness, and fell on the floor, swearing—

Another voice was raised up, crying Reswen had no idea what words. As he rolled to a standing position again, he looked over his shoulder and saw Lorin standing there behind him, looking more terrified than even Reswen had ever seen him, eyes squeezed shut so that he wouldn't have to look at the looming terror in the middle of the circle—but standing with arms raised, chanting. *Can words look like something?* Reswen thought, for there seemed to be bright movement in the dark, throbbing air where Lorin stood, bright shapes lancing away from him almost too fast to see. They arched through the air like fired arrows and buried themselves in the barrier that had stopped him. It wavered, flickered with pale light and with colors, as if the two kinds of words warred with each other—

Perhaps they did. Reswen saw the look of amusement turn into fear on Hiriv's face, and the priest fumbled what he was chanting, faltered, began chanting something else, a hurried sort of litany. Pale fire began to drive out the colors in the circle barrier. But Lorin kept on chanting, louder; and Hiriv made the mistake of looking up at the dark thing that lowered over him, seeing the malice and balked hunger in its eyes—

There was suddenly a patch of barrier that wasn't pallid at all, but all colors. Reswen took his moment, dove through it, and crashed into Masejih, knocking him over and away from Laas. She fell to the patterned floor, choking and coughing, her eyes bloodshot with the near-strangling and her face bloated out of its usual shape. All this Reswen noticed with the anguish of love, but he had no time to do anything about it. Cold pale eyes were on him. He rose up and put himself between the lowering shape and the stones and bottles of water.

It bent its eyes on him, and he started to freeze with terror. The thing smiled at him, a smile that promised worse than death, much worse—a long, leisurely sucking-

dry that would leave him a little dried-out husk after what
would seem centuries, but would actually be only minutes. And after that it would do its will on Laas anyway.
There was nothing he could do to stop it—

Its arm reached toward him. Reswen, sick with fear,
still did what he could to protect his city: one last blow—it
would not get at the stone and water without at least that.
The rose-and-gold knife swung, gleamed in the paleness,
drove into the thing's arm—

And with the quick jolting hesitation of a perfect stroke,
it went through! In astonishment Reswen heard its high,
awful scream, watched it flail and bleed darkness in great
gouts. Its face was full of rage and astonishment. It reached
for him with the other arm; he slashed that too, at the
inside elbow where the blood vessels are closest to the
surface—

Something grabbed his arm. "You can't do that, it's
impossible!" Masejih screamed. "Invulnerable to iron and
fire—"

Reswen, bemused, looked at the knife with affection
despite all the madness going on around him. "It's not
iron," he said. "But it *does* work as a knife." And to prove
it, he put the knife right up to its hilt in Masejih, underneath the collarbone—an incapacitating strike, not a killing one. *He'll live long enough for questioning, anyway,*
Reswen thought, and turned his attention back to the dark
shape in the circle.

It was writhing and screaming, an awful high thin
sound. *Good,* Reswen thought, and crouched to pick up
the stones and bottles of water. He pitched them out of
the clear patch in the circle. The stones shattered; the
bottles smashed and the water ran out, blots on the rammed
dirt of the floor.

The screaming that began now made all the rest look
paltry. It came to Reswen that this was an extremely good
time to get out. He picked up the still-gasping Laas and
half hauled, half carried her out of the circle through the
narrowing patch of color. *Masejih's going to have to take
his chances. "Seal it up! Seal it up!"* he shouted at Lorin.
Lorin simply stopped chanting.

And the circle was all pale fire again, and the dark,

screaming shape in it looked for someone to wreak its vengeance on. It threw itself against the bounds of the circle, found there was no way to get at Reswen and Laas and Lorin—then turned, and looked long and lovingly at the two who were trapped inside with it.

Laas was kneeling retching on the floor; Lorin was running up the corridor and out of sight, all his courage done with. So only Reswen saw what happened to them. He didn't stay for more than a few breaths, just enough time for Laas to recover herself. But it struck him as amazing how much blood a fat mrem like Hiriv had in him. . . .

He picked her up, then, and ran as best he could. When Laas struggled in his arms, he put her down and let her lean on him, and they ran, or rather staggered, together. The screams coming from behind him were getting more and more terrible. They lurched up the stairs together, out into the main hall on the ground floor level, found one of the windows onto the garden unlatched by Lorin, and tumbled out through it. The urge to simply lie there, in the cool green grass, in each other's arms, was very strong, but Laas this time struggled to her feet and helped Reswen get up. They ran for the back of the garden.

They were barely on top of the garden wall when the front half of the building simply shattered itself like a beer keg with too much ferment in it, knocking them down on the other side. The explosion rained stones and glass and wood down on half the city. All around, after the initial terrible roar, they could hear the clatter of stones hitting cobbles, hitting houses, the occasional distant scream as they hit mrem, or almost hit them. One thing went up and did not come down: a pale-eyed shape like a black wind, black even against the night, which went up screaming with satiated hunger and vanished, melted into darkness.

Reswen and Laas sat there on the pavement and put their arms around each other, and simply wept. Strength would be required tomorrow, but in the meantime, this was more important . . . .

▲

She rose up in her wrath. She felt the spell which she had commanded her pet to enact come apart like an old torn skin, she saw her mission go to tatters, and worst, she felt her pet die, devoured by the wretched little vermin-god. That should have been *her* prerogative, none other's. The rage rose up in her, blotting out even her terror at what would happen to her now that she had failed her masters. She would wreak her vengeance on this place at least; they would wish, those few of them she might leave alive, for the fate which was now denied them, that of simple slow starvation. They would beg her for their lives yet, and she would deny them all—

▲

"Get up," Lorin said. "Oh, for pity's sake, get up. This is no time for it. Come *on!*"

"If you don't shut up," Reswen muttered into Laas's fur, "you're going to go to gaol, do you know that?"

But Lorin was in no mood, apparently. *"Reswen, get up!! You've got to do something!"*

"About what?"

"About *that!*"

Reswen looked up, unwilling, and then became befuddled. There seemed to be a pillar of fire rising up from somewhere across town. "What the—"

"The liskash," Lorin said—and his voice dropped to a whisper, as if he was afraid it might hear him.

Oh gods, he did see it, Reswen thought. All his fur stood up on end at once. *What the hell do we do about that?*

"Come on," he said to Laas, and helped her up. "He's right, we *do* have to do something—"

She looked off toward the sudden violent brightness in the sky, and shuddered. "How could it be?" she said. "They're extinct—at least, we thought—"

"We were meant to think so," Reswen said, brushing himself off hurriedly. "Come on, we have to get out of here and *do* something about that thing—"

But what? he thought, as together he and Laas and Lorin picked their way over and through the rubble that had showered down from the Lloahairi Embassy. The place was a dead loss; the Lloahairi were going to have to rebuild it from scratch—*and this time*, Reswen thought, *I'm going to insist they build it on bedrock, by the gods!* The street in front was knee-deep in rubble. Mrem were running around and screaming, and other mrem, far enough off down the street not to have been involved, were standing in their gateways and staring curiously at the uproar. A few constables were trying to dig about in the mass of fallen stone and masonry. Reswen's heart tightened in him as he saw a half-crushed leg and tail underneath a stone. But he felt no qualms whatever about grabbing the arm of the young constable who was trying to pull the stone off the extremely dead mrem underneath it.

"Forget that just now," Reswen said. "It's Miav, isn't it? Miav, leave this and get you down to the constabulary. I want half the available force here. Everyone else who can be spared must go straight to Haven. No one is to try to deal with what they find there. Just surround the place and keep people out of it. Understand me? Then get going!" He pushed the youngster hard in the back. Miav stumbled, and headed off. "*And call out the city cohorts!*" Reswen shouted after him. "Get them there too!"

Miav waved, didn't stop running, turned the nearest corner leftward and dashed out of sight. "Come on," Reswen said. "We have to get there first."

"And do what??" Lorin cried.

"You tell me," Reswen said, grabbing him by the arm and starting to run himself. Laas leapt after him, lithe and easy even after everything she had been through. "What can you do about a liskash?"

"*Me??*" Lorin laughed as he gasped, and started running along in earnest. "What makes you think—there's anything I can do? This is a liskash—this is what almost made an end—of our people—"

"But they didn't," Reswen said, gasping too, and not caring, as they turned the corner and pounded down through the Whites. "We must have—done *something* right—"

"They died out!" Lorin said, panting, desperate, as they turned a corner. "They just died—"

"Nothing just dies! There had to be a reason! Magic—"

Lorin shook his head desperately. Laas came up on the

other side of him from Reswen, took his arm, helped him run. "Their magic is more powerful than ours, they've mastered fire—"

Reswen was watching the glow in the sky ahead of them grow, and was secretly wondering whether there might not be something to this. "And we have other masteries. Don't we? Why would a liskash have come here at all unless we had something it needed?"

Lorin panted and ran on a distance between Reswen and Laas before gasping, "Possible. Our gods are different—"

"And our magics are different. Aren't they, Lorin? Here's your chance," Reswen said, and gasped for air himself as they turned another corner. Was the air hotter here? Certainly the light was growing ferocious ahead of them. All of Haven might have been on fire. *Oh, my people underneath . . . please be out of there, get out!*— "Here's your chance to legitimize magic forever in this city. Get rid of this thing and no one will say a bad word about it again, not ever. You can practice your trade in the open—"

"Get *rid* of it! What do you think this is, some kind of bug I can swat?" Lorin said, nearly laughing with his desperation, and then coughing. "These things ruled the world— "

"But they don't any more! Lorin, I mean it—"

And then they turned the last corner, into the street down which Haven lay. . . .

The smoke billowed out at them. Trees burned like candles. Stones were blackened with smoke, gates of houses nearer the burning melted. Haven was all one great blaze. The cries of mrem could be heard in the background, but none in that street dared cry out, or make any sound at all.

She lay there in the middle of the road, in a nest of flame, like one of the fabulous beasts of myth; the stones themselves burned under her. There was no doubt that the creature was female. There was no doubt, either, of its power. Flame wreathed and coiled about her, and left her unhurt. In the heart of it all, her skin, when she moved, glittered dimly as if it were gemmed. Easily eight times the size of a mrem, she was like one of the tiny lizards of the desert, but writ large: Her claws were curved like knives, and as long as knives; the fangs in the jaw she dropped in an awful mockery of a smile gleamed in the light of the fire. Her tail twitched and coiled slowly, thoughtfully, as her eyes rested on them.

Reswen felt his blood literally running cold as the liskash looked at him and contemplated his death. His fur stood up on end, and it was with the greatest difficulty that he resisted the urge to run right back around that corner again. The thought occurred to him that if he did not do it right away, he might not have the chance. But he was damned if he was going to run from a lizard, from something whose day in the world was over, no matter how many of his people it might kill—

Laas's paw crept into his. He gripped it tight and looked the liskash in its terrible eye, and would not look away. He could think of nothing else useful to do. He glanced over at Lorin—

Lorin took a slow step forward, as if fascinated. And another. Reswen would have put out a paw to stop him, but suddenly found it too much effort to even raise the limb—

Lorin shook himself all over. "Nay then," he said, very loud, his voice shaking, "you can do better than that. I challenge you, child of fire."

There was a long slow hissing from the liskash. "What sort of challenge do you think to field against me?" she said, and Reswen shuddered all over at the sound of that voice—cold and leisurely and humorous, the hissing wrapped all around each word it spoke, like the hissing of a struck gong. "You are one alone. The Three know nothing of you, and will not help. They cannot. You have forged no links with them before this, preferring to hide, and it is too late for that now. What do you think to do?"

Lorin said nothing at all, merely walked right forward into the fire.

Reswen watched him with astonishment. He felt heat, smelled the smoke of burning, but the flames that leaped and curled about the liskash, and flowed down the street, blackening the stones, did not fasten on Lorin. They wreathed about him and did him no harm. Reswen thought

he could see Lorin's mouth moving as he walked, but
whatever spell he was saying didn't carry.

The liskash watched him, smiling still, a terrible, oblique
look. It lifted up its head, and suddenly Reswen found that
he couldn't move. Beside him, he felt Laas's muscles
trembling with the effort to shake off the sudden paralysis.
But up there, in the fires, Lorin just shook his head, and
paused a moment, and made a gesture like someone scat-
tering something along the ground.

Reswen never saw how it happened, but suddenly he
could move again—and the street was awash in water. A
foot deep, it came rushing out at him like a flash flood, and
he pulled Laas close to him to brace her against the rush
of it. The liskash looked about it in sudden astonishment,
its tail lashing; the fangy mouth closed, losing the parody
of a smile. The liskash hissed in anger as its fires went out,
and the only burning left in the street was that of Haven.

Quite suddenly the liskash was not there. Reswen staggered to one side of the street through the water, pulling
Laas with him out of the flow of it. Over its rushing he
could hear Lorin shouting, "You make light work of controlling those who don't know about you, snake, but when
someone faces you down, you run and hide! You can't bear
direct opposition, can you! We're all supposed to just fall
over and shake at the sight of you—or walk into your
mouth like frightened birds—"

He just managed to jump aside from the gigantic clawed
foot that came slamming down into the stones. The water
went away as suddenly as the fire had. Lorin scrambled to
one side of the street on paws and knees as the huge
fanged maw came down, hunting him along the cobbles.
"Two can play at that," he gasped, packing himself up—
and suddenly a titan reared up over the little street,
sidestepping the trees, stepping over walls as if over curbs:
a mrem a hundred feet high, glowing faintly as if lit from
within, feinting with bared claws at a liskash that could
have eaten all of Haven at one gulp. Jaws snapped and the
huge golden eyes glinted, terrible with rage, but Lorin in
his ragged clothes leapt and swiped and batted, and the
liskash jerked its head back as he struck with his claws at
the hypnotic eyes, and they grew translucent with fear.

The liskash was cursing in words that hurt Reswen's ears. "Barbarian," it shrieked, finally, "vermin, unsubtle insect—"

"Not subtle, no," Lorin said, striking at her eyes again. "But direct. You can't cope, can you, snake? One 'vermin' wizard is enough for you, in the body! Oh, out of the body you're big stuff indeed—walk the overworld, make yourself cleverer and prettier and stronger than you really are—but in the body, where *real* magic is done, where it counts, you can't do it! You daren't!"

"Liar!" The liskash shrieked, and two more houses down the street exploded into flame. "Vermin liar!"

"Ah, there we see how strong you are," Lorin said, striking at the liskash's eyes again, and again she pulled back. "Very brave you are at burning poor mrem in their beds that can't fight with you. But you can't do anything about *me*, can you! You dare not meet me in the body, just as you won't come to grips with me here—"

She snapped at him, a snap that should have taken Lorin's arm off, and instead mostly got his sleeve. Like a gutter scavenger the liskash worried the giant sleeve until it tore, and flung it away, and still Lorin laughed. "You don't dare!" he cried. "Lizard! Lizard!"

And suddenly the giant shapes were gone, and there were just Lorin and the liskash, circling one another in the street. *He's going to die,* Reswen thought, terrified. *And I drove him to this—* "Lorin!" he shouted, and as Lorin turned, he threw him the rose-and-gold knife. *Maybe it'll do some good—*

Lorin turned, caught it out of the air with the practiced motion of someone used to catching thrown money at the fighting pits, and turned back to the liskash, all in one fluid motion. The liskash had no more glow about it; its magic was confined for the moment, from anger or perhaps exhaustion. Its sides were heaving. Its jaws were open, no more in a smile. It circled Lorin, and he it, and Reswen mourned at the sight. The thing was eight times Lorin's size, and the knife, glinting in the light of Haven burning, looked like a silly pin—

"Come on then, lizard," Lorin was saying. "Come find out why your kind died out. Come find out why you live in damp caves now, when your kind once lived in cities and ruled the world. Come find out about mrem!"

The liskash was beginning to hiss again, a sound like water pouring onto fire. "Come find out," Lorin said, as they circled closer. The thing was three times his height. It could surely fall on him and crush him, but it did no such thing. "Come find out what we have that leaves us free to let magic be for the most part!" The rose-and-gold knife glinted. "I feel you feeling for my mind; but maybe The Three know more about me than you think, eh? Maybe you're trying to get out of yourself even now, into the overworld, but you find the way is blocked! Maybe you're stuck in your poor body, and you're going to have to discover that we're better at living in our bodies than you are—!"

He slipped in and struck—to slash, not to stab; the rose-and-gold knife went black along that vicious edge. Reswen held onto Laas for all he was worth, hearing, with one ear, the sound of the fire brigades coming—the rumbling of their big water carts along the cobbles a couple of blocks away. Lorin was shouting again, now, but this time shouting words that Reswen couldn't understand, another spell, Reswen thought. Next to him, he felt Laas shuddering. He pulled her closer. To his surprise, she pushed him away.

"No," she said. "He's going to die, Reswen! He's binding the thing with his spell, it's a death spell, he's going to let it kill him, and his death will seal its own—!" The tears were rolling down her face. "We have to stop him—"

Reswen held her regardless, and his face grew hard, though his heart cried out in him. "No, we don't," he said. "If he can kill it that way, let him—it's more than we can do. He's got it bound into its body now. Don't distract him—if it gets loose again it'll burn all Niau." And the tears ran down his face too, but he dared pay no attention to them. "Let him do what he's doing. It's his choice—"

Lorin kept chanting, backing away from the liskash. It followed him, its eyes always on him, hateful, waiting its moment. And then he stopped, and looked up at the liskash, and opened his arms, the knife in one paw, and held quite still.

Slowly it reared up on its hind legs before him, the huge tail bracing it, the great jaws opening, the terrible front claws outstretched—

The bolt thudded into its back with a wet thick sound almost too large to believe, and then another, and another. A cranking, ratcheting sound came from down the street, by Haven, as the liskash screamed and rose up and up on its hind legs, and then turned to face what had struck it—turned into the teeth of the repeating "stinger" catapult set up at the end of the street. Two more bolts hit the liskash in the gut in the time it might take a mrem to breathe, and then three more, one through the chest and two through the head. The liskash fell down, writhing, and kept writhing for a long time after it should have been dead.

Lorin dropped the knife and simply sat down on the wet cobbles and started to cry.

Reswen and Laas went to him, bent over him. "I'm all right," he said, sobbing, and wiping his nose on his sleeve. "I'm all right." And he cried harder.

Reswen patted him, leaving Laas with him for the moment, and picked up the knife. Then he went off slowly down the street to where the repeating catapult stood, with the mren who had armed it and fired it, and the beasts who had drawn its big cart down the little streets in such haste, and Sachath, leaning on the frame of the thing, and smiling at Reswen.

"Been waiting to use this thing ever since we bought it," Sachath said. And he poked Reswen good-naturedly in the arm with his baton. "So much for the Arpekh," he added. "Let 'em tell *us* anything about defense spending, eh?"

Reswen smiled and went back to Lorin, and Laas.

EPILOGUE

$\blacktriangle$ —————————————————————————— $\blacktriangle$

The explanations naturally were not over in a day, or ten days. Reswen began to think he should simply move into the Arpekh—put a bedroll on the floor of the council chamber perhaps.

They were outraged with him at first, especially Mraal, and on the day immediately after the explosion, Reswen thought he might be in for that famous view from over the city gates. The evidence was, he had to admit, a little damning. The Lloahairi Ambassador assaulted, the embassy broken into, and then blown up by means no one understood— Theories for this among the Arpekh ranged from the opinion that Reswen had gone mad, to the rather more cockeyed idea that he was himself some kind of wizard who had been planted in the Niauhu police force by the Easterners.

But Reswen produced his evidence slowly, carefully, and in good order, and slowly the Arpekh began to realize that they were not going to get to spike him up, that they in fact had a hero on their hands. About the first thing he had said when getting back to the constabulary in the middle of the night was, "Go arrest Choikea." His people had done that, and had been delighted to find the mrem in the process of packing to flee the city by night. His papers indicated he was heading to Zashikeh, where (as intelligence had recently reported) there was another Eastern group requesting stone and water of that city. Choikea had proven most amenable to questioning; he was the sort of mrem to whom you merely show the knives and irons, and all sorts of fascinating things start coming out. He confessed immediately to Shalav's killing—for his memory of it was much more complete than the liskash had suspected—and also to having set up the previous ones to cover himself, since it had been his intention (and mission) to murder various Niauhu mrem anyway. The liskash had merely made use of what was already fertile ground. Choikea independently confirmed that by this and other means, the Easterners had long been intending to set the Lloahairi and the Niauhu at one another's ears. With the two of them warring, their lands would be easy pickings for an expeditionary force.

The natural result was that the signed agreement was torn and torn again, ceremonially, in the presence of the merchant Rirhath, now senior surviving member of the Eastern delegation, and he and his (those that were left; some had died in the burning of Haven) were told to be out of the city walls within five days. All the Easterners became quite quiet, especially when Rirhath inquired about Hiriv, and was presented pointedly with the several scraps of slashed and singed fur that were apparently all that remained of him. Reswen discussed the plot rather scathingly with the Arpekh, and got many sheepish looks and a commitment to a much stronger armed stance. "There's no chance they're going to stop this kind of thing," he said. "Sooner or later, they or the liskash will try it again—if not through magic, then by war. I would prefer to be ready, my lords. I wouldn't want to see what happened to the Lloahairi Embassy happen to the Arpekh. . . ."

The matter of the Lloahairi was also on their minds, and Reswen's. Their soldiers were packed up and sent home, with messages for the Lloahairi government that implied they had better look to their relations with the East—some cities apparently thought of Lloahai as nothing better than a pawn to be used in their expansionist schemes. There was also a polite request for another ambassador, since the old one seemed to have been lost in the explosion that the Easterners had engineered.

Reswen sighed over that, late one night some time afterwards. "We may have another war on our hands," he said to Laas. "They may not believe us." He toyed with his cup of sherbet, and sipped a little. "But we'll deal with it when it happens."

They sat in the Green Square together again. It was evening, and they had just finished a small haunch of ennath, one of the little desert beasts, with a sauce so hot it had practically paralyzed their mouths. Laas drank a little of her sherbet, put the cup down, and looked at it wistfully. "I'm going to miss this," she said.

Reswen's heart ached inside him. It had been aching for days now, and all the business and bustle hadn't distracted him from it. "There must be some way I can change your mind," he said softly.

She shook her head. "I have to go with them," she said. "Reswen, what would I be here but a housecat? This is no place for a magic-worker to live."

"No one would bother you, not after—"

"Ah, but they would, specifically because the chief of the police, not to mention the H'satei, can't be married to an Easterner, who might be a spy, or something worse . . . like a charismatic. No one here is going to give up their prejudices against magic so quickly, no matter what Lorin did the other night. Otherwise you'd have called him up before the Arpekh to be rewarded by now—isn't that so? But you've been playing it quiet so far. Sooner or later the truth about me would get out, and then mrem would start saying that you were using my talent to influence people on your behalf—or even that I was doing it without consulting you." She shook her head sadly, squeezed his paw. "Darling one, no. I have to go."

Reswen held silent for the moment.

"Besides," she said, "the Easterners are still going to try this kind of thing, with other cities. You know it as well as I do. Someone has to be in a position to stop them, to keep it from working. My people think I was out messing around, that night. No one but the Arpekh knows I was there, or what I was doing, and they certainly won't tell. I'm in a perfect position to foul the works for a long time to come." She sipped her sherbet again. "No more starving," she said. "No indeed. Someone has to keep it from happening."

Reswen felt like shouting, *Fine for them not to starve,*

but what about how I feel about you? Aloud, he said nothing for a moment, then nodded. "I suppose I see your point," he said. "But Laas . . . I still don't like it. I want you to stay here and be my mate."

"I know," she said. "I want to stay and be your mate, too. But what I want and what I need to do seem to be two different things at the moment. . . ."

He stared at the cup, looked up again. "Stay with me tonight?"

"Of course."

And she did.

I've got to stop this crying, he thought at one point. *I'm the Chief of Police, for the gods' sake.* But somehow he couldn't seem to stop. The feeling of her in his arms clashed so horribly with the knowledge that tomorrow, his arms would be empty, and probably forever. Oh, she might visit. But how often? Who could tell whether she would be spared more than once every couple of years? And what if some accident happened, what if she died—

Oh, stop it. You'll get over her. But it was a lie. He never would. Nor would he find anyone else, he knew. Reswen was stubborn that way. He was not one to find a jewel and thenceforth make do with glass. He would sooner go through the rest of his life with empty paws.

Which was exactly what would happen. . . .

"Reswen—darling, what are you thinking about?"

"Nothing," he said. But he knew she heard the lie. He bit Laas's neck gently, starting to make love to her again, and hoped she wouldn't notice that the fur was getting wet.

In the morning, the Easterners left. They tried to leave early, since the feeling against them in the city was now as high as it had ever been, if not higher. But even though they were at the city gates just after dawn, there was also a crowd there to heckle them. So no one found it particularly surprising that a contingent of constables should be there, with the chief of police to supervise.

There were few courtesies to observe, nothing to be done but open the gates and see them out. The chief of police stood in his worn, everyday harness, watching the loads on the beasts being checked, watching the litters being hoisted to the shoulders of the bearers. One litter he did not look at, and at that early hour, no one remarked on it.

The gates swung open, and the first litters went out, followed by lowing beasts and the Easterners' servants, leading or switching the creatures along. One by one the party passed out, and one last litter. The police chief's eyes seemed to linger on it, with an uncomfortable look. Mrem standing around thought that he was glad to see the back of it, and he turned away briskly enough when the gates shut behind it. Briskly he walked off, and mrem standing around muttered to one another that it was good to have a decent police force, even if you couldn't always get them to look the other way when you were lifting something. . . .

He leaned on his elbows on the old crumbling black wall and looked down at the city, at the desert beyond it. He could see them down there, a tiny group against the immensity of the desert. The night had not been very cool, and already the day was hot; waves of heat shimmered, made the little figures down there look somehow unreal. It would be an hour or so before they would be out of sight. He would watch them from here, with only Sorimoh for company. She wouldn't care if he wasn't up to making conversation.

His eyes were dry at last. He had his own work, after all; married life would be something that would have interfered terribly with his schedule. He was married to Niau, he supposed, and that was sufficient. There was going to be so much work to do in the days to come. After this mess with the Easterners, about twenty people in the department were due promotions. He was going to have to work out where to slot them in, how to supervise them. And his star seemed somewhat in the ascendant with the Arpekh at the moment—there were hints about increasing the number of constables, adding more people to the H'satei— He rubbed his eyes wearily. More work, but at least it would be interesting.

He glanced down at the departing group, and rubbed his eyes again. They paused, or seemed to—it was hard to tell, with the shimmer of heat that had come up. *Going to be a hot one today,* Reswen thought. Then they went on again, but one of them seemed to have turned back. *Probably forgot something.*

One of them had turned back—

He was down from the walls in a flash. He was out of the old fortress and pelting down the hill and down to the road to the city quick as a kit chasing string. When he got to the gate he was panting and gasping for air like a mrem about to die of a heart seizure. He didn't care. He cared nothing for the looks of the guards on the wall. He gestured the gates open like a king and stood there, panting and impatient, as they swung slowly toward him.

The litter stopped in the gates. Laas flung herself out of it, dismissed the bearers, ran to Reswen, and threw her arms around him. "I'm an idiot. You're an idiot," she said. "I forgot something."

"What?"

"To marry you, you fool," she said, and bit him on the neck right there in front of all Niau.

An admiring cheer went up from the soldiers on the walls, and there were yowls and cheerful suggestions about Reswen's prospective sex life. Reswen glowered at them all—it was a friendly glower—and said, "Shut the gates, you half-wits. There's only one of her, and she's mine!"

If there were more cheers then, he ignored them. "Come on," he said, "let's go see the Arpekh about a wedding license."

And paw in paw they went off together, to start their lives at last. . . .